"Tell me ........... plan to overcome my resistance."

He looked at her steadily, the trace of a mocking smile curving his mouth. "If you were a woman, it would be easy, but virginal children are an unpredictable lot."

Merrit's eyes flashed hotly. Her hands came to rest on his shoulders, then slid up his neck to bury themselves in his dark hair. As her face lowered to his, his eyes closed, a sudden longing making his pulse jump with anticipation. When her kiss did not come, he opened his eyes to see her taunting smile.

"A child, Captain? Is that truly how you see me?" she chided, seeing the desire she had stirred vanish in an instant.

"You play games like one," he said with a frown. Then a slow smile spread across his handsome features. "If you could meet my kiss with disinterest, then perhaps I would believe you a woman."

Determined to prove herself, Merrit bent down to bestow a chaste peck on his lips, but he caught her chin in his hand and held her still while his mouth slanted across hers with a bruising insistence that was far from chaste and impossible to resist. Stunned, she sank down on his lap, her knees unable to support her under the weakening onslaught of emotions that robbed her senses of reason and her mind of will. No amount of pride or vengeance could force her to relinquish that sweet taste of passion. . . .

# The PIRATE'S CAPTIVE

## DANA RANSOM

ZEBRA BOOKS

Kensington Publishing Corp.
475 Park Avenue South
New York, N.Y. 10016

First printing: August, 1992

Printed in the United States of America

## ZEBRA BOOKS
## KENSINGTON PUBLISHING CORP.

ZEBRA BOOKS

are published by

Kensington Publishing Corp.
475 Park Avenue South
New York, NY 10016

First printing: August 1987

Printed in the United States of America

# Chapter One

The captain of the square-rigged merchant ship wasn't alarmed by the rapid approach of a smaller sloop. Not at first. Wearied by the four-week voyage from England, beleaguered by foul weather and the endless complaints of queasy passengers, he was eager to meet with a certain tow-haired lass who waited with a cool mug of ale. He gave the sleek vessel barely a glance, assuming it was bound for the Chesapeake Capes as well. Expecting it to easily pass his lumbering 280-ton commercial ship heavily laden with cargo and passengers, he experienced a mild curiosity when the craft slowed and came alongside. By the time he realized the danger, it was too late to order evasive measures. He was knocked off his feet as the vessels collided, the rapierlike bowsprit of the sloop slipping across the bow to tangle in the rigging of his ship.

Cursing vigorously the incompetence of the other ship's master, the captain picked himself up. At the same time, his eyes surveyed the errant vessel. The English flag had been lowered. Standing in mute terror and indecision, he watched a banner rise rapidly, an ebony ensign that unfurled in the wind to display its message of death, the bold imprint of a grinning skull above crossbones.

The sight of the *Jolly Roger,* and the lack of orders from her captain quelled resistance on the larger ship. Not a shot was

5

fired, and the nineteen-man crew of the merchant vessel was no match for the three-dozen men who dashed across the bowsprit, swarming over the deck and brandishing their weapons and howling wildly. It was as if the gates of hell had suddenly swung wide to release its denizens. The captain and crew had no wish to risk their lives to protect the cargo against this barbarous onslaught, so the merchant ship was secured in a matter of minutes, the pirate captain, with an arrogant swagger, crossing the bowsprit bridging the ships to inspect his captured prize.

"Be Gad, Captain Whitney," a seaman gasped in a wondrous awe. " 'Tis the Spanish Angel hisself come to claim us."

Captain Whitney swallowed hard, trying to stiffen a backbone that suddenly had the consistency of cold porridge. He had heard much of this daring Spanish captain and his swift vessel aptly called the *Merry Widow*. For more than two years, this pirate had been successfully plundering ships as they funneled through the narrow mouth of the bay between Cape Charles and Cape Henry, always avoiding capture by vanishing into the haven of the Caribbean.

The pirate captain spoke briefly to one of his men as his eyes scanned the chaos on deck—the captured crew and passengers were being herded into a trembling huddle by a bristling ring of sharpened steel, while the lower decks were being scoured for possible treasure—and his wandering gaze paused when it met the English captain's. A slow smile lit the handsome features that had earned him his sobriquet. Cold rivulets of fear ran through Captain Whitney, but he forced himself to appear calm as the Spaniard drew his cutlass and approached him purposefully.

The pirate pressed the tip of his broad sword to Whitney's throat, making blood trickle down the captured captain's neck.

"Good day, Captain," he said pleasantly, his low voice heavily accented. "A good day to make your peace on this

6

earth before departing it." He lifted the sword slightly forcing Whitney to bend his head back at an awkward angle. As the helpless merchant captain's pasty face glistened wetly, the Spaniard's smile widened upon reading the other's terror, but his words were a chilling epitaph. "Look well into the eyes of the dark angel before you go to look upon your God. Look well and see death."

A shout from below broke the pirate's unwavering stare, and called his attention away from his cold purpose. Yet the Spaniard's cutlass remained steady and kept Whitney at bay, while he looked to his dark-skinned quartermaster.

"A problem below requires your attention, Captain."

"What is it?"

"A matter of some delicacy," the coffee-colored man stated with a veiled smile, provoking a curious frown from his captain. "It requires your — um, diplomacy."

The Spanish Angel nodded, then his gaze returned to the sweating Englishman who once more grew rigid under his close scrutiny.

"It seems there will be a slight delay, Captain, but do not despair. I will not forget you or keep you waiting long." His eyes held a promise sharper than the blade he carried, and only when both dropped away was Captain Whitney able to draw a breath.

"What is it, Rufe?" the pirate asked again as he followed his friend down into the belly of the ship.

"A bit of resistance we could not agree on how to handle," Rufe replied cryptically as he pushed his way through the buccaneers to clear passage to the open doorway of a stateroom.

The captain's brow rose in surprise. A stocky woman stood before the group, regarding them all unblinkingly over the yawning muzzle of a blunderbuss, which held the amused pirates back momentarily. That the only spark of resistance on the entire ship came from this large, handsome female had them all nonplused.

7

"Be ye in command of these brigands?" the woman demanded fiercely, the wide, dark bore of her weapon aimed at a spot on the pirate captain's chest.

"I be the captain, my lady," he said with mocking formality.

"Then I be telling ye the same as these other rogues. Not one of ye vermin will set foot in this room or I'll be putting a hole in ye big enough to see daylight through."

The captain extended a placating hand, and smiled charmingly at the desperate woman. "Put down that weapon. We mean you no harm. We've no designs on your virtue, lady, only on your valuables."

Her dark eyes flashed to the wardrobe she guarded, then returned to the pirate. "Stay away, I say," she warned menacingly. "I'll not be believing such honeyed words from the likes of ye."

The captain's look went speculatively to the armoire. "That must be some fine treasure for you to be so bold in the face of so many."

The woman's features tightened in sudden alarm, and her gaze swung about to follow his. In that brief, unguarded second, the pirate took a quick step forward, thrusting aside the blunderbuss with one arm and spinning the cursing woman to Rufe with the other. While she showered him with colorful expletives, he jerked open the doors of the armoire, the avarice in his eyes being replaced by shock.

"A treasure, indeed," he murmured as the other pirates crowded in behind him in the hope of spying great wealth.

Crouched in the cabinet beneath a covering of cloaks and gowns, a young woman fearlessly looked up into the eyes of the pirate captain. It was impossible to discern much about her form due to her cramped position, but her face was perfection. Beneath a heavy mass of chestnut curls, large dark eyes dominated its creamy skin. A fringe of long thick lashes made them appear enormous by comparison to her small upturned nose, bowlike mouth, and delicately pointed chin which had a determined tilt. The captain was so caught up in those depthless eyes, he failed to see the dagger she clutched. He was reaching out to help her from her tortuous hiding place when a flash of silver and a fiery streak of pain awakened him to the danger she presented. His bloodied hand snapped out and fastened on her wrist, jerking her to her feet and then up against his unyielding chest. He bent her arm behind her back, crushing her to him while he twisted the dagger from her grasp. Though relieved of her only means of defense, she glared at him in open defiance, showing none of the trepidation that his presence had instilled in the English captain. Such undaunted, albeit foolish, courage softened the pirate's glare and brought a smile of begrudging admiration to his lips.

"If you be determined to carve out my liver, I'd have a name from you," he said softly, the Spanish intonation giving a crooning lilt to his words.

"Merrit Ellison," she replied coolly, "and if it was your liver I'd wanted, I'd have it."

The roar of laughter from behind him brought a wider smile to his swarthy face. "A brace of hellcats befitting Calico Jack," he remarked, bringing more laughter from his men.

Though she didn't understand his reference to the pirate John Rackham and his bloodthirsty ladies, Anne Bonny and Mary Read, she recognized the derision in his tone and knew he mocked her. With an angry cry, she struggled to free herself from his embrace, but to her dismay, her ineffective wriggling against his hardened frame brought a new light to his startling green eyes. Now she was afraid. Her rescue came from a puzzling source, and it would be a long time before she understood why her maidservant's words evoked such a powerful reaction.

"Unhand Lady Merrit at once, ye blackguard," Mildred raged. "Mind ye, ye maul Lord Winston Whitelaw's betrothed."

9

The captain released Merrit so abruptly, she stumbled and nearly fell. Looking into his face, she thought in panic, he's going to kill me. Mildred's disclosure had brought a look of near madness to the man's green eyes, but it quickly cooled to thoughtful menace.

"If she be the lord's betrothed she must be packing a right-sized fortune as her dowry," one of the pirates cried in greedy excitement, and the others all shouted in agreement and anticipation.

The Spanish captain continued to stare at the apprehensive maiden while he sucked the blood welling from the stripe she had laid across the back of his hand. Finally, he turned to his men and ordered crisply, "Take them up with the others and search this room. Lord Whitelaw would exact a heavy payment in taking a bride. I want it found." With that, the captain strode from the room, leaving his men to gleefully ransack the cabin.

Pushed among the others on deck, Merrit shivered in the circle of Mildred's comforting arm, the same sturdy arm she had clung to since childhood when her parents had engaged this outspoken lass to govern their spirited child. Mildred had seen Merrit through all the crises of her young life. Never had she faltered or failed her charge, and Merrit took great consolation in her nearness.

"What do ye think they'll do to us?" one of the younger sailors whispered, his quavering voice ill concealing his thoughts.

His older companion pointed to the afterdeck where the pirate captain had come into view with his dark-skinned quartermaster. "That be the Spanish Angel. Me thinks we ought to be saying our prayers."

"Think you that they plan to murder us?" the boy yelped in panic, his eyes large and round.

"That Angel, he be a vile one. I heard tell that on the last ship he took, he raped the women and then laughed whilst he slit their throats."

Feeling Merrit stiffen beside her, the older woman turned and cuffed the sailor sharply. "Hold yer tongue," she snapped. " 'Tis lies ye tell so keep them to yerself."

Shamefaced, the sailor fell silent but his grim words were already working on the girl's impressionable mind as she recalled the passion and hatred in the pirate captain's green eyes. Were they the eyes of a man who could commit such atrocities? She began to pray in earnest that they were not. When she cast a timid glance toward the afterdeck, she felt chilled at finding those bold eyes upon her.

"What sort of vengeance is it that you're planning, Colley?" the dark quartermaster asked bluntly, with the easy familiarity long friendship allowed. When no answer was given, he pressed further. "Would killing her satisfy your thirst for revenge?"

The captain turned, surprise registering for a fleeting instant on his features before they became dispassionate. "The loss of his bride would not harm him as much as the loss of his hoarded wealth." He studied the fragile figure of the girl. "What do you think he'd buy a pretty piece like that for?"

Rufe followed his gaze and his thinking. "If he'd ever laid eyes on her, I would think a tidy sum."

They were interrupted by one of the men who growled disappointedly, "No sign of a dowry, Captain. We tore the floorboards up, and couldn't find a farthing."

"No matter," the Spanish Angel said, waving a hand to dismiss the loss as insignificant. "I've other riches in mind."

The anxious group on deck watched as several pirates climbed the masts, puzzled as to their intent until the boatswain sang out joyfully, "They be topping the masts. They plan to release us."

"Thank the merciful Lord," Mildred breathed in relief, patting her ward's shoulder and feeling it sag wearily. "We may be a bit late but we'll get ye to yer Lordship."

The relieved sailors began to talk among themselves, to

11

joke and boast of how they had never really been afraid, all knowing the falseness of their bolstering words. Only Merrit remained silent as she watched the pirates gather, apparently for some sort of vote. A lusty roar announced their decision. Smiling, the Spanish captain approached them, his glance sweeping over Merrit before he spoke to the English captain.

"As you may have surmised, we have voted to let you and your crew continue on to Virginia, less, of course, your cargo."

The captain nodded quickly, willing to accept that concession without complaint. After all, it wasn't his loss and those who would bear it could easily afford it. They were leaving him with his life, his crew, and his ship. What more could he ask?

"And," the pirate concluded with dramatic flair, "one of your passengers."

There was a stunned silence as his green eyes shifted to Merrit Ellison.

"Nay, ye bloody devil," Mildred shrieked, thrusting a stunned Merrit behind her. "Ye'll not touch me pet. I'll not stand by and let the likes of ye paw at this sweet child. I say nay to ye."

The swarthy captain made a motion and his crew rushed in, tearing Merrit from her protesting guardian and drawing their cutlasses to daunt any brave soul who considered interfering. It took two stalwart men to restrain a determined Mildred, who cursed and called down all manner of ills on their heads.

"I cannot allow this," Whitney stammered. "The lady is under my protection."

A single cutting glance halted any further heroics on his part. "The lady sails with us. If you object I'll have every member of your crew tossed in the sea and then I'll burn your ship around you."

"That will not be necessary, Captain."

They turned in surprise to hear such a strong voice from one so slight. Merrit shook off the burly hands that held her, and boldly faced the pirate captain. "I will go with you. You need not resort to savagery." She flinched, but her gaze did not waver at Mildred's cry of protest.

Green eyes assessed her thoughtfully, then turned back to the pale English captain. "Go, and be thankful. The lady has spared your worthless lives. She will come to no harm. She is under my protection." He made a gesture and Merrit was escorted onto the *Merry Widow*, her back stiff with prideful resignation. Only Mildred's sobbing marked her departure. Eyes puffy with grief, the loyal woman still managed a hate-filled glower when the Spanish Angel came before her. Then she spat at him in heartfelt contempt.

The captain wiped the offending spittal from his cheek, and to Mildred's amazement, he actually smiled. "If the likes of you made up the crew of this ship, we would have been cut to ribbons before we boarded," he said in a quiet voice meant for only the two of them. "Your lady will be well cared for. Have no fear for her safety. I would have you relay a message to Lord Whitelaw. Tell him we value your lady's company at one hundred and fifty thousand pounds and ask him if he is of the same mind."

"If he be any kind of man, he will be. But if he is not?" There was an edging of fear in Mildred voice, and she eyed the pirate with open distrust.

He smiled again, his eyes crinkling mischievously. "Mayhap then I will think her worth the price." He bowed cordially in the face of her wrath and went to join his men.

Once the pirates went about their business, it took them little time to strip the merchant vessel of its cargo. Riotous shouts rang out at the discovery of a cache of liquor, and even the appropriation of clothing and books was met with enthusiasm. Their captain watched the proceedings with a satisfied smile and when the ship had been sacked, he tipped his hat to the dour-faced Mildred and turned to the English

13

captain.

"It seems it was not your day to die, Captain," he said jauntily. "Perhaps we will meet again and set things right."

Captain Whitney was able to meet his stare, but couldn't muster the fortitude to speak the angry words that burned bitterly in his throat. He still held his life above his pride. Perhaps he would meet this man again, he thought as his crippled vessel was released.

# *Chapter Two*

Merrit cowered on the brass-trimmed sea chest, her earlier courage fading as her situation became painfully and frightfully clear. She was alone for the first time she could remember, with no one to call upon to ease her fears and soothe her doubts. At seventeen, she knew little of life outside of her family's manor house. This had been her first venture into the world, and now her childlike excitement at the prospect of adventure had turned into an anguished longing to be once more among things familiar and with those she loved.

Drawing her feet up and hugging her knees, she looked about the cabin in which she had been placed. Her prison was a small, sparsely furnished room, its paneled walls relieved by a papering of maps and charts and further broken by a multipaned porthole that ran the entire length of one wall. The door was guarded, but not locked—there was certainly nowhere to go. Though she had not looked out the porthole, she knew what she would see. Water, endless miles of it, an unbroken expanse of blue. The chest she perched upon occupied one corner of the room, an unmade bed set on a pedestal of drawers the other. Purposefully, she kept her eyes from lingering on the latter piece. The only other furnishings were a crude table with four plain chairs, wash stand, and a commode.

She wondered tremulously when he would come, the Spanish Angel whose reputation had her agitated to the point of faintness. The sailor's careless remark echoed through her frantic mind. Rape . . . murder. Was that what lay in store for her? If not, why then had she alone been taken? Did he plan to exact some dreadful vengeance for her brazen attack on him before his men? Had he taken her for his own pleasure or to seek retribution? She didn't know which she feared more.

A slight movement in the mussed bedding made her cry out, but her fear dissolved into nervous laughter when the largest cat she had ever seen languidly stretched, then regarded her steadily with luminous green eyes. It was a mammoth animal with a sleek black coat and a frame that weighed at least twenty pounds. Its cocked ears were badly mangled, and when it hopped from the bed with a heavy thud, it moved with a distinct limp. She put down a hand, intending to touch the cat's questioning nose, but withdrew it when a low raspy rumble of warning came from the creature. Woman and cat regarded each other for a moment, then the feline, apparently bored with her, leapt up onto the ledge beneath the porthole and began a fastidious grooming.

The click of the knob turning brought her eyes back to the door. Her breath, even her heart, seemed to stop in that brief instant when the captain entered the cabin alone and closed the door on the raucous sounds of revelry coming from the upper deck. He seemed unaware of her as he crossed to the table, set an unopened bottle on it, and placed his hat next to the liquor. Then, brooding and silent, he faced her.

Across the scant distance of the room, Merrit had her first opportunity to observe her captor closely. If beautiful was a word she could use to describe a man, the pirate captain was truly beautiful and at the same time overwhelmingly masculine. His raven black hair was close cropped, but an errant

16

lock formed a dark comma above one of the heavy black brows set above his short, straight nose. His eyes were glimmering emeralds, yet Spanish blood was evident in his dark complexion and in his high, well-formed cheekbones which ran smoothly down to a strong, squared chin. His mouth had a sensual fullness, a generous line that she knew could quickly and cruelly turn thin. He dressed with a theatrical bent, in a scarlet coat with brass buttons and deeply turned-back cuffs, a black shirt, and loose-fitting trousers. Polished jackboots rose to the bottom of his knee breeches, their leather gleaming from careful attention. His shirt was open nearly to the heavy belt that bore his cutlass, exposing a broad expanse of smooth, tanned chest, and a scarlet neckerchief was knotted at his throat, above the heavy gold chain that matched the hoop dangling from one of his ears. He cut a dashing figure, a fact he was well aware of, for his vanity was apparent in his immaculate appearance. When Merrit realized he had purposely paused so she would admire him, she dropped her eyes quickly and flushed.

"I trust you have made yourself comfortable," he said in his low, richly accented voice. When she made no reply, he added, "Consider yourself my guest."

Up to that point, she had been contemplating falling before him to beg for mercy, but his taunting words touched a rebellious nerve in her and she brought her head up so she could eye him boldly.

"Guests are not wrested from their loved ones and forced to remain where they do not wish to be," she corrected sharply, lifting her chin defiantly.

"True," the captain agreed with a brief smile. "If you prefer it, think of yourself as my prisoner."

His summation was brutally true. She was his prisoner, and whatever mercy she hoped to receive would not be won by sparring with him. She lowered her eyes in a semblance of meekness, but started fearfully at a sudden loud pop,

17

relaxing only when she realized he had pulled the cork from the bottle. Through the heavy fringe of her lashes, she watched as he drew two glasses from the deep pockets of his coat.

"Join me, my lady?" he asked, gesturing to the French brandy. At her silence, he shrugged and filled one glass, sipping from it appreciatively as he let the smooth liquor roll over his tongue. As he leisurely finished his drink, he assessed her huddled figure with open interest. She was a lovely little creature, the blush of her youth offset by the ripe maturity of her well-rounded, though petite, figure. He guessed her to be some ten years his junior, though the quick challenge of her gaze spoke of an uncanny wisdom in one so obviously untried. Her wealth and social standing was apparent in the costly fabric of her gown and in her poised manner. Even though she tried to convey it, she was no timid miss, not the type of groveling weakling he despised. He recognized character in her scathing glance, and that piqued his interest and respect. Perhaps the voyage would have its amusements after all.

Under his scrutiny, her dark eyes lifted once more to his, uncertain yet still unabashed. "Why have you taken me?" she asked, her voice not as steady as her eyes. If he meant to harm her, she would prefer to know it now rather than spend needless hours dreading her fate.

Her straightforwardness made a smile play across his full mouth. "For what reason do you think?"

Deep-rooted indignation overrode her anxiety, making her words crisp and combative. "Do you plan to rape me?"

The captain blinked at her bluntness, then gave a low chuckle. "It was not my intention, my lady, but if you have your heart set on rape, I could easily accommodate you. I never disappoint a lady."

She drew back, clasping her knees to her chest, and saying quickly, "That is not my wish."

He smiled crookedly. "I thought not. Rape is so unneces-

18

sary when women succumb so easily to persuasion."

Merrit frowned at his insinuation, righteous anger at his arrogance erasing her fear. "Not all women, my lord pirate," she said searingly.

"Oh ho, deny if you will, but your eyes say differently. Perhaps I should be the one to fear rape."

"You flatter yourself, sir, if you think I would ever welcome, let alone desire, your presence. You are my jailor, Captain, not my chosen. Do not mistake the two."

Any trace of good humor left his handsome face as he considered her rebuttal. Again, Merrit was stirred by a prickle of alarm. When he spoke, his word were soft and chilling. "Madam, you wield your tongue as sharply as your dagger. Take care that you don't cut too deeply."

She swallowed nervously at his warning, her eyes dropping to his crudely bandaged hand. She must control her temper lest he goad her into evoking his anger. Though he chose to play the genial host, his meaningful suggestion told her that could easily change. She relaxed her threatened pose somewhat, lowering her feet to the floor, unaware that her skirts had caught on one of the trunk's fittings, leaving an expanse of shapely calf bared to her host's gaze. Noting the direction of his glance, with an irritated flip, she dropped her skirts to conceal her flesh from his avid stare.

At her withering look, the captain's humor returned and he chuckled to himself as he filled both glasses, then pulled out one of the chairs.

"My lady, I am sure it is not as grand as you are used to, but 'tis far more accommodating than that chest."

She stared at him blankly, for his heavy accent had given way to the King's English. "Spanish Angel, indeed," she snorted. "You are as British as I am." She slid from the trunk, and skirted him warily on her way to the proffered chair. "You, Captain, are a sham." As she passed him, she was surprised to note that he was not as tall as she'd thought. When she had first seen him, fear had made him soar above

19

her.

" 'Tis no sham. At least not completely. I am a bit of both lands. I speak both tongues equally well."

As he seated her, his hand fell lightly on the top of her head, caressing her wavy chestnut locks for a moment.

"As I thought. Like finest silk," he mused softly before she jerked away, her eyes flashing in renewed fear. She started to scurry from the chair, but he stilled her with a quiet laugh. "Do not fret. I will behave myself. It is hard not to permit small indulgences when you've been so long at sea."

Mollified but not totally at ease, she settled back onto the chair, eying him cautiously as he dropped onto the one opposite her. She would not again make the mistake of lowering her guard. She was a prisoner, not a guest. Her hand was slightly unsteady when she lifted her glass for an experimental taste. Though it burnt, it was pleasant.

"I ask again, Captain, why have you taken me?" Merrit demanded, emboldened by his casual pose as he drank deeply while watching her closely with those emerald eyes.

"In truth, my lady, you are indeed a treasure, a treasure your betrothed will forfeit for your return."

Merrit was silent. Finally she asked, "And if he does not?" The faintness of her voice conveyed what her words did not.

"Pray that he does" was the level reply.

She rose from the table, agitated, and crossed to the porthole as the pirate admired the gentle sway of her skirts. When she leaned on the ledge, the huge cat spat in irritation and vacated its preferred spot to seek consolation on the lap of its owner. The captain absently stroked the creature's thick coat as he thoughtfully watched the tense figure highlighted by the light shimmering off the water. In his profession, he knew all the aspects of fear, knew how to instill it and how to use it to his advantage, as he had with the English captain. The greater the fear, the less the chance of violence and resistance. Hence his carefully constructed legend; the mere mention of his name wreaked more havoc than a show of force.

And he was using fear to control this girl, by leaving her in doubt of her safety and of her future. Had she known that the articles he sailed under prevented him from harming her in any way, that he had every intention of releasing her whether the ransom was paid or not, he guessed he would have to tie and gag her to control her spirited will. He knew she was badly frightened in spite of the bold front she used as a shield. Such bravado moved him more than her unsettled plight. Had she resorted to hysterics and wailing, he would have played the game without compunction, but harrying such an admirable woman, a child really, tweaked his usually inaccessible conscience.

The captain thought of the Whitelaws and a scowl darkened his handsome features. She was on her way to become one of them, to willingly join that hated clan. Therefore she was to be despised. A hard smile twisted his mouth when he thought of how the Whitelaws would greet the news that the Spanish Angel had snatched up their pretty virgin on her way to the marriage bed. Let them be tormented by all manner of terrors at the thought of the dainty miss left unprotected in his supposedly bloody hands. He no longer saw Merrit as anything but a tool for vengeance that would be sweet, oh so sweet.

Merrit turned at that instant to catch his look, and an insurmountable panic seized her heart and mind. The unmasked hatred in his expression was gone in a flash. Once more he was the handsome captain with the mocking smile and the teasing eyes. The change in him was so startling that she wondered if she had ever seen such evil in that swarthy face. She prayed not, prayed that this angel was not a devil in disguise.

Tremulously, she asked, "Where do we sail to, Captain?" to ease the tension of the moment more than her curiosity.

The pirate leaned back in his chair, still stroking the large, contented cat. "Our hold is only half-full. We'll stay in

21

these waters a while longer."

"Looking for more victims?" The harsh words escaped before she could curb them, but he seemed to take no offense at her swift condemnation.

"Perhaps." He chuckled. "You might as well settle yourself in. This will be your home for the time being."

Any further conversation was halted when the cabin door was pushed open without warning and a scraggly face peered in. The odor of strong drink permeated the small cabin.

"Captain Angel, the men would like to see the baggage to assure themselves of its worth." The sodden man slurred his words, and his grin was twisted.

The captain smiled easily as if undisturbed by the intrusion. "By all means, Mr. James. Take her up. Let them see what Whitelaw's money buys." He sat back while James took the lady's arm none too gently and propelled her from the room. Her eyes flashed to his in an instant of frightened supplication before she was urged onto the deck. He responded with a moody frown, then rose to follow them at a measured pace.

The liquor casks they'd seized had been tapped and the pirates reeled about the deck in drunken celebration. Unlike their well-groomed captain, they were a mangy lot clad in ill-fitting clothes, and for the most part unwashed and sporting tangled masses of hair from crown to chest. Their eyes were hard, and blurry, their teeth were bad, and they wore their wealth upon them: ear hoops, necklaces, rings, and fancy armaments stolen from their unfortunate victims. At the sight of their dainty captive, they formed a rough circle into which she was pushed amid crude catcalls and raucous observations.

Merrit felt naked under the lusting stares of the crew. Trembling inwardly with humiliation and rage, she nonetheless held her head high as she was paraded about to be ogled and jeered at. She was painfully aware of the low neckline of her gown, which left her creamy shoulders bare, as bold gazes feasted hungrily on her, and the bearded, leering faces blurred as she fought back hot tears of humiliation.

Only two of the men refrained from the ribald laughter — their unusually solemn captain and his quartermaster. Only Rufe was truly aware of the degradation Merrit was feeling. He remembered all too well his time on the auction block, knew what it meant to be appraised as merchandise rather than a human being. And it was those bitter memories that prompted him to turn to the captain in disgust.

"Colley, why do you allow this barbarity?"

The green eyes never left Merrit's rigid back as his captain answered with seeming nonchalance. "Let them have their fun. They do her no harm and perhaps it will take some of the starch from her sails."

Rufe looked at him closely, hearing the whisper of anger behind his glibly spoken words. He knew well that his captain had no power to interfere in the distasteful proceedings unless they posed a threat to his prisoner. Only if they did so, could he step in with any real authority.

Merrit gave a sharp cry as her escort stumbled, sending her into the drunken arms of several crew members. Fumbling hands caught at the bodice of her gown and rumpled her skirts as she reeled, nauseated by the sickening stench of sweat and drink. She failed to see the captain take a quick step forward, then halt when she jerked away from the pawing hands with a shriek of rage, her palm connecting with the closest cheek. Her defiant action provoked a roar of approval from the men.

"Captain, methinks you didn't price her high enough," one of them shouted.

"Aye. I'd even give one thousand pounds for her, and I already gots meself two wives," called another.

"I'd sooner see a bit more of the wench before I'd open me pocket," vowed a bold soul, lifting the hem of her gown with the point of his cutlass. When Merrit snapped her skirt

23

down, the razor-sharp blade slit its fragile fabric nearly to her hip, laying bare the clean line of her leg to those who stared. With a colorful curse she'd learned from Mildred, she tugged the cloth together, her dark eyes blazing with resentment.

"Take your bloody hands off me, oaf. I'll stand for no more of this filthy mauling," she spat out. Whirling to face the pirate captain, she mistook the reason for his smile. She marched to where he stood blocking the stairs and shoved him hard. "Out of my way, Captain Fool."

A hush came over the crew at her harsh words, and Merrit feared she had gone too far. The anger in her eyes was tempered by a degree of uncertainty as he gripped her arms in a strong but painless hold and brought her up against his lean form.

"Careful, my lady," he whispered softly. "I enjoy a good jest but I'll not have you unman me before my crew. Tread softly."

"Is your manhood so fragile that it could be damaged by a mere female?" she jeered, loudly enough for her words to be heard for she was unwilling to submit to his quiet threats. His face flushed and his hands tightened on her arms, but when she would not recant, he released her so she could regally retreat below.

"What ho," cried one of the more drunken men. "A lady untouched by the Angel's charm?"

The captain smiled at the man who spoke. "Watch your tongue, lad," he cautioned in the heavy Spanish accent. "You've no bonny face or rounded bosom to hide behind."

The awkwardness of the moment passed as the crew chuckled in amusement, but a foolhardy pirate would not let the incident lie.

"What say, Angel, a wench not moved by your pretty looks?" The taunt came from the back of the group, and the men turned to the tall, blond sailor whose joking words had held a biting edge. The captain met his challenger's eyes, a

24

spasm of anger pulling at his mouth before he smiled coldly.

"A wager perhaps, Durant?"

The other smiled agreeably. "Remember the articles, Captain. She must be willing."

"Willing and wanting before she's turned for a profit," the captain vowed with an arrogant lift of his dark brows.

"I think not, Angel. She be a spirited wench, not like your other docile ladies."

"Would you care to let your share of the next prize ride on your words?" The captain's congenial grin did not warm the cold glitter in his eyes.

The enormity of the stakes had the crew agog and muttering among themselves as Durant's self-assured smile faded. "That is a great deal to place on one woman, Captain," he murmured hesitantly, for the Spanish Angel's power over women was well known.

The captain shrugged and was about to turn when Durant called out, "Done."

The captain paused with a grin. "I shall enjoy collecting both."

"Willing, Captain. Willing," was Durant's reminder as he stepped below.

As he closed the door, Merrit refused to turn from where she stood at the porthole, hugging her arms about her as if she could shed the feel of those hot, damp hands on her flesh, rid her ears of the sound of laughter and tearing cloth. Never had she borne such crushing humiliation, and the prickle of incipient tears made her throat ache drily as she fought to contain them. She was determined that he would not see her bend beneath his mockery, determined to be strong and fight for her dignity. She had only to keep her head high until the Whitelaws paid the ransom . . . if they paid it.

Seeing her shoulders tremble, the captain was moved to

ask, "Are you all right, my lady?"

Dashing a quick hand across her eyes, she spun to glare at him. "You dare ask that after you play the host then throw me to your jackals?"

"I was not aware that you desired me to be your protector," he replied smoothly, not liking the direction of their words. How could he woo her into submission when she was so eager to tear out his eyes?

"If I am the recipient of further ill use, I'll not rest until I see your feet dancing on the breeze."

He gave a half-smile as he advanced into the room, shrugging out of the bright coat and filling his glass. "You are not alone in that wish, my lady." His eyes were drawn to the rent in her skirts through which a rounded thigh peeked out in tempting innocence.

"Stop your leering," she hissed, pulling her skirts about her. "I am not some wanton who welcomes your attentions. I would like my belongings brought to me so I might change and escape your goggling."

He tipped up his glass and drained it in a single gulp, the bouquet he had savored earlier now too bitter to enjoy. "You have no belongings," he said shortly.

"But I saw them brought aboard," she protested in confusion, then scowled. "I forgot you were thieves."

The captain dropped his eyes, curiously wounded by her barbed words. He spoke softly, trying to placate her and to explain without apologizing. "I could not get them for you if I wanted to, not until all is shared out equally."

"Forgive me, Captain, but I cannot imagine any of your men looking fetching in one of my gowns, even one so pretty as yourself."

There was no softness in the eyes that rose to meet hers or in the brutal truth he flung at her. "But they will look fine on the backs of New Providence's whores."

Merrit's lower lip quivered briefly before she turned away from him. Her next words startled him with their meekness.

"I beg a needle and thread from you so that I can make myself presentable."

"That I can manage," he agreed quickly, eager to lessen her antagonism toward him.

She turned in puzzlement. "You are the captain, are you not? You should be able to manage anything you like."

He smiled indulgently. "You do not understand. We are pirates. I am captain only as long as they allow me to be. When it no longer pleases them, they will elect someone else. I have no special privileges, and my orders carry weight only in battle. That is our way."

She digested this and frowned. "What honor is it to be called captain then?"

"I have these elegant quarters," he said, with a disarming grin. "And a double share of any plunder. And your fair company." His sudden movement made her take an involuntary step back. "I will return in a short while. I suggest you stay below while the men are in their cups." At her rebellious pout, he added, "Or your wish for rape may be realized. But that is only my suggestion."

She nodded jerkily then sat heavily at the table when he had gone.

# Chapter Three

The captain leaned against the raised gunwhale, accepting a mug of rum from his quartermaster in companionable silence. The crew's riotous drinking would continue throughout the night, the noise of their revelry carrying far out over the darkening waters. He gave a sigh of contentment as he watched the blue of the sky deepen. Twilight was a time that never failed to stir his soul when he was at sea. Its infinite magnitude and peace quieted his restless spirit. Knowing his moods, Rufe waited for him to speak.

"Was it a good take, Rufe?" he asked finally, the pleasure of the moment dissolving as the sky faded to black and the stars winked on like distant lamps.

"Not bad. Some marketable goods that should turn a tidy penny. Not much in the way of coin though."

The captain hesitated briefly then asked, "I would like some of the lady's things for her."

"Colley—"

"As a favor to me, Rufe," he concluded softly.

"All right." Rufe studied his captain's profile curiously. He had never known his captain to use their friendship to gain anything extra, for to do so was to compromise the oath that bound him. Equal shares for all was the most zealously guarded rule of the pirates. It must be the woman, Rufe thought. A nagging obsession with her had pushed Colley to ask for more than he was allowed.

"Forget I asked," the captain said quickly, having seen his friend's thoughtful frown. "I should not have. I have no right."

Rufe waved off his chagrin and said, "I will give them to her." He felt more than saw the slighter man relax. "Captain, your bet with Durant was an unwise one."

"You doubt my appeal to the lady?" There was mild disbelief in his voice.

"I doubt your motives. What madness moves you, Colley? You need be wary of Durant. He has a taste for your cabin. If he should win this foolish wager, the crew's favor may no longer be with you."

"Then I will step down," he replied simply.

"Durant would not allow you to stay, and your pride would not accept the demotion."

"You are treating me harshly, my friend," the captain complained, albeit with a smile.

"Why risk so much for a romp with a vixen?" Rufe continued, knowing he was the only man on the ship who dared to speak so frankly to the captain. "By God, Colley, she's but a child and not to your taste in female companionship. You'd risk your ship and your title for a piece of skirt? That's not like you."

"No." The single word conveyed more than endless explanation.

" 'Tis the Whitelaws again that goad you toward an insane vengeance."

"Oh, but a vengeance so sweet. To send them back their bride an innocent no more, and if she presents them with a bastard babe, so much the better." His voice was low and it shook with harsh emotion, its Spanish lilt no affectation. Only Rufe had heard him speak so, from the tormented heart that lay beneath his flashy, carefree facade. In this mood, he was like a demon possessed by vindictiveness, a dark angel. Rufe shivered in the night.

"What about Lady Merrit? Would you use her so heart-lessly?"

Green eyes turned to him, gleaming in the darkness. "I care not for her troubles. There is no place in my heart for a woman who goes willingly to make her bed with them."

Rufe's voice was soft and without criticism. "You have no heart, Colley." To stave off any denial, he concluded simply, "Good night."

Flinching as he entered the cabin, Merrit ceased her restless pacing to evaluate the pirate's mood. In the muted glow of the lamp, he truly looked like an angel, his perfect features almost painful to behold, his skin deeply bronzed and his eyes luminous. Without sparing her a glance, he lifted the bottle of brandy and swallowed the remaining liquor in a few measured gulps. Weighing the empty bottle in his hand, he assessed his captive long and silently. Despite her slight proportions, her figure was pleasingly full, her ample bosom apparent. Although her waist was small enough to make her appear fragile, he could find no flaw in what he had seen of her slender limbs. He remembered the luxurious feel of her hair, thinking how good it would be to bury his face in that tousled mass which lay loose about her shoulders. He avoided her too expressive eyes, studying instead her lips, so red and tempting, seeing their edges curve down slightly. Would they taste as sweet as they looked? He was suddenly assailed by an aching loneliness that smothered him in its cold, empty embrace. Was it the liquor or the echo of Rufe's words that filled him with such unaccustomed melancholy? To break its spell, he looked up into her large dark eyes, seeing her mistrust and unvoiced fears.

"You are a pretty little wench," he murmured almost unconsciously. She said nothing, puzzled by his strange quiet. "Has your intended ever seen you?"

"We've exchanged likenesses."

"And how does he strike you?"

Merrit thought hard for a moment, trying to conjure up the features of the man she would marry. "He has a fine, noble face."

"As handsome as mine?"

She looked at him candidly, then said plainly, "I've never seen any one as handsome as you, Captain Angel, but then in your vanity you did not need to be told that."

Oddly, it didn't please him to hear her reluctant praise. With a sigh, he unbuckled his cutlass, dropping it onto a chair.

"The light needs to be put out at eight," he said quietly. " 'Tis nearly that."

"Why douse the light?" she asked.

"Because we are sitting upon enough powder to blow us to the gates of hell and I am in no hurry to see them just yet."

As he reached for the light, she said in a rush, "Where do I sleep?"

"This is the only bed, my lady. I am sorry if it does not meet with your standards."

The comfort of the bed was not her concern. "And where will you go?"

The captain raised an arched brow. "Madam, this is my cabin. I am generously offering to share its meager comforts with you."

"How kind," she said drily, "but I think not."

He frowned in irritation, too tired to argue over maidenly convictions. "Then take a hammock in the hold with the rest of the crew, but I guarantee you'll get more sleep here. It matters not to me."

His brusque retort brought a vivid blush to her face as she stood chewing her lip in indecision, her eyes scanning the rumpled covers apprehensively. The bed looked fearfully narrow and she had never shared one with anyone, let alone a pirate jailor.

31

"Decide, my lady. I've no more patience with foolish virginal hesitancy. I assure you, I have no plans to rape you this night, in my bed or no."

"Your word as a gentleman?" she asked cautiously.

"My word as a pirate, for I am no gentleman." With that sharp comment, he blew out the light, plunging the room into darkness. He paused to get his bearings, hearing the rustle of her gown as she moved across the room. When he took a step forward, he was rewarded by a yowl that made him stumble. "Wretched animal," he growled at the scurrying shape. By the time he reached the bed, his eyes had adjusted well enough to discern her figure beneath the covers. No further sound coming from it, he sat and pulled off his boots and shirt. With a bleak smile, he lifted the sheets and slid beneath them, encountering a bunched mass that made him grumble, "Is it your intention to sleep fully clothed?"

"It is."

He tossed for a moment, then sat up, declaring irritably, "Out."

At his black tone, she hurriedly complied. Did he mean for her to sleep on the floor? Perhaps she would be safer there. She stood hesitantly, awaiting word from him.

"Take that gown off," he commanded. At her horrified gasp, he reasoned, "It would be irreparably crumpled by morning, and I will not abide it tangling about my feet all night."

Timidly, she did as she was bid, unable to argue with his logic and frankly uncomfortable enough to be thankful for an excuse to shed the heavy gown. Her fingers were unusually clumsy as they worked down the ribbons that held together the stomacher of her dress. Finally she slipped out of her gown and discarded the full petticoat as well, having forgone hoops for the voyage. Shivering slightly in the thin batiste of her chemise, and hoping he could not see in the dark as well as his cat, she turned to the bed once more. He had shifted to the side nearest the wall, but he held up the covers for her invitingly.

"I thought you would prefer to sleep on the outside. That allows for an easier escape should you feel yourself compromised. That also means you'll not be crawling over me in the middle of the night for fear that I am trying to take advantage of you whilst I sleep."

Though pricked by the sarcasm in his tone, she was nonetheless grateful. She lay down on the edge of the mattress, rigid with distrust, only to hear him snort loudly.

"I trust you do not snore, my lady," he mumbled, placing his back to her. "Sleep well." He listened for a time to her quick, frantic breathing, then smiled as it slowly grew more normal. The first challenge had been met. There would be many more nights. He could feel the brandy coursing lazily through him, warm and thick, lulling him into quick easy slumber.

For Merrit, there was no rest. She lay on her back, eyes open and hands gnarled with tension. It was a struggle to remain on her side of the bed, for the weight of his body created a dip that threatened to draw her closer. To fight that pull, she kept one leg over the edge, her knee securing her position. She started at his every movement, afraid to close her eyes lest sleep overtake her and leave her vulnerable. On the deck above, the sounds of merriment finally gave way to a deafening silence; the creak of the ship, the rush of the waves, and the quiet breathing of the man beside her the only sounds. In that stillness, her resolutions gave way to the exhaustion of mind and body.

Within moments, however, her eyes snapped open to darkness. Uncertain as to what had awakened her, she sensed a lumbering movement at her feet. The large cat was settling on top of the sheets. She lay motionless for a moment, choking back a cry of alarm, for the pirate had rolled toward her, the shifting of his body bringing hers against him. The heavy weight of his arm rested on her rib

33

cage, his hand curling about the curve of her breast. After her panic subsided, she realized that he was not awake, not about to ravage her, and that the placement of his hand was accidental. Pulses racing, she gave his shoulder a slight push, toppling him onto his back. She was instantly on her feet unable to control her trembling. Realizing she could not return to the subtle dangers of the bed, she crossed to the porthole, resting her head in her hands as she stared over the empty ocean. Unbidden, tears came, and soon she was shaken by weary sobs.

"You've no cause for such tears," said a low voice behind her.

"No cause?" she choked out, feeling his closeness without turning. "I have every cause. I've been taken from the security of my oldest friend, shamelessly pawed by drunken beasts, leered at and laughed at. All my clothing has been taken from me to be used as barter for prostitutes. I have been closeted in a room with a man who threatens my life and my virtue, and I have no way of knowing if my ransom will be met. If not will death or dishonor await me? Tell me, Captain, will I be used as ship's whore in that case? I would prefer a merciful death to that."

His hands moved to her shoulders, felt her cower beneath his touch. As she shivered, he said softly, "Merrit, no harm will come to you. My promise on that."

"Your promise?" she shrilled hysterically. "I do not believe you. Thief, murderer—why not liar as well?"

He spun her somewhat roughly to face him, his voice urgent and persuasive. "I am speaking the truth. I never planned to harm you. I am sorry if you were frightened. Believe me." Even as he assured her of the emptiness of his threats, hoping to soothe her fears, in the back of his mind a small voice was telling him perhaps trust would gain him more than fear with this one.

"Then let me go," she wept. "Please. Set me ashore anywhere you like or put me on another ship. Just let me

34

go. Only then can I believe you mean me no harm."

His fingertips touched her wetly shining cheek. "I cannot," he said softly. "I will not."

"Then let me be," she cried, pushing aside his hand and shrinking back. "Just leave me alone."

He took several steps back to assume a less threatening pose. "If that be your wish. Get yourself some sleep and we shall talk in the morning."

Her eyes, large and apprehensive, went to the bed.

"You may have it to yourself, my lady. I will not disturb you."

After gauging him warily for a moment, she wiped her eyes and returned to the bed, crawling beneath the covers and falling asleep before fear had a chance to seep into her thoughts.

The brightness of day brought Merrit new hope. After a deep, untroubled sleep, her spirit was restored and the bleakness that had brought on her tears had lifted. She stretched languidly, provoking a low growl when her feet came into contact with the warm lump at the foot of the bed. Clutching the sheet to her scantily clad bosom, she looked about for her captor, relaxing when she saw him seated at the table, his dark head pillowed on his arms. Quickly, she rose and pulled on her gown, unwilling to be caught in a state of undress now that the cabin was flooded with revealing daylight. Once she had secured the gown's ribbons, she spied the inviting bowl of water on the wash stand and lifted a self-conscious hand to her hair, feeling a tangled mass that had slipped down in several places, its stray tendrils reaching past her shoulders. She looked about but, seeing no mirror, gave a wry smile. The vain pirate was certain to have one somewhere.

As she walked quietly to the basin, her shadow crossed the table. The sleeping captain gave a start, one hand flying out to jerk free his cutlass. The air sang as the broad blade sliced a rapid arc, coming about to meet the cringing young woman. For a moment, neither she nor the pirate moved, then he let out his breath in a heavy rush.

"I am sorry. I had forgotten you were here," he murmured in apology, setting aside the instinctively wielded sword and rubbing his sleep-swollen eyes. "I am unused to people creeping about me in the wee hours of the morning."

The paralysis of fear left Merrit in a visible shudder, for she had recognized death in that brief instant, and she remarked acidly, "Then you must not entertain as often as your legend suggests."

The captain chuckled and leaned back in his chair. "You are the first, my lady. Beelzebub alone has warmed my bed up 'til now."

She realized he meant the cat and pursed her lips. "The lusty Spanish Angel with no willing women?"

His humor faded slightly at her cool reply. "When we are about our work, we drag no willing wenches along. To this point, madam, you have proved no exception to that rule."

"Nor will I," she assured him tartly. At his smug smile, she demanded, "Something amuses you, Captain?"

" 'Tis unnatural for someone's eyes to be so bright so early in the day."

Flushing beneath his warm stare, she observed, "Perhaps because they are not clouded by last night's drink."

"Always the sharp tongue," he mused, before stretching and then rolling his head and shoulders to loosen the cramping aches of his uncomfortable sleep. When he stood, she noticed for the first time that he wore only loose breeches. He paid no heed to her flustered discomfort. Going to the wash stand and plunging his face into the cold water of the basin, he rose up to run his fingers through short black locks until they lay flat against his head, gleaming with a damp, satiny sheen. He drew the inevitable mirror from the stand's drawer, hung it from a nail in the

36

wall, and after observing his even features for a moment, began to scrape the dark stubble from his chin with the dagger he had taken from her.

Merrit stood a short distance away, watching with guarded interest as he plied the the blade down lean cheeks. The dagger halted in midstroke, and she found herself meeting green eyes in the reflecting glass.

"Wishing for me to cut my throat, my lady?" he asked mildly, then returned to his toilet when she flushed hotly and dropped her gaze.

Within moments, however, her attention was directed to his bare, bronzed back, drawn not by its sinewy sleekness but by the multitude of scars that could only have resulted from the touch of the lash. The marks were old, their marring stripes nearly blending with his tanned skin. She wondered with queazy horror what he could have done at such a young age to earn such a punishment. Most likely it was some crime akin to his present profession and the stripes were well deserved.

His careful grooming complete, he stepped back to allow her a turn before the mirror.

"I've a brush in the drawer you may use," he told her, seeing her dismay upon greeting her reflection. While she worked her chestnut tresses into order, he went about his dressing, pulling on jackboots and a simple white linen shirt, then pushing the sleeves up over his forearms and not bothering with the majority of the buttons. The white cloth contrasted starkly with his dark looks.

"Captain, did you mean what you said before?"

The slight catch of doubt in her voice brought his gaze to hers. "About what, my lady?"

Merrit turned to face him directly, not trusting such an important question to his image in the glass. "That you had no plan to harm me."

He spoke quietly, eyes steady and sincere. " 'Tis what I said. 'Tis what I meant."

"The truth?"

He came up to her slowly, moving carefully so as not to alarm her. "Lady Merrit, you will suffer no abuse while on my ship, not from me or from my crew. You've my word on the articles that rule my life. If that does not convince you that what I say is true, perhaps this will." He reached out and took up her hand, pressing the handle of her dagger into her palm and curling her fingers over it. "You have my protection until the price is met for your return."

He was standing very close, hands warm about hers, as he held her uncertain gaze. Looking up into those clear emerald eyes, she felt suddenly calm, drawn by the magnetism of his nearness, his warmth, and lost to the heartrendering appeal of his handsome features. She wanted to believe him, desperately wanted to believe him.

"And if the price is not met?" she pressed in a low voice, unable to break away from the swirling spell of those green eyes.

"Then you will be taken safely to wherever you wish to go." At his words, he felt her hand tremble slightly, and her body seemed to sag as if she were drained of all but a weak relief. Still there was an edge to her dark eyes.

"And if you lie, Captain?"

He brought up her captured hand until the sharp edge of the dagger touched the pulse in his throat. "Then you may use this blade for whatever purpose you will."

Slowly his hands released hers, leaving her free to hold the knife at his vulnerable neck, his gaze never faltering. Unblinkingly she drew the blade across his throat until its tip rested beneath his chin. Though he did not show it, he was plagued by a brief icy shock, thinking he had misjudged her. The point of the dagger nudged upward, pricking him.

"I shall remember that, Captain," she promised, slightly intoxicated by the power he had placed in her hand. As she lowered the blade, she smiled, showing a row of perfect white teeth. "You are very brave, my lord pirate."

"Or very foolish," he returned, with an answering grin. In this easy moment of truce, he fought the urge to sweep her up and bear her to the bed, though certain she would succumb to the persuasion of his kisses. He had noted the earlier softening of her defenses, but then he had felt the nick of her blade as well. If he pushed too hard, her screams would seal his fate. He had no desire to feel the biting kiss of the lash once more or to paddle in the sea, a morsel for the fish. Better to wait. There was time and she had nowhere to go.

When the captain was gone about his ship's business, Merrit felt a strange mixture of relief and regret. What sort of magic was he plying her with? Was he only trying to subtly bend her will, leave her vulnerable to his promises? Was he only telling her what she wanted to hear, and would the lack of ransom bring a different look to his handsome face, a look she had glimpsed fleetingly before?

She went to the bed and smoothed the sheets as her thoughts traitorously recalled the heat of his nearness, the feel of his hand upon her. Recalling his guileless touch evoked a turmoil of foreign sensations. With a frown, she walked purposefully to the porthole, refusing to dwell in the dangerous untested waters of emotions whose smooth and inviting surface hid the treacherous eddies below. Captain Angel was like that. She would not fall prey to his veneer of charm when she was not certain of his intent. She could not afford to forget that he was a pirate, a thief, a master of chicanery. Whatever else she thought she saw in him, that would not alter those basic truths.

She examined the wicked piece of metal that lay in her hand, a wry smile on her face. How false was her feeling of security? He had disarmed her easily before, so what defense could this blade afford her?

A tap on the door saved her from further contemplation, and as it opened, she found herself clutching the dagger in the deep pocket of her skirt. She relaxed somewhat when she

39

saw Rufe.

"Pardon, my lady. I have brought you a bite of breakfast and some other trifles."

Her eyes passed over the tray of hot food, then took in the colorful garments draped over his shoulder. "My gowns," she cried in delight, forgetting all else as she hugged them to her. "But how? The captain said he could not get them for me."

"He could not. I could," Rufe confided, with a broad smile.

As she stroked the elegant satins and silks, she found herself staring at the quartermaster curiously for she had never seen a black man up close before. He was tall and muscularly built. His skin, the color of well-creamed coffee, revealed a mixed heritage. Only his wide flaring nose and close-cropped mass of tight curls betrayed that he was other than a darkly tanned white man. His eyes were light, more golden than brown, and his broad prominent nose seemed to accent the large smile that split his face. When he raised his brows questioningly at her lengthy perusal, she flushed hotly and stammered, "I am sorry to stare. I meant no offense."

"None was taken, my lady," he said easily. "I would ask something of you, though. If mention is made of the gowns, they were my doing, not the captain's."

"Why is that, Mr. Rufe?"

He smiled again. "Just Rufe, my lady. The captain has no right to any goods taken until they are divided amongst all. What he asked for your sake posed a risk for him, but all goods are in my care, to dispense as I see fit."

She lay aside the gowns, wishing to satisfy her curiosity. "Is that because of the articles he speaks of? What are they?"

"They are our laws, our governing rules. They bind all who sign them at the start of each voyage. To break one is to meet with punishment most severe."

"And what are these rules that govern the lawless?" Merrit

40

was puzzled. She would not have thought to find such discipline among the thieves of the sea.

"You know of the equal distribution of clothing and fresh provisions. There is an equal vote as well. In return, all are expected to keep their weapons ready for battle, and are forbidden from striking one another. It is death to desert in battle. Those are some of the rules we sail under."

She was encouraged enough by his openness to ask, "And which of these applies to me? The captain said the rules prevented me from coming to harm. True?"

"Misuse of prisoners is forbidden while they are in the captain's care," he said, his eyes evasive.

"And?"

A faint smile flickered across his face. "Perhaps you should ask the captain."

"Would he tell me the truth? I am asking you."

"To meddle with a prudent woman without her consent is punishable by death," he said flatly. Perhaps it was better that she knew that. He had no desire to mete out such a verdict, however, and hoped she would not misuse the knowledge.

"Oh," was her soft reply. "Thank you for setting my mind at ease."

"If you need anything, my lady, come to me. If it is in my power I will grant it."

"I thank you again, and my name is Merrit."

"Lady Merrit," he declared with a smile as he bowed to take his leave.

Before giving way to the insistence of her stomach, Merrit changed into a gown of saffron silk, its open skirts revealing a quilted petticoat of the same shade, its stomacher decorated with a graduated series of ribbon bowknots or *échelles* of contrasting chestnut. The fine ruffle of her chemise peeped coyly from the gown's square neckline which was set low enough to offer an innocent yet tempting sample of bosom. The fresh gown did much to revive her humor and

41

optimism, but she told herself she wasn't taking extra care with her appearance to please a pirate rogue.

Nonetheless he was pleased when he returned, and he paused in the doorway to admire her much as she had admired him earlier. The color of the silk did much to accent her beauty, making it hard to think of her as a child, but only a child could be so unaware of the havoc she wreaked on a man. Before he could break from his appreciative trance, she'd spun about to give him a warm smile, stunning his senses with her surprisingly unspoiled charm.

"Captain, I want to thank you for your kindness," she gushed. Then, when a shadow of uneasiness shaded his features, she added, "Rest assured that I shall be discreet about their appearance."

The captain hesitated before returning her smile with less enthusiasm. He was hot and tired after a day in the airless hold cataloguing the plunder and bearing up under Rufe's ribbing at his lack of tolerance for the heat. In the presence of Merrit's crisp freshness, he was uncomfortably aware of his own sticky appearance. He ran his hand through his damp locks to restore some order to them and then spread out the sheaf of papers he was carrying, ignoring the cold portions of his noontime and evening meals to pour himself a liberal dash of rum.

"I trust you did not find the day too tiresome, my lady."

"Not as much as you apparently," she commented, seeing him stiffen as his vanity was pricked by her words. The shallowness of his conceit made her smile at the knowledge that if she could not wound him with the dagger, she could always cut him through his pride.

"Have you dined already?" he asked coolly, annoyed and little inclined to conceal it.

"Hours ago, Captain."

"Then get rid of this," he ordered, gesturing toward the food. As she cleared the plates, he drew a heavy ledger from his chest and placed it in the midst of the scattered papers.

42

With quill and ink at one elbow, a bottle at the other, he began to transcribe hastily scribbled figures into the leather-bound volume. Feeling dismissed by him, Merrit wandered the small cabin for the thousandth time, finding nothing to interest her as much as the man at the table. She lit the lamp and hovered about, while eying him covertly. Seemingly unaware of her, he continued to copy the figures for some time, pausing only to refill his glass. After he'd had several drinks, the persistent ache in his temples began to pulse behind his eyes, making the numbers blur and waver. He leaned back wearily.

"What are you doing?" Merrit asked curiously.

Willing to be diverted from the increasingly arduous task, he pointed to the loose sheets of papers. "I keep a list of all the plunder taken and its source."

"Are all captain's so concerned?"

"Only careful ones" was his cryptic reply.

"Careful of what?"

He merely smiled noncommittally before lifting the pen once more. But he drew a quick breath as Merrit leaned over him to scan the pages, warmly brushing against his shoulder. She did smell good, he thought wryly, most certainly much better than he did.

Startled by the heat that had coursed through her as she'd brushed against him, Merrit pulled away. "You look all in, Captain. Perhaps I could finish this for you," she offered to cover her retreat.

"You can cipher?" he asked in surprise, the knowledge raising her even higher in his esteem.

"My father is a merchant with five daughters and a growing business. He believes in the practical rather than the fashionable, and so we all were educated. In turn, we helped him whenever possible. I am no stranger to ledgers," she said, her fond smile hazy with remembered emotion.

"You would do this for me?" he questioned in mild astonishment.

43

"I would be grateful for something to do," she admitted, then suggested hesitantly, "You should eat something."

He shook his head wearily. "I only need to rest my eyes for a moment."

As she took his place before the ledger, he stretched out on the bed, to be immediately joined by Beelzebub whose throaty purr created an extra pressure in his head. As his eyes drifted shut, cutting off the sight of the woman bent over his table in the soft glow of the lamp, he felt a puzzling contentment that would plague him long after.

Merrit worked diligently over the log, engrossed in what it revealed. One section listed the coin taken from each ship seized, registering staggering amounts of doubloons, guineas, louis d'ors, crusadoes, pieces of eight, and crowns. While the average seaman made one pound per month, these pirate raiders netted one thousand five hundred to fourteen thousand pounds per ship. It seemed as though the wealth of the New World was being channeled into their greedy hands. The rest of the ledger concerned property taken, and whether the goods were shared out or sold to purchase staples for the ship's maintenance. She was astounded by the Angel's thoroughness, and frowned when she saw her name linked with the Whitelaws'.

His notation, "dowry unrecovered," sent a chill through her.

Finally, the figures transferred, Merrit looked to the captain for instruction but found him lost to sleep though still fully dressed, his handsome features heavily etched with fatigue. Lacking the heart to wake him, she gathered the papers into a neat pile as eight bells sounded. Lights out. Obediently, she extinguished the lamp, but after a long day of inaction she felt no need to seek rest. Instead she went over to stare out over the calm, now black, waters.

In the darkness, a sadness rose up in her, bittersweet and painful. She longed for her beloved home and family. She had missed them greatly after she'd left England, but

Mildred's presence had eased the choking homesickness. Now there was no Mildred to recall those happy ties—only an empty ache of loneliness that would not be stilled. Poor Mildred would be frantic with worry.

Sighing deeply, Merrit left the porthole, then cast a glance at the bed. She could see the outline of his sleeping form, but his features were lost in the dimness. Deciding that she needed to clear her head after the confinement of the small cabin, she thought of the fresh air above. Quietly, she slipped from the cabin and stole up on deck. A few crewmen were about, manning the watch or drinking and casting lots, so she kept to the shadows and began to stroll along the gunwale, drawing in deep lungfuls of sweet-smelling salt air. She could almost imagine herself on the deck of the *Chesapeake*, safe and with her own, and that illusion made her careless. She did not see the stealthy movement in the shadows.

# *Chapter Four*

The captain awoke with a start, totally disoriented for a moment, then he remembered Merrit and sat up, intending to apologize for letting his brief rest become sleep. But the cabin was empty. Alarm quickening his movements, he buckled on his cutlass. Had she foolishly ventured above despite his warning? No sensible woman would expose herself to such danger. But, he reminded himself, she was not woman but a child, ignorant of the evil that could stir in a man when temptation was great, and Merrit Ellison was tempting.

A sharp female cry from above brought to life his worst fears. With a curse and an edging of panic, he charged up the stairs.

Merrit was taken totally by surprise when a large hand covered her mouth, smothering her scream of fright as she was pulled roughly back into the darkness. Her flailing arms were seized, making her struggle against the man at her back futile, and a bearded face loomed before her out of the blackness.

"Hold her Freddy and take care she don't yell out," the man before her hissed. She recognized him as the one who had slashed her skirts only now in the dark of night, his harmless if crude joke had become sinister and dangerous. His eyes seemed to glow with heated intent, his teeth flashing briefly like those of some savage beast.

"I don't like this, Bob," the pirate called Freddy protested, his youth evident in his voice, but his iron grip didn't lessen.

"Just some fun, Freddy," Bob soothed. As his rough hand tangled in Merrit's hair, her eyes rolled whitely and her struggles increased.

"I don't like it," Freddy whined. "Angel'll keelhaul us when she tells him."

"She won't be telling him anything." The low confident voice made Merrit freeze. A new horror was dawning on her, exceeding even her fear of the impending rape. "If she was to throw herself over the side, Angel'd carry on over the money, but we'd have gotten our shares, eh?"

"I don't want no part in killing a lady," the youth vowed, his grasp loosening slightly.

"Then you'll have no part of what comes before either."

Aware of her captor's slackening grip, Merrit flung herself forward to break momentarily free. She took three steps before the back of her hair was caught, jerking her up short. Her scream was stilled as she was flung to the deck, and before she could scramble up, a heavy weight was upon her, a hand was at her throat, and another was forcing up her skirts. She managed a single cry before the fingers tightened, cutting off her air and bringing swirling darkness upon her. In wild desperation her hand went to the pocket of her skirt, closed about the handle of her dagger.

By the time the captain arrived, the scene was awash with lantern light. The boy, Freddy, was held between two men, his youthful face pale and terrified. Merrit was huddled on the deck, hugging her updrawn knees, and at her feet, her attacker stared up at the stars through sightless eyes, the hilt of her knife protruding from his chest. For a moment, the captain's mind went blank. Then a boiling rage swept over him. With a harsh cry, he swung his fist at the petrified boy.

Before the forbidden blow could connect, Rufe gripped his captain's shirt collar, pulling him back with a sharp jerk and then shaking him until reason returned to his blazing eyes.

"Colley, no," the quartermaster said shortly. "Leave his rightful punishment to me. I don't want to take you to task as well."

Breathing hard, the captain shook off Rufe's grasp, his features composed and under control once more. He put a boot on Bob's chest and pulled out the blade, wiping the crimson blood on the dead man's shirt. After giving the boy a long look that had him trembling, he gripped Merrit's arm, hauled her to her feet, and propelled her forward, leaving the grisly circle of light behind.

Once they were inside the cabin, he thrust Merrit from him, leaving her to stumble to the bed. He lit the lamp with an unsteady hand, then, with sudden violence, stabbed the dagger deep into the wooden table top. As it quivered, he struck it with the back of his hand, snapping the blade in two.

Mistakenly believing his rage to be directed at her, Merrit cowered on the bed, shaking with shock and unable to lift her eyes to the man who began a harsh, ranting tirade.

"Foolish child, what were you thinking? Did you believe you were strolling in a quaint London park? Didn't you have the brains to realize you were twitching your skirts around pirates, not your tame gentry? What did you expect to happen when you dangled a sweet before them? Did you think it wouldn't be snapped at? Damn you woman." He didn't realize that his anger was stoked by the fear that he could have been too late, that if she had not been lucky in using the dagger she would even now be cruelly used by a man who had no care for her innocence. If her frightened weeping failed to reach him, it was because he was imagining that scene, and her present fear paled beside that stark picture.

"Never venture on deck without me or Rufe, unless you

48

were so stimulated by tonight's events that you wish a repeat performance with a different finale. Do you hear and understand me?" he shouted, gripping her chin to force her to meet his gaze. She nodded dumbly, too numbed to speak. He looked at her dark eyes, puffy with tears and anguish, and at the dark bruises that began to emerge on the tender flesh of her neck, and his fierce determination crumbled beneath a flood of compassion. The release of this strong, foreign emotion shook him to the soul, creating sudden sweet panic. The hand that had roughly seized her became instantly gentle as he sat next to her and tried to draw her to him in an instinctively comforting gesture. But Merrit let out a hoarse strangled cry and struggled to pull away, turning his sympathetic embrace into tightly binding opposition.

"Don't fight me, Merrit. I'm only trying to help you," he insisted gruffly as she twisted in his arms, fearing he was intent on making her submit to more abuse. The calming words that came so easily when he was insincere were difficult for him to voice now. "Trust me. Just for this moment, trust me."

Then he was kissing her, drawing her close, using strength to overcome her protest until she was crushed to his chest, her head tipped back over his arm. At the first touch of his lips, she stiffened in denial, but as his mouth moved warmly and persuasively over hers, her struggles ceased and she allowed his lingering caress to continue. Feeling her submission but aware of her lack of response, he pillowed her head on his shoulder, letting the scalding heat of her tears dampen the fabric of his shirt as he slowly rocked her to and fro. No heart, Rufe? he questioned silently. Then what was this awesome wrenching in his chest, the hammering of his pulse which frantically tried to match the thunderous beat? If not from his heart, from what did these surging sweeps of powerful anguish come as he sought to quiet her?

Torn by her grief and afraid to deal with the growing

49

turmoil within his breast, he held her from him, breathing unevenly as he regarded her serene beauty. Then he sought her sweet lips, his kiss speaking more of longing than passion. Encouraged by the slender circling of her arms about his neck, he used his weight to press her down on her back. Though he was shaken by emotion, his thoughts were not on conquest but on the wondrous feelings she was awakening in him. He kissed her mouth, her eyes, her throat, then through swirling, engulfing warmth, he heard her whisper softly.

"Hold me. Please just hold me."

Quickly compliant, his arms swept her up, and then they lay side by side not moving or speaking until finally the lamp sputtered out, its fuel supply used up.

Wakefulness came to Merrit slowly as if unconsciously she sought to protect herself from what the new day would bring. She floated briefly between the two states enjoying a deep and welcome peace. As awareness gradually ebbed back, she snuggled back into her cocoon of warmth until that encompassing blanket began to stir and mutter.

Merrit's eyes popped open, surprise making her gasp when she found herself face to face with the Spanish Angel. It shocked her to find their arms entwined as if they had fallen asleep in an embrace. He seemed just as surprised as she. Before she thought to pull away, he quickly released her, and without a word, stepped from the bed to go about his morning ritual of washing and shaving, oddly silent and avoiding her gaze.

Merrit sat up more slowly, puzzled by the aching rawness in her throat. Remembrance returned with a sudden stab that twisted through her with sickening clarity. On the table top was the broken tip of her knife still bearing traces of the blood of the man she had killed. Her widened eyes shifted to the man at the mirror, agonized doubt in them. She had slain one of his men and had evoked a violent fury in him. And tenderness as well, she remembered in confusion, her lips parting slightly as if they could still feel the touch of his.

The door of the cabin opened to reveal the face of the handsome pirate Durant. His eyes went to Merrit in the rumpled bed before going to his captain.

"Angel, they be wanting her on deck," he said briefly, masking the speculation in his expression. True, the lady was dressed, but there was noticeable tension between the pair that made him wonder if the captain had taken what the unfortunate Bob had not.

The captain nodded once, then waved him out before facing Merrit reluctantly. Seeing her on the bed, her questioning large eyes carefully holding his own, he felt a vague stirring that reminded him of last night's surging emotions, and it left him feeling vaguely disturbed.

"What awaits us on deck, Captain?" Merrit asked quietly.

"The trial of Freddy Moffit. Bob is by far the luckier of the two," he remarked grimly, his eyes hard and accusing.

"I did not ask them to attack me," she said staunchly in her own defense, though she felt none should be made.

"So you say," he bluntly declared.

Her temper flared at this outrageous turn of events, and she experienced an odd twinge of betrayal because of his callous behavior. "So it is your belief that I should not have resisted."

Her statement brought a dark glower to his face. "No, of course not. 'Tis just an ugly affair I'd have rather avoided." A persistent, nagging inner voice kept reminding him that if he had not fallen asleep the carnage would not have occurred. His voice a low growl, he said, "Ready yourself, and show no emotion. Your part in this allows you no room for squeamishness."

"As you wish, Captain Angel," Merrit replied coldly. She drew herself up proudly, her dark eyes as emotionless as his own.

51

As they walked down the passageway, he informed her that aboard this ship business was always conducted in public and a majority vote decided the outcome. Discipline was left to the quartermaster, the captain's vote carrying no more weight than any other. As the *Merry Widow* drifted on the gentle sea, they joined the crew gathered on the main deck to decide the fate of Freddy Moffit. The boy was subdued, more by an excess of strong drink than by fear, and he swayed in the hands that held him. His eyes, vacant and uncaring, were the only ones that didn't turn to Merrit as she stepped on deck, her head held high as she preceded their captain. The men's faces didn't hold anger or a craving for retribution, but an odd mix of respect and sympathy.

Rufe spoke to her in a tone that carried to all who stood by. "Lady Merrit, you know the penalty for abuse of a woman aboard our vessel. Is Mr. Moffit guilty of that offense?"

She answered in a level, sure voice. "I cannot vouch for his original intention, but he did not harm me and he did refuse to be an accomplice in the other's plan."

"Still his conduct cannot be condoned. He was a part of it all. A touch of Moses' Law should teach him some manners."

Merrit felt the captain flinch at her side. She did not understand the punishment chosen, but sensed its severity by the murmur that rippled through the crew. As she'd promised, she stood impassively while the dazed boy was shackled to the mast and the shirt was torn from his back. Then she understood. They were going to flog him. A solemn Rufe stripped off his shirt to reveal a hard muscluar chest before he reached out to take the lash from one of the men. He shook out the whip, the long coil snaking out on the deck like something dark and deadly. Then it hissed through the air, a dangerous adder, that struck at the boy's unprotected back. He gave a startled yelp more from surprise than pain. Then, before he could draw a breath, the lash sang again and this time his cry was one of pain.

Merrit took an involuntary step back, protest rising in her and insisting she turn away. She gasped as her hand was crushed in another's. Held motionless, she swallowed the bitter taste that rose in her throat, and forced herself to close her ears to the increasing screams as she watched Rufe's arm move tirelessly in an unchanging rhythm. As the count rose toward the far distant thirty-nine lashes called for, the pressure on her hand tightened until her bones were ground together painfully. She turned her eyes on the stoic figure beside her.

Each crack of the whip brought back memories that bled as fiercely as the poor boy's flesh—the feel of the mast's cool wood against his cheek, the warning whistle that sounded a fraction before the fiery sizzle boiled across his skin, the horrible ache in his jaw from holding in pleas that would not be heeded, and the panic of loosing count and not knowing when it would end, thinking it was done then hearing that whistle.

Merrit was alarmed by the strangeness in his faraway eyes and the growing wetness of his palm as he clutched her hand unsteadily. Finally, she tugged on his sleeve to catch his attention.

"Captain, please end this. I am satisfied. Please," she said urgently.

"Rufe, the lady is satisfied if you be," he called out evenly.

The quartermaster paused with only half the punishment dealt out. Then he began to coil the whip, murmuring, "Cut him down and see to him."

In his cabin, the captain sought surcease in the bottle. He was already into his second glass when Merrit asked softly, "For what offense were you flogged?"

He bolted down the remainder of the harsh rum before answering. "Failure to carry out my captain's order."

"Which was?"

He sat down heavily, filling two glasses but not offering one to her. "It was early in Queen Anne's War. We had taken a Spanish vessel, and no one on board was to be spared. I refused to fire on the women and children. My last charitable deed — one I paid dearly for." He stared into his glass broodingly, the faces of those brutally murdered people as torturous as the memory of the agony that followed.

"Were you a pirate then?"

He gave her a cynical glance and laughed. "I was in the Royal Navy. Do you think pirates are the only jackals? Had it not been for Rufe, I might not have survived."

"He saw to your wounds?" she asked innocently.

"He did the flogging."

"Yet you call him friend?" she cried in confusion.

"A good friend. A lash in the hand of an enemy can kill, maim, or disfigure most cruelly. He did his duty and for that I cannot fault him."

"But some would have."

They both turned to Rufe who stood in the doorway, buttoning his shirt. The captain held the second drink out as if he'd expected him.

"Colley was only grateful that I did not mar his pretty face," Rufe joked, winking at Merrit to relieve the soberness of her expression. He touched his glass to his friend's.

"And what will happen to Freddy Moffit?"

"His wounds will be tended, and when he is able, he will be given light duty," Rufe explained.

Merrit was perplexed, for these pirates fit none of the bloodthirsty tales she had heard. Theirs was a strange democracy with a high regard for justice if not for life.

"Angel, a ship," Durant called from the open door, bringing keen looks of anticipation to the faces of both men within the cabin. The captain was off his chair in a trice, running to the deck to take the spyglass.

"What be she?" he asked quickly.

"English, Captain, and heavy in the water."

"Run up the Union Jack and ready all to greet her," he called out, sending the men scurrying in his wake.

Merrit met the captain at the door with an anxious, "What is it?"

"Business, my lady," he said simply, but his eyes were afire. They glittered brilliantly as he pulled open his trunk and began to dress for his role in battle. Merrit watched in fascination as the Spanish Angel came to life by donning the elaborate coat of the Spanish admiralty, heavy with braid and medallions, then adding an extra brace of pistols to his lean hips, as well as a cutlass. He turned to her, his expression serious. "Stay below. I'd not like you to be hurt."

"Or to escape," she added drily.

"That too." He grinned, then left to take command on deck.

The *Merry Widow* was a clean-lined ship. Her gunwales were raised for the protection and concealment of the crew, and her deckhouses were razed to leave the decks flush, to create a sleek silhouette, and to lessen the threat of flying splinters. As her captain strode among them, the crew lashed their hammocks along the gunwales as an extra measure against small-arms fire. Rum was freely passed to give the men spirit, but the Spanish Angel touched none of it. He needed no liquor to stir his blood. His eyes were on the round-sterned, broad-beamed flute with its large cargo area.

Merrit sat below, hearing the Spanish-accented voice ring out loudly for "two-headed angels," chain shot through the rigging to cripple the prey's maneuverability. The wild, undulating cries that had chilled her marrow when first she'd heard them arose as the infamous pirate flag was hoisted.

The ship, a rich prize heavy with gold as well as stores, was speedily taken and plundered, and the pirates were exuberant as the sloop cast off. Heads were knocked out of hogsheads of claret and French brandy, the victors dipping bowls into them while letting off their guns to the accompaniment of pagan howls. Cutlasses were wielded to nick off the necks of liquor bottles as the riotous revelry continued well into darkness.

The cabin was lit by its single lamp when the captain stumbled in, his mind reeling from strong drink and the generous praise of his crew. He was brought up short when a vision of unequaled beauty rose up from his bed for, until that moment, he had truly forgotten his captive's presence. Seeing her in the hazy light through even hazier eyes, his senses clouded under the pressure of a urgent desire to taste her sweet lips and to feel the velvety warmth of her skin against his own.

Merrit wasn't alarmed at first. Relieved to see him after long hours of tense worry over his safety, she did not note the glow in his eyes or the stagger in his walk. She had no way of knowing that the shots she'd heard had been by the crew during their merrymaking, so when the captain had failed to appear, she'd been shaken by a creeping fear that he might be injured. To assure herself that he was indeed whole, she approached him quickly until the reek of alcohol and his heavily slurred speech gave her pause.

"Good evening, Lady Merrit. Do I sense a concern for me in those lovely eyes? Have no fear, for I have survived to seek greater treasure."

She gave a squeak of surprise as his hands gripped her forearms, bringing her roughly up against his chest where the odor of gunpowder and liquor was overpowering. She was too startled to evade his first hasty plundering of her mouth, but outrage quickly replaced shock.

"Captain, please," she protested angrily, twisting her face to one side and pressing her palms to his shirtfront to force a distance between them.

"Aye, I am eager to please you, my lady," he mumbled, his viselike embrace crushing her to him once more.

"Release me at once," she demanded, still more enraged

56

than afraid.

"I will give you release, a sweet release to paradise," he crooned, actively seeking her lips once again but managing to find only an ear. His ragged breath rasped against it hotly.

"Captain, I shall scream," she warned, wriggling to gain some leverage. But she was unable to pry him from her due to his greater strength.

"As you wish, but no one will come. I am the soberest of the lot." He chuckled. "Enough talk. To bed."

"Captain," she shrieked indignantly, jerking backward. Her sudden movement caused his feet to tangle, bringing them both to the floor. His weight momentarily knocked the breath from her, and he was encouraged by her apparent acquiescence. What did it matter? he reasoned. For his purpose, the floor was as good as the bed, and it was far more steady. His kisses burned hotly across the flesh of her neck and shoulders while she struggled to draw air. Then his weight shifted slightly as his surprisingly agile fingers began to work to release the series of bows on her gown.

"No," she wailed, finding her voice. "Get off me, you drunken fool. I'll not play the willing whore for your panting lust."

Not in the least affected by her harsh words, he returned his lips to hers, whispering against them, "Yield to me, Merrit. Yield to me."

The touch of his full, persistent mouth quelled her rebellion for a brief time as strange, dizzying sensations—the first awakening of desire—stirred lazily within her. Her emotions were as glorious and frightening as the lips that sought a response. Part of her yearned to yield and learn what treasures paradise held, but she could not forget who he was . . . or that she had killed a man who had tried to use her thus.

"No," she spat, cuffing him sharply and rolling to one side. Having succeeded in escaping his arms, she clambered quickly to her knees, but he was quick as well. Cloth tore as he tried to catch her; then she was abruptly released.

Panting heavily, she glared at the captain, but his eyes were no longer on her. She followed his rapt gaze to the floor where creamy pearls the size of hail pellets lay scattered about, freed from encasement in her hollowed busks. He reached out an unsteady hand and scooped up several, rolling them between fingers and palm.

"By God, there must be a fortune here," he breathed faintly; then his eyes rose to Merrit's. "Your dowry."

With a desperate cry, Merrit hurriedly began to recover the flawless pearls until he stopped her by placing large hands on her shoulders.

"Are there more?" the pirate demanded hoarsely, his eyes glimmering like the brilliant stones they resembled. "Of course, a fortune sewn into all your gowns. How clever and it almost worked."

"Captain, please," she cried brokenly. "It is everything my family owns. I cannot marry without my dowry. You mustn't take it."

Even then he was prying the pearls from her hands, not seeing her tear-stained face, his eyes lost in passionate avarice. Knowing she had to sway him from this disastrous course, she took his face in her hands, forcing his green eyes to meet hers.

"Captain, I beg you to leave me my future. I will yield to you, only do not take my family's fortune. I will be your willing mistress until the ransom is met."

He regarded her long and pensively, and for a moment as his gaze traveled down to the rent in her bodice, she thought he would relent. When his eyes returned to hers, she realized she had lost. He took her hands gently but firmly and held them away. "I am sorry, my lady. I cannot keep such bounty from my crew." Closing his heart to her weeping, he rose to rummage through the rest of her gowns, ripping open the stomachers to reveal their hidden wealth.

Tipping the pearls into his upended hat, he started for the door, only to have an anguished Merrit grasp his hand. A flash of irritation went through him at the brief feeling of sympathy and desire her pleading ignited, yet he hesitated.

"Is there no way I can make you understand? Take what is there and leave the rest. Leave me something," she pleaded.

Was there no emotion in him? She had reached him once, and had known the tenderness of his touch. But his eyes were as hard as green glass, and unmoved by her tears, he pulled his hand free and closed the door upon her sobbing.

Rufe gave a muttered curse as he was roughly shaken awake. Opening his eyes, he saw his captain kneeling beside his hammock. "What is it, Captain?" he asked in alarm only to be shushed and conspiritorially motioned to follow. Once he was in the empty corridor, he grumbled, "What's wrong, Colley? Has your cat fallen overboard again?"

Silently, the captain extended the hat, watching as a puzzled Rufe dipped in his hand. Then his quartermaster's golden eyes rose, amazement in them.

"Where did you get these?" he stammered softly.

"There's more."

Rufe blinked. "I must be dreaming. I thought I heard you say there is more."

Moments later, kneeling on the floor of the hold, the two men looked up at each other, taking their eyes from the scattering of torn fabric. A wealth of pearls finally lay in a flour sack.

"Have you any idea of how much all this is worth?" Rufe asked faintly.

The captain shook his head, unwilling to think of the pearls' worth to their owner.

" 'Tis Lady Merrit's dowry, is it not?"

"What does that matter. 'Tis our fortune now. The White-laws will never see it."

Rufe looked closely at his friend. "There are some who will ask how you came by this treasure."

Grasping his meaning, the captain frowned. "Not honorably, I fear."

"Idiot. Fool," Rufe pronounced harshly. "Is it worth all the meat on your back? Return it to the lady and ask that she say nothing. We will consider that none of this happened."

"No," he gasped in protest, drawing the precious bag to him. "I'll not surrender it to them. Are you forgetting that if it were not for their treachery, I would be in their place, perhaps waiting for my bride to bring me these. No, Rufe. They made me what I am. They put me on the seas, put this bitterness in my heart. If it were not for them and their greed, I would have been a different man, one who could have afforded to be kind to an innocent girl. But greed begets greed and they will suffer for theirs through mine."

Knowing there was no dissuading him when that touch of madness lit his eyes, Rufe said heavily, "You know if the lady decries all, I will have no choice."

"I will pay the price," Colley vowed unblinkingly.

"Your price is getting ever higher. How much more can you afford to pay?"

"All, Rufe. All."

# Chapter Five

The cabin was dark and without sound when the pirate captain returned. He could make out a vague shape huddled beneath the covers, but he knew not whether she was sleeping or simply avoiding him. She had every right to hate him, to seek revenge. Why did he feel that uncomfortable stirring now that it was too late to change the cast of the die? Did he regret declining the offer of her virginity or ignoring the pain in her dark eyes? Either way, it didn't matter now.

It was all Merrit could do to remain still when she heard him move about the room. Anger and an urge to commit violence swelled painfully within her breast. He may have left her her virtue but he had taken something he had rightly seen as more valuable, deliberately ruining her life. There was nothing left to her now. Without her dowry, the White-laws would not accept her, and how could she return home after shattering the long-planned hopes of her father and the dreams of her mother and sisters? Hate was not a strong enough word to describe the emotion that made her tremble helplessly. If she had her dagger, she would wield it with pleasure. She cursed silently at the memory of his casually offered throat laid bare to her blade. As she listened to him pace the floor with his light, aimless tread, she began to plan all manner of revenge, smiling at her own creative savagery as she drifted off to sleep.

The moment he had dreaded throughout the night came with the break of dawn when, turning, he caught sight of her red-rimmed eyes staring back at him.

"Good morning, my lady," he said evenly, testing the water to see if it was calm or turbulent. The chill he felt was immediate. Wordlessly, Merrit got up from the bed, mindless of her disheveled hair and of the torn bodice that exposed the thin chemise beneath it. Even under these perilous circumstances, that glimpse of her evoked a flare of desire in him. But he wisely remained silent while she bathed her face and assembled her gown into makeshift modesty. When she turned to him, however, he drew a low breath. The waters had suddenly become treacherous. She crossed to him in a few short strides, cracking her palm against his cheek, all the force of her hurt and anger behind the blow. He faced her emotionlessly.

"Would you have the other as well?" he asked mildly, then blinked as she smote the other cheek with equal vigor. He couldn't help but marvel at her beauty as she stood there, the color high in her oval face and her eyes molten with inner fire.

"If you would like to exact a heavier toll without bruising your hand, you can have me fileted before your eyes for my treatment of you. I apologize for my weakness as a man, but not for being what I am."

"I can forgive you for being a man, but not for being a thief. I have no wish to see you flogged. My vengeance will be more subtle, Captain."

The next few days they practiced cautious avoidance. Merrit had the cabin to herself, while he withdrew to the hold. Despite the crew's ribald speculation, Merrit was treated with great deference because of the wealth she had inadvertently brought them. When she was on deck in

62

Rufe's company, she was gallantly and gently received, the men vying for her favor like clumsy suitors. The most eager of them was the boy, Freddy Moffit, who was always underfoot in his effort to please and earn forgiveness. That Merrit was generous with her smiles to all but their sullen captain was a source of great amusement to the pirates, and he bore the situation with ill humor merely watching his men fawn over the woman who refused to spare him a glance. She seemed to be wherever he looked, her name included in every conversation. She had bewitched his surly men, and he chafed at being excluded from her warmth.

So vexed did he become, however, that when the jaunty Durant approached him early one morning, he was edgy and annoyed beyond further endurance.

"Ho, Angel, have you given up on the wench? It will be hard to win your wager with your hammock in the hold. If you care to default now, I will accept gratefully."

The captain scowled darkly, his vanity as sorely ruffled as his pride. "I had been considering raising the stakes."

Durant blinked dumbly. The whole crew was aware that the lady had shut the captain out of his own cabin. How could he expect to sway her now? "To what end?"

"My share of the pearls," he said calmly. "Before morning."

"Angel, ye be crazy, but I'll not let such madness pass. Done. If you fail to woo the lady by morning, I will welcome your fortune."

Within the hour, the ship was alive with news of the wager. Rufe sought out his friend in disbelief but one look confirmed the worst.

"I know, this is madness," the captain said to him. "But I shall be free of her one way or the other by morning."

"That is not what worries me."

Green eyes eyed him curiously. "What then?"

"That once you get close to her, you'll not be able to get away."

The captain laughed. "I've no heart, Rufe, remember."

"But she does, so go softly, Colley. She's become a great favorite with the crew. To have her with you is dangerous to you. To have her against you is dangerous to your position. Be careful. She'll have heard of the wager by now with all these wagging tongues. Do you think she'll fall into your arms?"

"I can hope, can I not?" he said with a grin.

"Fool." Rufe spoke with fond irritation.

"Aye, Captain Fool."

Merrit met his arrival in the cabin with a decidedly cool glance, noting his unshaven face and rumpled clothes with wry amusement.

"Good morning, my lady," he said easily before attending to his morning ritual before the mirror as nonchalantly as if he had not been absent for nearly three days.

Merrit eyed him warily. Freddy had told her of his bold bet, the controversial pearls staked against her honor. It was ironic that he had chosen one over the other only to risk his wealth now on that which he had dismissed. She wondered how he planned to gain her trust and virginity in such a short while. Did he have such a monumental belief in his own charm or such little regard for her will? Would he ply her sweetly or with aggressive force? Unbidden, she remembered his kiss, the way it had sweetly dominated her lips, unleashing disquieting emotions. He turned to catch her intent on that thought, her eyes half-closed, her lips moist. That unexpected softening of her features stunned him for a brief second, making him think of Rufe's warning. Boldly, he pressed onward into whatever danger lay ahead.

"Have you breakfasted yet, my lady?" he asked, sitting at the table in his fresh linen shirt. He noticed wryly that Beelzebub had taken up residence on her lap.

"No, I've not. Would you care to join me, Captain?" Her cordial reply couldn't offset the wariness in her eyes.

Freddy brought the meal, eying his captain with displeasure when he was safely out of his view.

"You've won quite a following with the crew, my lady," Colley observed when they were alone.

"Including yourself, Captain?" she countered. With him so near, it was harder to control her feelings of rage. Her palm itched for the feel of his smooth cheek, her lips for the feel of his.

"Would the Spanish Angel fall prey to a woman?" he teased, favoring her with a slow smile that warmed his eyes to a glowing luminescence.

So he meant to court her sweetly. That knowledge frightened her. She was not sure she could deal with his charm as easily as his boldness. To restore her guard, she asked bluntly, "Tell me, Captain Angel, how do you plan to overcome my resistance by morning light?"

He looked at her steadily, the trace of a mocking smile curving his mouth. "If you were a woman, it would be easy but virginal children are an unpredictable lot."

Merrit's eyes flashed hotly, her injured pride demanding that she challenge his observation. Slowly, she stood and, smoothing out her gown, one of those least damaged, came around the table. He turned in his chair to watch her progress with veiled amusement, looking up as she came to stand between his knees. Her small hands came to rest on his shoulders then slid up his neck into his short, dark hair. Unexpectedly, his breath began to quicken, the teasing light in his emerald eyes mellowing to a questioning glow. As her face lowered to his, his eyes slid closed, and sudden longing made his pulse jump with anticipation. When her kiss did not come, his eyes slitted open to see a taunting smile.

"A child, Captain? Is that truly how you see me?" she chided, seeing the passion she had stirred vanish in an instant.

"You play games like one," he said with a frown. Abruptly, his thighs tightened, trapping her between them, and a slow smile spread across his swarthy features. "If you could meet my kiss with disinterest then perhaps I would believe you a woman."

Determined to prove herself, Merrit bent down to bestow a quick, chaste peck on his lips, but he caught her chin in his hand, holding her still while his mouth slanted across hers with a bruising insistence that was far from chaste. Stunned, she sank down on his lap, her knees unable to support her under the weakening onslaught of emotion that robbed her senses of reason and her mind of will. No amount of pride or vengeance could force her to relinquish that sweet taste of passion. It mattered not who he was or what he had done, that only he had the power to inspire in her a yearning that grew into a desperate fear that she would surely die if he were to stop kissing her before she had explored more of this wondrous dream. She moaned softly as he sought the warmth inside her mouth, his tongue parting her lips for a lingering perusal, this exciting new realm of sensation more devastating than the last.

At a sharp rap on the door they broke apart, hearing the cry "A ship, Captain."

He gave a pained groan and then stood, setting her on the chair as he did so. Breathing in quick pants, his eyes dark with smoky desire, he kissed her again, quickly murmuring, "Do not move. I will be right back." His fingers traced over her cheeks in a light caress, then he was gone.

Merrit sagged bonelessly in the chair, unable to slow the runaway gallop of her heart, her senses spinning in a giddy delight. What a silly child she was. He had only to touch her to make her his own. How could she ever have imagined herself immune to his experienced persuasion? She was a silly untested virgin left shivering at the first heated kiss. He had known she would be, and had taken advantage of her innocence, awakening stirrings of womanhood without thinking of the turmoil he would leave in his wake. She had no right to learn of such things outside her marriage bed, but with the loss of her dowry, her wedding might never come to pass. He was offering to teach her now, and did she really want to learn from any other? Could she still deny that she had wanted it to be him since she'd first seen him? But could she afford a repeat of what had just occurred? Perhaps his interest lay in the wager alone. How could she give her trust when she knew he was not worthy of it?

Her thoughts were interrupted when the cause of her torment reentered the cabin and began to dress for battle. Once he was satisfied with his preparations, he drew a pistol from the brace he wore and extended it to her.

"In case we are boarded and you are not asked if you are here by choice," he explained, noting her uneasy glance. His eyes grew suddenly sultry as he pulled her close and searched her face. He must have sensed her hesitation, for he released her without pressure. "I will be back soon."

The approaching merchant ship rode low in the water, hinting at a full hold. If the Angel hadn't been distracted he might have been warned by how quickly the vessel came about, apparently suspicious of the trimmed-out sloop. Before the Jolly Roger reached the top of the *Merry Widow*'s mast, the merchant ship fired its cannons.

Merrit gave a cry as the sloop shuddered, cannon balls tearing into her hull and deck. Clutching the pistol in both hands, she crouched in terror as screams sounded above. This would be no easy capture. When the door to the cabin burst open letting in a rush of acrid smoke, she rushed to Rufe who staggered in under the burden of his captain.

"No," Merrit sobbed in panic. "He cannot be dead."

"It's a miracle he's not," Rufe told her. "Had a ball drop almost right on his feet." He slung the still figure down on the bed, then caught the frantic woman by the shoulders. "Steady now. 'Tis not as bad as it looks."

Merrit gave a wailing moan as she looked upon the motionless figure. His face was smudged with black powder and crimson bloodstains streaked it as well as his shirtfront and torn coat. Through all the soot, it was impossible to tell the source of the bleeding, but he was a grisly sight. Green eyes flickered open, at first vague, then sharpening in alarm.

"Lay still, Colley," Rufe said firmly. "I don't know how bad it is."

Ignoring the warning, the Angel struggled to sit up, clutching his temples and grimacing. "The ship," he mumbled. "Who's in charge?"

"Durant was calling for the Budge Jack," Rufe said stiffly.

"That fool. How could he call for no quarter. We have to cast off. Dammit, Rufe, let me up." Free of restraining hands, he tottered to his feet, swaying as explosions rocked to and fro in his head. Gratefully he accepted Rufe's steadying hand as he said tersely, "Get me up on deck before all is lost."

Pandemonium greeted them. The seasoned crew had scattered when their captain had fallen. Durant had succeeded in getting the two ships lashed together, but the crew of the merchant vessel fought against being boarded with frantic desperation. Enraged by their resistance, Durant ordered the heavy cannons to be fired into her hull. When he saw the battered captain return to the deck, bloody but on his feet, he cursed fiercely, for the crew instantly turned to him for direction.

"Cut loose and steer clear lest we go down with her," Angel shouted above the gunfire. "Cut loose."

The merchant ship was aflame and her shattered hull was letting in tons of water. From her tipping deck, the captain glared across at the pirate leader in a last defiant gesture then watched in puzzlement as the dreaded Spanish Angel drew his cutless and swung it at the mast, snapping one of the ropes. The bloody flag sailed out over the water, fluttering one last time on its severed cable before falling into the sea.

The sailing master skillfully manuevered the *Merry Widow* free of the floundering craft, putting distance between them before the other ship was blown apart when flames reached the powder in its hold. She sank quickly her debris littering the water.

The pirate captain's shoulders sagged briefly as he fought the pounding in his head that demanded he seek rest. He stepped away from Rufe to wind his way along the splintered deck. Such a waste of life and cargo was no victory. All about him were the screams of the dying and the smell of death, but he could not afford to hear or see the wounded, the fate of the ship was still uncertain. He ordered the stores in the hold shifted to one side to create a list that would raise the shattered part of the hull out of the water. Now if they could only limp to the safety of one of the nearby islands before meeting any other vessel, they would have a chance.

Merrit was choked by the smell of smoke as she cautiously stepped from below. Her eyes sought a single figure, and once she was reassured, she crossed the rubble-strewn deck to see how she could be of help. The injured were being brought to the forecastle where the ship's surgeon was working feverishly to save those he could. Swallowing the bile that rose in her throat, she began to circulate through the wounded, binding minor cuts, mopping foreheads, giving water and where there was no hope simply holding the gnarled hands of the dying as tears washed down her cheeks. She listened to the prayers of those who could manage to say them and spoke the words for those who could not, while she tried to shut out the wails of those on whom the surgeon plied his tools, tools that made him ship's carpenter as well. And she kept her features steady though her soul screamed in anguish.

Watching her from the afterdeck, the captain was stirred by a wave of emotion that weakened him in a way none of the horrors of that long day had. There, kneeling in pools of blood, in the midst of all that agony, she was a true angel, one of light and mercy not of darkness. She saw to his men tenderly, ignoring her own weariness and the kind of men they were, seeing only their need.

"Quite the lady," Rufe said softly at his side, as he watched

69

emotions play across his friend's face.

"Aye," Colley answered simply, not trusting himself to say more. There was nothing more he could do. The ship was secured and now at the mercy of the sea, so he conceded to Rufe's urgings that he go below and see to himself. Casting a last look at Merrit's slight figure, he saw her folding still hands over a motionless breast.

Merrit labored into the darkness. Under the torchlight, the scene seemed a horrible nightmare. She looked up vaguely as a hand fell on her shoulder.

"Come, my lady," Rufe said softly. "You've done all you can. Go below and see to yourself and the captain." He lifted her to her feet, giving her an admiring smile. Even with her bloodied gown, smudged face, and tangled hair, she was arrestingly beautiful as she smiled wanly in return.

Merrit found the captain seated at the table, dozing fitfully. At the sound of her approach he woke with a start, an expression of pain crossing his features because of the thundering in his temples. Without speaking, she brought the basin to the table, dipped a cloth into the cool water, and pressed it to his forehead. He gave a soft sigh of relief, his eyes closing as she rinsed away the layers of filth with a gentle hand. The deep gash at his hairline was now darkly clotted. When she touched it he tried to pull away, but she steadied his head with a hand beneath his chin, holding him still while she purged the wound. The moment she finished, he turned his cheek into her palm. As he pressed a light kiss to her fingers, his green eyes, edged with pain, fatigue, and sorrow, were also softened by emotions he was too tired to conceal.

"Thank you, my lady," he said quietly, "for all you have done for my crew and for me. I must go now. I had not planned to stay so long, but I wanted to see you before retiring."

When he began to stand on shaky legs, she stilled him by placing her hands on his shoulders. "Stay, Captain. It is

70

your cabin. Can you walk as far as the bed? I can not carry you, and you should lie down."

He clutched her forearms for balance and stood, swaying as a swirling dizziness threatened to rob him of his senses. Noting his abrupt pallor, Merrit steered him quickly to the bed, sitting him down on the edge and forcing his head down to bring the blood back to it. Within moments, he straightened on his own, the giddiness conquered, but his color was still not good. Merrit loosened his coat and shirt, which smelled of gunpowder, then slipped them off while he grimaced in protest. His chest was colored by bruises and scrapes, but none looked too severe. She pulled off his boots, bringing a soft chuckle from him.

"This is the first time I can remember a lady undressing me since I was old enough to do for myself," he murmured.

She smiled faintly up at him. He looked so tired and helpless, battered past the edge of exhaustion, but that warmth in his gaze persisted, his eyes following her as she went to the table for a bottle of brandy. After he took a long drink, she followed suit, blinking as the alcohol burned her throat and then kindled a soothing glow in her stomach.

"What is your name?" she asked suddenly.

He looked surprised then suspicious. "The name I once had was lost when I became the Spanish Angel."

"Rufe calls you Colley."

"That goes back to a different time and a different man," he said, firmly but evasively.

"And what kind of man are you when you are not the arrogant, vain Angel?"

He gave a snort of a laugh, a bitter twist to his lips. "A man you would not want to know and one I do not like to claim." Before she could press him further, he growled, "Leave off, Merri. I am what you see. Prod no deeper lest you wake something in me you do not wish to see."

What was he warning her of? What lay hidden beneath this man's swaggering surface? She had seen brief snatches of violence and tenderness, which both repelled and intrigued her.

"I fear I have already awakened something, or surely the bold Angel would not tremble so at my touch." As her hand lingered on his cheek, he pressed his face into it, his green eyes closing in contentment.

"Merri, don't," he whispered hoarsely. That slight spark of resistance faded as her soft lips touched his with shy hesitance. He knew in her innocence, she had no idea of what she had begun, but her inexperienced kiss forced noble thoughts from his mind. If she was determined to cast away innocence, he would not dissuade her. He didn't have that strength of character, nor did he want it at that moment.

"The light," he mumbled against her lips. " 'Tis after eight." As she crossed the room, he lay back on the bed. He would give her one more chance to alter her course, to change her mind and save her chastity. Why he did not know, for unselfishness was as foreign to him as the strange tightening in his throat and chest. He watched Merrit's trim silhouette as, in the darkened room, she unfastened her gown and stepped from it. He slid over in the bed to give her an extra measure of room, offering her another opportunity to forestall what was to come, but she did not take it. Instead she leaned over his chest to find his lips.

For Merrit, nothing existed aside from this moment. Whatever happened, she would have the memory of this time. She rushed toward womanhood without compunction, little knowing what to expect but aware that by morning she would be a child no longer, trusting in this man to guide her along the way. She kissed him with artless enthusiasm until his hands came up to catch her face, stilling her so his mouth could move slowly and gently under hers, savoring her lips and setting a more leisurely pace for their lovemaking. His fingers freed her hair so it spilled down on his chest in a silken wave, the scent of smoke not quite overwhelming its perfumed fragrance.

He shifted his weight, rolling up onto an elbow so she was below him, his lips leaving hers to brush over her delicate cheek and then slip down the slender column of her neck to feel her pulse as rapid and fragile as that of a captured bird. His hand began to tug at the tiny laces of her chemise, fumbling until she came to his assistance and parted the wispy bodice for his touch. The sudden warmth of his hand on her breast made her gasp at the flood of sensations that light caress triggered, her breath catching in an excited moan as his mouth followed his hand, releasing trembling ripples of pleasure as it teased and tasted. Her fingers curled in his hair as the feelings he aroused made her writhe, and she begged him not to stop. His hand swept lower, slipping beneath the floaty edge of her chemise to the satin sleekness of her thighs. As his touch grew more bold in intent, he felt her arch up against him, and he knew he had reached the heart of her passions.

Slowly, slowly, he kept telling himself, as for the first time he fought the rough passion that usually ruled him. He knew she was different. He didn't know why, only that seeing to her carefully would yield him far greater pleasure than a quick release of his own demanding needs. His lips returned to hers as he explored her inner warmth and softness, bringing her tortured breathing to a near frantic sobbing. Struck by a sudden stab of conscience, he ceased his caresses and waited until her eyes opened to meet his.

"Merri, is this truly what you wish?" he asked huskily, torn by the naive yet sultry allure of her beauty, and not certain he could stop himself if she asked it of him.

"Love me, Colley. Please love me," she whispered faintly, then kissed him with an insistent longing that lay the question of her willingness to rest.

After a brief pause during which they freed themselves of their clothes, his weight came down on her, his smooth hard chest crushing her breasts. Her hands moved over his shoulders and down his back, holding him, then clutching him as his knee parted her thighs and she felt the first bold press of his manhood.

This was as far as her innocent dreams had ever taken her. She had no knowledge of a man's body or of just how the taking of her virginity would be accomplished. Her mother and Mildred had thought to shield her from that basic knowledge until her marriage was upon her. Their careful consideration of her naiveté was no help to her now as that strange heated probe touched her, igniting fear and a panicky reluctance. What was she doing? It was all too stark, too suddenly real. Her romantic notions fled to be replaced by desperate alarm as she looked into the face of this man, this stranger who was about to do whatever it was men did with women in the dark privacy of the marriage bed. But here was no lawful husband come to claim his due. He was a pirate, a renegade, her abductor. His face in shadow, his eyes closed, he saw none of her confusion. Her head swirled with the masculine threat of him, the harsh scents of gunpowder, blood, and sweat; the strange feel of a naked man's body crushing her, all hard unyielding muscle pressed upon her inch for inch. Stifling panic raced through her, making her suddenly uncertain and terrified by what she did not know and could only fear.

She began to struggle beneath his smothering weight, rising up in an effort to escape yet succeeding only in bringing him to her with a tearing force that he had never intended. Sudden, burning, foreign pain made her panic that much more intense.

"Don't hurt me," she cried in a small voice, her tears salty and damp under his kisses.

With a tender turn of emotion, he kissed her mouth and then her tears, murmuring softly, "Don't be frightened, love. I am sorry. I did not mean to. It will only be for a moment, I promise you. That is the way of it the first time but never again. Did I not promise you paradise?"

His gentle, stirring kisses and the caresses of his fingertips

74

made her fears and tension ebb, and soon, as he had promised, the pain was gone, muted to a strange warm ache. He was no longer a shadowed stranger on the verge of plunging her into a realization she wasn't prepared for. The low familiar voice that caressed her with a husky whisper of Spanish words brought back her desire for him, the green-eyed thief who had stolen away her resistance. And she wanted him, wanted this.

When he began to move, she whimpered softly then all thought of discomfort was pushed aside by a tingling heat and a growing anticipation. She heard his breath catch; then his lips ground down on hers with a sudden violence that soon became a lingering sweetness. When he had been gone from her, she had wanted to protest the loss, knowing there was more, but now that yearning was replaced by blissful peace and she held her lover with a happy contentment.

He drifted for a long moment as if on a gentle tide, until a hand moved through his hair sharpening his awareness. He opened his eyes slowly, reluctant to leave the encompassing warmth, to find it only a dream. The source of the heat was Merrit's lush body which was pressed closely to his, the feeling of security came from being in the circle of her arms.

"How long have I been sleeping?" he mumbled thickly.

"Not long," she assured him quietly, uncertain and a bit embarrassed by this new intimacy. What could she say to a man who had just known her as fully and completely as a man could know a woman? An awkward timidness would not allow her to call him by the name she had spoken so easily in the height of passion. To ease her discomfort, she murmured, "Some brandy, Captain?"

"Thank you." He stretched, feeling her withdraw slightly from the brush of his bare skin. Sensing her confusion, he wanted to touch her, to kiss her, to say something warm and reassuring, but he was at a loss when it came to such tenderness. Did she expect him to don his clothing and slink off, an unwelcome robber of her innocence? Would she cry

75

rape to protect her honor? He was vulnerable to her whims for the sheets would collaborate any charge she might make. He waited, not knowing what to do. He had never taken a virgin before, or a lady either for that matter. Recalling tales of such women's hysterics and clinging, he had purposely avoided them, seeking uncomplicated relief from undemanding whores who cared not if he was gentle or if he kissed them or if he left them without a word as long as he left coin. Had he been wrong to let his obsession for this dark-eyed girl sway him into ignoring his previous precautions? Would she fly at him in a rage or become dewy-eyed and cloying, expecting this union of their flesh to become something more than he would let it be?

He sat up as she slipped nervously from the tangled sheets, regretting the movement because it drove spikes of agony through his temples. The sight of Merrit gliding about the darkened room helped him fight the faintness that threatened. He even managed a slight smile when she returned to sit at his side and pass him the heartening amber liquid.

"There you are, Captain," she said in an odd, breathless voice.

"Regrets, my lady?" he asked softly, sipping the brandy and trying in vain to discern her expression. It had been long years since his name had been spoken by a woman, and he was sorry she was no longer calling him by it.

She was silent for a some moments, then she shyly looked into his eyes. "None," she whispered. His silence made her wonder how he viewed her now. Well, she wasn't about to sit there blushing like a confused imbecile.

"How is your head?" she asked lamely. Did she sound as foolish and awkward as she felt.

"Bloody awful," he confessed, the hint of discomfort in his tone bringing her fingertips up to brush his temple in an unthinking gesture.

An unpleasant stickiness matted his hair, and he flinched

76

at her touch. The thought of his pain brought back surges of tender feeling and an urge to hold him close, but suddenly she was afraid of such emotion. What was wrong with her? This was the man who had ripped her future security from her gown. Oddly, she couldn't force that complaint into focus. Instead, she said in a rather stilted voice, "I am sorry I proved to be the virginal child you suspected I would be."

"No," he countered softly. "You were not at all what I expected." He leaned forward, meaning to give her a light kiss, but her lips clung to his, her slender arms encircled his neck, and her gentle bosom pressed against his chest. Her candid desire shook him. "I'm sorry I hurt you," he heard himself saying huskily.

Her fingers brushed his lips. " 'Tis not the pain I remember."

"I apologize for not showing you the promised paradise," he whispered, kissing those soft fingertips.

"Didn't you?"

He smiled at her obvious surprise, wondering if he had ever been so ignorant of life. No, he had never had the luxury of innocence. How long had it been since he had experienced the thrill of being with a woman, the quivering of emotion and the shortness of breath, the need to share fully touch for touch, joy for joy? He never had done so. Oh, he had enjoyed nights of pleasure in the arms of countless women, taking that effortless ride to physical release, but none had seared his soul like this guileless, child — a woman now.

"Let me show you now," he crooned silkily, taking her willing mouth as his palm moved over the silken curves of her body. She shivered, then pressed eagerly against his touch. This time there was no halting his caresses until he lifted her to the ecstatic state he'd promised.

While she was content to languish there, she felt his heaviness above her and drew a quick breath lest he be wrong about the pain. He wasn't, and she welcomed him with a soft cry of renewed wonder, matching his movements until that sweet, undeniable friction made her the epicenter through which thousands of shock waves rolled and she shook with the wrenching force that could move the earth and the heavens. Tremulously she sobbed his name as he, too, was swept into the tidal pull of her fulfillment.

# Chapter Six

Their awakening was abrupt as well as rude. A bearded face peered in, then quickly withdrew to call a message through the closed door.

"Captain, the islands lay ahead. What be your orders?"

"I'll be right up," he answered without a thought. Then he cursed reluctantly and buried his face once more in the satin web of Merrit's chestnut hair. He felt her lips press against the top of his dark head as her fingers teased at the nape of his neck.

"Don't go, Colley," he heard her whisper, her breath stirring his hair and her words, his heart. "Not yet."

With a jolt of determination, he told her simply, "I must," and got from the bed.

Merrit rolled onto her stomach to watch him dress, feeling no embarrassment, only an admiring warmth at the sight of his sleek nakedness. She gave a tiny sigh, knowing that once he left her side the Spanish Angel would take the place of this man. He buckled on his cutlass and came to kneel at the bedside to touch her lips with his in a bitter-sweet kiss. Then he was gone.

Merrit rolled over into the warm hollow his body had made, hugging the covers to her and closing dreamy eyes. So this was the womanhood she had sought, a new sense of completeness, of belonging that linked her with emotional bonds to a man whose name she did not know. She refused to consider the consequences, jealously clinging to the moments they had shared as if time had stopped and nothing could touch them. A silly dream, perhaps. She was a woman now, initiated into this state not by just any man but by the Spanish Angel of the heavenly face and the devilish reputation.

Chiding her self-indulgence, she rose to wash and slip into a fresh gown. Refusing to let a frown linger when she touched the roughly mended bodice, she went about brushing her hair to a glossy sheen. Her reflection in the mirror seemed subtly changed — her cheeks were infused with color, her eyes were soft and glowing, her lips were red and slightly swollen. Was this a woman's face, one that hinted at some smug secret yet was sparked with a new confidence? She smiled at the face that was young but no longer youthful.

The appearance of their captain drew many a speculative glance, and there were some throaty chuckles for news of his relationship with the Lady Merrit had preceded his arrival. He did not hear or chose to ignore the gossipy murmurs as he crossed to the sailing master, instructing him to find a secluded cove for their careening. His eyes were intent on the approaching shoreline when Rufe pressed a hot tin cup into his hand. He merely smiled and sipped from it gratefully. Rufe was puzzled. Not diplomatic where women were concerned, Angel was usually boasting and full of exaggerated tales of his prowess after a new conquest, especially after one as lucrative as this. But this morning he had nothing to say and his friend became worried.

"How do you feel this morning after nearly shaking hands with the devil yesterday?" Rufe asked with forced lightness.

The captain put a hand to his head. It still throbbed with a persistent ache. "Better than many others," he remarked grimly, his eyes going over the splintered, blood-spattered deck. "At least I am whole."

Respecting his melancholy, Rufe said nothing more. When he saw Durant approaching, he tried to wave him off, sensing the man would be wise to keep his distance after such a costly blunder, but Durant was ever tactless.

"Morning, Angel. We are waiting to hear how you fared last night," he called boldly, attracting the attention of curious ears and a pair of cutting green eyes.

"Comfortably," the captain answered calmly, his even tone contrasting with his glittering stare. "I am touched by your concern."

"If what I hear is true, you have no need for such modesty."

"And what, pray, have you heard?" The brittle snap in his words brought a frown to the other's face.

"Perhaps we should ask the lady if she was indeed willing."

Only Rufe's cautioning hand restrained a rash response. "Ask her nothing."

"What kind of woman lets you steal her fortune and then her virtue? It makes me wonder about your truthfulness or the lady's honor."

"Wonder no more."

The men turned in surprise toward the petite woman who'd uttered those cold words. Merrit was enraged. Eyes black with fury, she railed, "Perhaps you would like the stained sheets to run up your shrouds as proof for all to see. And as for the question of willingness, we can lay that at rest as well."

She strode up to the wary captain, meeting his stare with angry directness and deliberately taking his face in her hands and kissing him fully. He remained unmoving, aware of the wrath and humiliation that provoked that hard, passionless gesture. It was not the time to reassure her and soothe her ruffled pride. When she stepped away, he realized his error. He should have spoken some word to hearten her, but now her dark eyes forbade him to.

"Collect your wager, Captain. You seem to have won it."

Had the captain followed her to the cabin, her anger and hurt might have been dissolved with a tender word, but he

81

remained on deck to see to his ship and she was left to nurse her wounded pride. She waited for him to come to her, to explain that he had not lain with her simply to collect his wager, and in his absence, her anger grew. Had she been more experienced, she would not have doubted him, but the new, fragile emotions she was feeling were crushed by her certainty that it had all been a game to him. Why indeed should he be moved by the passionate union that had so shaken her? He was no untried lad. She was just another one of his many conquests, just a pleasant diversion and a profitable one at that. She paced and cursed and fought back hot burning tears. He would not make her cry. He would never again make her cry. Why had she tried to convince herself that there was more to him than she could see?

The crippled ship limped into a shadowed cove on one of the many tiny, lush islands found in the coastal waters from Virginia through Florida. It was an ideal spot for repairs, with a deep sandy bottom and sturdy overhanging trees. The pirates quickly set about the task of shifting their guns ashore and mounting them on hastily constructed earthen mounds so the helpless ship might be protected. When the top masts were removed, the crew went ashore to wait out the repairs. Block and tackle was strung from masts to the trees at the water's edge and the *Merry Widow* was slowly rolled almost onto her side to expose her badly encrusted and battered hull.

Merrit was taken ashore in the first boat, and she sat on the shady beach glaring sullenly at the ship as repairs commenced and her sides were scraped. The tropical air did little to warm her temperament, and only Freddy Moffit dared approach her with an offer of lunch and refreshment. He followed her icy stare to the beached sloop, seeing the confused mixture of desire and fury in her expressive eyes as they feasted hungrily on his captain who worked alongside

82

the others, shirt off and feet bare as he helped piece together the shattered hull. Freddy could have told her a thing or two about the Angel, that he was a good and fair man to sail under, that he was popular with the men, bold in battle, and most importantly, he was lucky. What he most wanted to tell her of was the Angel's way with the ladies. The man could be most charming and attentive, but once he became bored, he was gone — and he never looked back. That is what he would warn her of, if he thought she would listen. He had only to look at her to know she would not. Wordlessly, he left her to her stormy brooding.

The pirates basked in their island stay, building a large fire over which they roasted fresh game and around which they pulled their corks. With the repairs to the ship almost completed, the rum flowed generously and spirits were high despite their costly encounter the previous day. To them, life was fleeting at best and held cheap. With the promise of adventure and gold before them but not a lengthy future, they dwelled only on the day. As an outsider filled with hope and anticipating a long life, Merrit found their revelry callous in the wake of such a loss. She noticed that their captain held himself aloof from the merriment and stood at the edge of the water. Leaning back against a palm, a bottle of rum in hand, he stared out across the calm water bloodied by the setting sun. In spite of her anger, she felt a painful stir of emotion, for even hurt did not stop the wanting. She wanted him and wanted to discover if what had taken place between them was real or part of a cruel charade. Part of her didn't care which was true. It was willing to be used by him if only he would come to her again and awaken that soul-wrenching passion. But her pride and common sense would not allow that. They demanded that she hold back and seek a sign of his sincerity. There had to be more to him. She wanted that to be so.

The serenity of the Angel's twilight watch was broken by a jeering voice.

"Once sampled, have the lady's charms lost their appeal?" Ignoring the captain's cold, green-glass stare, Durant continued. "Or could it be that the brave Angel is afraid to face her after bearing the brunt of her scorn? Has the lady made you soft, Angel?"

The captain took a long pull at the bottle, then said almost congenially, "I do not like you. I have never cared for your loose mouth, so take care how you flap it in my presence lest I be moved to close it for you."

"Captain, I would like a word with you," Rufe called out. He sensed trouble brewing. Hostility had always existed between those two, and it was becoming dangerously apparent that the barnyard was too small for both of those strutting cocks.

"We will speak another time, Angel," Durant said flatly, his pale eyes narrowed and threatening. He would not behave rashly before the burly quartermaster who was known to be the captain's man.

"Be thinking of where you will sign on when we reach New Providence," the captain told him coldly.

"I was about to tell you the same," Durant confidently replied before he swaggered back to the fireside.

Rufe regarded his friend closely as they shared the rum. Then he spoke solemnly. "I would pay heed to his words. He has gathered a coterie about him and has been building support with the crew in order to turn them from you. I have no wish to serve under him, but I will not promote your cause if you refuse to. Some feel your interests no longer lie with the men but that you follow softer pursuits." His meaning provoked a warning frown that was ignored. "Colley, you cannot afford moodiness. Go make your peace with the lady, then join your men and court them like they were the prettiest whores."

Merrit looked up suspiciously as the captain approached, feeling a sharp tug at her heart as he drew nearer. He stopped at a cautious distance from her, his expression

84

betraying none of his thoughts.

"My lady, have you need of anything?" he asked with simple courtesy. He himself needed only one thing—to look upon her pretty upturned face, the face that had plagued him throughout the long day. Now that evening had come, he found himself desiring her company. He had never sought out a woman for that purpose, finding companionship among his men, but now he would have preferred a quiet talk with this lovely woman to the easy comradery at the fire. How strangely she worked on his mind, her lingering sweet promise just beyond his reach.

"I am fine, Captain. You have done quite enough for one day."

Her tart reply froze the warmth in his eyes and turned down the generous corners of his mouth. Tired and uncomfortable on her sandy bed, she did not welcome his taunting presence.

"As you wish, my lady," he responded coolly, giving her a slight bow before he took his place with his men.

Repairs were completed on the *Merry Widow* by late afternoon and the smell of the cooking tar, sulphur, and tallow that would be used to seal her hull hung heavily on the scorching air. The day had become unbearably hot and humid, so the once-jovial pirates were surly because of throbbing heads and short tempers. The ship would not be ready to sail until morning, and they were stranded far from the cooling sea breezes until then. Durant and the captain had been circling each other throughout the day like wary wolves seeking a weak flank. Their cautious antagonism came to a head when Durant began boasting of his quick action in taking control of the sloop, his eyes on the pacing captain as he addressed a small gathering of his chosen companions. He'd made sure Rufe was out of earshot before beginning his needling commentary, and he felt a smug satisfaction when the captain turned on him, his face dark

85

with rage.

"You speak boldly for one whose foolishness cost us a wealthy cargo. If you had not waved the Budge Jack, quarter would have been given. The loss of that ship marks your carelessness and poor leadership."

Durant's features became mottled, and he rose to his feet with menacing intent. "If your mind hadn't been on your whore, we could have escaped all harm," he cried harshly. "You should have seen it coming. At the first sign of danger, you should have flown your true color, a bright yellow, calling for us to cut and run."

"If that be my color then yours are red for the blood of your crewmen needlessly spent and green for the whining envy you show as you wallow in my shadow."

The captain was rocked back by the force of the blow that split his lip. Tasting the saltiness of blood, he struck out, catching Durant's jaw with the back of his closed fist and knocking him to the sandy beach. Bored and testy, the crew formed a quick circle about the two men, shouting and catcalling as Durant charged off the ground full tilt into Angel and sent them both rolling as they exchanged buffeting blows. Before an advantage could be gained, a booted foot flashed out, met Durant's ribs, then was planted firmly on the captain's chest to keep him from pursuing the attack.

"Enough," Rufe roared, bringing an abrupt halt to the confrontation. He released his friend and both men scrambled up, their eyes shooting venom. "Since the two of you seem to have so much energy and it is too hot for me to flog you both, decide between you how to settle this quarrel and then have at it."

"Pistols and swords," Durant demanded fiercely, and his opponent quickly nodded his agreement.

The skirmish brought Merrit from her isolated retreat. Her relief at Rufe's intervention was short-lived, for a brace of pistols was soon split between the two combatants. When she started forward, a hesitant hand caught her arm.

86

"Don't interfere, my lady," advised Freddy Moffit. "It would not be welcomed."

Realizing he was right, Merrit swallowed hard to force down the dry knot of fear that had lodged in her throat. Seeing her distress, Freddy patted her hand awkwardly.

"Don't fear for Angel, Lady Merrit. They'll not kill each other. 'Tis only to first blood."

It was in her mind to deny her concern, but she saw how foolish that would be. She was petrified, staggered by the thought of the emptiness the loss of him would bring. She vowed that if he survived this exchange, nothing would keep her from him, not her doubts, not his indifference. Life was too short. The pirates had taught her that, and she would waste no more precious time by keeping herself from the man she wanted.

The two men faced each other, heavy pistols primed and lifted. Durant managed the first shot, his ball whistling past the captain's ear in what was clearly meant to be a killing shot. Angel's cool green eyes sighted down the barrel. His finger tightened on the trigger, then he frowned. Killing Durant outright in this fashion would serve no purpose, would give him no satisfaction. He sighted down, his shot kicking up the sand between Durant's boots.

Durant smiled craftily and drew his cutlass. "Come on then, Angel. I'll enjoy carving my mark on your pretty face."

Their duel was not the delicate dance of fencing. The cutlass is a broad, brutal weapon made to chop through flesh and bone, and the two men wielded the heavy blades savagely. Without thinking of finesse, they sliced and jabbed, the sound of metal on metal resounding along the narrow beach. Durant had the advantage of size and strength, but not of cunning and agility. While Merrit stood frozen, the pirates yelled out their encouragements, and money changed hands as the two men circled each other, wet with sweat and breathing hard. Finally Durant's weapon flashed out in a short two-handed chop to the flat of the captain's blade, knocking it from his foe's numbed fingers. Smiling and wanting blood, the blond man bore down on his unarmed opponent. Angel side-stepped the thrust, caught Durant's shoulder, and brought his knee up into the bigger man's stomach. Then he scooped up his sword while his opponent gasped for breath. Using his advantage, Angel wielded his blade, piercing Durant's arm, and then kicked the feet out from under him with a quick swipe of his boot. Straddling the wounded man, the winded captain pressed the cutting edge of his cutlass to Durant's throat.

"Yield or I'll have your head," he snarled.

"I yield. I yield," Durant wheezed faintly, seeing no hope of quarter in the captain's glittering eyes.

Amid much cheering and back thumping, the captain was lifted from his defeated foe, and a bottle of rum was placed in his hand. Using the stained blade, he nicked off the top and drank deeply from the broken neck while, unnoticed, Durant picked himself up, his eyes still hot for vengeance, and Merrit sank weakly to the ground.

The water was so cold it nearly shocked the Angel sober as he waded out into its icy darkness, the still surface a black mirror reflecting the moonlight that played between the sheltering trees. He gave a contented sigh as the clear water washed away the caked layers of dirt and the day's heat as it soothed his aching shoulders. A surprisingly poor swimmer for one who had spent more than half his life on the sea, he paddled awkwardly about the shallows, finally rolling lazily onto his back to float, eyes closed and rum-soaked mind drifting in pleasant emptiness. The touch of hands on his shoulders was such a surprise that he sank beneath the surface, and water rushed in to choke off his cry of surprise. Unable to draw a breath, he floundered in sudden panic, not certain which way was up until the other swimmer rescued him. After such close contact, there was no mistaking his assailant's identity.

88

Sputtering and coughing, he rubbed the water from his eyes, then made out a pale gliding shape swimming across the pond with smooth measured strokes. Smiling as he thought of her silken nakedness against him, he waited for her return, but she stayed out in the deep center of the pond, playing about in the shadowy darkness like some mythical nymph of sea. Teasing glimpses of her skin and the sound of her soft laughter were inviting. His perception dulled by drink, the distance didn't seem too far so resolutely he pushed off from the bottom and splashed ineffectively to the spot where he had last seen her. But she was no longer there. Winded and alarmed by the pull of the water, he called to her and she came to him, slipping her arms about his neck, her lips warm and wet on his own. He ceased his floundering, her buoyancy keeping him afloat. Coquettishly, she pushed away from him, and water closed over his head in a dark rush. He managed to return to the surface, struggled to keep his head up and call to her in an unsteady voice. He hated the helpless sound of his words, but the thought of drowning in a calm pond angered him more especially when it would happen because he'd chased an elusive sylph who didn't take his panic seriously.

"Over your head, Captain?" she taunted, smiling as he gripped her forearms with a desperate strength. "It's not far to shore, and it's easy to learn how to swim."

"Don't let me go. I don't wish to learn now. Don't let me sink."

She grinned at his shaky tone. "Why, Captain, I think I rather enjoy having you at my mercy." The deviltry in her eyes made him frown anxiously. "Even a child can learn to swim." She glided away, leaving him to paddle frantically, his agitated movements making him swallow a good deal of water.

"I am not enjoying this," he clipped out angrily. "Stop your games, Merri, before I drown." He caught her hand gratefully, unwilling to let her escape him again.

"Relax, Captain. Trust me. Is that not what you are always saying? Trust me?"

"You have a remarkable sense of humor, my lady," he growled, but he was forced to place his safety in her hands. She swam to the shallows with strong, easy strokes, towing him with her. Once his feet touched bottom, his confidence and humor returned, and he pulled her roughly to him.

"I'll teach you to toy with a poor drunken fool in fear of his life," he scolded harshly, then savaged her mouth with a twisting kiss. When she melted against him, her arms entwining about his neck in willing surrender, his kiss softened to linger over her lips while his fingers sought the wet tangle of her hair. Merrit's head fell back as his mouth moved hotly down her arched neck, her coral-tipped breasts pressing against his chest and her slender hips molding to the bold urgency of him.

"Oh, Colley, I want you so," she whispered hoarsely, meeting his lips as his arm swept behind her knees to lift her easily.

He carried her to the grassy edge of the pond and placed her on the soft earth, covering her with his warmth. His kisses caressed all of her, burning where they touched and making her moan with mounting desire. She caught his dark head between her hands, pulling him down to her, her mouth devouring his with an intensity that made his reason swirl. His passion was a molten ache when she came to him, drawing him into an endless darkness of hot flashing sensation. His heart thundered like roaring cannon fire, and his breath rushed out in the raspy gusts of a gale over calm waters. Above those deafening sounds, he heard her voice, a low sweet whisper against his ear, begging, "Love me, Colley," and more surprisingly his husky answer. "I do."

# *Chapter Seven*

"If this be a dream, don't wake me from it." The lazy murmur was voiced by the man who lay stretched out on his back, his dark head pillowed in Merrit's lap. She wore only his linen shirt, her drying hair hung loose about her shoulders, and the sight of her warmed him the way the rum had earlier.

"Then close your eyes, milord pirate," she replied softly and her fingertips traced the smile that curved his full lips. Though her body felt heavy and relaxed, languidly peaceful, her thoughts were in a turmoil. Looking down on his features, she felt a soft flutter of hope then purposefully crushed it. What did she want with the love of a pirate? She was betrothed. She had obligations to meet. She shouldn't even be sitting here in the still tropical darkness holding his head and caressing him with her eyes, but no power on earth could make her move. She had followed him purposefully to the secluded pond just to have this moment, and she would not be cheated from it. The need she felt for him frightened her with its bold flaunting of all she believed.

As she brushed back the dark lock that strayed across his brow, she asked hesitantly, "Have you ever been in love, Captain?"

Without opening his eyes, he smiled and replied jauntily, "I have loved many but have never been in love." At her long silence, he looked up warily, seeing the uncertainty of her expression. How young she looked and how vulnerable. "Do not fall in love with me, my lady," he cautioned softly. "I will not be tied and I will not be changed."

"You flatter yourself, Captain Angel," she quipped lightly to cover the sudden painful wrench of her heart. "Why would I take a vain pirate rogue when I am pledged to one of the wealthiest men in the Colonies?"

There was an abrupt stiffening of his features, and his eyes closed but not before she saw a strange hard glimmer in them. His voice betrayed no hint of his thoughts when he retorted, "But I make a satisfactory lover, you must admit, even for a roguish pirate."

"Most satisfactory," she agreed huskily, bending to kiss him. His response was slow in coming, then his hand rose to caress her cheek and run down her neck to disappear inside the open shirtfront. For a moment her words were halted by the quivering surges of pleasure his touch gave; finally she asked, "Colley, when are you going to release me?"

"You seem anxious. Have you found our hospitality wanting?" he asked drily but he still would not open his eyes, afraid of what they might reveal to her.

"Don't be mean. You have been an admirable gaoler."

"Soon, my lady. We sail for New Providence in the morning."

"Oh," was her faint reply.

He slit his eyes to peer up at her, finding her pale and troubled in the dim light. Frowning, he asked, "Do you fear I will not keep my word and let you go?"

Hearing the slightly injured chiding in his voice, she answered quickly, "No, of course not," but there was still a sadness to her that disturbed him.

"What then?"

"You have left me an uncertain future, milord pirate," she said quietly. "You send me to my intended with nothing to offer, no dowry and no chastity."

"And I regret taking neither," he admitted with a grin. To his dismay, her eyes began to shimmer with tears. Again, he felt the inexplicable need to comfort her and his voice grew deep with emotion. "Merri, no man could look at you and say you have nothing to offer. No man."

The tears began to fall, slipping in silent anguish down her cheeks to fall like salty jewels upon his face. "If he will not take me, I don't know what I shall do," she whispered, not stopping to realize she was confiding her fears to such an unlikely source, the man who had caused all her grief and who would not be moved by her plight. She wanted no sympathy, just someone to vent her worries on as if voicing them could ease the pressing torment of panic in her breast. "If he turns me out, I'll have nowhere to go. My family put everything into the dowry contract. Without the marriage my father will be ruined and all hope will be gone for my sisters to make a good match. There will be no money to bring me home even if my family wants me to return after I have betrayed their trust."

"None of the fault is yours," he soothed gently. "They cannot blame you."

"No?" she cried wrenchingly. "Do you think they would approve of my willingly taking my captor in my arms, giving him what by right should be my husband's?" Her eyes sparked with sudden horror as she stared down into his handsome features. "What if I should already have conceived your child?"

He frowned at the abject terror and denial in her tone, his vanity bruised by her harsh rejection. "I think we should make an admirable child between us."

She let out a stricken wail, and wept all the harder until he could bear no more of her distress. He sat up, embracing her tightly and pressing her damp face to the warm flesh of his shoulder as he stroked her glorious hair. "Enough," he murmured with an easy tenderness. "The past cannot be changed and the future will come in all good time. The only thing you have in your hands is the present. Take what pleasure you can from it, enjoy each moment for there is no promise of what is to come. You bemoan, like a child, that which you cannot reach. Grow up, Merri. There is no time to waste on what could or might be. Seize the present and leave the future to itself."

Her weeping stilled and she leaned against him in silence for some time before her hands moved up his scarred back, fanning out across tanned shoulders, then gliding into short black hair. Her face tipped up to his, her dark eyes liquid and glowing, her lips parted to welcome his.

"Colley, I am yours for this night without regret or reservation; the future be damned."

She felt his smile against her lips and sighed as he bore her down to the mossy ground.

Propped up on an elbow, he was still for a long while, looking upon the serene beauty of her sleeping features as the island came slowly to life about them. The heat of the sun became a warming caress, and the sounds of the water and of the tropical birds were a soft orchestration of nature. Fearing to touch her lest she awaken, he was content to admire her—the thick glossy hair tousled about the creamy perfection of her face, the feathery lashes that hid eyes which could burn with such passion, the soft red mouth, now innocently parted in sleep, that had tormented him so with its hungry insistence. His gaze slid lower to the slight but womanly figure engulfed by his shirt, the hint of a full ripe bosom rising above the top button and long, trim legs curled beneath it. He was provoked by a sudden desire to wake her, to feel that satin skin, to taste those eager lips, and to soar on her breathless whispers; but there was too little time. The peace of the moment was about to end and he selfishly wanted to savor it while he could.

He had no name for the tender swelling of emotion that had become an inescapable ache in his chest, and had someone put one to it, he would have called that person a liar. He knew nothing of the subtle stirrings of love. Blissful in that ignorance, he was certain he could not be moved by such a weak emotion. But weak it was not. Catching him unaware, it had seized his heart and mind in a powerful, crushing grip, refusing to be casually dismissed under the guise of simple pleasure. He had sensed something dangerously wrong at the first touch of Merrit's lips, but he wasn't truly afraid until he heard himself saying those unplanned words. "I do," he had said. That simple admission terrified him and so did his inability to convince himself that it meant nothing. His pride and sensibility demanded he put aside such thoughts, insisted that he disavow the curious feelings of longing and contentment, but deep within him a quiet voice overrode their protests with the epitaph, "Too Late." Too late he had realized what her subtle revenge would be, and he writhed beneath its cruel torture.

A movement caught his eye and he looked up into the dark speculative eyes of his quartermaster. That brief glance called him back to what he was and what he could never have. Without a word, Rufe retreated. With a last quick look at the sleeping figure, he dressed and hurried after his friend, joining him at the edge of the gutted fire for a tin of harsh black coffee.

"We'll be releasing her within the next few days, Colley," Rufe said.

"I know."

Golden eyes met his chidingly. "Do you? Do you really? Have you given it any thought at all? The woman is our prisoner, and when the ransom is met, she will return to her own life and you to yours. She is not here of her own volition. She did not choose to be with you. Her choice lies elsewhere. Let her go, Colley. Now."

"I cannot get away, Rufe," he admitted wretchedly, eyes on the smoldering fire, seeing in those sputtering coals the flickering of his own will gasping for life.

95

Seeing the play of emotion in his green eyes, Rufe asked, "Have you forgotten your vengeance then and the plans you have made?"

The fire in his eyes blazed to life. "No."

"Have you forgotten to whose bed she is going? If you need to be reminded, look upon this." He pressed the miniature he'd found in Merrit's belongings into the captain's hand, his usual reluctance to encourage his friend's bitter rage overshadowed by the threat of Merrit Ellison. She was by far the more dangerous of the two.

The captain looked down at the tiny portrait, his eyes narrowing. Winston Whitelaw. As he glared at the arrogant face, the familiar boiling hatred flooded through him, burning open the festering wounds time had failed to heal. For a brief moment, he thought Merrit was the balm that could free him of that persistent poison, but the realization that she was a part of it only made the wounds more painful. His fingers clenched about the gilt-edged frame, and his hand shook with the force of his anger. Damn you, Merrit, he thought fiercely. Damn all of you.

Waking to find herself alone in the sheltered copse, Merrit quickly dressed, and, hugging the linen shirt to her with a sense of peaceful warmth, hurried to find its owner. She ran through lush foliage, along the twisting path which opened onto the sundrenched beach where the pirates were already busy transporting their guns back to the mended sloop. Their captain stood at the water's edge dwarfed by Rufe's large form, both men staring out over the tranquil blue-green cove. A smile softened her expression as she gazed at him, remembering the tenderness and smoky desire in his eyes. But the eyes of a stranger turned to her, freezing her heart with a glare that held all the cutting force of his slashing cutlass. She took a step back, uncertain now and fearful of the unrestrained hatred in those glittering eyes.

96

The *Merry Widow* got under way smoothly. To Merrit, the small cabin was almost welcoming, for the lop-eared cat immediately wove his way about her feet. When she sat down, he gracefully jumped up to deposit his full tonnage on her lap. Great rapturous purrs came from him when she absently stroked his glossy fur, her troubled thoughts returning to the unsettling encounter on the beach. Colley had refused to look her way a second time, but the memory of his scathing glance still cut through her.

Freddy brought her noontime meal, exclaiming cheerfully that they would reach New Providence by morning light. To him, the island had all the allure of a pagan playground, for it was a place where anything could be had for a price and the ship was heavy with riches.

Merrit knew their arrival would bring a speedy end to her captivity. She had no doubt that she would be released regardless of the ransom. What confused her was her strange reluctance to go. She told herself it was the uncertainty of her future and the prospect of coming to a new land that made her hesitate, when in truth it was not what she was going to but what she was leaving that had her upset. Forcing herself to think of what awaited her in Williamsburg, she felt a pang of joy at the prospect of seeing Mildred again, but the rest was shadowed by apprehension. She knew nothing of the family she was going to join except that they bore an old established name and were very wealthy planters. She was to bring a touch of that prosperity to her own family. For the first time the idea of that arrangement made her frown — it was almost like being sold into bondage for a tidy profit.

She shook her head sharply. How could she even think of attributing such a motive to her father? Hadn't she been the one who'd begged to go, to help them recover the losses they had sustained in that devastating fire? The trade her marriage contract assured would see to that. Her father had always made every effort to see to her happiness and security. It was she who was betraying him with her wanton desires.

Eight bells came and went, and Merrit lay in the darkness with only Beelzebub's company, longing for warmth of a different nature. The sleek heated warmth of her captain's bronzed skin, the searing warmth of his mouth, the smoldering warmth of his gaze, and the heavy warmth of him beside her when they slept. Why did he stay away when their time together was rapidly coming to a close?

On deck, Colley was bedeviled by the same thoughts as he paced restlessly and stared out over the dark water, knowing Merrit to be below in his cabin, in his bed. His soul was afire with a tearing anger, spurred by hatred and bitter rancor. He was thinking of the Whitelaws. He tried to force Merrit's face among theirs, to make it something to be spat upon and despised, but the memory of those melting eyes kept preying on his vindictive mood, easing away the sharp edges and muting the violence within him. He would have his vengeance. She would not soften him against it. So why not have it and her as well? Why couldn't he enjoy the sweetness of his vendetta? She was willing to play the innocent pawn, so why not use her? While his mind dwelt on revenge, his heart gave him other more traitorous reasons to seek her out.

Merrit murmured sleepily as her lips were gently claimed and the mattress dipped to receive her lover. Her arms came up instinctively, and with a soft sigh she held him tightly as he loved her with a concentrated fierceness, bruising but never hurting her as his rough demanding anger slowly ebbed and his kisses became achingly sweet, his caresses almost reverent. He slept in the curve of her arms, the deep undisturbed sleep of a child, waking to an almost panicked disorientation until he heard the familiar rhythm of her breathing as she lay curled trustingly against him.

Angered by his weakness for her, he rose from the bed, his abrupt movement waking her as well. She watched groggily from the warmth of the bedcovers as he went about his morning routine, then dressed in the scarlet coat that accentuated his dark looks. He seemed to be studiously avoiding her until she slipped from the bed, padding on silent barefeet to where he stood before the mirror, her arms encircling his middle and her cheek pressing against his shoulder. She heard his harsh intake of breath as his body stiffened at her touch.

"Colley, what is it?" she asked softly, feeling the runaway tempo of his heart with her hands.

"We dock within the hour," he told her with forced evenness, struggling to deny the emotions her closeness aroused. Whatever she had awakened in him had to be forgotten. She was taking her tender charms to his hated enemy. That was the future he had to face. "Rufe will come down for you. Stay with him, my lady, and no harm will come to you."

"Can I not go with you?" she asked with a small degree of alarm.

"No." His curt reply struck her with the force of a slap. Feeling her flinch, he scowled in ill-humor at the part of him that would soften to her. As he turned to face her, his pulse gave an odd skip at the sight of her silken nakedness. Taking her in his arms with unintentional roughness, he pulled her to him, his mouth coming down to plunder the willing softness of hers. He heard her draw in breath as she rose up on her toes to meet his kiss more fully. Then their mouths came together with hungry yearning, sharing the same breath and the intimate dance of their tongues. For him it was half-heaven, half-hell, and his senses reeled as he surrendered to the mysterious control she wrought over him, letting desire and the ache of longing sweep through him, searing his mind and heart, leaving nothing in his world save the woman whose kisses burnt through to his

99

soul.

Merrit moaned softly beneath his savage yet sweet mouth, so hot, demanding, and devouring upon her own. Her arms tightened about his neck in a possessive circle that sought to bind him to her forever. His hands warmly stroked the gentle curve of her back, then cupped her buttocks, pressing her hips to the hardness of his passion-inflamed body as he moved against her with a slow deliberation that kindled a need in her to feel the smooth, muscled warmth of him upon her, to reach for those spiraling heavens together. She held his dark head with one hand while the other fumbled eagerly with his shirt buttons.

Merrit gave a gasp of surprise when he pushed her away, leaving her atremble with unmet desires while, panting unevenly, he stared at her long and hard. His full lips were moist from the touch of hers, but his emerald eyes were cold and distant.

"Try to forget me when you welcome your new husband to your bed," he challenged in a low angry voice. Then he turned and strode quickly from the cabin.

# Chapter Eight

New Providence was a pirate haven, a jewel of the Caribbean, its high coral hills ringing a snug harbor too shallow for any but the sleek buccaneering vessels to enter, yet large enough to accommodate as many as five hundred ships. It held half that number when the *Merry Widow* glided in, attracting many a cautious eye until her well-known captain came on deck and brought hails of welcome from anchored vessels and from the growing crowd on shore. While the crew made ready to take their shares of the plunder and the saleable cargo ashore, the captain was busy scanning the harbor to see who else was in port. He recognized Benjamin Hornigold's sloop *Mary* and Henry Jenning's *Bathsheba* as well as several other vessels. The stay promised entertaining tales and free-flowing spirits. He avoided Rufe's shrewd gaze, knowing he couldn't explain his weakness where the lady was concerned, why she had become a temptation he could not resist when others could lay no claim to his thoughts minutes after he left them. How could he explain that he, the Spanish Angel, had been moved by the tears of a girl, to the point where he had considered returning her dowry to earn her favor. There was no understanding that kind of madness. She would soon be gone and with her the wrenching emotions her presence stirred. He could again be carefree and indifferent. No heart. No ties.

With a moody frown, he turned, unprepared to face the dark eyes that gazed up at him, looking for some sign of reassurance, asking more than he could give before his crew and his perceptive quartermaster. He fought to keep his expression neutral while their eyes held for a long moment, then he put his back to her, calling to his men to begin the transfer of their booty to shore.

After the captain's cool dismissal of her, Merrit looked uneasily toward the town of Nassau as Rufe helped her into one of the landing boats. She had become at ease on the pirate ship, but this wild town filled with dangerous strangers made her fear return. What she saw was a seamy tent town sprouting from the white sand beach and the coral outcroppings of the busy harbor. Tattered-sail tents housed games of chance and games of lust. Scraggly men staggered about in a haze of rum, while those who were sober eyed her petite form with bold interest as Rufe handed her onto the hot beach. She didn't need to recall the captain's warning to stay in Rufe's giant shadow as they followed the jaunty Angel up the beach to the shabby town in a ragtag procession.

Their passing drew much attention, most of it directed at the flamboyant captain. Painted whores ran out to greet him, and he met their hot kisses enthusiastically before passing them back to the others who eagerly latched onto the willing tarts.

Rufe felt a satisfied relief when he saw the girl at his side stiffen with rage and hurt at her lover's brazen sampling of the local charms. She didn't understand the casual game Colley played, not knowing him well enough to see that his interest in these women was superficial, calculated to enhance the image he'd created, that of the dashing, arrogant Angel. His promises were mostly for show. Rufe knew he would seek out none of their favors and that even as he fondled the buxom creatures, one on each arm, his thoughts were on monetary figures rather than softer ones. Not that the captain would turn away a persistent wench who caught his fancy, but his moments with her would be fleeting at best. These things Rufe would not tell the young woman at his side. It was better that her anger grew.

The procession from the *Merry Widow* ended where it usually did, on the streets that housed the only permanent structures—stores, taverns, and brothels. The crude, often palm-thatched buildings attracted pirates as well as merchants and traders who came to purchase plunder and smuggle it to the Colonies.

Upon entering one of the taverns, they were greeted by a tall blond woman who shrieked, "Angel," and rushed to cast her arms about the grinning captain, giving him a long, fiery kiss. Stepping back from her, his smile tinged with her bright lip rouge, the captain gave her cheek a fond caress.

"Hello, Pru. Have you a room for me?"

"Aye. There's always room for ye," she answered, her voice throaty with promise.

"And Rufe as well?"

She smiled over his shoulder at the large mulatto. "Rufe is always welcome." The woman's smile faded into a look of perplexity as her gaze fell on the lovely young girl at the big man's side. Assessing her fragile beauty, she sensed a threat. "And the lady? Is she yer lady, Angel?"

Without turning, he replied indifferently, "She's part of the plunder. Can you manage a place for her as well?"

Prudence eyed the girl, thinking of the dank cellar far away from the handsome captain. "Aye, if it pleases ye."

"Now fetch me and the men something cold and filling."

"And later something warm and filling," the blonde crooned, moving her skirts provocatively against the Angel. He gave her bottom a sound whack to prompt her return to the kitchen.

Merrit sat at the corner table Rufe steered her to, seeing nothing through the bitter rage that choked her. How dare he flaunt his passion for that overblown whore right beneath her nose as through he cared not that he trampled on her emotions and on the wondrous memory of their nights together. Didn't he know how he hurt her or did he simply not care? Part of the plunder, he had called her as if she were

103

as inanimate as the pearls he had stolen from her, just another item to be bartered for the greatest gain. She glared at him as he wove his way through the crowded tables, greeting friends with his charming smile and accepting their offers of drink, feeling certain she would soon hate him with as much vigor as she desired him.

It was a long night of heavy drinking and enjoyment for the pirates, and one of mighty profit for their captain and Rufe for they were negotiating with a merchant for the sale of the stolen goods. The captain smiled at the man's fat face wondering why he was the one to be called pirate and thief. At least he was honest in his trade. He listened and watched blearily as Rufe haggled, his eyes and thoughts drifting to the corner where, under Freddy Moffit's zealous guard, the Lady Merrit nodded sleepily. He admired her unspoiled beauty even more amid the surrounding corruption, of which he was a part.

Slowly his eyes left her pretty face to dip lower and scan the creamy skin displayed above the low neckline of her gown. His attention was riveted on the tempting valley that had known no exploration but his own. The memory of the feel of her silken freshness beneath his hand, the clean smell of her, the warm taste of her left his mouth dry and his temples hot and pounding. If she had looked up and met his bright, hungry stare, he would have borne her quickly and without a thought up to the nearest bed. Shifting uncomfortably, he closed his eyes, willing her taunting image to leave him in peace. Oh God, he wanted her. Was there no escape?

A large hand closed on his arm, giving him a rough shake that brought his green eyes up in a foggy, wandering stare.

"Colley, go outside and let the air clear the rum from your head," Rufe advised. He had never known the captain to lose himself to drink before all business was settled, but something was interfering with his greed this night, that something the ever-dangerous Merrit Ellison. He had seen the desire burning hotly in his friend's eyes. It had to be stamped out before Colley was seared its by uneven heat. Burns of that nature were painful and hard to heal.

Obediently, the sodden captain rose and wove his way to the door in a staggering path, stumbling out into the crisp, cool night in a fever of drunken longing. Everything was hot and shivery and out of focus, and he reached out blindly trying to grasp onto something solid to steady his tipping world. His groping fingers found only air, then he landed full length on the hard-packed earth of the street. His only thought as he lay in a swirl of rum was to find Merrit and plead with her to show him some mercy, some kindness, some of her tender loving — anything that would ease the painful insistence of his need.

Suddenly, she was there for him, lifting him off his face and onto shaky feet, accepting his awkward kisses and mumbled apologies without a word.

Prudence had eagerly rushed after the captain at Rufe's suggestion, to find him sprawled in the dirt in a stupor. His sudden passion was a surprise and a delight. Though she couldn't understand his slurred words, she accepted his kisses with a half-starved hunger. She clutched his hands as they began to tug impatiently at her clothing.

"Upstairs," she whispered into his urgent kisses. He stumbled and leaned heavily on her sturdy shoulders as she led him through the crowded tavern to the stairs, where he turned to her, eyes smoky with passion. His hand came up to cup her coarse cheek, and he murmured something low and husky before claiming her lips.

Merrit gave a soft gasp of pain upon seeing their empassioned embrace. While she watched, feeling heart-crushing hurt, the pair climbed the stairs in each other's arms and went into one of the rooms above.


"I'm sorry, Pru. You don't deserve such a disappointment."
Prudence turned to the man who lay at her side staring at

the ceiling, his even profile visible in the dim light. She put a hand on his smooth chest, rubbing it lightly.

"Ye're never a disappointment, Angel. We have always been better friends than lovers," she assured him warmly.

Green eyes slanted to her, brows raised in disbelief. "You have found me lacking as a lover?"

She gave a low chuckle at his offended pride. "Ye are a fine lover, but, like all your men, ye are selfish and stingy about giving of yerself. Still, I cannot complain for it is good to have a man share my bed. Ye have always been special to me, Angel."

His eyes dropped away with a guilty flush. His memory was vague and clouded by spirits, but he knew somehow he had confused Prudence with another and, in realizing his mistake, had made a fool of himself. Prudence, too, was aware that something had happened to put an abrupt end to what she had hoped would be an evening of unequaled passion. When they had fallen naked onto her bed amid heated kisses, his green eyes had suddenly snapped open in stunned surprise. He'd stared at her in open-mouthed shock as if he had awakened to find himself in some unknown place, and his ardor had cooled in a frigid wash, leaving him to make awkward apologies for he was unwilling to tell her that his failure was due to finding himself with her instead of the one whose place she could not take.

"It must be the rum," he explained lamely. His head did ache dully.

"Or the lady downstairs," Pru concluded with a smile, feeling him flinch in a manner that would overrule any objection. "I've known some men who belong to only one woman, but I would not have thought it of ye."

"Come now, Pru. You know me better than to think that," he protested without great conviciton. She did know him well, too well.

"And when ye said 'I love you. Don't leave me' were ye speaking to me? I think not. We may be good friends, but ye

106

never loved me. Do ye care for that meek little girl with the big calf eyes?" There was a touch of spite in her voice. She had loved him for many years, hoping, always hoping that she would someday sway him, taking comfort in the fact that no other woman could. Then, in swept this sweet-faced little chit to steal his heart. It was jealousy pure and simple, an emotion that rarely touched her.

He laughed softly, a warm sound. "She's far from meek. You'd like her, Pru. You really would, but it matters not for she will be gone soon." He rolled onto his stomach, chin in hands, expression somber.

"She would leave ye knowing that ye love her?" Prudence asked in amazement. It was inconceivable to her that any woman would not want him.

"Why would she stay? I took her on her way to her fiancé, used her selfishly, stole her fortune. I am a pirate, a thief, as she so readily pointed out. She has at her feet all of Williamsburg. Would she trade all that for a rogue, a villain; live here like a common — I'm sorry, Pru."

" 'Tis all right, Angel. I know well what I am and I am not ashamed. Why should ye be of what ye are?"

He frowned but said nothing, the truth of her words making him uncomfortably aware of what was happening. His feeling for Merrit was making him try to change what he was, making him feel lacking, ready to forget his purpose, his one goal. There was no place in his life for a woman like Merrit Ellison, someone who would confuse him and preoccupy his thoughts. Better she should go. If he had lain with her this night and spoken to her the words he'd mistakenly mumbled to Prudence, he knew he could never have escaped her, but fate had intervened, leaving his course clear. It couldn't be love he felt for her. If it were, he would be willing to make sacrifices for her and he was not. Better for them both that she should go before he succumbed again to the madness she evoked in him. He sighed heavily and closed his eyes as Prudence rumpled his hair.

"Would you see to her for me, Pru?"

107

"For ye I will. Rest here until I return."

He nodded, settling himself deeper into the bed and letting the weariness and rum rush over him and pull him into sleep.

Prudence went downstairs. She fended off the noisy revelers' bawdy questions concerning her and the captain with a grin and a sharp retort that it was none of their affair but there was no vacancy in her bed that needed filling. When Merrit's large eyes rose to hers, she felt a twinge of pity for the poor, worn-out girl while wondering at the same time what the Spanish Angel saw in that youthful face to move him to such great feeling. The girl's eyes were filled with a sullen anguish that gave Pru pause. Could it be that she returned the Angel's emotion? How would she greet the knowledge of his love for her? Would knowing make any difference? Prudence selfishly decided to say nothing and leave things as they stood.

"Come with me, missy. I've a room for ye. Ye'll be resting better there than in the middle of all this riff-raff."

Silently, Merrit rose to follow the captain's chosen whore up the narrow stairs. She was tired, too tired to convince herself that his callousness didn't matter. It bruised her to the quick. Perhaps the new day would provide her with the strength to bear it with dignity, but for this night she could summon up none. When she was finally left alone in a small dingy room, she fell onto the bed, surrendering to the bitter tears that had threatened throughout the evening, weeping out of loneliness, hurt, fear, and mostly loss.

Outside the door Prudence frowned to herself, reluctantly sympathetic. Then she returned to lie beside the sleeping pirate, taking comfort from his presence if not his love.

# Chapter Nine

The entire first floor was a shambles when Merrit ventured down early in the morning, tables and chairs overturned amid a random scattering of half-empty bottles and glasses. The air was heavy with the sour smell of liquor. Holding her breath, she quickly flung open the windows to let in the purifying light and the breeze. Then, after binding her hair in a colorful kerchief, she began to pick up the littered tables, more to keep herself busy than anything else. The physical work soothed her troubled spirit, and soon she was unconsciously humming as she applied a harsh soap to the sticky table tops. She was unaware of the figure that paused on the stairs to watch her in silence.

At first he had thought her some new cleaning wench, but there was no mistaking the slender figure he had held close in his arms. A half-smile on his face, he enjoyed watching her move about doing the common chores with an uncomplaining ease and grace. Again, he felt the alien warmth of contentment. With a snort of denial, he continued down the stairs, the sound of his boot heels bringing her eyes about in startled alarm. She stared at him for a long moment, a multitude of half-expressed emotions flickering over her features before they became carefully guarded.

"Good morning, Captain," she said softly, her melodic voice catching at his heart. "I did not expect to see you about before noontime."

"How could I sleep with you down here banging about," he grumbled. "Why are those bloody windows open? Have you no respect for the dying?"

She pursed her lips in reluctant amusement, seeing his angry, swollen eyes, now a cloudy green surrounded by red rather than white.

"They look worse on this side," he remarked. Falling into a chair with a groan, he lifted one of the discarded glasses, eying its contents for a second before bolting them down. He shuddered as the warm harsh rum tore down to curdle in his empty stomach.

"Some breakfast would serve you better, Captain. I'm not sure what the kitchen yields, but I'm certain I could find something better for your stomach than that."

He looked up at her suspiciously, then growled, "My head will not alow me the luxury of chewing." Speech was difficult enough with the echoing thunder it unleashed.

Favoring him with an uncharitable smile, she stepped behind his chair, giving him an abrupt start as her cool fingertips brushed his throbbing temples. "Relax, Captain. It is not my intent to torture you unmercifully," she chided.

"That remains to be seen," he murmured, yielding warily to her touch, fearing not the pain but the pleasure. His eyes slid shut as she lightly rubbed his temples bringing an almost immediate ease to his head but kindling a more insistent discomfort elsewhere. Her gentle massage moved over his closed eyes, then to the knotted muscles of his neck, coaxing a low sound of pampered enjoyment from him.

Merrit looked down at his upturned features, feeling a flash of irrational annoyance because he looked so content. He gave a muffled cry as her soapy rag slapped over his face, and reaching out blindly to catch her arm as she tried to flee, he pulled her roughly into his lap, where she struggled against him giggling mischievously. Abruptly, she was still, her panting bosom pressed to his firm chest and his

110

steel-like arm circling her tiny waist. Her hands came up to rest on his shoulders as their eyes held, each seeking some sign of encouragement from the other, some reason for this magnetic pull that kept drawing them together with an undeniable force.

"Merri, you promised not to torture me," he said softly, his free hand rising to her smooth cheek.

A soft sound behind them broke the hypnotic attraction that held them motionless, and with a shaky relief, Merrit hopped from his lap, using the interruption to halt the inevitable. Her hurt was still too recent; she could not forgive him so easily. She looked toward Rufe gratefully as she hurried to the kitchen.

Rufe sat across from his surly friend, paying no heed to the dark murderous glare that greeted him.

"You could have found a more convenient time to arrive," Colley grumbled ill-humoredly.

"To me, it looked very opportune," Rufe countered with a grin.

"No lectures. I'm in no mood," his friend declared irritably, still feeling slightly overwarm from Merrit's unexpected closeness. Had Rufe not arrived he would have been sampling her soft lips. There would be time to steal a moment later, and she did not appear eager to resist him. That thought brought back some of his good nature. He gave Rufe a sudden smile that made the quartermaster instantly suspicious.

"Did you arrange for the sale of all the goods?" Angel asked finally, his mind returning to business.

"All was settled after your abrupt absence last night. I had the bulk of your share taken aboard and kept this out for your immediate use."

As the captain opened the proffered pouch, a frown creased his brow. He drew out one of the large flawless pearls, rolling it thoughtfully between thumb and forefinger. When a plate was dropped in front of him with enough force to endanger the worn crockery, he looked up into Merrit's stormy eyes. All trace of softening was gone from her youthful face. Caught in a position where he was helpless to placate her ruffled anger, he merely met her glare with calm aloofness as her eyes sparked with remembered betrayal. Without another word, she set a plate before Rufe and then marched back to the kitchen.

"Ah, damn," he muttered softly, returning the offending pearl to the pouch and dropping it into his coat pocket.

Merrit was vigorously scouring one of the pots with a concentrated violence when she heard someone approach. She whirled about wielding the pot, intending to give his head a reason to ache.

"Oh," she blurted in surprise when she came face to face with a puzzled Prudence still tousled and bleary-eyed from sleep. "I beg your pardon," she stammered. "I prepared Rufe and Colley a meal, and was cleaning up after it."

Colley? Prudence drew a painful breath. As far as she knew, Rufe was the only one Angel had ever let call him by that name, but this girl used it with familiarity. She forced a smile and advanced into the kitchen. "You needn't have, missy. I would have done it meself."

"It is not my nature to take advantage of someone's kindness," Merrit corrected quietly. "I was an unwilling prisoner on the ship, but you have taken me in as a guest and I would repay you for that."

Prudence frowned. Angel was right. She did like the chit though it was not her intention. The girl had a natural unaffected dignity that was most disarming. Angel's other women had not treated her with any degree of courtesy, yet this one, who had the most to gain by doing so, seemed to bear her no malice. It was hard to understand.

Merrit felt awkwardly embarrassed under the other woman's stare. She observed Prudence with a timid eye, finding her attractive in an earthy way. With her bold heavy features, large round blue eyes, and full red lips, the blonde

112

was every inch a woman. The ample curves brazenly displayed by her yellow gown made Merrit painfully aware of her own girlishness.

But Prudence gave her a generous smile that eased her fears. "If ye be willing to help, I'll gladly let ye. This place can be a fair wreck when a ship puts in. I be Pru."

"And I'm Merrit," she answered with a hesitant smile.

The captain let out his breath when both women emerged from the kitchen apparently unscathed. Normally, he made it a rule never to be in the same place as any two women he'd been with—his crew could learn something of savagery from women at odds. But it seemed as though the older woman had taken the younger under her wing. Neither spared him a glance as they tidied the large well-aired room which would be filled to capacity within a few hours' time. As he listened to Rufe talking his eyes followed the trim figure about the room. Would she be content to remain here under Pru's protection while he was at sea? Would she be happy as his mistress, satisfied with the few days out of several months that he was in port to lie with her and let him shower her with riches? Could he trust her to remain faithful in his absence? He did not dare to dwell on the realization that, though the idea of Prudence taking up with any other man bothered him not, the thought of this slender girl welcoming another brought dark anger.

"Colley."

Rufe's sharp voice broke through his pleasant musings, bringing his attention back to the matters at hand, but within minutes he was drifting again, a small smile playing about his mouth. He had never kept a woman before, though he knew several of his men did and found benefits in such an arrangements. He wondered if that unbinding attachment would change things, but one look at Merrit gave him his answer. Knowing she was here would make his voyages that much shorter. Ransom and vengeance were forgotten as he enthusiastically plotted his wooing of Merrit

Ellison.

By early afternoon he saw his chance to catch her alone as she went to the kitchen, and followed her, warmed by the thought of being with her again. He paused outside the door when he heard her speaking with Prudence. Their topic made him frown.

"Tell me about yer intended, Merrit. Is he handsome? Is he wealthy?"

"Quite handsome from what I can tell, and very well established."

"I envy ye yer happiness. Ye are happy to be going to him, aren't ye?"

"I had thought so at first, but now I fear I will not be well received."

"Because of Angel?"

"Damn his black heart, he's stolen the basis for my future. If I find no happiness, the blame lies with him."

"He winced at the harshness of her tone. She would not forgive him easily, but he could not fault her for that.

"He will not take ye lest ye give him the pearls?"

"I pray he will, that I can convince him of my worth. I will not give up without a fight. It is what I want, what I am entitled to, and I'll not let that thieving blackguard cheat me of it because of his selfish greed. Let him keep my wealth. Let him buy an early grave with it. Word should come soon releasing me from my unwelcome imprisonment; then I can return to a normal life. All I have ever wanted, dreamed of, was to be the wife of a good man. I can only hope that the captain has not ruined that for me. What man wants spoiled goods?"

Prudence laughed. "He need never know of it. Men are too wrapped up in their own pleasure to notice us much. If ye pretend it is yer first time, he will never know the difference."

" 'Twill be a welcome change to be with a true gentleman."

The remainder of their conversation was unwitnessed for

the captain returned to his table to delve into his bottle of rum, his foolish notions regarding the Lady Merrit tossed aside.

Prudence looked at the younger woman as she chopped the vegetables for the evening stew. She smiled gently, not fooled by the girl's vehement protests. "And ye care nothing for Angel?"

Merrit set down the cleaver, unable to continue because her eyes were clouded. "Oh, Pru, he confuses me so," she confessed. "I should hate him, but I cannot. I cannot keep him from my thoughts. A future without him looks so bleak."

"He is a beguiling man, but I am not the one who can tell ye how to escape his charm. Ye are so young to try to understand a man like Angel. My advice to ye is not to risk your heart on him until ye know more of the world. Try to find yer happiness where it is safe to do so. Try for that good life ye deserve first."

Drying her eyes, Merrit looked curiously at the big-boned woman. "And what of you? Did you never want the good life?"

Prudence laughed and stretched her arms wide. "This is it for me. In Good Mother England, my husband Dickie found hisself at the short end of a rope and I was sold as a bond servant to a colonial merchant. A bad one he was, with nasty evil ways. Our ship was sailing to the Chesapeake when Angel raided it. Most of the crew signed his articles, and he brought me with him when I told him my circumstances, gave me this place so I could make my livelihood, never asking nothing in return 'cept that I always had a place for him to stay when he was in port. He could have asked for anything," she confided with a smile, and Merrit nodded wrily. "Well, this be my home now and I be happy. There's always a warm and willing man to keep me from missing my Dickie too terribly much, and pirates can be a generous lot if they fancy ye."

Merrit smiled, suddenly envious of this woman who knew how to be content with what she had. And she had the Spanish Angel. With a sigh she turned back to her chopping, musing over what it would be like to live among these lawless thieves. But she would be different from Pru. For her there would be only one man.

The captain was in a dark mood by the time Merrit reentered the taproom to refill mugs of ale and to laugh with the members of the *Merry Widow*'s crew. As he looked upon her pretty smiling face, his temper grew blacker yet. He was unused to being fooled by a woman, and with this one he had been willing to venture much. He scowled and pulled deeply at his bottle. So she was anxious to begin her life with Winston Whitelaw, eager to become his bride and to please him with what she had learned. She would do well in that family for she had a cold, whore's heart. On the surface Angel owed his mood to wounded vanity, but it was also true that the thought of losing Merrit plagued him. To think she had lain beneath him whispering his name in rapture only to curse him and call him a black-hearted thief. She had been right. It was a subtle vengeance. He would have preferred a flogging. At least once the agony of the lash was over it was done with, but thoughts of her continued to tear at him without mercy.

Merrit frowned as she looked at her moody lover, wondering about his new turn of temperament. No man had a right to look so fair, to have such a flawless surface cover such a multitude of imperfections. He was vain, arrogant, cruel, tender, greedy, charming, without morals or conscience — and she didn't know where she could ever find the excitement he stirred in her. *Do not fall in love with me*, he had warned. Was it too late to heed the warning?

Her attention was drawn away from the handsome pirate by the arrival of a boisterous tart with impossibly flaming hair and a ripe figure arduously squeezed into one of

Merrit's finest gowns. The gown alone was enough to provoke her temper, but what sparked fury in her was the delicate gold chain clasped about the tramp's neck, its small cameo nearly buried between her swelling breasts. Eyes on that shiny pendant, Merrit strode purposefully to the hussy, her features rigid with outrage. The painted woman regarded her with amused curiosity until Merrit reached for her throat.

"Give me that," Merrit demanded fiercely, only to have her hand slapped away.

"Here now, missy. What be ye talkin' about?"

"That necklace is mine. Give it to me."

The strumpet raised an eyebrow, and her red lips curved into a jeering smile. "I don't recall ye helpin' me earn it," she said, bringing a bout of laughter from those who overheard.

"My father gave that to me," Merrit continued doggedly, unable to bear the thought of the treasured gift being worn like a trophy by this brassy harlot.

"Perhaps I got it from him, missy."

With a snarl, Merrit's hand whipped back in a closed fist, but its forward motion was abruptly halted by a steely grip. She whirled to glare up into Angel's chilling green eyes, enraged by his interference.

"Enough, my lady," he said in a low voice. "Do not abuse our hospitality."

"Let go of me," she hissed. "I only want what is mine."

Making his words deliberately cruel, he said, "You forget yourself. Nothing here is yours. Nothing. You have no right to demand anything. If you cannot remember that and cease to cause any further trouble, you'll be confined upstairs. What be your pleasure, my lady?"

Her eyes glimmered for a moment, threatening to spill over in anger and hurt, but she blinked them back and said in a brittle voice, "I will accept the fact that you have stolen from me all that I hold dear, but do not expect me to be charitable about it."

117

He gave her a slow smile that was without mirth as his hand rose to stroke her flushed cheek. "You did not protest the loss of some things half so much," he said bluntly, then caught her other hand before it could find its mark. "Now sit down and be silent."

She dropped into a chair at his table, lips thinned and eyes dark with fire. Unconcerned by her mounting wrath, he turned to the indignant whore, using his forefinger to press the locket between her generous breasts.

"I suggest you not flaunt that until the lady is gone lest she be tempted to part your head from your shoulders."

The woman pouted her red lips, then, giving him a saucy wink, sauntered off to find another source of gifts.

Rufe looked questioningly between the two stiff figures at the table. While the captain had no great regard for a woman's feelings, it was unlike him to treat one harshly before others. It was not like him to let his silky façade slip, to show his inner violence. Rufe noticed that while his captain's curt actions were applauded by those who saw Lady Merrit as a spoiled wealthy aristocrat, the members of his own crew were strangely silent, for they remembered the gentle woman who had knelt on the bloody deck to see to their dying. The lady's presence was becoming a serious threat.

The reprieve came sooner than expected, with the arrival of a new ship fresh from pillaging the Capes. Its captain entered the tavern calling, "Ho, Angel. I've a message for you."

The Spanish Angel straightened in his chair, his eyes bright with expectation. "What be the message?" he urged, pouring a generous glass for the bearer.

"Whitelaw will pay you nothing, and warns that he will hunt you down like a rabid beast if the lady is harmed."

For a moment, Angel remained unmoving as if he hadn't heard Merrit's small gasp or Rufe's curse. While he appeared calm, inside him a blinding rage was exploding.

How dare the man cheat him and make such bold threats? Whitelaw had called his bluff and was smugly awaiting his reply. The abrupt knowledge that Merrit was lost to him, as was the fortune he'd expected to be paid, provoked an even deeper rage. Since the Whitelaws were out of reach, he struck out at the nearest substitute, his opaque eyes turning to Merrit, the anger and resentment smoldering in them meant for more than her.

"Well, my lady, it seems you are no longer of any value to me. I have overestimated your worth, unless someone here would care to buy you to cut my losses." His voice rose in a taunting offer. "Anyone here care to purchase this pretty baggage and take her off my hands? I can vouch for her better qualities."

At the ensuing laughter, Merrit reddened, then paled in sudden horror and doubt. Was he so angered by the loss of his money that he would do such a thing? Did he hate her so much? She remembered the pawing Bob and his lusting eyes. Was that what awaited her?

"Captain, please," she said in a small uncertain voice. "You promised you would release me."

His dark brows rose even higher, then came down to meet over the bridge of his nose in a heavy line of anger. "Did I? You call me liar and thief and yet you expect me to be honorable? Stupid child. I don't care about you. You were only important for the money you could bring me and the distractions. Now it seems no one wants to meet your price." He took a savage delight in the pain he saw in her eyes. He wanted to hurt her. His voice took on a deeper timbre and a heavy Spanish cadence that only Rufe recognized as no part of the dramatic joke the others thought he was playing. "Your husband should pay me well for enduring your clinging passions for the sake of my vengeance. At least he will have the benefit of my teachings. And if your wedlock should bear immediate fruit, let him wonder from whence the child came. God save me from foolish virgins."

119

"Perhaps I can save the pretty Angel from that problem," she said in a soft voice. His words had torn her asunder, shattering her naïve hope and faith and leaving her with the hard edge of a scorned and humiliated woman. Rufe saw the danger a second too late to keep her from seizing an empty rum bottle and smashing it down upon the table's edge with all the force of her outrage behind it. Seeing her unexpected movement, the startled captain made an attempt to stand and take hold of her. That fateful reaction placed him in the path of her arcing hand, and the upswing of the bottle caught him across the face. The force of the blow knocked him back, and he reeled to the floor with a short cry of pain and surprise.

Rufe twisted the broken bottle from her hand, and caught her about the waist with a massive arm, pinning her in a crushing embrace as his captain struggled to get his knees under him, then to shakily stand. The Angel's hand was pressed to his cheek, and bright crimson spilled between his fingers to run in rapid rivulets down his arm. Eyes slightly dulled by pain and shock, he stared at Merrit, seeing her horror and fury. This was what he had wanted, something that would make their parting easier.

"Let her go, Rufe," he murmured thickly, the agony of speech nearly robbing him of his senses. "We stand even now, my lady. We've both drawn first blood." With a last look at her stricken face, he said, "Take her wherever she wants to go."

# Chapter Ten

At her first sight of the Virginia Capes, Merrit felt a touch of alarm. What kind of savage wilderness had she come to live in? The coast was drab and endless, its wide empty beaches bathed in the golden shimmer of sea oats. Sand dunes, shifting in the constant turmoil of sharp ocean winds, crowded the shoreline, yielding only saltbush, bayberry, and live-oak trees. The rest of what she could see was low, flat, and marshy. Was this desolate place the golden land of wealth and plenty?

As they continued up the bay, the view became even bleaker. The beaches thinned to marsh, and gangly cypress trees crouching on widespread gnarled fingers were bearded heavily with silvery Spanish moss. Pine forests rose sheerly from the shoreline creating a stark, unyielding profile for her dismayed eyes. She half expected to see mahogany savages lying in wait in the trees. She puzzled over the occasional dock that seemed to lead nowhere, unaware that plantation houses were set well back out of view from the river to lessen the threat of marauding pirates.

Abruptly Merrit's glum doldrums were lifted when she saw a frantically waving figure at one of the docks. She let out a wailing cry as she recognized the sturdy woman, and soon she was rushing in to that familiar crushing embrace.

"Oh, me lamb, me pet.. I feared I'd never see ye again,"

Mildred sobbed.

"Here I am, safe and sound," Merrit soothed, feeling it strange that she was comforting the older woman.

Mildred stood back, still steadfastly clasping Merrit's hands while her puffy eyes looked closely at her charge. The girl did look well, a bit tired about the eyes but she bore no sign of the ill-use that had tormented Mildred's dreams. In fact, with the girlishness gone from her features she looked more beautiful than before. It was as if she'd been brought to adulthood with a rude shock. Mildred could only hope that the transition had not been too cruel.

"Be ye truly all right, me lamb?" she asked with a sniff as she dried her eyes on a large square of cloth.

"Truly, Mildred. And very happy to see you again."

Mildred beamed, her tears forgotten, and she embraced the girl quickly. "Get yer things. We just got word that ye were arriving and they be waiting up at the house to give ye a look."

Merrit plucked at her worn and mended gown with a wry smile. "This is everything."

"And the pearls?" Mildred gasped in horror.

"Gone" was the flat reply.

"Well, there's no help for that now, though herself will not be pleased. Come then, pet. Let's say our hellos and get ye into a hot bath."

The Whitelaw dwelling was situating on a grassy crest on the other side of the pine copse, an impressive brick structure with many ornate gables and a stepped roofline. It was as spacious and grand as any manor house she had seen in England. The Whitelaw family, with one exception, met her in the parlor.

Thaddeus Whitelaw came forward to clasp her hands warmly, a welcoming smile lighting his round face. He was a short, rotund man with red pudgy cheeks and buttonlike brown eyes, and he appeared almost comical in the elaborate full-bottomed wig he had been forced to wear.

"Lady Ellison, how good to finally meet you after such a dreadful ordeal. What a terrible welcome to our country and our home. I assure you, 'tis not all quite so savage."

"Thaddeus, you are rambling." The sharp voice brought him instantly to heel. Merrit turned to look at the woman Mildred had coolly referred to as 'herself.' Sophia Whitelaw was a tall, slender woman with an imperious bearing, her once-handsome features having thinned with age to give her a face as sharp and commanding as her voice. Her pale hair was dressed in a style too fussy for her demanding visage. It accentuated the severity of her ice-blue eyes, her thin razor-sharp nose, and her tight unyielding lips. Her critical gaze measured every inch of Merrit until the young woman felt like squirming in discomfort, painfully aware of her tattered apparel and her much discussed arrival.

"Welcome to Whitelawn, Lady Ellison," she said cordially, but there was no convincing warmth in her eyes or in the thin hand that shook Merrit's loosely.

The two Whitelaw daughters ogled her with wide-eyed interest. Gabrielle, who was a year younger than Merrit, had her mother's features softened by youth, while twelve-year-old Letitia was a bright cherub and the image of her father. Conspicuously absent was Winston Whitelaw, her intended.

"I am very sure you are weary after your long and arduous voyage. Your maid will show you to your room. Dinner is at eight sharp."

Sophia's words carried the weight of an order, so Merrit dipped into a curtsy, mumbled something awkward, and followed Mildred to a wide flight of stairs. She held all her questions in until the door of the guest room was closed behind them.

"Well, what did ye think of her majesty?" Mildred remarked acidly as she readied a bath in a large metal tub.

"Is she always so overbearing?"

"Ye've seen her at her most charming."

Merrit smiled fondly at the older woman, her relief so great at being reunited with Mildred that nothing else could dampen her spirits.

"The others, they be fine," Mildred continued, measuring oil and scent into the water. "The mister is like a friendly pup on a short lead. The older girl be a bit hoity-toity but not a bad lass. The little one, now she be full of sassy charm. Reminds me of a little chit I once knew, she be so full of mischief." She chuckled and tapped Merrit under the chin. "Into the tub with ye."

Gratefully, Merrit shed the soiled clothing and stepped into the steaming water, sighing as she sank down into its perfumed embrace. She leaned back, eyes closed, while Mildred soaped her luxurious hair as she had done since her childhood. However, her tranquil enjoyment was ended by Mildred's blunt question.

"I'll be asking ye now for I know herself is bound to. Were ye abused by those pirates, me lamb? Ye need not fear telling me."

"No," Merrit replied softly, keeping her eyes shut lest Mildred read more into her answer. "I suffered no abuse."

"And that sweet-faced captain with the devil-green eyes?" the older woman pressed, recalling the man's lusty interest in her ward.

"The captain respected my wishes in all things, Mildred."

The dour-faced woman heard the evasive caution in the girl's voice, and was piqued to find her less than truthful despite their many years together. Merrit had been a scamp of a child, but never had she lied. Why had she begun now? "I didn't truly think he would keep his word," she murmured, closing watching the girl's face.

"He was most honorable for a pirate," Merrit said coolly, her features betraying no emotion. Better to keep the truth from her beloved friend than to confess all and awake the bitter pain once more. "Where is my fiancé?" she asked to distract Mildred. Her tone was a bit sharp, for she recalled his refusal to pay for her release when he had no assurance that she would not be harmed.

"Haven't laid eyes on him yet. Hear he's up the coast on some sort of business."

Merrit felt relieved upon learning of the postponement of their meeting. With her emotions in such a shambles, she wanted no part of the man for a while. At least time would have a chance to ply its healing before she was introduced to her husband-to-be. Perhaps the haunting image of cold green eyes would fade and she would be free from the constant torment of longing and hatred. She only needed time.

Dinner at the Whitelaws' was a formal, unbearably stuffy affair with little conversation. Merrit tasted none of her meal, for she was too uncomfortable in her position across from Sophia. She gave a start as her hand was squeezed under the table, and looked at the impish Letitia who gave her a cautious smile.

Once the china was cleared, Sophia rose to signal an end to the meal.

"Lady Ellison, if you are not too tired, I would speak to you in the parlor," she said, in a tone that would accept no excuse.

Though she was fairly faint from fatigue, Merrit replied in the affirmative, then followed Sophia who regally settled herself on a print chaise before gesturing to a chair. The woman's pale eyes narrowed speculatively as she examined her son's prospective bride.

"You are indeed a pretty child. Winston will be pleased," she commented, seemingly to herself. Merrit remained silent, hands clasped docilely in her lap. "You look fit for having suffered such horror at the hands of the renegades."

"I was treated quite gently, my lady. Aside from being afraid, I came to no real harm," the younger woman said quietly.

Sophia's lips pursed as if she suspected this to be untrue.

"One hears of the great atrocities performed by these pirates."

"Thankfully, they are exaggerated," Merrit murmured a bit stiffly, but she kept her eyes down to conceal the spark of irritation in them.

"You must realize that this is a small community, and though we are far removed from the mother country, we are still very civilized. Talk of your abduction is widespread and has caused much, shall we say, speculation. We have high hopes for Winston's political future and therefore the woman he takes for his wife must be above reproach. We would not wish his good name or that of his first child to be the topic of gossips. There must be no question of parentage. That is why, and I am sure you will agree, we cannot announce a betrothal until we are sure there is no question."

Merrit sat rigidly, but she forced her tone to be mild. "I see. There must be no supposition that I bring a pirate's bastard into the family."

Sophia frowned at her indelicacy but said calmly, "Exactly."

"I will advise you when my time arrives," Merrit said flatly, feeling more humiliated at this moment than she had when she'd been paraded before the pirates. She was also more than a little alarmed. There would be no passing off a wrongfully conceived babe. Sophia Whitelaw was a shrewd, careful woman.

"Now, there is the matter of your dowry."

Dark eyes rose in anguish. "I have none to bring. All was taken from me, even the clothes I carried," she admitted faintly, her worst fears realized when the harsh-faced woman drew a long breath.

"I see," Sophia stated slowly. "We will discuss this at a later time when you have had a chance to rest. I assume that all you have is what you are wearing."

Merrit nodded, clenching her teeth to hold back a sharp retort. Would there be no end to this agonizing interview?

She felt as though her dignity had been torn from her like a filthy rag.

"Well, we cannot have you running about in that. I suppose you can wear something of Gabrielle's until we can have you fitted properly."

"Please. You needn't go to that trouble," Merrit begged, unable to withstand further mortification.

"Don't be silly, child. We must keep up appearances."

"Of course." The offer was not made out of compassion but vanity. One couldn't have a future family member running about untidy. Sensing that her fury was reaching the danger point, Merrit said softly, "I am feeling very weary. Would you please excuse me?"

"Certainly, child. We will continue our talk tomorrow."

One glance at Merrit's flushed face told Mildred how her charge had fared. Without comment, she sat her down at the dressing table and began to brush out her heavy chestnut waves, using long, tireless strokes until the soothing methodical care worked its charm and cooled the fires in Merrit's dark eyes. The face that Mildred saw in the glass gave her a shock, for it was that of a woman of mature age, with troubles too great for her darling's slight years.

"Be we staying or going, me pet?"

Merrit's chin dropped into her hands as she moodily regarded her image. "For the time being, we've no choice. I've no money. We may be forced out soon enough."

Mildred frowned, her irritation at the Whitelaws rising with the Merrit's distress. How dare these people bring such glum lines to her lovely face! "They would not do that, me lamb. Ye've a contract to bind them."

"Without the dowry, it may not once the time Lady Whitelaw has given me expires."

"What be ye talking about, lass?"

"The lady insists I provide her with proof that I have not already conceived. My word to her was not enough."

The older woman puffed out like an enraged adder,

cursing and fuming indignantly. "Who does she think she be to so insult me pet? Her high- and mightiness needs a good setdown, and if she be determined, I'd be glad to oblige her. True, she be bold as brass to ask such a thing, but you've only to wait a short time unless—"

Merrit's sudden forlorn tears stilled her words and brought her arms about the shaking shoulders of her charge.

"Did he rape ye then child?"

"He did not have to," Merrit admitted in a choking voice, closing her eyes to the memory of Colley's handsome face. "He was very persuasive." She could chance revealing no more lest the whole tale unfold and destroy Mildred's respect and faith.

"That fiend. To prey on your innocence and leave you to face the possible disgrace. 'Tis no man but a soulless demon." The lines of her face grew stern and formidable. "If there proves to be a child, there are ways to see it does not flourish."

Merrit's eyes grew round with shock. "No. I would not destroy his child."

"But, me lamb, a pirate's bastard babe—"

"I don't care," she wailed, tears coming in a steady stream of grief and loss. "Don't you see. I went to him. I wanted him. I still want him after all that's happened, and if he called, I would gladly go. I will cherish any part of him, and be there a babe, I will love it with all my heart because it is his."

"Quiet now, pet," Mildred soothed, holding Merrit's glossy head to her sturdy shoulder so the girl couldn't see the dismay in her features. "What's done is done. If there be a child, I will stay by you. Don't fret. Could you go to the papa for some help?"

She shook her head with a grievous sob. "He does not want me, so he would not welcome my return or the presence of his child. No, I could not go to him. I would not." There was a sudden strengthening in her voice as her uncontrolled weeping was stilled by the force of will. "Damn him to hell. He'll not hear of my sorrow," she vowed firmly as she sat up, tears oddly placed on her solemn face. "There is no need to worry until we have cause. I would like to sleep now, Mildred. It has been a long exhausting day."

Eyes filled with unvoiced concern, Mildred merely stroked Merrit's chestnut hair before leaving her to her private fears. Silently she cursed the bold pirate for stealing away more than the dowry, for taking that most precious orb of all, the pearl of blissful innocence.

129

Merrit awakened to a sensation of loss and disorientation before an impish face peered around the door and brought everything back to her. She sat up with a smile, and with that encouragement, Letitia scurried in to bound up on the side of the bed with a childish excitement. Her curling brown hair swinging as she did so, she tucked her bare feet beneath the hem of her Indian cotton night dress.

"Good morning. I'd hoped you'd be awake so I could see you without Mama's sharp eye on us. You are so pretty. I wish I were. I think I shall like having you for a sister. We're not all as stuffy as Mama. Well, Gabi can be," the girl rattled on cheerfully, as she sat, legs crossed in a most unladylike fashion. With a painful wrench of longing, Merrit was reminded of her own sisters and of their secret chatty talks.

"Why, Letitia, I think you'll be very pretty, and I shall enjoy having another sister as well."

The child flushed, unused to compliments. She put a chubby hand to her baby-full cheeks. "You think so?" she asked in shy hopefulness. "I always thought I would be the goose to Gabi's swan."

"Oh, nonsense," Merrit pronounced, and accepted Letitia's impulsive hug with a smile. Perhaps life with the

Whitelaws wouldn't be so bleak after all.

"Tisha, what are you doing in here bothering her ladyship?" The soft scolding came from the open door.

"I'm not bothering her. We were just getting acquainted," Letitia said grandly. "You're just jealous because I beat you here."

"Come in, Gabrielle. I should like to know you as well," Merrit called, seeing the older girl hesitate before stepping inside.

The invitation prompted Gabrielle to enter and close the door behind her conspiratorally. She was carrying a gown over her arm. "Mama said I was to lend you something to wear because of your unfortunate circumstance," she said primly, looking every inch her mother and bringing a flush to Merrit's face.

"Oh, Gabi, you carry on so," Letitia scoffed. "You're just afraid she's going to outshine you in your rags."

Gabrielle made a face, immediately becoming a girl instead of a shrewish woman.

"I thank you for your kindness," Merrit said diplomatically, "but I doubt I can do the same justice to the gown as your sister."

Gabrielle stood taller beneath that bit of praise, the haughtiness of her expression softening as she regarded her contemporary whose arrival she had so dreaded. She'd worried that Lady Ellison would upstage her in the household, but then perhaps this pretty dark-eyed girl wouldn't treat her as meanly as she herself treated her younger sister.

"Tell us about the pirates, my lady," Letitia demanded with enthusiasm, flopping on her stomach gracelessly, chin in hands.

" 'Tis Merrit and what do you want to know?"

"Are they really like devils with tails that drink blood? Did you see them murder anyone? Did they try to make you walk the plank? Did they ravish you?"

"Tisha!" Gabrielle exclaimed in horror as she, too, succumbed to curiosity and sat, an avid listener, on the bed.

"Such wild tales." Merrit laughed. "They were just men, only talking worse and drinking more than most. They are thieves, not killers, and I was treated well while in their custody and under the protection of their captain."

"The Spanish Angel," Letitia sighed. "Is he truly as handsome as they say?"

"More so," Merrit admitted softly, her thoughts full of that beautiful face.

At Gabrielle's snort of disbelief, Letitia teased, "Pay her no mind. She thinks no one could outshine her Captain Seward. You shall get tired of his name as I have. He's Gabi's intended."

"Hush now, Tisha," Gabrielle insisted. "You cannot compare my captain to a pirate."

"No, your bewigged fancy would pale before a real man."

Gabrielle flushed indignantly. "And what do you know of real men?"

"About as much as you," the imp countered, instantly grinning at the embarrassment the remark caused.

Merrit chuckled with enjoyment. "It is like being home with my own four sisters. You have made me feel most welcome. But off with you now. I must get dressed and go down for breakfast. We can talk later."

"If it had been me, I fear I would have fallen in love with the Spanish Angel," Letitia vowed dreamily out of an innocence Merrit could no longer share.

"No, you would not, because in spite of his charm and his fair face, he is a dangerous pirate who thinks only of his own greed."

"But I should have anyway," the child persisted, then scampered out in the wake of her sister, leaving Merrit glumly reflective.

"Good morning, Lady Ellison." From the head of the table

132

where she sat, Sophia coolly assessed Merrit's appearance in her daughter's gown. The girl lacked Gabrielle's height and slenderness, so the hem dragged and the bodice was pulled taut across the bosom. "You shall go into Williamsburg this morning to be fitted for some proper things. When you return, I wish to see you."

"Yes, my lady," Merrit murmured docilely, but with a streak of rebellion she wondered if anyone had ever dared refuse one of this formidable woman's requests. Not in this household, certainly; her daughters were too young and her husband too cowed. But what of her son? Was he like father or mother? Would Sophia rule him and their marriage? Merrit suppressed a frown. If that was the case, there would be storm clouds gathering, for she was determined to be the only mistress in her house. But she would play the meek miss until she met with Winston; then she would know what the future held for her.

"When will your son be returning?" she asked finally. "I understand he is on some business in the other colonies."

"Yes," she replied shortly. "He should return in three weeks' time."

Three weeks. So long to be uncertain. By then the shrewd woman would know if her son's bride was indeed unburdened by a child before going to the altar. Of course, her son's business trip would cause no curious talk. How carefully arranged it was.

"Gabrielle will accompany you into the village. Can your lady servant be trusted to chaperone you?"

Merrit's eyes flashed hotly. "My father trusted her enough to accompany me across an ocean."

"And to what an unpleasant result."

"Mildred can hardly be blamed for that. It would have changed nothing for her to have forfeited her life to protect me."

Sophia sniffed at the unexpected fire in the girl. "I suppose we need fear no pirates in Williamsburg. I will have

133

the carriage brought round in an hour. You can be ready by then."

The ride to Williamsburg was a pleasant one, the true beauty of Virginia unfolding about them in a colorful panorama. As spring ripened into summer the land was awash with color. Bright spots of pink dogwood, white flowering plum, magenta Judas tree, yellow Scotchbroom, purple wisteria, and pale jasmine dotted the scenery. Large plantation houses lay scattered along the James, their crop lands and pastures alternating with pine forests, blending civilization into the wilds. It was a new and exhilarating land, and Merrit found herself longing less for England as the miles went by.

As they traveled the bumpy roads, Gabrielle rambled on about her favorite subject as Letitia had forewarned. Merrit listened wistfully to the girl's excited tone. She wished she could speak of her own fiancé in the same manner, but she could not pretend to feelings for a man who was a stranger, a man whose arrival filled her with unease instead of anticipation. She wanted to be in love with the man she married, wanted to yearn for the day of their wedding and the pleasures to follow. But she didn't love Winston White-law and she felt cheated of happiness.

She sighed, looking at Gabrielle's flushed and animated features. How much in love she looked. Oh, to look that way again. Again? No. She had never been in love. He hadn't stolen that from her as well.

Williamsburg was a pleasant little village of some eighteen hundred inhabitants, its streets lined with sturdy warm brick buildings that gave an impression of solid permanence. Their arrival was greeted with many a curious look, and Merrit cringed inwardly. Were these people all wondering if she was the pirate's captive, speculating upon how she had fared upon his ship? As if her manner alone could still their tongues, she held her head high and adopted her brightest smile, nodding pleasantly to those who stared

134

openly and giving most cause to flush and hesitantly return the smile. Surely this vivacious girl could not have suffered all the horrors they'd imagined, not when she greeted them with such unconcerned charm. The local feeling about Merrit Ellison began to change.

Despite her many troubles, the trip to the dressmaker proved to be a most happy distraction. Merrit lost herself in the rich feel of fabric and delicate lace. Gabrielle had a surprising eye for color and soon their two heads were nodding over the choice of materials and trims. They selected fresh, clear, and feminine colors of shell pink, pale apple green, dove, soft lilac, and powder blue in delicate silks and damasks and Indian cotton. Over twenty yards would be needed to make the fluid, loose saque gowns with double or treble Watteau pleats that were all the vogue in the newer issues of *La Bagatella*. In addition to two of the popular saques, they ordered material for two open-robe gowns with embroidered petticoats and beribboned stomachers, several full pleated mantuas with open skirts piled behind into billowy bustles, and a selection of simple calicos. Panier hoops, filmy chemises, linen and silk neckerchiefs, wisps of lace and lawn to cover the head, fans of satin and ivory, and a rocket cloak of white serge-like material completed their order.

Loaded down with packages, and having been promised that the remaining items would be delivered within the next few days, under Mildred's watchful eye the girls returned to Whitelawn in a spirit of gay comradery, discussing fashion like the best of friends. Their light mood slowly faded as they neared the estate, Gabrielle becoming once again the sober, reserved miniature of her mother. Merrit thought of her own loving mother who had guided and encouraged rather than manipulated and controlled. She felt sorry for the repressed girl, vowed to take more time with her. Letitia would not need such nurturing for her spirit was far too strong to be crushed. Perhaps Gabrielle's Captain Seward would whisk her out from beneath her mother's overbearing influence so she could blossom. She wondered if Winston would prove her own salvation from the domineering Sophia Whitelaw.

Merrit wasted no time, but hurriedly changed into the gown the dressmaker's assistant had adjusted for her while they had been fitted, a fetching silk of softest lilac with lace trim. The frothy creation had not been picked up by the woman who'd ordered it made, and Merrit had decided its dainty, helpless appearance would waylay her more stubborn tendencies. With Sophia she must use any device that might sway her and spark some sympathy in her heart. As it proved, her effort was a waste.

Sophia regarded her with a satisfied nod, then got right to the purpose of their meeting. She was not a lady to waste time or sentiment. Or sympathy.

"This is not pleasant for me, but I cannot see letting you maintain false hope. Without a dowry, your marriage to my son will not take place." She raised a thin hand to halt Merrit's gasp of dismay, and continued smoothly as if she were not delivering news that would ruin the young girl's life. "Without the promised pearls, the agreements concerning the marriage and the business arrangements with your father are voided. You must understand that Winston's political future is dependent on the dowry he receives, so we must waste no time in arranging another suitable match unless you feel there is hope the pearls may yet be recovered."

Merrit shook her head numbly, unable to believe that it all could be crushed so neatly and impersonally — her future, her father's company, her sisters' hopes for good marriages, her mother's dreams. Gone. And all because of the greed of a man who would show her no mercy.

"I have dispatched a missive to your father advising him of the complications. You will, of course, remain here as our guest until we receive word from him."

"Thank you for your kindness," she murmured faintly, because it was expected of her. In truth, she wanted to scream and wail, to berate the injustice of her lot, to curse the pirate who had crushed her future in his avaricious hands. She wanted to scratch and tear at the remote woman who so casually sat in judgment. Instead, true to her good breeding, she rose silently and climbed the endless stairs, holding back her tears for the privacy of her room.

The following days were a painless limbo for Merrit, she seemed to wander through some cloudy, uncertain dream. Her stay at Whitelawn was awkward for them all. Thaddeus regarded her with sad, helpless eyes as if to assure her it was none of his doing. Letitia spent much time trying to cajole her into good spirits, while Gabrielle remained distant, being old enough to feel Merrit's unhappiness but too young to know what to do to ease it. Only Sophia remained unchanged, her attitude that of a cordial hostess toward an unwanted guest. Merrit tried to be as inconspicuous as possible, creeping about the house so as not to disturb its normal functions. It was a gloomy existence by day, but the long, quiet nights were worse. She would awake to dark stillness, her pulse racing as she clung to the vivid dreams that left her trembling. Then she would lie in the cool darkness, hatred festering for the man who ruled her dreams and desires.

It was during one of the tedious evening meals that her cocoon of indifference was torn asunder. In a breach of table etiquette, Gabrielle blurted out, "When I was in Williamsburg this afternoon I heard the most surprising news."

Ignoring her mother's severe glance, Letitia begged to hear more.

"They've captured the Spanish Angel. He is to hang in Charlestown."

A loud buzzing rose in Merrit's head, rocking her senses

until she feared she would swoon. *Colley*, her heart cried in anguish as her mind spun with crazed grief. She took a quick swallow of water to cool the fever of her panic. She had to stay calm. She had to think.

"When are they to hang him?" she asked in an oddly level voice.

"In eight days."

Eight days. So little time. She had to see him, if for no other reason than to lay her personal demons to rest. Perhaps if she saw him now, she would not be moved by the same stirring of passion, and her heart would be free for one more deserving. In truth, nothing mattered except looking on that handsome face one last time. She had only to get to Charlestown.

"Lady Whitelaw, may I speak to you for a moment."

Sophia looked up from her tatting, gazing directly at the lovely girl who hesitated in the doorway. Laying aside her work she called Merrit in.

Not knowing how to broach the subject gracefully, Merrit plunged in with a desperate directness. "I must get to Charlestown. There is a chance that if I can speak to the pirate captain I can recover the pearls for my dowry."

Sophia regarded her coolly for a long beat. "Not much of a chance, you must admit."

"No but a chance is all I have to restore my life, a life you were willing to risk when you told the pirates you would pay no ransom. You owe me this chance, my lady, in all fairness."

Sophia so admired the girl's tenacity, she permitted herself a small, rare smile. "I must admit that if you recover the dowry it will spare us the trouble of locating another suitable girl."

Merrit stiffened, holding her temper with difficulty. There was too much at stake to let pride rule.

"All right, my girl. You have your chance. I will arrange passage to Charlestown on tomorrow's coach. I truly wish you well, but do not place too much hope in the hands of a pirate."

To reclaim your dowry, is it?" Mildred said drily as she brushed out Merrit's soft, heavy hair. "Is that the only reason?"

"Reason enough," the girl snapped, immediately regretting her harshness when the face of her longtime friend tightened. "Forgive me, Mildred. I've no reason to be cross with you. You know me too well for pretense. Yes, I want to see him again, if only to assure myself that he is cut out of my life and heart. All these troubles are his doing. If he were to right them now for my sake, I would say a prayer for his soul, though I think he would rather I didn't. Mildred, I hate the man. He has lied to me to gain my favor, has used me as a fool before all. I wish to spit on him for what he has done to me, but first he must tell me what has happened to the pearls. They are what is important. They are my future."

But as she lay beneath the sheets that night, her thoughts were not on pearls but emeralds, the green of his beautiful eyes that she'd never thought to look into again. What if he would not see her? And would she be able to control her own emotions on seeing him? She could never again be fool enough to believe what she saw in his fair surface. She knew what lay beneath, and it was vile and ugly. That was what she would remember, the bitterness of his deceit and cold treachery. And when they hanged him, he would be out of her life forever, no longer a taunting shadow.

The Spanish Angel was the sole occupant of the Charlestown gaol, a small windowless cellar beneath the county meetinghouse. The guard undid the lock and bar, and lifted a lantern high to guide their way down crumbling stone steps to the earthen floor. It was foul and dank in the airless space with barely enough room to stand erect. Merrit shivered in revulsion at the thought of being caged in such a place.

As the solitary figure still cloaked in heavy shadow turned to them, she knew that no amount of talk and convincing could have prepared her for that first sight of him. There was a sharp rasp of hastily drawn breath, then a low, even voice.

"My lady, this is indeed a surprise."

Her pulse gave an uncontrolled leap at the sound of the heavy Spanish accent, and she steeled herself as if bracing for battle as he came forward into the circle of lamplight, his features sharpening into focus. How could she ever have foolishly believed she would be able to deny the dark fascination he held for her? Memories surged back to torture her senses—the crisp smell of the sea and the harsh scent of gunpowder that clung to his short black hair, the taste of salt on tanned skin that was like warm satin beneath her touch, the sweet heaven of his firm mouth moving on hers, and the feel of his large roughened hands on her body. Even now he claimed her heart and mind. He stood before her in heavy chains, but she felt no satisfaction in his humbling. If he had made the slightest welcoming gesture, she would have cast herself into those strong arms in helpless abandon, but the Angel's emerald eyes were as cold and expressionless as his words.

"Have you come to see me hang then? How comforting to know there will be a familiar face among the crowd. I trust the entertainment will not disappoint your thirst for vengeance."

At his mocking words, her self-control returned in an icy rush, her brief pulse of desire turning to anger as she noticed the ring in his ear had been replaced by a single flawless pearl. Fighting to remember her purpose, she said calmly, "I came only to speak with you, Captain, if you will listen."

His lips twisted into a sardonic smile. "I have little else in the way of amusement. I will listen. Welcome to my humble dwelling. I would protest the conditions, but it appears they are temporary."

Wincing at his blunt summation, she turned to the guard. "I would speak to him alone." When the man hesitated, she added impatiently, "If he had meant to harm me, he would have done so long ago. Leave the lamp."

The man shrugged and, after casting a wary look at the notorious pirate, made his way up the stairs, replacing the bar and listening for any sounds of distress.

Once they were alone, the captain spoke caustically, all traces of an accent gone. "Perhaps you are mistaken to think yourself safe with me. After all, you have left me with a face that would not move even the most desperate virgin."

At her puzzled look, he turned his face, and Merrit gasped. Crisscrossing his cheek were several half-healed gashes that marred its perfection. These were cuts that would leave scars. The worst of them curved down from the outer edge of his eye to the corner of his mouth in a wicked crescent. This slash gave him a sinister look; he was now more demon than angel.

Merrit swallowed hard. Though she was aghast at the aftermath of her impulsive act, she would not apologize. This was a cruel justice that gave her no satisfaction.

"So, my lady, what brings you here if not to witness my departure from this earth? Has your husband come with you, or doesn't he know you are here meeting with your defiler?"

"And you have faulted me for being sharp of tongue," she chided softly, trying to find a halfway cordial ground on which to pose her request. "Do not tell me the Spanish Angel has lost his considerable charm."

141

He stared at her for a moment as if making some decision, then smiled, his green eyes thawing and softening. "I beg your pardon, my lady. 'Twas not my intention to disturb you with my rude speech."

She pursed her lips thoughtfully unable to tell if even now he was mocking her. But at least he was making an effort to be agreeable. "I am sorry for your situation," she said with quiet sincerity. "Is there anything I can get for you?"

"A last request? A fast ship and twenty more years," he said with an easy smile as if the shadow of the gallows was not over him. "Truly, my lady, I have every comfort, but I am sure the comfort of my last days is not what's brought you to me. Why did you leave the bosom of your new family? The truth, Merrit."

Her eyes dropped uneasily to his shackled feet, for she was afraid to voice the aim of her mission. When he remained silently waiting, she began in a low, unemotional tone. "I have no new family, nor can I return to the old. I must have my dowry back. That is why I have come." She ventured a glance at him, seeing a flicker of disappointment skirt his eyes before they became carefully opaque.

"The pearls, of course. Did you think I would have them, that my gaolers would let me take them with me to eternity?" His fleeting good humor was gone as he scolded her sullenly.

"But you know where they are," she prompted.

"Why would I tell you?"

She held his eyes, looking long and deeply into them as if trying to see into his soul, to find the man who had treated her gently and passionately. "Because I asked you. Because it is important to me that you do this last charitable act."

That brought a genuine smile to his lips. "Ah, but that proved costly in the past."

"What have you to risk?"

His smile widened. "True enough. But what have I to gain?"

Merrit's eyes grew heavy, and her hands came to rest on his soiled shirtfront. "Much," she murmured.

Eyes narrowing into glittering slits, he took a quick step back, away from her touch and out of the light. "Offer me something I have not already had," he said with a blunt harshness. Seeing her hands clench as if she longed to strike him he added, "If you are waiting, I do not plan to turn the other cheek this time."

"Your life, Captain," she spat fiercely. "Is that offer tempting enough?"

He was silent, then replied, "Tempting . . . but not possible."

"You underestimate my determination," Merrit countered shortly.

There was a flash of white teeth, as his hand rose to his torn cheek. "I confess I have in the past, and have regretted it. All right, my lady, arrange my freedom and I will retrieve your dowry."

Merrit let out her breath in a gush of relief, her eyes closing briefly in an unvoiced prayer of thanks. He would help her. Nothing else worried her. "I will return as soon as I can."

"I will be here, my lady," he retorted lightly. As she turned to go, there was a rattle of chains, and he stepped quickly after her, saying in a rush, "One last request, in case it is out of your power."

She looked back at him, eyes lifted questioningly. "What is it, Captain?"

His manacled hands rose to cup her soft cheeks, holding her face still as his mouth came down to hers. Any thought of protest fled from her the instant their lips touched, awakening slumbering emotions and erasing all the barriers between them except for the length of chain that kept him from embracing her as he longed to do. His kiss played across her parted lips with a searing intensity, draining her of all awareness save of the delicious things he was doing to her with that single caress of his mouth. Merrit's nerves were afire as a molten desire poured through her to warm every fiber of her being. It was as though contact with him had restored her soul from a lifeless prison. Her restraint buckling under that powerful surge of feeling, she relaxed her control, letting the tip of her tongue lightly explore the shape and warm inner contours of his mouth. until the painful bite of his fingers on her jaw and the back of her neck returned her to her senses.

Feeling her hesitate, he instantly released her, slowing his breath with difficulty as he looked down into eyes now warm and languid with wanting. "I only wish I could ask for more, but I shall be content with that," he said in a low, throaty voice. "What happens now does not matter. I will be satisfied with what you have just given me."

In a confused whirl, Merrit stepped away from him, agitated and at a loss to understand his shifting moods. Frowning slightly, she turned and hurried up the stairs as he looked up from the darkness, slowly licking his lips to savor the taste of her still on them.

"Me lamb, what is it? What has he done to you?" Mildred insisted upon seeing her charge's wild breathless appearance when Merrit returned.

"Nothing. Nothing," the young woman assured her as she struggled to control her panting and the careening race of her heart. "We came to a bargain is all."

Mildred's eyes narrowed suspiciously. She noted Merrit's bruised lips and the finger imprints along her jaw. "What sort of bargain, miss?"

"He will get the pearls if I can get him released," she explained, bathing her face in the cool basin to lessen its heat.

"No," Mildred said sharply. "Merrit, stay away from him. He is a dangerous scheming man who hopes to prey on yer weakness for him. Do not be fooled again. He will only hurt ye."

"You are wrong. I will be very careful," she protested firmly.

"What kind of protection can ye put up against a man ye'd let make love to ye when his neck is in a noose?"

Merrit frowned at the critical truth, then gave her a winning smile. "That is what I have you for, dear Mildred. You will protect me."

## Chapter Twelve

Colonel Alexander Spotswood looked up interestedly from the scattering of building plans as the daughter of his old friend was announced. She had grown from a small, skinny child into a beautiful young woman, but the teasing dark eyes had not changed.

"What a surprise, my dear. I was not aware you were in the Colonies or I would have sought you out immediately," he vowed fondly, crossing to take the tiny hands she extended with a smile.

"I've only recently arrived. I bear my father's wishes."

"Is he still pushing himself as though a thousand demons were at his back?" the large, bewigged man asked with a chuckle.

Merrit's smile was a bit strained. "Only one pursues him now, and that is why I am here."

"Sit down, my dear. If there is anything I can do to help you, name it," he insisted.

She took a large leather-covered chair and looked hopefully to the man who had shared their table on many a night as she grew up. He was now the powerful governor of the Colony of Virginia. "There is a name for it," she began quietly. "The Spanish Angel."

"The Pirate?" Spotswood asked curiously as he settled himself behind his desk and pushed aside the plans for

146

building on his estate in Williamsburg. The construction had occupied his thoughts for the last weeks.

After he poured two glasses of claret, Merrit related her tale, beginning with the fire that had ruined her father's business and the marriage contract that was intended to end their troubles. From that point on, she gave him a chaste version of her abduction, and the older man frowned, then scowled as she told of the Whitelaws' indifferent treatment of her. It was difficult if not impossible for Merrit to keep anxiety and upset from creeping into her voice.

"So you see," she concluded, her eyes moist, "I must have my dowry to regain my self-respect. Without it, I might as well turn to the streets for I could never return home and face my family."

"Nonsense, my dear," he interrupted gruffly. "I will speak to that puppy Whitelaw. He aspires to my office, but he will accept you without the dowry or he'll hold no post in my jurisdiction."

"No," Merrit cried in alarm, for her honor was prompting her to bargain for the return of her dowry while her heart wanted her to save the life of the pirate.

"It must be done this way to save my family's honor. I'll not have it said that we'd knowingly break an agreement. You know my father. I am like him in that respect."

"An admirable but somewhat difficult trait, pride," he murmured, then leaned back to consider all he'd heard. "You know we've gone to considerable effort to capture this pirate. He has been bleeding our coast for an indecent amount of time. I cannot release him just to aid the daughter of an old friend. I must consider my political future."

"Of course. I would not expect you to help me if doing so would put you in jeopardy. I propose an equal exchange of information, and then there would be my gratitude when I marry Winston."

Spotswood looked at the girl and smiled at her shrewdness. She was right. Whitelaw was a bothersome problem. He was young and vital, and would hold sway with much of the populace. Yet, with Merrit to intercede between them, his own deposition could be delayed, perhaps until he was ready to retire from office. In addition, her father was not without influence in England, and he would remember a favor tendered. But to release the pirate on these grounds would provoke a cry of outrage.

"What exchange do you speak of, Merrit?"

"I gathered much information during my stay with the pirates, about other captains and their plans for future raids. If I tell you all I know and you attribute the information gained to the Angel, no one can protest your pardoning him. I understand it is becoming a common practice in Charleston to release the one to gain the many."

The governor rested his hands on his portly belly, and nodded. He, too, had heard such talk and was considering the use of pardons to tempt the buccaneers off the seas and to ease the financial distress of the Colonies. "This renegade, this pirate, can he be trusted?"

"As much as one can trust a pirate. He has proven that he keeps his word and I know he will see me safe from harm." She looked up with large hopeful eyes. She had said all she could. Now it was up to Spotswood; her future and the captain's life were in the governor's hands.

The Spanish Angel ceased his restless pacing as the door of his prison opened. He had been unable to calm his thoughts after Merrit departed. Half-mad with desire for her, he was, at the same time, longing to cheerfully throttle her for coming back into his life. When he had first seen her standing in the poor light of his dank tomb, he'd feared he had truly gone mad, that his insistent dreams of her beauty had made her come to him as an apparition to taunt him in his few remaining days. But this had been no dream, no haunting ghost of his longing, but the lady herself, come to

148

tease him with the dangling offer of her sweet favors and with escape from the gibbet. Was there any truth to her words or was she playing some cruel joke on him? Surprisingly, he didn't care. Her unexpected visit and the eager press of her lips had lifted him from an abyss to a plateau of daydreams and memories.

In those weeks after she had sailed from him, he had tried to concentrate on the pain of his wound rather than that caused by her loss, seeing his marred cheek as proof of his foolishness in weakening for a woman. But he had been unable to get her out of his thoughts when everything brought back the image of her beauty. His cabin was a torture—he saw her reflection in the mirror, her slender back bent over his ledger in the soft glow of lantern light. He would awaken abruptly in the night thinking he had felt her fleeting touch or heard the whisper of her skirts. Even the constant agony of the wound on his face brought back the look in her dark eyes, the accusing glare of hatred, the hurt that would not give his conscience ease. In the clammy darkness of his earthen prison, he had envisioned her going into her new husband's arms willingly as if no other had come before. He had writhed at that picture, damning her for so easily forgetting their nights together, for coldly using what she had learned in his arms to please another while he lay imprisoned in a dark, airless hellhole, waiting to be released from her torment.

When she had come to him, for a moment he had been swept up in the idea that she had come only to see him again before he died, prompted by whatever feelings he had been able to awaken in her. The true reason for her appearance was yet another bitter blow. She had come to use him. Part of him rebelled, insisting that hanging was better than freedom under those circumstances.

"Come up, Angel. It looks like your lady was true to her word," the guard called from the top of the stairs.

The captain blinked in surprised disbelief, then permitted

149

himself a brief smile. He had underestimated her again. Once he stood in the fresh, clean air, eyes squinting against the harsh daylight, he saw her waiting in an open carriage, her delicate brows arched in smug satisfaction. He gave a slight bow out of respect for her ingenuity, before climbing awkwardly into the equipage and seating himself next to a glowering Mildred. He gave the woman his most charming smile, and murmured, "How good to see you again, madam."

"Keep yer distance, pirate," she growled, unimpressed by his courtliness.

Grinning, he settled in beside her. When his eyes rose to meet those that boldly watched him from the opposite seat, his smile faded. "I am in your debt, my lady," he stated flatly. He was uncertain of her, remembering her response to his kiss and her fury that had scarred him. Dare he trust her?

"See that the debt is repaid, Captain, and we will owe each other nothing," Merrit replied crisply.

He nodded, eyes shifting to the man at her side. His dark brows lowered as he considered that hard face. "Captain Neville, if I am not mistaken. As I recall a good part of your crew signed our articles when we took your ship. I trust you remember me."

Captain Neville fairly seethed with hatred as he clipped out, "Yes, I remember. You are in my hands this time, so go carefully. My greatest pleasure would be to see you fitted for a noose aboard my ship. It is revolting to see you acting the free man when you should by all rights be waiting to swing, but my orders come from the governor himself. Play me false and nothing will keep you from my judgment."

The pirate regarded him with unconcerned disdain, then raised his manacled hands. "If I be free, why am I yet chained?"

"The chains remain until your part of the bargain be met. I haven't the lady's trust in your honor," Neville sneered contemptuously.

The Angel smiled and, with his thickest Spanish accent, said, "A pirate's word can be trusted more than that of an English captain who is a greater thief."

With a snarl, Neville struck the Angel's mocking face sharply, and was rewarded with an amused chuckle.

"Captain Neville, you forget yourself," Merrit said harshly. "The captain is in my care, not yours, and I will not tolerate abuse of him while he is my . . . guest. If you are not man enough to hear him out without such displays of violence, I advise you not to encourage him to speak. Is that understood?"

"Yes, my lady," Neville said with icy formality, as the pirate grinned at him.

"And you," Merrit continued, looking coldly into the green eyes that softened perceptively when they turned to her. "Do not try me with your bold arrogance. You are not the strutting Angel here. I have had your life spared for my own purpose, and I can easily change my mind. Behave as a guest or be treated as a prisoner. Is that understood?"

Colley's chin lifted slightly, and he turned away from her without deigning to answer, presenting her with a view of his ruined cheek. Repressing a sigh, she dropped her eyes. She disliked redressing him publicly, but she couldn't afford to show her true feelings for she must maintain a tenuous balance between the two men. She would bear the brunt of his silent fury in order to keep him safe from harm until he could be released. However, with his swaggering arrogance, it would be no easy task to keep him from offending the naval men he so despised.

Their swift brigantine lay waiting in the harbor, sporting ten cannon and a sixty-man crew. There was no mistaking the hostile threat in the eyes that followed the pirate aboard. With a nonchalant air, he moved easily among the seamen, seemingly unaware of their murderous glares as he went to stand at the bow of the ship. Breathing deeply of the salt air, his eyes scanned the horizon eagerly. Watching him, Merrit felt her emotions take a tender turn. Enthralled by the sight of him, she was nonetheless apprehensive about having him so near, especially when she was unable to reach out to him. Shaking off those wistful feelings, she went below with Mildred, to settle into their small cabin.

"He's a cocky one, that pirate," Mildred said with begrudging respect as she hung Merrit's gowns alongside her own. "He'll be lucky to survive the trip in this company."

Merrit frowned thoughtfully. "I will see to his safety."

Mildred gave her a long look. How the girl had changed. She'd been spirited as a child, but her handling of the two battling captains and this new voice of authority showed a strength and wisdom that had come lately. She wondered how much of that maturing was due to the pirate. She had seen the wary looks the pair had exchanged, and she hoped distrust would stave off the passions that had simmered in those covert glances. Determined to keep Merrit from getting hurt again, she decided to see that they were not left alone together so those sparks could ignite. She wanted Merrit to safely return to the path planned for her.

"What happened to his pretty face?" Mildred asked idly. "Some drunken brawl or perhaps a jealous wench?"

Merrit stiffened, looking decidedly uncomfortable. "It was my doing," she said softly, overcome by a sudden sense of guilt at her rashness.

Mildred could only stare in open-mouthed surprise. Her gentle pet so violent? It was inconceivable, as if the child she had nurtured were suddenly a stranger.

"Do not ogle me so, Mildred. 'Tis nothing I am proud of, but it cannot be undone so no more talk of it," Merrit snapped irritably, then took a long breath to compose her rattled thoughts. "When we are under way, ask that the captain be brought down to me. Do not scowl. You may hover over both of us to soothe your fears.

"That I will," Mildred assured her smartly.

* * *

With the arrival of the pirate, the cabin seemed overly crowded. Merrit, painfully aware of his presence, was unable to avoid his questioning green eyes.

"You sent for me, my lady?" he asked with a touch of mockery.

Making her voice unnecessarily cool in the watchful presence of Mildred and the first mate, Merrit said, "I thought you might like to clean up after your confinement. I brought you some fresh things."

His eyes registered pleased surprise, but his reply was noncomittal. "You are very kind to have considered me."

"I was considering myself. Your presence is noticeable long before you arrive," she remarked, wrinkling her nose saucily.

His brows lowered in abused vanity, then he gave a sudden flashing smile that lit his features and revived his magnetic charm. "How unkind of you to say so."

They shared a brief smile, their eyes warmly holding until she turned to the mate and ordered, "Undo those chains."

"But Lady Ellison," he protested.

"How can the man dress when he is so trussed? Release him and go. You may return for him in a half-hour." When the ship's officer still hesitated she said sharply, "Do as I say. He'll not escape. He can't swim so you needn't fear he'll go over the side."

The captain frowned at that disclosure, but he held out his wrists, rubbing his chafed skin as the irons were removed. He watched Merrit as she filled the basin with fresh water and then turned to him, brows raised. Without reluctance, he stripped off the offensive shirt under her hungry gaze, then reached down to unfasten his breeches.

Merrit frowned sullenly as Mildred gripped her arm and spun her about, giving him cause to chuckle as he finished disrobing. The splashing of water followed by a long murmur of contentment drew Merrit's eyes to him in a quick glance, her breath catching at the sight of his sleek, manly

153

form now clad in close-fitting, white canvas trousers, his skin dark in comparison. Fascinated, she watched the smooth play of muscle and sun-warmed skin as he vigorously scrubbed layers of grime from his chest. A desire to touch that bronze back rose in her, sudden and strong, and she dug her nails deeply into her palms to fight off that impulse. He slipped into the loose linen shirt, breaking her trance-like admiration. Rolling up its sleeves, he left it unbuttoned to expose a lean expanse of tanned chest and flat midriff.

Picking up the razor she provided, he regarded his face in the mirror, hesitant to begin the torturous task of working around the scabbed-over gashes. He started when the blade was taken from his hand, looking to Merrit in puzzlement.

"I'll do it. You'd most likely tear all those cuts open again," she told him quietly, then smiled in reassurance. "Do not look so nervous, Captain. I have done this for my father on many occasions when his hand was none too steady."

He returned her smile somewhat apprehensively, but obediently took the chair she offered, sitting stiffly as she knelt between his knees and began to ply the blade with a firm, practiced touch. He was uncomfortably aware of Mildred's disapproving glare and of the havoc Merrit's nearness was causing, so he kept his eyes on her studious face, lovely in concentration as it had been when she'd labored over his ledger. He held his breath when the razor paused against his throat, noting the frown that clouded Merrit's face before she continued her task. When she had finished, he turned to catch her eyes, found them darkly shimmering.

"I am sorry," she whispered faintly. "I did not mean to hurt you so terribly."

"You did" was his soft, enigmatic response. Then his eyes left hers and he raised a hand to test his smooth cheeks.

Merrit rose on shaky legs, choked with emotion and bitter regret, for she realized how costly her anger had been for

154

him. She turned away to draw on her inner strength to calm her features, then asked, "Will you sup with me, Captain?"

He was silent for a moment, his eyes questioning. Then he gave her a twisted smile. "No, my lady. 'Tis not my intention to hide behind your skirts. I can take care of myself, and I promise to behave like a congenial guest. I will give you no cause for sleeplessness."

He was wrong in that, for she spent a restless night tossing on her lonely bed and thinking of him so near yet so impossibly distant. He was such a confusing collection of personas—the jaunty fearless Spanish Angel and his demonic counterpart with the piercing cold eyes, and the man she called Colley who seemed so sincere and warm. How could they all be embodied in one form and how could she have one without taking all? Which was he in truth? What if the man she desired was but a façade like the flashy Angel, and he was really the dark, angry vengeance seeker?

Still unable to rest in the pink light of early dawn, Merrit rose and quietly dressed so as not to awaken the snoring Mildred. Then she crept up on deck to clear her thoughts in the crisp, salty air of the new day. After fetching a mug of the aromatic coffee she'd developed a taste for aboard the *Merry Widow*, she began to stroll the deck, stopping in puzzled surprise when she came across a sleeping figure propped against the gunwale.

"Captain?"

He was instantly awake, rubbing his eyes and stumbling to his feet amidst the tangle of his leg irons. "Good morning, my lady," he muttered, momentarily stunned by her appearance. She was as fresh and crisp as the cool morning breeze, her silk mantua of palest silver blue shimmering in the early morning light like a perfect evening star.

"Did you sleep out here all night?" she demanded in outrage. "Weren't you provided with a place below?" If she found that to be the case, heaven help Captain Neville.

He smiled at her concern and explained simply, "I found

it to be healthier up here."

On closer scrutiny, she could see slight discolorations about his face and lumpy swellings along his jaw. Seeing the dark flush of rage that crept into her cheeks, he said easily, "I but fell, my lady, but do not fret, I was very well behaved in doing so."

"Who struck you?" she fumed, furious to think that anyone would abuse a man who was defenseless and in chains.

"I cannot think of anyone who did not want to, my lady. Calm yourself. I am a pirate, a murderer of children, a ravisher of widows. You can see why I am not beloved by these men. They toil and sweat under the threat of the lash to scratch a few coins together while I sail free and am my own master, possessed of more wealth than they could dream of. Of course they hate me as I would were I in their place. I accept that as you must. Do not fear. I have no wish to have my throat cut in the night. Say no more or it will only go harder on me."

Her hands trembled slightly as she extended the coffee to him, unable to be so casual about his dangerous position. He took the cup gratefully, his eyes sweeping over her in warm appreciation.

"You are more beautiful than I remembered. How can that be possible?" he mused.

"Captain—" she began uneasily only to have him wave off her protest.

"My name is Nicholas. I can be no captain without a ship. Call me by my name."

"Colley." She said it like a caress, warmly and lingeringly. On her lips his name was an intimate endearment whispered in the throes of passion. The sound of it, low and inviting sent an abrupt chill of anticipation through him, and he knew with a certainty that it would be only a matter of time before she came to him for a taste of the heady aphrodisiac they created together. Knowing that, he gave her a slow smile that brought panicked confusion to her face.

"Is there more of this?" he asked finally, extending the tin and releasing her from his disconcerting spell.

"I will get us both some," she offered quickly, eager to escape and gain much-needed prospective.

She returned a moment later and, passing him one of the warm cups she carried, leaned on the rail beside him in a moment of easy silence.

"Captain, where is your ship?" she asked. "How is it you alone were captured and sentenced to hang?"

He took a deep draught of the coffee before answering, his eyes taking on that hard brilliance. "Not by accident, my lady. We had taken a fat prize, ripe and easy. We were all spirited up for the boarding." What he didn't mention was that he had seldom been sober since her departure, but had eased the ache in his face and in his heart with massive doses of rum. "The flute's masts were topped and we had put out when something was laid across the back of my head and I was in the water. No one on board could hear me over the celebrating, no one save Durant; but it was not his plan to pull me in." The hands holding the tin cup clenched until their knuckles went white, but Colley's tone was still casual. "The crew of the flute fished me out, a fine catch to be sure. The rest you know."

"No one came back for you? Not Rufe? They would just leave you?" she asked in astonishment.

"We never go back. We cannot afford to. Not for anyone. That's what being a pirate means. There is no time for thought of anyone else, only what's best for yourself and the ship."

"But to have no loyalty? Rufe was your friend," she protested, unable to understand the primitive code that ruled his life.

"He still is, but there can be no loyalty, just survival. Life is short enough without taking extra risks. You have given me back some of that precious time I thought I'd lost, and I would thank you for that now."

His hands rose to lightly touch her face, her pulse jumping in quick response to what she wanted, had been waiting for. Her eyes drifted closed in dreamy willingness; then, abruptly, his fingertips were snatched away. With a startled gasp, her eyes sprang open to see one of the navy crewmen spinning the captain about and using the chain that joined his ankles to jerk him off his feet. When Colley met the deck with a force that momentarily winded him, the brawny sailor turned to Merrit, a leering grin on his face, his eyes boldly sweeping over her.

"If it be a man yer wanting, there be plenty of us good ones more than anxious, so you needn't dirty yerself with the likes of that. What say you, missy?"

Merrit quickly glanced at the fallen man, meeting the silent question in his hot, angry eyes. "I say it is too much to expect good behavior in such a case as this," she said coolly.

With a savage snarl, Nicholas kicked the backs of the sailor's knees, felling him with a surprised cry. The pirate was on him in an instant, wrapping a length of chain about his neck with a brutal twist, bringing the gasping seaman up to his knees.

His voice harsh and nearly unintelligible due to his thick accent, Colley hissed, "Never again lay a hand on me, and never — ever — speak disrespectfully to the lady." As he jerked the chain taut to further emphasize his words, Merrit noticed that a crowd of curious men had begun to gather and she saw in this a chance to set things right.

"Hear me well," she told the sailor as his eyes bugged due to the constriction of his throat. "Only two men have ever tried to abuse my good nature. One of them, the captain had flogged. The other I sent to his just reward with my knife in his ribs. Think on that before you rape me with your glances."

There was a surprised murmur from Mildred who had joined the group, but Merrit refused to sooth her with a glance, she was too angry about the sailor's treatment and the interruption of the kiss she had been longing for.

The crew parted for their captain, who, after assessing the situation, drew his pistol, and leveled it between upraised green eyes. "Release that man," he demanded with chilling severity. "You were warned, Angel, and now you will be flogged."

The pirate unlooped the choking coil and stood, drawing himself up with proud arrogance, his eyes darkened by contempt and his generous mouth twisted in an insulting smile. No trace of fear or intimidation showed on his handsome, mocking face.

"Captain Neville, don't be a dolt. He was but defending my honor," Merrit interceded crisply.

Neville gave her a cold glance, seeing his opportunity for vengeance fade. In frustration, he said snidely, "From what I understand, it was our chivalrous captain who soiled your honor to begin with."

Merrit went white with shock, but she clung to enough presence of mind to place a hand on Nicholas's chest to halt the pirate's hasty advance. While she struggled to think of some rebuttal, the stocky Mildred came to her rescue, cuffing the offending captain with a heavy hand.

"Ye be apologizing to her ladyship. After all she's been through the likes of ye should cast no slur on her name," she declared furiously.

Neville turned to meet Merrit's stricken eyes, and made a formal bow. "My apologies, Lady Ellison. Anger loosened my tongue. Forgive my churlish words."

Merrit drew a shaky breath before responding, her voice tremulous with emotion. "How dare you expect forgiveness. When I was a captive I was given every courtesy, yet I am scorned and treated cheaply by supposedly good men who are in the service of the Crown. You, Captain, could learn something of manners from the thieves you despise. I am shamed that you would allow the captain, pirate or no, to be so abused on your ship after he extended me every care while I was aboard his. That is not how I choose to repay him. I want those leg irons removed, and I want your promise that none of your men will raise a hand to him. I will hold you responsible if he comes to any harm, and believe me, Mr. Neville, you will be taken to task. Now disperse your gawking crew and get out of my sight."

Once she was alone with Mildred and the partially freed captain, her outer strength began to crumble, giving way to feelings of stunned outrage and weariness. Was there no end to the besmirchment she had to endure on every front? For one gently reared, the stigma of wantonness was difficult to bear. Was it everyone's belief that she had been the pirate's whore, and if so, why was she now trying to put her life back to rights?

Seeing those brave shoulders tremble, Nicholas reached out a hand to her, saying her name in a low voice filled with empathy.

"Merri."

Merrit's eyes flashed up to his, dark and wetly shining. "Go away, she cried in anguish. "Haven't you caused me enough grief?"

His hand dropped away and he watched in helpless silence as Mildred quickly escorted her below.

## Chapter Thirteen

"Do not cry, me pet," Mildred crooned, patting her shoulder in a motherly way. "We will have ye back to yer intended soon and all will be right again."

"I am not going to cry, and all will not be right again," Merrit said heavily. "Is the mark of harlot so plain upon my face that all who see me know I was his lover?"

"No. No, me lamb. Yer face is as lovely and pure as ever. His evil seduction has left no mark on ye," the concerned woman quickly declared. Strangely, she wished the girl would cry, for tears would be easier to comfort than this withdrawn grieving.

Merrit straightened, pulling herself out of Mildred's encircling arm. "Colley is not to blame. Not as much as my own weakness. He but offered. 'Twas I who accepted."

Mildred stiffened at her familiar use of the pirate's name and her quick defense of him. What sort of entangling web had he caught her up in? Would his continued presence bring Merrit even greater harm? Yet he had not boasted of their intimacy, and he had leapt to her defense at the peril of his own life. Could it be that he, too, was a hapless victim? Mildred wasted no further concern on him, for he was a man used to breaking hearts. She only hoped that Merrit would not confuse desire and excitement with emotions that were deeper and more lasting.

"I would like to rest now, Mildred," Merrit said quietly in a tone that made it clear she wanted to be alone with her thoughts.

"All right, me pet. Sleep well and believe that all things work for the best."

Merrit gave her a sad smile bereft of hope. "As you will," she murmured.

Outside the cabin, Nicholas faced Mildred with raised brows upon seeing the stormy determination in her stolid features when she wagged an accusing finger at him.

"Angel, be damned. Yer the Devil, a dark seducer who lures trustful souls with sweet words of empty promise."

"Madam, what are you talking about?" he asked, bewildered by her sudden tirade.

"Lady Merrit, as if ye didn't know."

He blinked in surprise, but did not deny what she apparently already knew.

"Ye are a dark, soulless man even for a pirate, for ye disguise yer rape of innocents with twisted lies that entice and trap. Evil is no matter how pretty it appears."

He cast a quick look about to guarantee that their conversation would not be overheard, then said in a low, flat voice, "If the lady has told you I raped her, 'tis she who is lying." Was that how she saw their acts of love? he wondered angrily, but he soon became uneasy under Mildred's hostile gaze.

"Of course, 'tis not what she told me. She is but a child."

"She is old enough."

"Not to know what it is she wants," Mildred protested hotly, disregarding his casual explanation.

"And she wants me?" There was a sudden quickening in the timbre of his voice as if the angry woman had just given him new hope.

"She wants more, more than you could ever offer. Do not deceive her into believing that lust and love are the same."

He frowned, disliking the topic and unwilling to be made responsible. "I gave her what she wanted," he said bluntly, whereupon Mildred's face beamed mottled with rage.

"Do not play the guileless pawn with me, pirate. Ye knew well what ye were doing, that yer fair face and tempting promises would sway an inexperienced child. Ye lured her into yer crafty bed like a sacrificial lamb. She knows nothing of men like ye who deal in half-truths. A curse on ye for letting her think that because ye are the first to open her eyes to what lies between a man and a woman ye be the only one she wants. What she needs is the love of a good man, and she has a good man awaiting her, one who can truly teach her the ways of love. Do not get in the way, pirate. Do not confuse her with yer conniving trickery. Let this be a warning to ye. Stay away from her."

He spoke with a steady calm he was far from feeling, his eyes sincere. "Believe what you will. I have no desire to harm Merrit, but she be no child and she well knows her own mind. If she comes to me, I will not turn her away."

A jolt of agony coursed up his face as Mildred's palm firmly slapped his injured cheek. Yet with an understanding smile that bore no trace of mockery, he bowed to her before he left her to her rage.

Merrit woke to almost complete darkness, surprised to find that she had slept so soundly after the bland evening meal. She could hear fierce winds raging as a tropical storm assaulted the ship. As rain battered the vessel which pitched about in the sea, she was content to nestle deeper into the covers, warm and secure despite the howling elements. But then she sat up and gasped.

"What is it, pet?" Mildred asked from where she sat hunched over the table, reading a torrid novella by the dim light of a lamp.

"What time is it?" Merrit asked hazily.

"About nine and a half past."

Merrit leapt from her bed, grabbing a heavy cloak to wrap about her thin chemise. "How long has it been storming?" she demanded in alarm.

163

"Several hours. Why? Where be ye going? Surely yer not thinking of going above?"

But Merrit had already fled the room, and was hurrying up the steps into the full fury of the evening. Gale-force winds tore at her, making her struggle to keep the cloak and hood closed against the chill of the heavy rain as she ran carelessly across the slick deck, her eyes searching desperately in the poor visibility until they found him huddled against the negligible protection of the gunwale, arms clasped about updrawn knees, head ducked into hunched shoulders. His eyes rose and widened in amazement when she knelt beside him, shivering in the tearing winds.

"My lady, what madness brings you here?" he demanded. "Go below. 'Tis dangerous here on deck."

"I came for you," she shouted above the roar of the crashing waves that dashed over the side, drenching both of them with their cold, salty spray.

"Merri, you are mad. Go back to your cabin."

"Not without you."

Seeing her determination, he shook his head and stood, holding tightly to her as they cautiously made their way over the treacherous upper deck to the safety below. Merrit stopped to fetch a pot of brewed coffee from the galley, then prodded him on to her cabin.

Mildred looked up in dismay upon the entrance of the two dripping figures, and shot the unwelcome pirate a harsh look before stripping the sodden cloak off Merrit, and unintentionally leaving her charge standing in a damp, clinging night shift that revealed more than it covered. Before she could rectify her error, Nicholas pulled a sheet from one of the beds and swaddled it about Merrit, his eyes appraising her warmly as he did so. She gave him a brief smile of thanks, then steered him into a chair.

"You're chilled clear through," Merrit scolded as she fetched a blanket to drape around him, her brows knitting as he hugged it to him with blue fingers.

"I am fine, my lady. I have weathered many a storm."

His assurances would have been better received had his teeth not been chattering quite so loudly. Still frowning, Merrit poured him a tin of coffee, and he took it in both hands, savoring its warmth as the liquid sloshed about due to his trembling. He sipped the brew gratefully, then held it so the steam thawed his nearly frozen features. But Mildred's unwavering glower was even colder than the storm so, reluctantly, he set down the cup.

"Thank you, my lady, but I cannot stay here," he said firmly.

Merrit swiftly interrupted him. "Of course you can. I'll not send you back out. You'll spend the night here."

"No," Colley and Mildred stated in unison, but Merrit would not be swayed.

"Have you eaten, Captain?" she asked, ignoring Mildred's pointed stare.

"Not for a time," he admitted, clutching the blanket as he was shaken by another fit of shivering.

"Mildred, fetch the captain something hot and be quick about it," she ordered.

Her expression showing her unhappiness at being forced to serve such an unworthy master, Mildred grudgingly complied.

Once they were alone, Merrit produced a bottle of brandy — Mildred thought she didn't know of its presence — and filled Nicholas's cup to the brim. As he enjoyed its potency, she grasped a towel and began to briskly dry his rain-slicked hair.

"Merri, it is best I leave. My being here is upsetting Mildred," he said finally as he relaxed under her care.

"It upsets me to think of you freezing on deck."

"Then I will find a hammock in the hold," he persisted.

"And have your throat cut?" She recoiled at the thought. She could not relax unless he was in her sight, and she was unable to keep the urgency she felt from her voice. "I will not allow it, Captain. I purchased your freedom, and you haven't the right to risk your life while our bargain is unmet." She felt him wince at the unintentional harshness of her words. As her hands fell to his shoulders, his muscles went rigid beneath her touch. Then, in a rush of anguish, her arms encircled his neck and she rested her glossy head against his. "Colley, please stay. I don't want you hurt. Please stay."

His voice was cool and distant. "Release me, my lady. I will stay in your sanctuary and not jeopardize your precious future." He shrugged out of her embrace, leaving the warmth of the blanket in an abrupt denial of any comfort she would give, and taking the bottle, he began to pace the cabin, avoiding her dark, unhappy eyes.

Mildred returned to find the air charged with tension, Merrit brooding and the pirate sullen. That suited her fine. She placed the heavily laden plate on the table.

"I am not hungry," Colley growled in self-denial, for he felt surly and pettish.

Mildred's palms slapped the table top causing him to jump. "After I go to the trouble of fetching it for ye, ye'll eat it, ungrateful wretch."

Considering diplomacy admirable, he seated himself and began to wolf down the food, swallowing almost without pausing to chew. After observing his gluttony with raised brows, Mildred asked sarcastically, "Do all ye pirates eat like vultures picking the bones clean?"

"It has been some time since my last meal," he replied through a mouthful of bread, not pausing to look up as he used the heel of the loaf to sop up anything that remained on the plate.

"How long a while?" she insisted with a growing frown.

He looked up then, eyes thoughtful. "I don't recall. Day before yesterday I think."

"No more of that," the dour-faced woman proclaimed angrily. "I care not if they hang ye, but I'll not see ye starved."

He flashed her a quick dazzling smile that seemed to fluster her for an instant before she recovered, frowned, and poured him more coffee.

Merrit watched the exchange, amused in spite of her low spirits. She had been the only one to wheedle concern from Mildred in the past, and it was odd to see her so charmed by a man she professed to loathe. But she knew it was easy to respond to him when he chose to be amiable. She noticed that his hands still shook as he raised the coffee tin, his damp shirt sticking to him. There was no way to remove it while he wore the shackles on his wrists. By the time he had finished the laced coffee and the majority of the bottle, his eyelids were drooping.

"Captain, rest on Mildred's bed. She can share mine," Merrit instructed softly.

"Thank you, my lady," he responded, his gaze unforgiving. "Be assured I will try not to die of grippe and break our bargain."

She flinched at his searing words, but said nothing as he flopped on the bunk still in wet clothing, and rolled away from them both.

Merrit lay in the darkness for a long while, listening to Mildred's hearty snores and the captain's restless tossing. Finally, she gave a resigned sigh and slipped cautiously from the bed, crossing on soundless bare feet to where Nicholas lay shivering fitfully. Touching a silencing finger to his lips, she pulled off his sodden boots and stockings. Then, under his questioning gaze, she withdrew her dagger and slit the seams of his shirt so she might peel it off him. As she began to tug down his wet breeches, he murmured low with an edge of amusement, "It will have to be rape, my lady, for I am too spent to oblige you this time."

"Rest easy, Captain. I'll not abuse you under Mildred's nose," she whispered back. Having stripped off all his damp clothing, she lay down beside him, gasping with shock as she

167

felt his cold flesh through her gauzy chemise. She pulled the covers over them both, pressing herself full length against his side so he might absorb the heat from her body.

"Better?" she whispered.

"I seem to have overestimated my weariness," he murmured in a husky tone, only to have her thump his chest sharply in reproof.

"Shh. Go to sleep, Colley."

She could feel the rapid tempo of his heart beneath her hand as he turned his head toward her, his green eyes luminescent in the dimness. Reading his intent in them, she put a hand over his mouth to halt its movement toward her own.

"No," she said simply, knowing that if he kissed her, she couldn't — wouldn't — stop the rest.

Without argument, his lips lightly caressed her fingers and he settled in beside her, raising his arm to slip it about her shoulders so she could snuggle close, resting her cheek in the hollow between his throat and shoulder. As her shared heat warmed his body, he closed his eyes, letting the slow caress of her hand on his chest lull him to sleep.

Fully absorbed in the smooth texture of his skin, Merrit let her hand wander, again familiarizing herself with the swells and contours of his upper body, unaware that her passion was beginning to flare. He felt so good to her touch and he was such a contrast to herself, all taut and lean, the only trace of softness to be found in him being his full mouth. She lightly kissed the slow pulse at his throat, tasting the salty sea brine on him.

"Colley?" she whispered, wishing him to hear her so the insistent urgings in her youthful body could be met, but he only muttered sleepily, his arm tightening about her before his breathing grew slow and regular again. Sighing, she nestled her cheek against him and let her passions ebb away.

## Chapter Fourteen

"What in the name of Jesus is going on here?"

At the sharp cry Merrit bolted up with a yelp of panic, to find herself caught on and nearly choked by Nicholas's shackles as she struggled to escape from his side and from the wrath in Mildred's voice. Unconcerned, he raised his arm so she could slip from under it and roll off the bed.

With the bearing of an enraged Brunhilde, Mildred faced them both, hands on hips, her expression dark as impending doom. She noted quickly that Merrit was dressed, though scantily, and the captain was not, her eyes running the length of him in candid appraisal. Undaunted by her piercing glare, he rolled onto his stomach and went back to sleep, leaving Merrit to quickly tug the covers over him before she turned to shrink guiltily from Mildred's chastising eyes.

"Merrit Ellison, shame on ye." Mildred snorted. "Sneaking about in the night to lie with him like a loose moraled little piece whilst I be sleeping in happy ignorance."

Merrit's chin jutted out in a sulky defiance, but her response was fainthearted. "I was not lying with him. I was lying next to him."

"With him, next to him, on him, under him," she ranted, her words accompanied by a series of dramatic gestures. "Do not bandy words with me, miss. Call it what you will, but the fact is, ye were coddled up to a man who is jay naked, fine manly form though he may have."

Merrit flushed deeply as the pirate murmured, "Thank

169

you, madam."

"Quiet, pirate," Mildred scolded.

As she began to smile, Merrit's eyes grew large and cajoling, and she plied her strict guardian with a sweet look to sway her anger. "You would not let him starve. Would you have me let him freeze?"

"Warmth is not what the likes of him is starving for," the stern woman stated crisply. "Let him curl up at the gates of hell if he be cold."

"Ladies, have a care," Colley grumbled. "I am trying to sleep."

"Begging your pardon," Mildred drawled, her tone sarcastic. "Just what were ye doing in the wee hours of the night to make ye so weary?"

"Mildred, enough," Merrit said, with an exasperated shake of her head. "No harm was done and none intended. Do not act the wronged party here. 'Tis not the first time I've lain with him and perhaps not the last."

"Mind your tongue, miss," Mildred warned severely.

The captain smiled to himself. Not the last. That was a promise he intended to see met, the memory of the soft press of her bosom and of the weight of her slender leg, the lingering touch of her hand wakened a languid passion in him as he burrowed deeper into the hollow in which they had passed the night.

"If you are finished with your tirade, please fetch us all some breakfast. I am positively weak from bearing up under the weight of your tongue lashing," Merrit stated pleasantly, her dark eyes teasing a reluctant smile from the older woman.

"Watch yer manners whilst I be gone," Mildred cautioned, wagging her finger.

Once the door clicked shut, Merrit prodded the reclined figure with her bare toe. "Get up, you unchivalrous lout. Leaving me to brave Mildred's accusations whilst you hide under the covers."

He rolled over to grin up at her disarmingly. "I would have interceded had you been in any danger. Besides, I was not eager to feel the weight of her hand on my poor face a second time."

Merrit frowned in puzzlement. "When did Mildred strike you?"

"We had a few words this past morning," he said mildly, struggling awkwardly to sit up because of his imprisoned hands.

"She must have a soft spot for you then, for you still have all your teeth." Merrit's amused smile faded as he rose up before her. Unable to keep her gaze from taking in the masculine splendor of him, she flushed with color.

"A blush, Merri?" he teased devilishly. "After all your bold words to Mildred?"

She shot him a pouty glower and flung his dried breeches at him, refusing to turn away in maidenly modesty as he donned them. They hugged his thighs and trim hips. Mildred was right, she decided. His was an exceptionally fine form.

As Colley picked up his torn shirt, he raised an eyebrow. "It seems I will have to tempt you a bit longer, my lady."

"Don't flatter yerself, pirate," mimicking Mildred, she stabbed his tanned chest with her fingertip.

"You'd best clothe yourself before I become too tempted by that teasing bit of lace," he murmured, warming her with a flash of excitement as the easy scrutiny of his green eyes proved he did not find her wanting.

When Mildred returned, she found Merrit plying the razor over the pirate's handsome face. She was bothered by the contented glow in the girl's expression and by his relaxed enjoyment, for it seemed the intimate domestic task they shared brought both a great deal of satisfaction. Somehow, she felt these brief moments of comfortable silence were more of a threat than the blazing hours of passion. Merrit had slipped into a fetching gown of palest shell pink, but had forgone the cumbersome panier. About to scold her for her unladylike manner of dress, Mildred suddenly felt a pang. She could no longer reprimand her as if she were a child. There was nothing childlike in Merrit as dark eyes met green and her hand strayed down the pirate's smooth cheek in a purposeful caress.

"Here be yer breakfast," Mildred growled, her voice strangely tight. "Don't be trampling me in yer rush for the table."

They rose as one, eyes still filled with each other until the smell of hot bread tempted his glance to slide away from hers. The two women watched in amazement as Colley consumed a massive quantity of food with urgent gusto. Finally becoming aware of their amused stares, he glanced up, flushing vividly, almost boyishly, before he continued in a more leisurely manner. As Mildred stepped behind him to refill his cup, she glanced down at his brown back, and a curious expression appeared on her face.

"Where did ye get yer many stripes, pirate?"

"Under the tender tutelage of the Royal Navy," he replied drily.

"For what cause?"

His eyes rose to meet hers, and he replied seriously, "For abusing innocent young girls and their watchdog nannies."

Merrit choked upon her coffee, and Mildred looked down at him, half-believing for an instant, then she lightly cuffed the back of his dark head.

"Ah, go on with ye now," she grumbled, turning away before he could see her good-humored smile.

With the last bite of bread, the captain stood saying, "I'd best be getting on deck before my fine shipmates take notice of my absence and start thinking I be down here ravishing you both in truth or that I've thrown myself over the side to save them the pleasure of hanging me." He gave Merrit a long troubled glance that she could not understand, then said flippantly, "Thank you kind ladies for taking in a poor

172

villainous excuse for a man such as myself." With that, he left them, Merrit looking after him, puzzled over his strange look.

When she went above sometime later in search of him, she spied him on the forecastle deck looking out over the rolling sea, standing straight and proud and every inch the Spanish Angel in spite of his chains. She felt a painful twinge at seeing him bound like some dangerous beast, yet he turned with a welcoming smile upon hearing her light step, his warm greeting quickening the beat of her heart. They stood side by side, looking out over the choppy slate-colored waters in the hazy sunlight that managed to filter through the ominous layers of rapidly moving clouds which presented the threat of more rain. With careful subtlety, he shifted behind her, his hands casually clasping her tiny waist and when she offered no protest, rising leisurely up the graceful curve of her back to gently knead her shoulders. Reflexively, she relaxed against his solid frame as his cheek pushed into her chestnut hair, his warm breath grazing her ear. The Angel's mocking eyes slid to the crewman who had thought to take his place, boasting of possession, tauntingly arrogant. Still challenging the sailor with his eyes, he began to nibble Merrit's ear, chilling her with a shiver of excitement.

"Colley," she whispered in a low sultry voice. "Stop teasing the crew with your bold fondling of me."

She heard him draw a breath of surprise, and his reply held a note of pique. "If you knew my purpose, why did you not stop me sooner?"

"I was enjoying it too much," she answered with candor, then pushed his hands away. "Now behave, before your friends decide to throw all to the wind and lynch you from the yardarm."

" 'Twas my intent. I've no wish to swing before an audience."

Missing the harshness in his tone, she teased, "What? The

theatrical Spanish Angel foregoing the chance to please a crowd?" When her jest brought no response, she twisted to look up at him and found his expression strangely distant. "Colley?"

"Oh, 'tis not the hanging. Dead is dead. I've no fear of that," he said quietly, his cool indifference in regard to his own life making her shiver. "When I was a lad, I saw them lead Captain Kidd from Newgate. 'Twas an elaborate affair marching him down to the water, the functionary with the silver oar over his shoulder to flaunt the authority of the admiralty, and everyone following. Kidd was so drunk he nearly fell off the gallows with a nosegay of flowers in his hands. When they'd hanged him, they didn't bury him face down in the sea. Oh, no. They embalmed him in tar and encased him in an iron cage, to hang from the gibbet as an example to all who passed." He closed his eyes and shuddered with the remembered horror of a twelve-year-old boy who had had to look on the grisly sight every day. "I swore they'd never do that to me, hang me out to dry in front of all those smug faces." He turned to Merrit abruptly, his eyes oddly bright. "You saved me from that, and whatever ill feeling may lie between us, I thank you for it, for the chance to be on the sea, to go boldly to hell at the hands of men who hate but respect me."

She looked at him blankly for a moment, then said, "Colley, what are you saying? You're not being taken back to Charlestown."

"They'll not get me that far. If they won't oblige me with the noose, I'll go over the side, but I won't go back. If I had known that was what awaited me, I would not have let them pull me out to begin with."

Still confused, she blurted out, "You speak as though you were not going to be released."

His smile mocked her with a gentle reproof. "Merrit, I am not such a fool as to think there was ever a plan to free me."

"But I gave you my word, my promise," she protested in

174

an effort to ease his unfounded suspicions, fears that to her mind had no basis.

"A promise meant to be broken, my lady," he said softly, without rancor. His finger lightly traced the line of her jaw. "I do not blame you, Merri. God knows, I've given you every reason to hate me. Do not fear. I will see my part of the bargain through. I give that much to you for the taste of your kiss, no matter how meaningless."

Merrit's brows lowered over hurt and angry eyes. "You think I lied to you, that I tricked you. How could you believe that? I gave you my word that you'd be freed. Do you think I would share your kiss and lie with you in the night if I were planning your death?"

He gave her no answer, simply looked at her through calm eyes. When her hand flashed back, he squeezed his eyes shut waiting for the stinging slap that didn't come. When he slitted them open to peer at her cautiously, he found her pale with distress, her dark eyes large and damp. Could it be that she was speaking the truth, that she truly didn't know? Could he believe that without being made the fool again? How could he trust her? Despite that sweet beautiful face so empty of guile, he could still hear the echo of her voice, low and vicious, damning him as a blackguard and thief.

"You are wrong, Colley," she told him, stricken now. "I will prove you wrong."

"Go to Captain Neville and ask him what he plans for the Spanish Angel. Ask him why he needs so many men to guard one pirate in chains. Ask him, Merri, then believe what you will."

She backed away from him. Her eyes, clouded with doubt and denial, searched his for some small sign of belief or trust. They found none. Without a sound, she whirled and fled the deck.

"Good day, Captain Neville," Merrit called pleasantly as the hard-eyed man opened the door to his spacious cabin. "I came to ask if I could join you for your noontime meal. It would be so nice to enjoy some gentlemanly companionship." She smiled up at him prettily, flickering her lashes as the door opened wider.

After a painfully long repast during which she flattered and cajoled the obnoxious captain until he was in a relaxed, congenial mood, she turned wide eyes on him and asked, "Captain Neville, what are your plans for that arrogant pirate once his purpose has been served?"

"What is your interest in his fate, Lady Ellison?" he asked shrewdly, having heard the whispers that she had been the Angel's lover and that she had taken him to her on the past night.

Merrit saw his suspicion and dropped her eyes, forcing a modest blush. "This is difficult, Captain, for a gently born lady such as myself. The pirate has compromised me in the past, and I find his presence embarrassing and offensive. Once I have my dowry, I'd be grateful to be rid of him and all the speculation he has caused."

Neville smiled without sympathy. What a cold, scheming woman, he thought admiringly, to toy with a man as ruthless as the Angel for the purpose of recovering her fortune.

"Rest easy, my lady. The Spanish Angel will cease to be an embarrassment to you."

"How do you mean?" she insisted, feigning a touch of frightened hopefulness while she decided Captain Neville was a loathsome man.

"We'll let Angel get us safe passage into Nassau's harbor, then you will get your dowry and I will hang the bloody renegade in plain view for all his peers to see."

Under the table, Merrit's nails dug into her palms, but she kept her features steady as the captain chuckled coldly.

"So you see, my lady, everything will be taken care of to our mutual satisfaction."

It was a tense, white-faced Merrit who waited for the

pirate to be brought to her. She had spoken not a word to Mildred, who was growing increasingly alarmed by her pet's distant, glazed eyes. Those dark orbs grew large and glistening when they met the questioning look of the man who stood in the door.

"Mildred, I wish to speak to the captain alone," she said, her voice barely a whisper.

Mildred started to protest, but seeing the urgent looks the pair exchanged, she shrugged, saying gruffly, "Ten minutes, no more."

"Well, my lady?" Nicholas asked softly when they were alone.

Her eyes met his, such depthless agony and despair in them he knew instantly that she was innocent of any suspicion. He crossed the room in quick strides to take her in his arms, awkwardly maneuvering his chained hands about her shaking form to hold her close.

"Oh, Colley, he plans to kill you," she sobbed into his shoulder, clinging to him as if the strength of her embrace could protect him. "He means to hang you in the harbor for all to see."

He frowned at that, his mind racing quickly as he caressed her thick mass of hair. Neville wasn't even going to attempt to return him to jail. What was the man up to? As Merrit shifted in his arms to look up at him, her loveliness broke his train of thought.

"I knew nothing of this. You must believe me. I meant what I said. I thought you would be released," she declared. "Colley, please, please believe that."

His eyes softened as he smiled. "I do, Merri. It seems we are both pawns."

Her fair brow furrowed. "What do you mean?"

"Come sit," he urged softly. Still holding Merrit in the loose circle of his chained embrace, he steered her to the bed they had shared and sat her down upon it, then faced her, putting enough distance between them to keep his emotions

177

from clouding all else. "Captain Neville is one step above a pirate. He uses this ship for his own trading ventures, charging excessive shipping rates and arming the vessel with naval guns and personnel to discourage attack. What he does is illegal, but here in the Colonies, he's far enough away to make his own laws. He plans to have me on deck when we enter the harbor, knowing that will keep anyone from firing on this ship even if they don't recognize it. Once we're in the harbor, I don't know what his plan is, but, Merri, he'll not let me leave the ship. He would not risk my escape. He hates me enough to forgo all to see me dead. If I cannot go ashore, there will be no return of your dowry."

She was silent for a time, absorbing this information with grim, unquestioning belief. He could not tell what thoughts lay behind her serious expression.

"So it was a lie," she said finally. "I cannot believe it of Governor Spotswood. He gave me his assurances."

"Perhaps Neville is acting on his own, without the governor's knowledge."

"I've been such a fool," she said bitterly, then she looked at him in bewilderment. "But you knew. Why did you come with me?"

"I but suspected. I felt there was a chance I was wrong until I saw Neville. I knew he would never set me free regardless of his orders. I once shamed him in front of his crew. He would not forgive me that. But I wanted to escape that damned swinging cage and be on the sea again. With you," he added in a lower timbre.

"But you thought I was using you, tricking you, making a promise that would not be fulfilled."

"It did not matter to me, Merri," he replied quietly, his green eyes dusky with emotion. "I cared not if you hated me enough to wish me dead, that you would use me without care. I wanted to spend time with you, whatever time you gave me. That was all that mattered."

He paused, but she said nothing, simply stared at him

blankly, her eyes large, lips softly parted. He continued uncertainly, for he found the words difficult, though they must be said. "I lied to you as well, Merri. I lied when I said the money was all that was important to me. I hurt you with those lies and I meant to. I am sorry for that, and I accept the price of my cruel words." He hesitated as Merrit's hand came up to lightly touch the deep gashes in his cheek. Her eyes shimmered, but she was silent. "I deserve to hang. I have done much in my life to lead to that end and I have no regrets. I always expected it to be so, I just didn't know when. It seems the time is now and I will meet my fate willingly. But you do not deserve this cruel turn of events. I am sorry my death will cheat you of the future you should have."

He waited for some response from her, uncomfortable under her unwavering stare that told him nothing. Then, surprisingly, she began to laugh, a high wild sound that broke into renewed weeping.

"My God, Colley, what are those pearls compared to your life?" she cried shrilly.

"You value my life too highly, my lady," he interceded quietly.

"And you value it not at all. How can you accept this end with a shrug, saying 'tis what I deserve? Have you no reason to cling to life, to fight for it? You give up too easily, pirate."

He touched her cheek with his forefinger, smiling mildly. "You don't understand, Merri. 'Tis life I fear, not death. Why prolong it?"

"I will give you a reason."

Her lips were hot and insistent on his, bruising, demanding a response, salty with her tears. Then she scattered kisses over his cheeks and closed eyes, seeking to stir passion in him, but he remained motionless, his breath coming light and quick.

"Colley, love me," she pleaded, through that shower of urgent kisses. "Take me now. Use me as you will. But, please, don't let them take your life."

His large hands came up to catch her glossy head and hold her still so he could look upon her face, his green eyes warm and resigned. "Merri, be still," he soothed. "Do not grieve for me."

His words brought more tears, and Merrit's voice shook with desperate anger when she spoke. "Damn you Colley. Do not tell me not to grieve because I care more for you than you care for yourself. You selfish—"

Her recriminations were halted by his lips, which pressed gently on her own, shaking her with the depth of his unspoken longing, giving her all the tenderness he had in his soul.

Mildred stood at the door, moved by the sight of them. Had their embrace been a passionate one, she would have stepped in quickly to separate them, but it was so poignant, so filled with pure emotion, that she was arrested by their strangely beautiful pairing. She must have made some sound, for Colley's eyes flickered and slanted over at her, registering neither surprise nor guilty dismay. With a heavy sigh, his lips left Merrit's, but she quickly looped her arms about his neck to keep him from pulling away.

"Colley, no," she cried. "Don't go. Let me keep you safe."

"Hush, Merri. Hush, now," he murmured huskily as he avoided her persistent kisses and tried to twist out of her embrace. "Let me go."

"No." Her protest was a wail, and her arms tightened about him convulsively.

"Release me," he demanded.

The sharp crack of his words had the desired effect. Her arms dropped like leaden weights, and he quickly stepped out of her reach. Then, with a gentle sadness, he whispered, "Forgive me, Merri."

Merrit gave a soft cry and raced after him, but he put Mildred between them, letting the stolid woman intercept her. "Colley, please," she moaned despairingly as she tried to

180

wrench free.

Touching her chestnut hair with an infinitely gentle hand, he said to Mildred, "Keep her safe, especially once I am gone. There could be danger then."

Mildred nodded without understanding, puzzled by Merrit's grief and his sudden show of quiet emotion. "Be assured of it, pirate."

He gave a bittersweet smile, hand reluctantly dropping and left them.

"Colley," Merrit cried desperately. Then she sagged against Mildred as if her heart was being cruelly torn from her.

"Here now, miss," Mildred crooned. "What is all this? What has the captain done to ye now?"

"They're going to hang him. They're going to steal his life after promising me that he would be safe. I cannot lose him now. Oh, Mildred, I love him so."

Though shaken by this tremulous admission, Mildred was wise enough to know that these were not the words of a fanciful girl. Merrit's voice had been rich with passionate feeling.

"Still yer tears, pet and tell me who is trying to harm our pirate."

The "our" brought Merrit's head up in grateful relief. She hugged the stocky woman fiercely before finding a chair to collapse in while she briefly explained what she had discovered.

"Bloody cur," Mildred muttered under her breath.

"Mildred, Colley's just going to wait for them to put the rope around his neck. He won't try to stop it."

The older woman patted her shoulder in sympathy. "Child, there is little he can do. He is one man and chained at that. What chance would he have against an armed crew eager to see the color of his blood? If he makes a move, they'll cut him to ribbons and he knows it. He be a brave man, pirate or no. Have a little of his courage, lamb. It be

181

over tomorrow."

"Tomorrow," Merrit echoed faintly. Tomorrow they would snatch that vital, passionate soul from her, robbing her of the man who had shown her love, taught her desire. "No," she said with sudden conviction. "I will not accept it. They'll not deliver him up to the devil without a fight." She got up to pace restlessly under Mildred's pitying glance.

"Lamb, there is nothing ye can do. He is going to hang."

"A fast ship and twenty more years," Merrit whispered to herself, standing motionless. Her eyes flashed up, bright and feverish. "They'll not have him."

"Merrit—" Mildred began uneasily.

The young woman gripped her arms desperately, looking into her solid, familiar features pleadingly. "Mildred, will you help me? Will you help me free him?"

Mildred hesitated. The man was a pirate, a criminal who had ensnared the love of the one most precious to her. He held in his unworthy hands Merrit's fragile feelings which he could crush without a care. If she aided him to escape, she was opening a Pandora's box of hurt, lust, desire, and pain—things she had struggled to protect this beautiful child from. Frowning, Mildred looked long into the up-turned face, so young, so inexperienced in the hidden dangers that threatened. And in the joys of life.

"Aye, I will help ye, child."

# Chapter Fifteen

The Spanish Angel brooded in the quiet twilight, staring at the horizon on which the silhouette of New Providence would soon be revealed. His outward posture gave no clue to the turmoil within as he searched for an alternative.

Merrit Ellison complicated the situation. But for her, his choices would be varied, and he would not be willing bait for Neville's trap, a shield behind which the ship would gain entry into the harbor. He could call some warning to those on shore and then take his chances in the water while the pirate guns blew the invading ship from the harbor. But Merrit was aboard. While he would sacrifice himself without pause, he would not willingly see her killed. However, if he allowed Neville's plan to proceed smoothly and gave himself over to the noose, Merrit might yet be jeopardized, for Neville would not hesitate to silence her if she protested his violation of her agreement with the governor.

Furthermore, the idea of hanging was beginning to trouble him for the first time. Facing the gallows in Charlestown had had no such effect on him, but now there was Merrit. He resented leaving her, being cheated of time with her. She had been right. It was harder to face her than to face the rope. The sorrow in her eyes tormented him. Did she truly mind his death that much, or was the loss of her dowry beneath it all? It was easier for him to credit the material over the emotional for greed was familiar to him.

Why had Merrit Ellison come to make his simple, pleasing existence, self-centered though it was, so confused? Thoughts and decisions which before had come to him quickly, naturally, he now labored over for fear of their consequences. Consequences. A strange concept for a man who had never considered anyone save himself. He couldn't control the doubts, the fears, the uneasiness—in a way, he was more naïve than the girl whose innocence he had taken. She could readily accept responsibility and could consider the feelings of others while he struggled with these burdens as though they were wild beasts about to devour him whole.

He was the Spanish Angel, a bold pirate. He had been safe behind that uncomplicated image for years until a mere girl had managed to wedge herself between him and that which he wished people to see, demanding things of him that he had no idea how to provide.

"Oh, Merri, what am I to do?" he whispered into the night, feeling as agitated as the threatening clouds that boiled overhead. "Tell me what to do?"

With a moody frown, he looked away from the turbulent waters to indifferently watch the approach of a youthful sailor. His expression grew puzzled, then alarmed, as the slender lad came closer, his large eyes lifting to rock him back with a stunned, "Good God."

"I've come to see my promise met, Captain."

In numbed surprise, he stood speechless while Merrit unlocked his manacles. For a moment he could only stare at her waifish form on which a seaman's jacket hung loosely over a linen shirt and full white canvas trousers. Beneath that outfit were extremely small bare feet. Above it she had bound a bright colored kerchief about her luxurious hair, and had placed a round crowned cap over that, tilting it down to shadow her delicate features. To the casual eye, she would appear a lad with a most provocative walk.

"Are you reluctant to seek your freedom then?" she asked

with a lift of her brow, amused by his almost comical disbelief.

Abruptly, he was the Spanish Angel once more, eyes bright and alert as they swept the nearly empty deck to see if her passing had been noted. Most of the crew was below eating the evening meal and the scattered few who remained above showed no interest in them.

"What have you in mind, my lady?" he asked crisply, willing to hear her plan if it would mean escape from his infernal dilemma.

"How far are we from New Providence's shore?" she asked in a low, excited voice, caught up in their conspiratorial endeavor.

"Too close for me to rest easy this night. We'll be in port by morning light."

"A fast ship and twenty more years, Captain." When he looked puzzled, she continued without explanation. "Could you manage a small boat that far?"

His reply was immediate, for he was beginning to understand her hastily conceived plan. "Aye; my lady."

They both started in alarm at the sound of footsteps, but Mildred appeared beside them, a smile upon her sturdy face. "No one will think to look for ye for a time, pirate. Some casks of rum mysteriously appeared for the crew's sampling. I don't think the welfare of a scurvy villain like yerself will be on their minds."

The captain grinned in genuine appreciation, though he was surprised and a bit nonplused that the dour woman was willing to aid in his escape.

"Quit yer lolly gagging, pirate. Yer not ashore yet," Mildred grumbled, flushing slightly under his warm gaze.

The three unlikely cohorts slipped quickly to where the small landing craft were lashed, but their plan was checked by the burly sailor leaning on the rail and puffing contently on a fragrant pipe. He appeared to have no immediate desire to move.

185

Merrit cursed softly in frustration. She chewed her lip for a moment, then asked, "Mildred, can you distract him while we set out in the boat?"

"We?" her companions echoed.

"Of course," she replied, a bit impatiently. "I am going with him."

Mildred recovered her surprise first, and scolded her. "There was no talk of yer accompanying yon pirate, miss."

"If I told you that, you would have refused to help me," Merrit concluded rightly. She caught Mildred's arm and hugged it pleadingly.

"None of yer sweet trickery, ye sly chit. Yer daft if ye be thinking I'd let ye be off on yer own with that man."

She found an unexpected ally in Nicholas who said firmly, "You'll not go, my lady. 'Tis too dangerous on the seas in a small boat especially with a storm brewing. I'll not risk your life in this."

"You both do not seem to understand. I am not asking permission. I am going. I have an interest at stake here. I will see my side of the bargain through, then you will comply, Captain. I will have my dowry back, and begging your pardon, sir, but I do not trust you to deliver it lest you have some prompting."

He frowned at her manipulativeness, and his eyes became dark with uncertainty. The dangers were real and would prove fatal to them if they were discovered before reaching the shore. Looking long on her lovely face, his reply came instinctively. "No, Merri. I'll not risk it."

She turned on him furiously, eyes snapping with determined anger. "Either I go or no one goes."

"It will have to be no one then."

Mildred let out her breath in a rush of relief. The pirate had surprised her by showing himself to be a man of honor, and she silently thanked him for it.

Merrit would not accept his valiant offer, however. She glared up at him, speaking in cool derision. "Is this the bold,

186

selfish Angel, this man who cowers at the thought of taking a risk, who will let Neville plunder his friends, possibly murder them while he waits like a whipped cur to be happily hanged? I think not. The Angel would seize any chance to save himself, to save his pretty neck from stretching so he could seek his revenge on the man who threw him to the sea. Who are you, pirate or coward, or are they one and the same?"

Colley could not control the deep flush that flamed at her spiteful words. Even though he knew the reason for her goading, her barbs had sunk deep. Was he the Spanish Angel who would use any means to save himself, or was he the man he wanted to be for Merrit, the man she called up from his reluctant soul, a man deserving of her, one who would see to her first above all things? If he ran at the risk of her life, he would be betraying all the strange wonderful feelings she had awakened in him, but if he stayed, he would be dead, an admirable martyr.

"We go," he said in a low, even voice, looking away from Merrit's pleased smile and Mildred's accusing stare. He couldn't change what he was; it was too late for that. He was a pirate.

"Well, I'll have no part in this," Mildred stated rebelliously. Damn the rogue, she thought. Let him hang. She had been foolish to think him worth saving.

Merrit looked up at her through cold, hard eyes that tore through the older woman's heart. In a voice meant only for the two of them, she said softly, "I love him, Mildred. If he dies because you would not help him, I will never, ever, forgive you and your name will be a curse to me."

In anguish, Mildred looked from Merrit's hostile eyes to the scarred profile of the pirate captain. The girl she had raised and nurtured had chosen between them, taking a vain, unscrupulous buccaneer above the woman who was devoted to her, and nothing could lessen the painful ache of that knowledge. "Aye, I will help ye," she murmured heavily, then endured Merrit's embrace with sad resignation.

"Do not fret, Mildred. The captain will see me safely back to you, won't you, Colley? Your word as a pirate?"

He looked from her bright eyes to those dulled with hurt and despair. "My word as a man," he replied softly.

"Not much comfort there," Mildred said gruffly, pushing Merrit away with a steady hand. "Ye keep her from harm, pirate or there'll be no hole on this earth that ye can drop into to hide from me."

He gave her a crooked smile. "I will return her just as she is."

Mildred thought that no great comfort since he had already taken Merrit, and she feared that the girl would choose to remain under his charming spell. Her charge did not fool her. She was not going after the pearls, she was going after the man.

Trying to lessen Mildred's somberness, Nicholas said easily, "I will save her from harm if it cost me my life."

"Like now?" the astute woman put to him acidly, and upon seeing him wince slightly, she added, "Aye, pirate, but who'll save her from you?"

Nonetheless, while the captain and Merrit crouched out of sight, Mildred strolled up to the brawny sailor at the rail.

"How does she plan to distract him?" the pirate whispered with surprising naïveté.

"The same way I got these clothes and the key to your chains," Merrit laughed, feeling a tingling warmth at his surly speculation. Soon it would be just the two of them alone of the sea, she and her captain. In her childlike anticipation, she did not envision the dangers, just the opportunities. She felt the now-familiar ache of desire rise to tease her and send a shiver of expectant longing through her. Eager to submit to his passion and to indulge her own, she was certain that nothing could stop them.

Though sturdy of build, Mildred was still a handsome woman, which was evident from the appreciative glance the sailor gave her as she approached him, exaggerating the roll of her hips and smiling congenially.

"Good eventide, mister. Be ye minding a little company?"

The burly crewman straightened immediately. "Who'd be refusing company so fair?"

"Oh, go on with ye now. Sure 'tis a hot and steamy night," she murmured, unfastening the first few buttons of her gown to bare her neck and the beginning swell of her ample bosom while she casually fanned herself. She paused for a moment to let the sailor feast on that sight, then made her eyes boldly inviting. "If ye be of a mind, I've some cool drink below to ease the heat," she said simply.

The sailor scanned the nearly empty deck, then he grinned and offered Mildred his arm. Her troubled glance touched on the crates that hid Merrit as she guided the eager crewman away from them, a teasing laugh escaping her lips.

"So that is how you got the key," Nicholas muttered sourly, irritation leaving him open to Merrit's ribbing.

"I learned all from her," she assured him with a grin. "Even how to tamper with a man's drink to woo him quickly into deep slumber. Shouldn't we be going, Captain?"

Quickly and silently they lowered the boat into the black water, and with the pirate at the oars, the craft skimmed over the surface into the concealing darkness until the brigantine was but a vague outline in the night. Seeing it fade behind them, Merrit gave a small sound of triumph. Clambering across the boat to where the captain sat, she threw her arms about his neck in a joyful hug.

"We've done it. We've fooled them."

He stiffened at the quick press of her firm breasts against his chest, angered by his sudden desire to bear her to the bottom of the boat and have her right then, and by his own unsettled guilt at having placed her in such danger. His words came out curtly as he shrugged out of her arms, never missing a beat with the oars.

"Stop acting the child, Merrit. We've too far to go to think

189

ourselves clever. Get back to your seat and stay there until I tell you otherwise. I cannot be bothered with you now."

She recoiled as if he had struck her, scurrying quickly back to her plank seat to huddle into herself, pouting. She was unable to understand why he was being so mean to her when she had saved his life. This was not how she had planned their escape. She'd expected him to be overwhelmed and eager to express his gratitude. Instead, he had snapped at her, berated her, and had thereby crushed her dream of an isolated, floating paradise. With a frown, she glared at him in the dimness, unable to see his expression as he plied the oars with a smooth strong rhythm.

Merrit woke abruptly, the sudden pitch of the boat knocking her head against the side of it. Uncertain as to how long she had been dozing, she straightened slowly, holding onto the seat as they were tossed from side to side. Above the rush of the wind, she could hear the harsh rasp of Nicholas's labored breathing as he struggled to fight the increasingly agitated waves. In dismay, she realized that her feet were wet, that water was sloshing about in the bottom of the boat.

"Colley, where are we?" she shouted over the roar of the sea.

"Less than a mile out," was his brief, winded reply.

"Are we going to make it?" Merrit clung to the boat as it tipped and plunged, more cold water flowing in.

"I don't know. I'm going to try my best."

"What can I do?"

"Take off my boots and bail. We cannot take on much more water."

She had to crawl along the bottom to steady herself against the violent pitching, feeling about in the darkness for his feet. For a moment, when she reached him, she pillowed her head on his knees, overcome by her sudden awareness that the rough unyielding sea sought to devour their tiny craft; then she quickly tugged off his boots. Kneeling, she began to frantically work against the continual surge of water, baling until her shoulders screamed in protest, but she was unable to make any headway for the sea rushed in at every dip of the boat. Her breath coming in low sobs, she doubled her efforts until firm hands gripped her shoulders, stilling her futile motions.

"Enough, Merri. 'Twill do no good. We're going down," he told her steadily, his voice betraying none of his panic as the cold, dark water rose about his calves. "Follow the direction of the current to shore. You should be able to make it."

"But you . . ." she cried in alarm.

"Merri, I cannot tread water on a smooth pond for more than a minute," he told her, brutally truthful.

She tried desperately to see his face through the darkness and the spray, but could not; the feel of his hands was her only link to him. "I did not risk so much to let you drown so near the shore," she protested fervently. Quickly, she pulled the bandana from her head, the wind catching her hair in a wild tangle. She knotted one end of the cloth about her wrist and the other about his.

"No, Merri," he said uneasily when he realized her intent, but she seized his hand in both of hers, bringing his whitened knuckles to her lips.

"Just hold on and keep your head up. I'm a strong swimmer. I'll get us both to shore," she assured him, the calm authority in her voice momentarily easing his doubts. Then they were in the sea, spilled roughly from the floundering boat into the chill water. The control and confidence that had served Colley while he was in the boat fled when choppy waves closed over his head as he floundered helplessly in water so cold it was deathlike. From somewhere close, he heard Merrit's voice raised above the raging wail of the storm.

"Don't fight. Just hang on. Colley, hold on."

The scarf became taut on his wrist, and abruptly her fingers caught his flailing hand. He clung to them, hoping

191

to steady his badly panicked nerves. She maneuvered closer, bumping him as the current surged and his free hand latched onto her forearm.

"Are you all right?" she called, feeling the tension in his grip. "Just stay calm. Fight me and we both go under. All right?"

"Tell me what to do," he sputtered as the water churned about him.

She smiled at the trust in his tone. "Just relax and let me carry you with me. Let me do the work. All you have to do is stay calm."

"All right."

Putting her arm across his chest, she rolled him onto his back, feeling him stiffen as water rushed over his head, then briefly struggle against his vulnerable position. Before she could utter assurances, he became still which she knew took great effort because she could feel the frantic tempo of his heart. Turning onto her side, she began to swim steadily against the hampering waves. In what seemed only a matter of minutes, she began to feel the effects of pulling his weight through the rough water. She was tiring rapidly. Her smooth strokes became short and broken, and in her weakening state, just keeping them afloat was becoming increasingly difficult to manage. The darkness yielded no sign of land, yet she struggled on in the vast emptiness that offered no encouragement.

"Colley, stay still," she gasped in alarm as he struggled from her restraining grasp to bob in the raging sea. "No, Colley, hold on. We can make it. Please. Hold on to me."

"You can make it."

His words were barely audible above the howl of the wind, but his meaning was very clear. She could make it alone.

"Not without you. It's not much farther. Please don't let go," she panted, fighting exhaustion and trying to get close enough to grasp him and put an end to his brave but foolish idea. Treading the turbulent waves, she began to draw in the bandana that bound them, but suddenly it gave. She stared in horror at the loose end on her wrist, dreading what it meant. The tie between them broken.

"Colley," she screamed into the fury of the storm. "Colley, where are you?" There was no answer, only the wail of the wind. "No. Colley, no."

The angry sea revealed nothing to her searching gaze, and after several minutes of anguished circling, Merrit had to admit that there was no chance she would find him. Sobbing, she began the surprisingly short swim to the beach.

# Chapter Sixteen

The blackness of the stormy night slowly yielded to the vivid pastels of morning as Merrit lay unmoving on the white sand, too numbed by grief and fatigue to think of what to do next. Her tears came in a steady stream provoked by a pain too great to consider in her weakened state. Mourning would come later when she could fully comprehend her loss. At that moment she knew only that she had tried to save him and had failed. Colley had drowned. That he was dead and she would never see him again hadn't yet seeped into her jumbled thoughts. The ache she felt just kept getting bigger and bigger, as awareness, like a wave that increased in size and volume, rushed over her. And when that wave of loss broke, it would leave her devastated.

Slowly, for no conscious reason, Merrit got to her feet, stumbling in a dizzy circle until her shaky balance returned. Only then did she take some faint interest in her surroundings. She glanced down the long stretch of empty beach backed by green uninhabited hills, and her wandering gaze caught a distant shape some several hundred yards down the waterline. Their boat. She started toward it, staggering but making the boat her destination because it linked her to what she had lost. When she reached it, she would rest and decide what to do.

As she came nearer to it, she drew up sharply, her eyes riveted to the hand that was extended beyond the other side of the boat, its fingers spread wide, motionless. A strange wailing sound broke from her lips, low and heavy with pain, but her tears were dammed up and the hard knot at the back of her throat made her breathing dry and difficult. A fitful trembling seized her as she stood rooted to the sand, half-wanting to run forward and half-horrified to think of what she would find. How could the fates be so cruel as to bring him to her, flaunting what she could never have and didn't want to live without? As she stared in stricken indecision, the fingertips slowly began to make trails in the wet sand as they were drawn up beneath the palm of the hand.

Her paralysis broken, Merrit sprinted down the beach to fall beside the prone figure lying face down. Carefully, almost fearfully, she turned him onto his back, aware of the scalding wetness on her cheeks. As she lifted him, limp and dangling, to a sitting position, he gave a choking gasp before he began to cough and spew out the massive quantity of salt water he had swallowed. Finally, his eyelids fluttered faintly, then opened to look at her in dazed surprise.

"Merri?" His hoarse croak brought on more racking coughs.

"Rest easy. I am here and we're safe," she soothed quietly, cradling his dark head in the crook of her arm, her tears further dampening his face as his hand rose unsteadily to touch her cheek questioningly.

"We must be alive for I cannot imagine us both residing in the same place in the hereafter," he muttered raspily, bringing a wan smile to her face.

She caught his hand and kissed it fervidly. "How could you do that to me?" she cried, relief letting her voice her anger. "You let go. I thought you'd drown."

"In truth, so did I."

"How did you get to shore?" she asked, her voice softening as she let one hand stray through his short black hair, which

195

slid damp and slick between her fingers.

"The boat," he mumbled, his concentration beginning to falter. "Held onto the boat and let the tide carry me in." His eyes drifted shut then flickered as if he were struggling to stay awake, but the pull of his weariness was too great to be denied. His last awareness was of her light kiss atop his head.

The cool of early morning gave way to the searing heat of midday as Merrit, unmindful of the discomfort, sat, propped against the boat, Nicholas's head on her lap. She was content just to look upon him as he slept, to be soothed by the soft sound of his breathing. Occasionally, her eyes rose to the sea, cautiously looking for the ship, but the water — flat, calm and empty — was the same pure depthless green as his eyes. Theirs was an undisturbed sanctuary, on which only the gentle wash of the waves and distant music of the tropical birds intruded. In spite of their difficult arrival, Merrit was where she wanted to be, alone with the man she had long coveted, and no amount of hardship could dampen her quiet joy. If only he could be made to care for her . . . Perhaps that would happen now that he didn't have to act the cocky Spanish Angel and she did not have to think about being the fiancée of Winston Whitelaw. He must care for her a little bit. If not, would he have untied the kerchief at the risk of drowning to save her life? But now nothing mattered except that he was alive and in her arms.

You will be mine, bold captain, she promised him silently. I'll let nothing stand in the way of that. You will be mine.

As if he had heard her thoughts, Nicholas stirred in her arms, waking gradually as if to protest his surrender to the heavy luxury of sleep. His green eyes opened briefly and he smiled up at her before he slipped again into the last languorous vestiges of slumber. Finally, he stretched to test the aches that plagued his overtaxed muscles, then sat up to a groggy swirl of darkness that slowly ebbed away.

"I feel awful," he murmured thickly, clasping his head with both hands to ease its throbbing.

"But alive and free," Merrit encouraged.

"Aye, that too." He looked out over the vast, deceivingly serene sea and then scanned the shoreline. "We must have been pushed miles off course. Can you make the walk, my lady?"

"Anything to get a bath and a change of clothes," she vowed without hesitation.

He looked to her then, taking in her disheveled appearance, the hair hanging loose about her shoulders in a wild tangle dulled by brine, the cheeks and nose pink from the sun. Her mannish garb was torn and stiff with crusted salt, but to him, no woman had ever looked more beautiful.

"We had better start out then if we plan to reach Nassau by nightfall," he told her somewhat gruffly. Frowning, he stumbled to his feet, annoyed by the weakness of his body and his heart. But Merrit extended a hand to him and her tentative touch was his undoing. He pulled her up against his hard chest, his mouth coming down crushingly on the lips she eagerly offered, tasting salt and the honeyed nectar of her kiss. The sudden press of her body filled him with a hot, raging desire, for his need of her had not been met since that last night aboard his ship. He groaned as if in agony and held her away from him, but the sight of her eyes, dark and hazy with passion, made his torment all the worse.

"Oh, Merri, sweet Mother of God, what are you doing to me?"

"Much the same as you to me, I suspect," she whispered huskily, his words kindling her hope; his touch, her desperate need.

"We will pursue this at a later more convenient time, my lady."

"Yes" was her emphatic response.

His eyes suddenly intense and bright, he caught her shoulders to draw her close once more. "Thank you for my

197

life, my lady. It is yours."

Before she could ponder his meaning, he was kissing her again, this time slowly and thoroughly until she trembled with breathless wonder. Her thoughts became scrambled due to her heady confusion, and she was intoxicated by what his words might signify. Hers. Hers.

Still in a euphoric daze, she walked down the beach at his side, close but not touching, matching his quick stride until awareness began to return and, with it, the agony of the scorching sand on her bare feet. He seemed not to mind it, for his own were toughened so she said nothing, not wishing to appear weak and complaining, but it wasn't long before her gingerly taken steps drew his notice and provoked a puzzled frown. Seeing her silent distress, he steered her into the surf, the salt stinging, then bringing her instant relief. The rest of the way they walked in the cool, wet sand at the water's edge, the miles disappearing behind his steady pace, somewhat slowed for her shorter strides.

As they made a turn about a spit which jutted out against the breaking surf, both nearly at the end of their strength, weary, hot and thirsty, Nassau appeared like a heaven-sent Shangri-la. Merrit's relief was tempered as she watched the man at her side subtly change, the slump of fatigue leaving his posture, the set of his jaw squaring, his chin tilting up, and his walk becoming a nonchalant swagger. His unconscious metamorphosis into the Spanish Angel became more apparent with each step. The distance between them widened both physically and emotionally as his brisk pace left her lagging behind. The fact that he didn't seem to notice brought a furrow to her sunburned brow, and a determination not to be ignored seized Merrit.

"Colley, I cannot keep up with you," she called, careful to keep any hint of petulance from her tone. He stopped and turned to her, the expressions of two different people skirting his features, the Angel's annoyance and Colley's apology, as if he wasn't sure of how to deal with her now that they had reached his element. Speaking slowly and without rancor, she said quietly. "You can go on if you like. I will meet you at Pru's."

He hesitated, looking from her to the promise that lay ahead, sorely tempted to continue to the seamy tent town on his own and to enjoy a welcome that would not include her. However, with a sigh, he held out his hand and waited for her to come and take it. Then he smiled, curled her fingers into the crook of his elbow, and escorted her into town on his arm.

His arrival occasioned a great deal of surprise, some of its more hearty celebrants certain they saw his ghost. Colley accepted the attention with smug pleasure, expecting due court to be paid, but despite his arrogant attitude, his hand was warm and caressing over hers as if part of him remained apart from the strutting spectacle he'd become.

When they entered the tavern, there was a loud clatter as a tray filled with drinks fell from Pru's numb fingers while she stared at Colley in slack-jawed amazement. Then, with a howling cry, she raced across the room to cast herself at his chest and shower his smiling face with kisses.

"Oh Lord, Angel, 'tis good to see ye," she sobbed. "We'd heard ye was dead."

"As you can see, that was a bit premature," he told her in amusement. Then he began to pry her loose, uncomfortably aware of the fingers that pinched his arm. "Pru, you are fair to strangling me. Leave off."

Suddenly seeing the reason for his cool treatment, Prudence stepped back from him, flushing awkwardly. The Lady Merrit's presence at his side could only mean that she was there by his choice, a choice Pru would have to respect.

"Hello, my lady. I was not expecting to see you again," she began a bit stiffly, but then gave Merrit a reluctant grin. If the girl made him happy, who was to hold a grudge? "But ye be welcome too. Ye both look fair to dropping. Come and sit while I fetch something to fill your stomachs and quench yer thirsts."

Merrit sank gratefully onto a chair, and when a man standing nearby handed her a mug of ale, without pausing for a breath, she let the entire drink glide down, wet and golden, under Nicholas's raised brow. "Another of these would do nicely," she called after Prudence.

When the tavern keeper returned, she carried a heavily laden tray and a huge black animal was at her feet.

"Hey, Bub," the pirate coaxed, which prompted the cat to leap onto his lap. "What brings you here?"

"Rufe left him with me. Durant was going to put him over the side, but Rufe convinced him different," Pru explained with a smile. "The creature and I but tolerate each other. The vile-tempered beast laid open three of my gentlemen friends. Ye be welcome to him."

Colley laughed and rubbed his cheek against the glossy black coat, his eyes narrowing thoughtfully. "Another thing to hold Durant accountable for."

As they ate, an audience gathered for word of the captain's unprecedented return quickly spread. Between mouthfuls, Colley told all those who came the tale of his capture and escape, overlooking Durant's part and embellishing Merrit's until she blushed furiously. But no one would heed her protests, so finally she gave up and good-humoredly endured his skillful fiction. As another round of ale was passed about and lamps were lit and shutters closed to the darkening sky, Prudence leaned over Merrit's shoulder for a whispered word.

"I've had a bath drawn for ye if ye'd care to soak a bit before retiring."

"More than anything," Merrit sighed in anticipation, and rising quietly, she followed Prudence upstairs. She was sure her presence wouldn't be missed amid all the bold talk and ample drink, but green eyes sought her out instantly to watch her ascend the stairs, half in admiration and half in speculation. He would give her time to herself before going

200

up to pursue what had started on the beach. Smiling, he drained his ale.

Merrit let the sailor's garb fall where it would, shedding it gratefully on her way to the metal tub. Seeing her trim figure and opalescent skin, Prudence could well understand the Angel's interest in the girl. She was a perfect flower, dainty, fragile, still in its unspoiled blush. And knowing himself to be the only one to have sampled her heady fragrance, could he fail to be stirred?

Merrit gave a low sound of enjoyment as she sank into the clear water, feeling it rinse away the caking of brine and perspiration. She looked up questioningly when Prudence approached with a small bottle of perfumed oil.

"Ye may use some of this scent if ye like. Angel always professed to favor it," the woman offered almost shyly.

Merrit held back the retort prompted by the scathing bite of jealousy, and answered with a smile, "You are very kind."

Smiling in return, Pru tipped out several drops of the amber liquid, causing a dusky smell to rise from the heated water. "I'd best be getting below. If ye need anything, just sing out."

"You have been a good friend to me, Pru."

Merrit's comment seemed to please the woman greatly and she flushed, bobbing her pale head before withdrawing.

Merrit leaned back and closed her eyes, breathing in the heady scent, sultry and mysterious, of the smoky oil, and thought of the night ahead, a night filled with promise. She could hardly wait for her pirate captain to come to her, at last to claim what she longed to give him. It may have been illicit to desire him so, sinful to want to consummate her love for him out of wedlock, and even shameless of her to forget her contracted betrothal; but none of these considerations could sway her from this mad, headlong tumble of emotion that could have only one goal, one end—to be in the arms of the man who had brought her the precious knowledge she sought to expand. The more she learned, the

201

more she wanted, her need of him becoming a powerful addiction for which there seemed no cure.

Wrapping her clean, wet hair in a heavy towel, she stepped from the tub to dry herself and squeeze the moisture from her thick chestnut locks, then looked with disdain at her filthy clothes, wrinkling her nose. Nothing could induce her to wear them again. Naked, she slid between the sheets, finding them coarse but deliciously cool, and with a smile of satisfaction and anticipation, she left the candle burning on the night stand to light the way for her lover.

Leaving the familiar ruckus of the taproom, Nicholas climbed the stairs carefully, giddy from all the drinks his friends had pushed on him and from the thought of the woman who awaited him. He missed a step and clutched the rail to keep from tumbling down the stairs, though he had weathered that fall many times before without breaking any bones. Drawing a deep breath to clear his head, he cursed the liquor he had consumed and the time that had slipped by. But it wouldn't have been right to leave a celebration in his honor. Besides, dawn was hours away and much could happen before then. Thinking of ways to spend those hours gave him the impetus to continue up the treacherous steps and purposefully stumble to the room where Merrit waited. Drawing himself up so he might appear presentable, he opened the door but did not enter.

In the soft aura of candleglow, her beauty was chaste and ethereal, light glimmering like muted fire in the thick hair spread over her pillow, her expression youthful and touchingly innocent in sleep. Her bare shoulders gleamed like creamy satin against the linen sheets, and as Colley leaned on the doorframe, absorbed in the sight of her fragile perfection, the lustful heat in his emerald eyes softened to a warm simmer. Just looking at her made him ache with the need to possess and protect her. However, at the moment, the only protection she needed was from him. He looked down at himself in chagrin, seeing grimy bare feet, knee breeches stiff with brine and stained with drink, his body layered with dirt and sweat. He reeked of alcohol and the lack of a bath. This was not how he had envisioned himself joining her beneath the clean sheets. He sighed and gave a reluctant smile.

"Not this night, my lady, but soon," he murmured. "Very soon."

He closed the door softly and, turning, came face to face with Pru's questioning gaze.

"Have you a place for me to spend the night?" he asked wearily.

"Haven't I always? And your lady?"

"She's already retired."

Prudence looked at him in amazement, envying Merrit more and more. Consideration from Angel? For a woman? "Come Angel, ye need to clean up and rest a bit. The lady will be all right."

He nodded and followed Pru to her room, where a bath had been drawn in hopeful anticipation. Without a thought, he let his clothing drop and stepped into the tub, the heated water drawing him in like an embrace. Eyes closed, he leaned back unprotesting as a cloth traveled over him, willing to accept that familiar service from Prudence as he had in the past. His thoughts drifted, never once lingering on the woman who knelt beside the tub, blue eyes soft and wistful.

Prudence smiled as she plied a razor down his handsome face. She couldn't in all honesty say the tragic scoring of his cheek had lessened his compelling good looks. No man could come close to matching his dark beauty. But if she were to assess him critically, she would have to call him coldly aloof, good-humored and charming when it suited his purpose, indifferent when he'd had his way. His friendship for Rufe, his affection for his surly cat, and his fondness for herself had been the only exceptions to that indifference; and she had clung to that privilege jealously. But now he had returned with the Lady Merrit on his arm, dashing all her hopes. Ah well, she reasoned, at least for this night she had him.

For an instant, he returned her warm kiss, eyes still closed but made no move to embrace her. Then he turned his face away, looking up at the blond woman, a half-smile on his face.

"Pru, you are a fine, generous woman, and you could have your pick of any man here," he began softly.

"But not ye," she concluded for him.

"Not me."

"I know that, Angel. Ye'll be breaking many a hopeful heart," she teased, well knowing that hers was one of them.

"They will soon find someone else to catch their attention," he responded, lightly dismissing her. Unmoved by affection for any woman but Merrit, he could feel no sympathy.

"But ye were the best of 'em, Angel, and 'twill be a great loss," she murmured, her hand lingering on his swarthy cheek as he smiled, flattered but doubtful. "You can sleep here. I'm sure I can find another welcoming bed."

"I don't deserve your kindness, Pru," he said with a sudden sincerity that flustered her.

"Nonsense."

204

# Chapter Seventeen

"Good morning, my lady. I trust you slept well."

"And you, Captain." Merrit's response was decidedly cool, and she sat up in bed, holding the sheet to her like an icy barrier. She observed him narrowly as he stood in her door, freshly shaven and dressed in clean clothing. Only red-rimmed eyes betrayed him.

"Would you care to come down to breakfast with me?" he continued, still unaffected by her remote attitude.

"I am hardly dressed to move among you pirates," she snapped, annoyed by his lingering perusal.

"I can find no fault in your appearance," he said with leering interest. "However, I will see if Pru has something that would suit you better than these breeches."

As he began to turn away, her sharp voice stilled him. "Do not disturb your paramour with my troubles, Captain."

He looked back at her, one heavy brow raised. "My lady is in a particularly ill humor this morning. Have you a cause?"

Face flushing, Merrit came up onto her knees, her dark eyes snapping with the anger and hurt that had been building in her since she'd wakened to find herself alone with a guttered candle on the night table. "Dare you ask that, you roving tomcat? You left me to cool my heels while you prowled the back alleyways on the hunt. Play the carousing Angel to the hilt if you like, but don't think you can stroll in and win me with a pretty smile. In what wench's bed did you wallow away the night whilst I foolishly awaited you?"

As she raged, his smile widened in amusement, stirred by the sight of her enraged splendor. With a low chuckle, he mused, "You have all the charm of a wronged wife, my lady. I was not aware you cared so much."

"Oh," she growled furiously, one hand clutching the sheet while the other flashed out to send the pewter candlestick flying at his head. He side-stepped nimbly, then quickly crossed the room while she searched for some other suitable weapon. "Get away from me, you roaming jackal. I want no part of your secondhand lusts," she spat out.

Dodging the fiercely wielded pillow, he fell across her, catching her wrists to prevent curled fingers from tearing at his face and pinning her under the weight of his body. He found Merrit's angry struggle an interesting challenge, and always ready for a contest, he chuckled. His response brought a savage wail from her. Then she redoubled her efforts to escape him, ironically trying to flee that which she most desired.

"Don't you laugh at my expense, you conceited rogue. Let me go. I've no wish to endure your brutish affection. Get off me."

He grinned down at her, his handsome face taunting, his hard frame pressing her to the bed while her tempting breasts rose and fell in rapid pants beneath his chest. "Conceited and brutish am I?" he mused. "You didn't seem to be of that mind earlier when you melted in my arms in your eagerness for me."

"Arrogant beast," she hissed. "I've changed my mind. Go find some simple wench to paw and stop rutting after me like a well-encouraged stag."

"So you were not encouraging me, eh, my pristine lady, chasing me about in a hunger to taste my kisses? I must have been mistaken to have thought you eager when you hugged me about the neck and moaned my name. 'Colley, love me. Take me now.' "

She shrieked at his accurate quote, writhing beneath him in a full-blown temper as he laughed at her attempts to topple him.

"Yield to me, Merri," he crooned, silkily. "Yield to me and let me love you. Let me become everything to you."

"Never. Never. Never."

"Never, love? Convince me that you mean it." He caught her mouth beneath his, moving his lips in slow, sensuous persuasion until he felt the fight ebb from her. When he released her hands, he was sent reeling as her fist caught the side of his head and the sheet was pulled over him. Before he could untangle himself, she was about to pull open the door, but his mocking words stopped her.

"How far do you think you'll get running stark naked through a nest of pirates?"

She paused, breathing heavily, to give that thought. He was right, of course, and that made matters all the worse. She had no way to escape the room and his odious, betraying presence. She met the green eyes boldly, seething as his stare burnt down her in casual appraisal, lingering over her full, rounded breasts, her trim waist, and the inviting curve of her hips.

"Come here, Merrit," he called low with a hint of impatience. "If I have to come get you, I may resort to brutishness."

"I'll risk that, for I'll not come to you like your other panting whores. Don't think me grateful for your vastly overrated favors, pirate."

He frowned slightly, then was off the bed with a speed that surprised her. Squirming and kicking, Merrit was tossed onto her back on the rumpled sheets.

"What happened to your precious code that calls for a lady's willingness?" she hurled at him scathingly as he held her down, the smug grin back on his face.

207

"That is at sea, my lady. On land we ravish whom we will without conscience."

He lay beside her still fully clothed, one of her arms trapped beneath him and the other held above her head. His leg rode heavily across hers to still her kicking. "You are more willing than you will admit. You cannot deny me, Merri. Yield to me lest I be forced to use sterner measures."

She shook her head vehemently, wondering with some alarm what measures he spoke of. Did he mean to hurt her? His means sometimes proved painful but in a most exquisite way.

While Merrit twisted in helpless rage, Colley's free hand moved slowly to cup her heaving breasts, his fingers leisurely teasing the nipple to excited tautness.

"Have you no shame," she cried in horror. " 'Tis broad daylight."

He smiled at her shocked sensibility but would not cease his bold caress. "My lady, the time of day is no measure of the flow of passions, and mine are now at full flood. Besides, I want to look upon you when you yield me all."

"I will never yield," she vowed firmly, her dark eyes sparking fire.

"So you say," he murmured, unconcerned by her fervency. His large hand moved lower, feeling the taut skin of her stomach flutter beneath his knowing touch. She gasped in protest as his touch grew more intimate, her struggle more with her own seditious emotions than with him as her body trembled and arched to meet his questing hand.

"Don't Colley. Stop," she insisted faintly, her breath coming hard and fast as warming ripples of persistent pleasure washed over her with growing intensity. "I hate you. I hate you," she moaned, struggling to stave off the swelling sensations he was teasing to life, using her own weak body to defeat her stronger will.

"I know you do, Merri," he whispered huskily. "But don't you love me just a little, too?"

"No. No," she decried, squeezing her eyes shut. "Not a little. With all my heart. I love you. Oh, Colley."

As he watched in awe her slight form was shaken by great rolling shudders, her fingers curling about his tightly as her breath caught in a tremulous sob. Then abruptly, she lay still and motionless as if drained of all strength.

"Do you yield to me now, my lady?" he asked, his voice rough with emotion.

"Aye, I yield," she whispered without stirring. "You do not play fair."

"I cheat. I am a pirate, remember?"

She accepted his kiss without reservation, giving him pause, however, when he felt a shiver of weeping run through her. In tender concern, he asked, "Did I hurt you, Merri? I did not mean to."

She would not open her eyes, but large tears welled at the corners and clung to her thick lashes. "You did. Why did you have to seek out another last night?"

He was too stunned to speak for a moment, then he wiped away the dampness from her hot cheeks. "Is that what you think?"

She nodded miserably.

"Merri, look at me," he ordered, seeing her open dark, shimmering eyes with reluctance. "Do you think I would go elsewhere when I have heaven on earth beneath my hand? Are you too naïve to see how you have tortured me with your nearness until I feared I would burst from wanting you? I've lain with no other since you last shared my bed. I seek no comforting arms but yours, no soft lips, no other sweet release. If you've any compassion for me, grant me the trust of your heart. I may be all of the many things you have named me, but I do not lie to you now. You are all I want, all I need. Merri, believe me. And love me. Please."

Merrit's hand stole behind his head bringing his lips down to hers. Her kiss pulsed with unabashed longing, her tongue flickering across his until its tantalizing dance brought a low moan from him. She rose up, shifting slightly, still savoring his warm mouth as her fingers unhurriedly parted his shirtfront to allow moist, nibbling kisses to trail down his tanned well-muscled chest.

" 'Tis daylight, my lady," he protested in a hoarse voice.

"Tell that to the tide, Captain," she said lazily, passionately. Then she kissed him softly and let her fingertips run over his features, pausing at the long curving slice she had scored in his cheek.

He observed her distressed expression, rebelling against the pity he saw there. Turning his face to one side to cover the ruin she had left in the wake of her anger, he said bitterly. "There are some who are not struck with repugnance at the sight of me."

Merrit took his chin and turned his head so he regarded her squarely. "Yours is a face of unholy perfection. I told you once you were the most handsome man I had ever seen. My opinion has not changed because your perfection is now flawed. In truth, I prefer this face to that of the pretty Angel. There was a falseness to its smooth beauty. I was thinking of how my rashness must have hurt you. That is why I was frowning."

After a second of careful study, his mouth turned up and his emerald eyes became heavy lidded. "You are either the best of women or an accomplished liar. I prefer the former."

"Now be quiet and love me."

His eyes darkened with passion as his mouth came down on hers, hard and hot, making her dizzy with the spiraling rush of feeling it provoked. His first thrust drove deeply, filling her with an aching completeness that made her moan his name in welcome.

Merrit held to him as her senses careened. It was nothing like she remembered. She was engulfed by the intense power and heat of him as he took control of her soul, drawing her into the whirlwind that spun faster and faster in ever-tightening circles punctuated by the rasp of his breath and the thundering of his heart. No memory could hold the magnitude of what he brought her, could tap into that sudden burst of desire that canceled all conscious thought until awareness filtered back like the return of feeling to a limb gone numb. Slowly, she sensed the heaviness of his motionless body, the damp sleekness of his hot skin, and the gradual slowing of his frantic pulse. When he stirred with languid reluctance, her hand came up to still his dark head against her shoulder, whispering, "Stay with me awhile." He relaxed in quick compliance, cheek nestling into the hollow of her throat and his breath becoming deep and steady.

They lay like that for countless minutes, desire sated but not their need for one another. Merrit didn't know if he slept or merely rested until he spoke, his voice gruff and unsteady.

"Don't leave me, Merri. To wake without you near me is to wake each day to darkness. You are my light. Please don't send me back to that blackness."

"I never wanted to leave you, Colley," she told him softly.

He raised his head to look at her, eyes brilliant as freshly cut gems. "You said you love me. Did you mean that?"

"I did" was the faint reply. Hesitantly, she touched his face. "And you, my lord pirate, do you care for me?"

The turmoil of doubt and cool reluctance flickered in his suddenly withdrawn expression, making her regret the impulsive question, but she wanted to know the answer, wanted it to be the same as she had given. She no longer was willing to settle for evasion.

"Merri, I feel great things for you, but if one of those be love, I cannot say. Love has never touched my life, so I cannot rush to lay claim to that which I do not know. I can say that I want to be with you, that I want you. That is more than I have said to any other. Can you be satisfied with that and not ask for more?"

Green eyes searched hers deeply, hopefully, as she nodded. For now, she said to herself, she could. She desired him too greatly to hold out for perfection. A slice of him would be enough until she could claim the whole.

Smiling, he rolled onto his back, drawing her close to his side and kissing her tousled head. His nose wrinkled at the musky scent that lingered upon her. It had suited Prudence's lusty free spirit, but it seemed too heavy and distracting on his delicate beauty.

"What is it, Colley?"

"I just miss the fresh, natural smell of you, 'tis all."

"Oh." That he had noticed pleased her, and she snuggled against his chest, listening to the rhythmic pulse of his heart, slow and lazy now that his passion had run its course. Her fingers drew circling patterns on his hard chest as her thoughts began to focus on what he had asked her. He wanted her to stay here with him, to leave all else and become his alone. While that idea thrilled her, her acceptance was held in check by a nagging question. She put it to him tentatively, feeling him tense.

"Colley, what of my dowry?"

"Merri, remember that you love me," he began slowly.

"You lied to me?" she demanded, trying to pull away, but his arms tightened to trap her at his side.

"Merri, do not be angry. It was the only way I could get you here," he hurriedly explained as she struggled in his embrace.

Her response was harsh and biting. "You mean it was the only way you could trick me into saving your miserable neck." Hurt surged back to freeze the warmth she'd felt, and she lay rigid in denial.

"That's true as well," he admitted quietly. "Is it your wish now that I had been hanged?"

As angry as she was, her reply was immediate. "No."

"Then why all this protest?"

"Because you lied to me, Colley. You used me. Why weren't you honest?"

"Merri, consider my situation. I was a condemned man. You offered me freedom at a price I could not meet. My

212

memory of our last meeting is hardly encouraging. I lied to you to become free, to convince you to love me, to be with me. Was I so wrong to do that? You know what I am, who I am. Would you have preferred me to go honorably to the gibbet or to chance your caring enough for me by the time you knew the truth that you would not wish it so. Do you love me enough to accept the man I am? I could tell you I will change, but that would not be true. Merri?"

Her voice was low and steady. "I love you enough to forgive you anything but more lies. Trust is a part of love as is truth. All parts must be there. I will forgive you because you did not know that, but I won't again. Don't lie to me, Colley. Trust me enough to be truthful. I will not stay with you if I am constantly in doubt."

"You will stay?"

He spoke with such enthusiasm she wondered if he had heard anything else she'd said. "Aye, Captain. I will stay. Without my dowry, I have nothing to return to. You have trapped me well."

He grinned and, unaffected by her chagrin, crushed the breath from her with a quick hug. "I'll give you everything, all the riches and finery you could desire. I'll—"

She put a finger to his lips, looking long into his eyes. "I want only you. I want you to learn to trust me and to love me." She saw the flicker in the deep recesses of his eyes, that cold denial, but it was far removed and she was not disturbed by it. After all, he couldn't be expected to learn overnight to open to that which he had shied from all his life. With an impish smile, she added, "And I'll teach you to swim."

He frowned at that but held her close, reveling in her nearness. Little else mattered as long as she stayed.

There was a small tap at the door, and then Prudence peered in, her face brightening with embarrassment and envy at finding them entwined on the bed. "Beg pardon," she stammered. "I did not know ye was here, Angel. I didn't

213

know ye'd left my room." She saw the jolt of shock run through the girl in his arms and quickly explained, "Before ye tear out his heart, I be telling you he stayed there quite alone. I found company elsewhere." She smiled as the girl relaxed and the captain let out a shaky breath of thanksgiving. "I thought I'd bring you some clothes more befitting a lady."

"Thank you, Pru," Merrit answered, uncomfortable at being observed in such a position with her lover.

But Colley didn't seem to mind. His hand skimmed down her bare flesh to familiarly caress her rounded flank. "Pru, would you fix us some breakfast? We'll be down in a bit."

"Surely, Angel," she replied. How much he had changed. Prudence had never known him to linger in bed with a woman once his needs had been met unless it was to sleep. She had never wakened to find him still beside her, yet he seemed reluctant to leave his lady. Ah, love, she thought with a sigh, closing the door behind her.

As they lingered over breakfast, his hand possessively resting over hers on the tabletop, there was a loud commotion. Looking up they saw a group of newly arrived pirates calling for drink. These men regarded the swarthy captain in stunned surprise, one of them erasing the contented look from his face with these words: "Angel, we just passed your ship. She was following us in. Should be docked in less than an hour."

The Spanish Angel straightened, his glittering eyes assuming a cutting edge. "I look forward to welcoming her return."

214

# Chapter Eighteen

Rufe entered the tavern heavy with fatigue and loss. They had returned with a nearly empty hold after a disastrous encounter with a brigantine that had nearly sunk them. The men were low spirited and restless because of Durant's incompetence, and he felt perhaps it was time to look for another ship. The *Merry Widow* wasn't the same anymore. Neither was this tavern, so full and yet so empty. He scowled down at the hissing cat that glared up at him. If the disagreeable creature hadn't belonged to his friend, he would have been tempted to put a swift boot to it. He watched glumly as the huge beast ambled off to run high-backed figure eights around a pair of jackboots. Catching his breath he slowly raised his eyes. The hateful cat coddled up to only one person.

A grin split Rufe's dark face as he crossed the room in great strides to lift a surprised man from his chair with a rib-shattering grip.

"Colley, by God. Be you real or angel in truth come back to haunt us?" he roared joyfully.

"Released me, Rufe, before you speed my exit from this earth," Colley wheezed. Then freed of the crushing embrace, he settled back in his chair.

Rufe rumpled his dark hair with a huge hand. "How is it that you're alive? We all thought you dead."

"I'm sure," Colley replied acidly, then his features softened as he turned to the figure Rufe had overlooked in his amazement. "My lady saved me."

Rufe's gaze shifted though he knew before he saw her who he would find. "Lady Merrit, I be grateful to you."

Her eyes met his in a challenge over the man who sat between them as if acknowledging their position as rivals. Only Nicholas was unaware of the tension. He reached out to each, lover and friend, with an easy smile of contentment.

"Sit down, Rufe. 'Tis not too early to celebrate with an ale. 'Tis not every day I return from the grave," he said happily.

"I brought the ship around when you couldn't be found, but there was no sight of you," Rufe was saying. "We were sure you had drowned."

"You went back?" Colley asked softly, moved and unable to fathom such devotion in a crew.

"We had to go on. You know that. We couldn't tarry long in those waters."

Colley nodded in dismissal, placing no blame where none was due. Slowly the green eyes rose, chilled and hard. "Where is your captain?"

"I am looking at him. That puppy who took your place should be arriving soon if he dares show his face. I came ahead of the rest. The stench on board was not to my liking."

Durant entered the tavern cautiously. The crew's disposition toward him was growing ugly, and he thought it would be diplomatic to avoid any confrontations. Searching the crowded tables, his eyes passed over the dark quartermaster, then returned in sudden alarm. Rufe was in amiable conversation with another man whose back was to him, the quartermaster's huge pawlike hand resting companionably on his cohort's shoulder. While Rufe was respected or feared by all, he called only one man friend.

"Damn him to the hell he's supposed to be in," Durant hissed. "I won't be so careless again." He drew the primed

216

pistol from his belt and coldly leveled it at the spot between the shoulder blades of his rival.

The rest followed rapidly. A scream of warning preceded the flash of powder as Nicholas was pushed from his chair. Rufe saw instantly to his dazed, though unhurt, captain while Merrit knelt beside Prudence. The buxom blonde had seen Durant's intent a brief second before he'd fired, and had taken the bullet in place of the man she so loved.

"Oh, Pru," Merritt cried, her voice low and broken. As the tavern keeper's blue eyes opened to gaze at her vaguely, blood seeped from beneath the hand she held to the courageous woman's generous heart.

Nicholas clambered to his feet, and spotted his assailant fleeing the building. With a snarl of rage, he jerked Rufe's cutlass free and ran in quick pursuit. Durant led him on a twisting chase through the teeming Nassau streets and up to the crumbling limestone fort, a relic of a one-time English settlement. There was a whisper of warning and Colley ducked as Durant's blade sliced through the air to spark against the stone.

"Come on, Angel. You seem to have as many lives as your bloody cat, but the count has run out," Durant prophesied, meeting the swing of his captain's sword with a quick parry.

" 'Tis you who has run out of time and soon life," the dark pirate promised. He bore down on the larger man with vengeful force, driving Durant steadily back until he was pressed against the buttress with nowhere to retreat. Then, with a hard, chopping arc, Colley knocked the weapon from Durant's hand, pressing the tip of his own blade to the blond man's throat.

"I appear to have beaten you again as I always have. But I tire of the game. This is our last contest, Durant. I'm going to kill you."

Durant sneered at him fearlessly. The Angel was well known for his mercy and his reluctance to draw blood unless he had no option. He preferred to charm his way out of a fight rather than kill. He hadn't the ruthlessness to slay an unarmed man. "You won't kill me, Angel. I know you too well," the arrogant pirate taunted, then the smile drained from his face as he looked into steady green eyes.

"You do not know me. My name is not Angel," Colley said softly. There was no hint of the good-natured Spanish Angel in the face that had twisted into an ugly snarl. And there was no trace of mercy.

Realizing his mistake, Durant reached for his dagger, fingers brushing its hilt as his life was swiftly taken.

As Merrit held the fatally wounded Prudence in her arms, the woman struggled to speak. "Do not leave him, Merrit. He loves ye so very much."

"Who? Colley?" she asked in bewilderment.

"That night before ye went away, he was only with me because in his drunkenness he mistook me for ye. He said he loved ye and begged ye not to leave him. I should have told ye then, but I was too blindly jealous. Forgive me, Merrit, for keeping you apart." She coughed harshly, the large red stain spreading out from beneath the hand on her breast.

"There is nothing to forgive, dear Pru. There was more between us than just that." Tears trickled down Merrit's cheeks.

"Angel, he be a good man if ye give him a chance. Promise ye will."

"I promise, Pru," Merrit choked out through her painfully constricted throat.

"I gladly paid the full price for him, but 'tis you he loves." Pru's eyes grew hazy and began to drift closed, her stained hand sliding over to clutch Merrit's tightly. "Love him."

"I do."

Smiling Pru closed her eyes for the final time, and with a sigh, she surrendered the life she'd sacrificed for a man who did not love her. Rufe rose from where he knelt beside her, deeply troubled by the words that had passed between the two women. If Prudence had spoken the truth and he didn't doubt that she had, his captain and the lady were closer than ever and the threat she posed was great. He had never heard his friend speak of love except with the utmost disdain, saying it was but a weak form of lust. Had the fragile lady touched off some feeling in the cold recesses of Colley's heart or was he but playing some calculating game of vengeance? It was hard to know what moved the man.

Rufe frowned as Merrit rose, Colley's name soft and low on her lips as she rushed to throw her arms about him and then hold him tightly as his dark head rested on her shoulder.

"Oh, Colley, are you all right?" she asked breathlessly, as he passed the crimson-edged sword to Rufe.

"I've killed Durant," he said heavily. "And Pru?"

When Merrit shook her head slowly, he drew a long breath and let it out in a shaky rush.

"Why?" he muttered softly. "Why would she do that?"

"She loved you, Colley."

He shook his head, confused. "But I gave her no reason."

"Love needs no reason to be. It just is," Merrit explained gently, but she felt she was explaining light to a blind man.

"If that be love, I've no use for it. 'Tis foolish and unprofitable and causes too much harm."

He pulled out of her comforting embrace, his eyes angry and aloof, and before she could speak, he turned and strode out into the dirty street. She made a move to follow, but Rufe caught her wrist.

"Leave him," he told her simply. When she glared up at him, his hand dropped quickly. "Lady Merrit, give me credit for knowing him better than you. Let him mourn in his own way."

Merrit nodded in grudging agreement. There was much she didn't understand about the brooding side of her lover. Perhaps Rufe did know best. She would give Colley time to be alone, and later when they were together, they could share their grief.

But later was a long time coming, after Prudence had been taken out to be buried and Merrit had fixed herself a lonely dinner. She had closed the tavern out of respect for its owner, sending the teary-eyed serving girls home with an extra wage. By nightfall, her spirits had lowered, and she was certain Colley had forgotten her now that he was reunited with his crew. Was this her lot, to wait for him to tire of wiling away his time with his men, to be his last, most unimportant stop? She sighed heavily seeing his absence as a desertion and wondering what she had done to warrant it or if he needed any reason to treat her so indifferently.

She looked up hopefully at the sound of approaching footsteps, then frowned in puzzlement at seeing the flame-haired woman she remembered from her last stay on New Providence. The woman looked hesitant and a bit sheepish.

"My name be Molly, missy, and if ye be remembering me, I be sure it be without any kind feelings. I came to bring ye this. I didn't feel right about having it after ye saved Angel and were such a friend to Pru and all."

Merrit looked in surprise at the gold chain and cameo, sudden tears pricking her eyes. "Thank you," she managed with difficulty.

Molly continued to linger, then asked brusquely, "Why be ye up here all alone when all are down at the beach celebrating Angel's return?"

"I was not asked to join them," Merrit said softly in a pained voice. The idea that Colley was celebrating while she waited brought a flush of anger to her cheeks. And to think she had felt stirrings of pity and sympathy for him, thinking that he was mourning Prudence's death.

"Ah, Angel's a selfish thoughtless cur sometimes," Molly summed up. Seeing the girl's distress fade to fury, she said, "Come on, missy. I be asking ye. Let's go fix up yer face and we'll go set yon pirates on their ears."

The sound of wild, pagan music rose up from the beach, the blare of horns and the pounding of drums. And a huge bonfire sent flames high into the calm night sky, casting bloody shadows over the tall masts of the ships in the harbor. With the indulating wails of the drunken revelers, this could have been a Dantesque inferno. The uneven light wavered on the motley group that had gathered about the tapped casks and the hogshead to indulge themself in every available debauchery. Drink and whores were greedily passed among them. Merrit hesitated outside the reach of the flickering light. Though she recognized the crew of the *Merry Widow*, there were many who were strangers to her and that made her hold back uncertainly until Molly propelled her forward into the midst of the wild throng. As she accepted a large mug of ale, her eyes searched for one face and when she found it, her dark eyes flared with a searing heat. Beside her, the redhead chuckled and shook her arm. Her captain stood with several other bandsmen, beating a steady rhythm on one of their drums. He wore the scarlet coat with no shirt beneath it, firelight gleaming on his bronze face and chest. About his neck was the slender arm of a pretty tow-haired whore who tipped a bottle of brandy for him to drink from as he played, laughing with him over some shared joke. Merrit felt as though she were that joke.

"Don't go on so, missy. The ladies they like Angel for his pretty face and easy manner, but he won't give 'em a tumble. We know whose bed he'll be falling into tonight," Molly chortled ribaldly, but she won no smile from the girl with the flashing dark eyes.

"Perhaps the pretty Angel will find himself unwelcome," Merrit vowed fiercely. "I'll not be so casually treated by him or any man."

Molly laughed again. "Ye be pure feist, missy. Who would have thought that on first seeing ye so proper and all.

If ye be mad at Angel, don't throw him from yer bed and cheat yerself of pleasure. It was long, long ago, but I still remember his touch and I wouldn't forgo it out of spite."

Merrit flushed hotly. Another one of his lovers. Was there no woman on New Providence who hadn't been with him? They all seemed to know and understand him so well, while she felt at such a loss.

"Merrit if ye be wanting to settle yer anger with Angel, give him a taste of what he be handing ye and watch him come round to your call."

Merrit pursed her lips. "What do you mean?" she asked.

"Look at yerself. He be not the only one fair of face and able to stir a lusty thought. There be many here who'd pant after ye given a touch of encouragement."

"But I don't want any other man," she protested, earning Molly's amusement.

"Ye don't let 'em catch you. Just tease 'em a bit."

"How?" Merrit asked determinedly, glaring at her man with a tight smile. *Play with my affections will you, Captain Fool.*

"Trust me, missy. I be an expert at it." She reached out to adjust the shoulders of the gown Merrit wore, and pulled the pins from her hair. "A few steps of the dance I learned from a Madagascar slave on the Gold Coast should turn the trick."

"But I know of no dance to music like this."

"Follow me, missy, and let yerself go."

The steps were easy to copy with the steady beat of the music. It was like no dance she had ever seen in the stuffy affairs in England, its movements more like those she'd learned beneath the pirate captain, slow, undulating, and with a clear inviting message. There was a step to the side, led into with the dip of a shoulder, a roll of the hip, and a shimmy of the bosom. Molly made it look so fluid and suggestive. Then she grinned and motioned for Merrit to join her and match her languid, rippling movements. As the two women danced the pirates began to cease their merrymaking to gather around them in a rough circle and to whistle and clap in appreciation. The tempo of the music sped up, growing louder and more insistent. There was no melody, just a throbbing beat, primal and instinctive, provoking the senses with its irresistible pulse. Like the beat of a heart or the surge of the ocean, it was steady, constant, unrestrained. It was the sound of the restless pirate soul and all moved as one to it.

Concentrating on his playing more than the caressing fingers teasing along the back of his neck, Nicholas glanced up at the circle of men to see what had caught their interest. Seeing Molly, he smiled, having seen her tempting dance before; then his smile faded, his jaw unhinging in surprise as he took in the petite figure mimicking her movements with a natural grace and a supple agility. Merrit? She looked as wild and untamed as any of the pirate women, clad as she was in a daring gown of emerald and black, its bodice tightly laced over her swelling bosom and its sleeves pulled down to display smooth, white shoulders. Her hair fell about creamy shoulders in a glossy mass, gleaming with fiery highlights, and her beauty was clear and sultry, without youthful traces of innocence. Dark eyes smoldered in her sun-warmed face, red lips were parted in soft allure. This was the hot-blooded temptress whose passions he had awakened, but the idea of her displaying such sensuality before all was oddly disturbing, as if he felt her dance should be for his private pleasure. Watching the hypnotic sway of her skirts, he wondered if she had any knowledge of the effect she was having on the men, but one look at her face told him she did. This was no child who knew no better but a woman well aware of her own seductive power, a power that held him spellbound and strangely awed. The gyrations of her body filled him with heated remembrance of those swelling curves pressed close in offering, an offering she seemed to be extending to all who witnessed the dance.

To Merrit, the sounds, the dance, the bold appreciation,

the lack of inhibition were exhilarating. She kicked off her shoes to feel the sand, hot and fine, between her toes, raising her arms to the dark heavens and spinning about like some goddess of the night come to dance before her moon lover. But there was only one lover she would have, and neither the moon, nor the stars could take his place. Bare feet shuffling to the rhythm of the drums, she moved to Nicholas he stood, reaching out to uncoil the whore's arm and push her away with a dark glare of warning. She swayed before him, an exotic, enticing Salome, encouraging with beckoning gestures, then whirling away when he reached for her, the taunting innuendo of her open seduction leaving him hot yet cold and confused.

The tempo of the music shifted to the light, tantalizing beat of the islands, and Molly found herself a partner among the many willing participants. Merrit ignored the first man who approached her and reached out a hand to Rufe. He regarded her skeptically for a moment as if he would refuse; then her tiny hand was engulfed by his and he spun her about easily to the quick rhythm. They made such a contrast—he so huge, she so petite—while they danced together in temporary compatibility. Rufe was moved to spare her his wide smile of admiration so he spun her away from him, and when she was reeled back, she met with a solid, familiar form. Frowning, she tried to pull away, but he would not release her, gliding her easily through the rapid whirling steps, holding her close against his chest, his green eyes bright and possessing.

"Did you miss me?" he asked above the music, his smile smug and confident.

"Did I appear to be pining away, Captain?" was her crisp reply.

"I was about to come for you," he began, reading the anger in her flashing eyes and hoping to placate her a quickly as possible. She had his passion running too high for him to waste time arguing.



224

"I will not grow old waiting for you. You are not the only man here who would be happy to serve as my escort," she challenged in the face of his unconcerned arrogance.

"But I am the only one who ever will," he concluded, her barbed attitude unwillingly pricking his vanity. "Everyone here knows you to be mine."

"Everyone apparently but you yourself. If you wish to lay claim to me, I suggest you cease fondling every available skirt. You give too little to ask so much. Think on that, pirate." She shoved him hard, sending him stumbling back as she seized the hand of another partner who seemed not in the least intimidated by the fact that she was the Spanish Angel's property. In fact, none of the dancers who claimed her hand seemed concerned about that. Even the members of the Angel's crew flagrantly courted her favor, lavishing praise on her and carrying on harmless flirtations while their captain stewed in a situation of his own making.

"Take a draught of this and stop panting after the lady for a moment," Rufe suggested. "She's only teasing you to make you act the fool. And she is succeeding admirably."

Miserable, Nicholas took a long drink from the proffered bottle then choked, his eyes watering as the harsh black rum tore through him. It was a moment before he could speak. "If I could only be certain 'twas just a game," he muttered, watching the laughing Merrit step from man to man. Like some free-spirited nymph, she smiled up at each face no matter how scraggly or unattractive.

"Find another wench to pass the time with until she tires of her tricks."

Colley frowned in protest, his eyes still following her, in them a mixture of jealousy and desire. What power did she have over him that she could twist his emotions inside out with a glance, a word, or the lack of either? He shook his head with a sigh. "I've no understanding of women. When they're not abed they're a damned confusing lot." He took another long swallow, blinking rapidly against the fierce burn.

"Don't try to. There's no logic to them. They love you one minute and hate you the next without rhyme or reason. They say they are mad for you, and all the while they are trying to think of ways to change what they tell you they love about you. They demand you get them more of everything, then complain when you leave them to get it. They're only happy when you are miserable."

He smiled faintly. "That does not sound very appealing." He braced himself for another drink. "Things were so much easier before."

"Why must they be different now? Nothing's changed. You are the same, as am I. You've your ship and the sea."

"And my lady," he added softly. "That's what's different. Nothing mattered to me before her. I didn't care about things. Women I took when they were there, and when they were not, I didn't miss them. They were just to be used like good drink, a heavy blade, a strong wind." He lifted the bottle not seeing Rufe's solemn expression, his eyes on the lovely face across the fire. "There's a difference now. When she's not with me, I feel her absence and I miss her, I want her. I'm afraid of her and what she does to me. I don't want it to happen, but I cannot give her up. Rufe, am I talking crazy?"

As much as he wanted to answer in the affirmative, because of their friendship, he said, "No, Colley. I think you've found you have a heart after all."

"If I do, then she's bruising it now."

Rufe smiled, clapping a hand on his friend's shoulder and thinking how oddly uncertain he sounded. "They are good at that, the women who would take us from the sea."

"Well, I want no part of it," he concluded firmly. He frowned abruptly at seeing Merrit dancing about in the arms of the moon-faced Freddy Moffit. Freddy Moffit? It was too much to bear. He passed the bottle to Rufe and strode purposefully through the crowd.

"Take your hands from her before I split you from throat to gizzard."

Freddy leapt away from Merrit at the cold threat, not needing to look into the Angel's emerald eyes to read the promise in them. He bowed quickly to the frowning lady, and scurried off.

"How dare you —" she began, but her words were halted by the long, hard kiss that rocked her into silence. When he stepped back, her eyes were still closed, her senses swirling in giddy surrender.

"Merri, you are mine, and I will not share that which I own, nor do I expect you to ask any less of me. If that meets with your approval, then kiss me for I am fairly starving for the want of a little kindness from you."

Her arms encircled him quickly as she rose to touch his mouth with her own eager lips which, too, had felt the hunger. Vaguely, they were aware of the crew's boisterous cheering; then there was nothing but each other, shared lips, shared breath, shared heat.


Several whole pigs were being roasted to feed the drunken pirates, the succulent scent of them heavy on the night sea air. Merrit sat comfortably in the sand, leaning back against his solid chest and hugging the knees that rose up on either side of her. His breath was warm and slow on her bare shoulders, punctuated with occasional nibbling kisses that left her shivering as they watched the dancing and merrymaking in easy silence. She reached up a hand to touch the dark head pillowed on her shoulder, feeling a sudden tension in his embrace.

"Colley, what is it?"

"Do you love me still?" he asked softly, almost doubtful of her answer.

"Of course, I do. That won't change."

"No?"

227

"What is it?" she repeated, clasping his hands in hers.

"I spent the afternoon on the ship, readying her to go out. The crew is anxious for the riches Durant denied them. They are eager to go. We must sail again soon, most likely day after next."

"Oh."

He felt her shiver briefly, and hugged her tighter yet. "Merri, I don't want to leave you," he admitted gruffly, his voice low and hoarse.

"Then like Anne Bonny, I will sail with you," she declared, feeling the lips caressing her bare shoulder break into a smile.

"If you only could," he mused. "But 'tis impossible. We must make plans for you."

"Hush, Colley. Not tonight. Don't speak of it tonight. I don't want to think about being apart, not when I still have you. Not just yet."

He kissed her bare skin warmly, then rubbed it with his cheek. "I wish I deserved you, Merri. Perhaps then I wouldn't fear losing you so much."

"You'll not lose me, pirate. I'm part of the plunder, remember?"

"Aye, my treasure."

Before they could reflect on that any further, they were pulled to their feet by the crew and made the center of countless toasts to his return and her courageous aid in his escape. By the time they started back for the tavern, Merrit was leaning sleepily against him, a silly smile on her face as they trod a wavering path. After mastering the tricky staircase, he placed her on the bed. Her arms reached up for him, and he was settling into their warmth seeking her lips, when there was a knock on the door.

"What is it?" he growled against her lips.

"Colley, come down for a minute. The crew has something for you," Rufe called.

"Tell them I've everything I want or need. Ah, damn. All

right." He kissed Merrit lingeringly, then murmured, "I'll be right back. Miss me."

"Do not be gone long, lest I be tempted to replace you," she teased, still holding him down, arms about his neck.

"As if you ever could," he scoffed, kissing her hard before disentangling himself from her embrace. "Soon. I promise."

She muttered sleepily and, with a nod, closed her eyes.


The entire crew of his ship was gathered in the taproom, pulling on mugs of ale and grinning.

"Angel," began Charlie Stuart, the bosun. "We all got together and took up a collection for your lady for bringing us back our captain. We want you to give it to her."

Curiously he took the bulging sack and looked inside. It contained pearls, Merrit's entire dowry, less his share. For a moment, he was too stunned to react; then, with an unsteady smile, he thanked them all. Only Rufe saw through Colley's smile. The cursed pearls surfacing again, a threat to his happiness with the lady. Green eyes met Rufe's, holding a sudden suspicion that was quickly dismissed. Then Colley turned and slowly climbed the stairs once more.

# *Chapter Nineteen*

Merrit lay curled on top of the covers, her cheek resting in her palm as if she were a sleeping child, her sandy bare feet tucked up beneath her rumpled skirt. He stood for a long while at the foot of the bed just watching the slow rise and fall of her breathing, the sack of pearls weighing as heavily in his hand as his heart in his chest. Oh, Merri, he thought glumly, if only I didn't love you so I'd know what to do. He was too distracted to realize the admission he had just made to himself, too obsessed with the thought of losing her.

He looked down at the heavy pouch, tempted to open the window and fling the contents out, but that was no answer. Someone was bound to ask if the gift was to her liking. He had drunk too much to think clearly or perhaps not enough to dull the pain of this decision. She had said she loved him. He wished he had enough belief in that uncertain emotion to trust her, but it was too abstract, too difficult for him to comprehend. Had she said she would stay only because she had no other option? If he gave her the pearls, would she be gone without hesitation, back to the bosom of the Whitelaws and her planned marriage? He felt a cold stirring of distrust and betrayal uncoil deep within him as he watched the sleeping woman. To trust her was to risk too much to the fickle workings of the female mind. He would have to give the dowry to her, but he could wait. She might be settled in and content here when he returned. Perhaps then she would be so happy to see him, the pearls would have no impact. His reluctance to be absent from her for a month or so was nothing compared to the thought of not having her here at all.

On the bed, Merrit gave a slight gasp at the sight of the shadowy figure staring down at her, then she lifted her arms in welcome.

"Colley, come to me," she called softly.

As he sat on the edge of the bed, he pushed the heavy pouch beneath it, then drew Merrit up to his chest for a desperate, crushing hug, his doubts momentarily suppressed by the eagerness of her embrace. He pressed his face into the thick tangle of her hair, breathing in its heady fragrance.

"Is all taken care of?"

"What?" he asked in a daze.

"Your business with your crew."

His arms tightened. "Aye. All is fine. Just some ship's business. Nothing to concern you." The lie came easily, but left a bitter taste when she nodded in quick belief. How readily she trusted him.

When she reached up to slip the coat from his shoulders and press hot kisses along his warm skin, he stilled her with his quiet words.

"I would like to just hold you for a time if that be all right with you."

She pressed herself obediently to him, nestling into the hollow of his throat, feeling the abnormally fast beat of his pulse and the rapid, uneven movement of his chest. "Colley, are you all right? Is something wrong?"

"I just don't want to be apart from you 'tis all." At least that was true enough.

"It won't be long, though it will seem so. Think of how sweet our reunion will be." Her lips moved leisurely against his neck in a tempting preview as his breath caught in a painful swallow.

231

"You will wait for me? You will be here when I return?"

Puzzled by the intensity of his questions, she made her response lightly teasing. "Where else would I go, Captain?"

She felt him stiffen, and his next words were barely audible.

"Would you go if you could? If you had your dowry?"

"I don't have it so there's no point in discussing that, is there?" When he was silent, she leaned away, looking up into his eyes with a warm smile. "I am where I wish to be, here with you. Does that satisfy your vanity, Captain?"

She looked so beautiful, so sincere. Believe her. Believe her, his heart cried above the protests of his suspicious mind.

"Merrit, I must tell you something," he blurted out in a rush before reason had a chance to halt the words. Trust, love, truth, she had said. Believe her.

"What is it, Colley?" He looked so serious, so anxious that she felt a prickle of alarm.

He hugged her to him, unwilling to let her see his face as he murmured, "I love you, Merri." He squeezed his eyes closed as he heard her gasp of surprise and delight. When she flung her arms about him, he knew he had said the words she wanted to hear, words that would keep her with him, even though he said them to serve his own ends.

"Oh, Colley, I love you so," she declared joyfully, and then she was kissing him, falling back onto the bed with him.

Their union was fired with a new intensity, Merrit's derived from joyful abandon and Nicholas's from a sense of desperation. Clothing was shed from flesh that tasted of sand and smoke, and with the exchange of searching touches and hurried kisses, their pulses began to beat with the primal rhythm of the drums on the beach, that throbbing tempo echoed in the movement of their bodies one against the other until it burst into the full song which can only be played on instruments of love.

In the aftermath of their passion, Merrit lay smiling in

the curve of his arm. She had thought she'd experienced the heights of pleasure with him but those brief words had changed everything for her, adding a new, deeper dimension to what passed between them, an element of confidence, of possession, that made paradise all the sweeter. Any doubts or uncertainties fell away in the face of that new encompassing strength. He loved her, by his own admission. All else could take care of itself. He loved her.

Languorous in the wake of fierce desire, Nicholas absently stroked her thick hair while he stared into the darkness. *Don't lie to me, Colley . . . She wants more, more than you could ever offer . . . what she needs is the love of a good man . . . You've no heart, Colley.* He closed his eyes tightly to those haunting words that would not give his conscience rest, feeling as though he were drowning in their accusation. He clung to Merrit's steadying hand while alternating waves of distrust and self-interest swept over him. Again, her frail strength was not enough to keep him afloat. He would not hurt her, he told himself defensively. He'd give her all he could, would do all he might to see her safe and happy. And he would try to learn of love and trust from her example. For her he would try to conquer the hostile suspicion that held him back from her, from experiencing the thorough enjoyment and peace he could see in her eyes. If his restlessness could be stilled, she would be the one to do so. A part of him continued to rebel against feeling secure with her, reminding him with insistent nudges of cynicism that it wouldn't last, that her betrayal was inevitable; warning him against making any concessions or changes for her, advising him to keep at least one foot on the firm ground of reason. No, he couldn't surrender to that blind, vulnerable trust she asked of him. He was too wary, too cautious to believe in the goodness he saw or to submit to the kinder feelings she inspired in him.

Suddenly he was looking forward to being on the sea again, where everything was predictable and simple, where he could lose himself in the easy comradery of his crew and in the shallow, uncomplicated life he had chosen — as long as he knew she would be here when he returned. He needed a brief escape from the turmoil she created as well as the security of knowing their parting was temporary. He needed to clear his heart and mind of all the cluttering doubts and desires so that upon returning he could face Merrit with his old confidence. Then he could afford to present her with the truth. If only she would wait . . .

The sound of an anguished moan woke Nicholas from what seemed too brief a rest, the promise of a glorious day brightening the room with a halo of light. The low, mournful sound came from the small figure huddled beside him.

"Merri, are you all right?" he demanded, suddenly concerned.

"I am fine. Just don't shout so." Her words were muffled.

Chuckling softly he turned her onto her back, whereupon she screwed her eyes shut against the piercing sunlight.

"Have mercy on me, Colley, and close the shutters. Oh, try not to bounce the bed so when you move," she groaned, clasping her temples with unsteady hands while he went to seal out the agonizing brightness.

"You'll never make a good pirate wench lest you can hold your spirits," he chided, the boisterousness of his voice making her wince. He lay back down beside her and attempted an embrace but she pulled away, jerking the sheet over her head.

"I don't want to be a pirate wench," she moaned. "Go away and leave me to my suffering."

A fleeting frown creased his features, then he spoke softly to her. "Merri, let me spoil you a bit. I know a sure way to ease your head. I learned it from a most captivating witch."

That brought the covers down enough for her to eye him skeptically before she gave a miserable sigh and lay on her back, at the mercy of his touch.

It was a surprisingly gentle touch. His fingertips lightly

rubbed the furrowed lines from her forehead, and as her throbbing tension began to ebb, she felt his warm lips brush her aching eyes, then slowly trail down to meet hers in an undemanding kiss that lingered until she responded.

"Shall we continue this, my lady, or would you prefer some time to recover yourself?" he asked in a husky tone.

Her eyes opened slowly to look into his. "Your touch is miraculously healing. I would prefer you to make me well."

In quick compliance, his lips claimed hers with tender savagery, and soon all thoughts of her aching head were gone.

"How do you feel now, my lady?"

Merrit looked up from the bed with a lazy smile, her eyes caressing his taut tanned body as he began to dress. She thought it odd that she should so enjoy the sight when a short month ago she had been terrified of him. She smiled when she said, "You have a kind touch, and I have been quite cured of any ills."

"Do I?" He frowned for a moment as he pondered that. "Then you find no fault with me as a lover?"

Uncertainty from the prowling Spanish Angel? She pursed her lips saucily. "I have naught to compare you to, Captain. If you want to be gauged for your prowess, you should ask one of your more experienced ladies."

Instead of smiling, his eyes grew dark and somber, making her realize with a sense of surprise how serious he was. "Pru told me I was stingy and ungiving. I did not want to be so with you. That is why I asked. It is hard for me to be considerate, for I am not a thoughtful man. I wanted to be sure you did not find me lacking."

She was amazed and flattered, knowing he did not often recognize any fault within himself. "Colley, come here," she coaxed softly, sitting up and opening her arms to him. He let her hold him for a moment, then knelt on the floor at her feet, his dark head pillowed in her lap. "I am greatly pleased with you, my pirate lord. You have been most generous and

235

patient with me in my ignorance. I fear I am the one who should apologize to you for knowing so little of how to care for you."

He gave a shaky laugh. "By God, Merri, if the whores here had your knowledge they would be living like queens."

"Should I find that a compliment, Captain?" she asked a bit stiffly.

"I meant it as such. Forgive my clumsy phrasing, for I have not had much practice in saying what I feel. I only meant that in your unskilled hands I have found a pleasure greater than I could ever imagine."

"I find that difficult to believe," she murmured as her hand played through his silken hair. She looked down at him curiously, but his eyes were closed and she could read no expression in his scarred profile.

"You give of yourself, Merri, and you do not know how rare that is. And you make me want to give in return, I who have jealously guarded my favors. While you demand nothing, I want to give you all the more. I want to make you happy, but I don't know how. I am selfish and shy of emotion, and you confuse me mightily with your control of my heart. I cannot lose you, Merri. You are the first woman I have ever sought out. I have never needed to be the pursuer before, and I fear you will elude me. Don't leave me."

Her hand trembled as it lay against his cheek, the depth of feeling in his hushed words shaking her. When he was quiet in spirit, she believed in all things, loved him with a fierce protectiveness, wanted to prove worthy of the fragile gift of trust he was extending to her with a cautious hand, eager for her to take it but reluctant to let go. She desired that trust almost as much as his love, sensing it was the harder for him to give.

"You have brought me from child to woman, and no other man can ever claim that. As no other can claim my love. All I ask of you is your love and truthfulness, and your trust when you can give it freely. I need nothing else. I want nothing more."

His hands tightened on her knees, though his eyes were still closed to her searching gaze. "Had you asked for the stars or England's crown it would be easier for me to give them to you," he told her slowly. "I would gladly surrender you all I own, but when you ask me to give of myself, you ask much. I will try not to disappoint you. That is all I can promise. Is it enough to hold you?"

"It is enough," she assured him, feeling the tension in his grasp diminish. He looked up at her then, eyes a smoky jade conveying much of what he had left unsaid.

"Would it suit you to remain here for the time I am at sea? When I return, I will find you a place of your own, be it cottage or castle, whatever you wish. If you like, I will have Mildred brought to you. Something tells me that despite her gruffness, she'd take to this hearty life as a pirate wench."

Merrit chuckled at that and, softly smiling, said, "I will be fine here. The room holds many memories of you and that will make the time speed faster."

"Not all of them good," he murmured.

"No," she agreed, her fingertips lightly tracing the curving scar on his face. "There is always a hint of bad in all things no matter how perfect we try to make them."

"I am far from perfect, Merri."

"I know well what you are, my vain, greedy pirate thief, but you are mine." She kissed his smiling lips to affirm her words, whispering against them, "I love you, Colley. Promise you will come back to me."

"That is an easy promise to keep. I will always return to you. Always. Now, before you distract me further, I must go see to provisioning the ship . . . if any of the crew has survived the night. I will try not to be gone long. I am jealous of the time we have together."

He stood and finished dressing, the strong and self-possessed Angel once more. Looking up at his handsome arrogant face, it was hard for her to see him as the man who had laid his head in her lap. The change was so swift and so complete.

He bent to kiss her deeply, fingers twining in her loose hair and tongue playing across her lips.

"Go quickly while I've still a mind to let you leave me even for a brief time," she warned huskily, pushing him away. She responded easily to his grin, her heart filled with the aching joy of love. "Do not forget me this time, pirate, or you'll find yourself at the mercy of the New Providence whores."

"I prefer to be at your mercy, my lady," he professed, pressing his lips warmly to her palm. Then, with a jaunty salute, he returned to the call of the sea.

The day was balmy, a cooling breeze whispering off the tranquil blue-green sea. Merrit stood barefoot in the sand, shading her eyes with a hand as she scanned the gently rocking ships that crowded the sheltered harbor, looking for the familiar sloop. A surprised and amused smile lit her face when she spotted it and several of its crew waved. The sloop had been rechristened. The Spanish Angel's sleek vessel was no longer the *Merry Widow* but the *Merri Fortune*. The knowledge that part of her would sail with him pleased her greatly.

"Good afternoon, Lady Merrit."

Merrit turned to the copper-skinned quartermaster, a guarded smile appearing on her face. She had been unable to shake the uncomfortable feeling that Rufe was a threat to her, though he had never given her reason to believe that he was.

"The captain is on board," he told her simply. "I can take you out if you wish."

She cast a longing glance at the ship, but shook her head. "No, I wouldn't want to interrupt him."

Rufe looked mildly skeptical, then nodded at her wisdom. He was silent for a moment as if making some decision. His blunt statement was a surprise.

"Colley tells me you are remaining here as his mistress."

She flinched as if unfairly struck, a frown clouding her expression. "I had not thought of it in that manner, but yes, I suppose I am." His mistress. What an ugly cast that put on their arrangement, but there was no denying the truth of it. She would become his kept woman, sharing his bed without benefit of the church's sanction, and any child she bore him would be deemed bastard. Her frown deepened. Somehow, when she thought of herself as his lover, it all seemed romantic and exciting, but there were those who would call her his whore and that disturbed her. She looked to Rufe, wondering if he had used that choice of words to provoke her.

"We sail tomorrow at first light," Rufe said finally.

"I know" was her soft reply.

"We may be gone for a month or more. Have you thought of what you will do in his absence? Life is not easy here for a woman left behind, even if she be under the protection of one like Colley. There are no fine amusements. There is no genteel company."

She bristled at his tone. "Why concern yourself?" she asked pointedly. "Do not spar with me, Rufe. I would know why you are so displeased by your captain's interest in me."

"My pleasure is not involved."

She flushed darkly at his abrupt censure. "I was not aware that you were Colley's guardian." She saw him frown at her use of his captain's real name and pressed on in annoyance. Rufe's friendship was not the only tie on the pirate captain. "I have his love. Have you a stronger claim on him?"

Rufe was momentarily taken aback, then he smiled wryly. "So he fancies himself in love with you." His chuckle brought an angry lift to her chin. "My lady, he has no idea what the word means. I say that not to be cruel or to belittle Colley, but to spare you further hurt. You know nothing about him, only what he allows you to see."

"And I suppose he has bared his soul to you," she said searingly, suddenly jealous of a friendship that had so many years behind it.

"Some, not all. He doesn't even trust me that much. I know enough to tell you as kindly as possible that you are a fool to think he loves you. He may lust after you or admire you or possibly even like you, but you'll never have more than that. Not from Colley."

"Perhaps you are the one who doesn't know him. Did he tell you he almost drowned to save my life?"

"It would be easier for him to give his life than his love."

That was too close to what Colley had told her. Defensively, she argued, "And how many others has he asked to stay with him? How many have shared his thoughts as well as his bed? Are there other women with whom he has spent more than one day?"

"You are the first," he admitted grudgingly.

"Then how can you be so sure, so positive that he has no feelings for me?"

"Because I know him well. The only emotion that touches his heart is hatred. Get in the way of that and he would cut you down as quickly as he would me, without thought, without warning. He walks on the dark side and he prefers to do so. Vengeance drives him and he will burn himself out to have it. When he does, if he does, he will give up his life, for it will have no purpose. My lady you have no idea what he is like when the dark side rules him."

"Yes, I do," she murmured faintly. "I have seen it." The memory of green eyes that burned and froze her in the same instant made her shiver. That was the part of him she had no wish to see again. The dark side. How well Rufe had summed it up. But she would not let him scare her off so easily. The good in Colley far outweighed the darkness. "You speak poorly of a man you call friend."

"Colley can be many things, the best friend a man could want and the best captain to sail under. He can be anything

240

that suits his purpose — charming, fearless — but beneath his façade he is ruthless and without conscience. That is what he doesn't let you see. You cannot afford to overlook that side of him because it may be all you have left."

"Why tell me all this? Why should you care? It is my risk," she said bravely even as his words seeped in unbidden to cloud her joy with the shadow of uncertainty. What if all he was saying was true?

"Merrit, you are so very young, and Colley can be very appealing. Look beyond that. You are refusing to see things as they are, him as he is. Do you know why we became pirates? Because we care for nothing but ourselves. When we want something, we go after it in the quickest and easiest way, without a thought to who gets hurt. If Colley wants you, you'll be hurt. He'll lie, he'll cheat, he'll do whatever is best for him, whatever he thinks he has to do. He's a pirate, my lady. Will you be content with living off what he brings you, knowing that he stole and perhaps killed to get it? And when he doesn't come back, what then? Who will take you in after you've willingly stayed with him? Your fiancé? Your family? What will you do when his obsession with you fades? Will you stay here to become like Pru and Molly?"

"No," Merrit protested, her firm assurance slightly shaken. "That won't happen."

"How do you know that, Merrit?" Rufe persisted. The hostility was gone from his voice, and the quiet gentleness that replaced it was even more disturbing. "You don't know him. Has he told you anything about himself, who he is, what his name is, why he hates the Whitelaws, and what part you play in his plan for vengeance?" When Merrit remained silent, her dark eyes pleading that he spoil no more of her dreams, he continued softly. "You asked me why I should care. You are a good woman, my lady. We rarely see that. You saved Colley's life, and for that I owe you. What he is, is a pirate and that you'll not change. If you force him to choose between you and the sea, it won't be

241

you he picks. He can afford no ties, living as he does. Let him go, Merrit, for your good and for his."

She turned away, squeezing her eyes shut, denying all he told her with a shake of her head. She couldn't let Colley go. She wouldn't give up the newfound happiness, the intoxicating desire, the sweet, poignant hopes. "I love him, Rufe," she said simply, as if that were the answer to all things, the rock upon which anything could be built regardless of the marshy ground beneath it.

"Then go quickly before your hurt deepens, while you still have good things to remember. Take the pearls and return to the life you were meant to have and leave this dream untested."

He saw her abruptly stiffen. "The pearls? What have they to do with this?"

Rufe paused, then answered, "Colley has them. He was to have given them to you last night."

There was a long, strained silence, then Merrit turned to him, pale but calm. "Rufe, take me to the ship," she said tonelessly.

242

# Chapter Twenty

Nicholas looked up in surprise, a welcoming smile lighting his face. He had only a brief flash of warning as Merrit's eyes lifted to his. Then her open palm connected with his cheek in a fearsome crack.

"Bastard. Whore's son. Liar," she spat into a face that was almost comically blank. "Rufe, take me back now. That's all I had to say."

As she began to turn about, all was shockingly clear to Colley. "Ah, damn," he moaned softly; then in a few quick strides, he caught up with her. "Merri, please."

But she would have none of him, whirling away, her eyes ablaze with fury and the hurt of betrayal. "I want no more of your lies," she shrieked, fighting him now in earnest when he pulled her to his chest. It took all of his strength to hold her without hurting her.

"Merri, listen to me. Please. Let me explain to you. Listen." His voice was panicked, low as he crushed her tightly to him, aware of the anger that seethed in her, of the stunned looks of his crew, and of Rufe's uncertain apologetic gaze. He had to calm her, but the cold terror that his words were coming too late shook him. "Come below with me. I'll not struggle with you here on deck."

She gave a harsh jeering laugh as he released her. "Oh, no. Don't let your men see the bold Angel humbling himself to a woman."

He frowned at her biting words, taking her arm and

leading her down to his cabin. He could feel her tense and trembling beneath his hand, but her expression was chiseled in ice. When the door closed, he rushed on.

"Merri, I would have told you."

She laughed, a sound so disdainful that he realized how little hope he had. "When?" she shouted. "Tonight in bed. Maybe tomorrow as you sailed? Next week, next month? When I was fat with your child? When it was too late for me to have anywhere else to turn? Is that when you were going to tell me?"

Seeing no point in trying to deceive her further, he answered quietly, "I planned to tell you when I returned."

"How thoughtful of you," she snarled. "Thoughtful and calculating. Why didn't you give me the pearls last night when you had me weak with passion. I wouldn't have left you then. Did you fear I would be as greedy for them as you once were, that I would forget you?"

"I could not take the chance," he replied stiffly. The imprint of her hand fused slowly with his rising color as he shifted uncomfortably under her scathing remarks.

"You mean you couldn't trust me." He said nothing, his eyes giving her the answer, and her voice deepened, growing husky with the pain that tore through her. "Why, Colley? I told you I loved you. I told you I would stay. All I asked was that you trust me, that you be truthful with me. Was that so much?"

"For me, yes."

She looked at him long and hard, seeing the beautiful face, the beguiling veneer he hid behind. Even now, the sight of him moved her strongly, almost enough to make her forgive him. Almost.

"What other lies have you told me, Captain? What other innocent fairy tales did you concoct to placate the stupid child who so foolishly wanted to believe in you? What Colley?" He winced at the contempt in her voice, and compressed his lips in damning silence. "How could you say you loved me? Or was that a lie too?"

"I said it to keep you with me," he told her with savage bluntness, tired of trying to meekly defend himself against her accusations. There was nothing to be gained by pleading his case before her. She was too incensed to hear him and her words cut too deeply to be ignored. Softly, he added, "But that does not mean it was not true."

Her dark eyes glimmered with tears she refused to shed, for she dared show him no weakness. Instead, she continued her attack. "What do you know of truth? Or of love? You who have no heart. You who think only of yourself. I told you I'd forgive no more lies. I told you that. Didn't you believe that either? How could you think so little of me that you could hurt me so?"

"I never meant to hurt you," he vowed.

"How could you think you wouldn't. Oh, Colley, I wanted so much to be with you, but it is time to wake from the dream."

He mentally tensed, bracing himself against her words, words he could not forestall. "Merri, please say no more," he pleaded hoarsely.

"I'm sailing with you, Captain, as far as Williamsburg. Leave me now. I've no wish to look upon you any longer. Just go."

He looked at her, his expression devoid of emotion. "As you wish, my lady. You may stay aboard if you choose. I will see that whatever you need is brought to you." He hesitated for a brief instant, his features softening with the pain of loss and sorrow; then the look was gone, wiped clean as he bowed slightly to her.

Rufe looked anxiously to his captain and friend as he returned to the deck, puzzled by the smooth, handsome face that told him nothing. Had he managed to talk the lady out of her rage?

"Assemble the crew, Charlie," the captain called to the bosun in a casual tone. "We sail on the late tide. There's no reason to linger." He walked quickly by Rufe to the bow of the ship, looking out over the waiting sea.

"Colley?"

Nicholas stiffened but did not look up as the quartermaster joined him. The calm look on his face never altered as he heard Rufe's question.

"Do I take the lady ashore?"

"No. We will be taking her back to Williamsburg. I must see to the ship. There is much to do if we are to be ready to sail." He spoke with an almost frightening smoothness that was betrayed only when he ran his hand ran through his hair. It was unsteady due to his inner effort to maintain control. He clenched it quickly into a fist and let it drop to his side in a denial of his weakness.

"Colley, are you all right?" Rufe asked in quiet concern, sensing his captain's underlying distress with a guilty pang.

When Nicholas answered, his words were still low and even. "Rufe, you would be wise to steer clear of me until we are under way lest I forget our friendship and tear your heart out for your part in this. I cannot easily forget what you have done to me." The green eyes rose slowly, dark with the suppressed violence that struggled for release.

Rufe took a quick step back. "I'll see all is ready for us to weigh anchor, Captain."

The immediate threat was gone as he nodded, his eyes returning to the still waters.


After Colley left her, Merrit stood for a long while, uncertain of what to do. The unpleasant confrontation had sapped her strength. Though her grief was monumental, she felt no urge to weep. Instead, she sat at the table and began to plan what she must do. There was no use looking back. The past held nothing for her. Its pain was still too fresh. She would return to Williamsburg and present Lady Whitelaw with her dowry. She would marry Winston Whitelaw, and be a good and proper wife to him, seeing to his needs and bearing children dutifully. She would be uncomplaining and without bitterness about her fate. Perhaps in time she would grow to love her husband when the agony in her heart eased. Even if she did not, she would be secure and well provided for, and she would be fulfilling her obligations to her family. She would not think on her own needs or wants. Better to let others take control of her life, restoring it from its present shambles to some semblance of order and peace. She would not think of pirates or promises.

Relieved that her course had been decided, she lay back on the bunk, refusing to let the blissful images it evoked come into focus. Exhausted, she closed her eyes and was able to drift into deep and undisturbed sleep, not waking until it was nearly dark and the ship was gently rocking. The *Merri Fortune* had put out to sea. The time for turning back was over.

She gave a start when she realized she was not alone in the room. "How long have you been there watching me?" she demanded of the figure that stood silent as a shadow by the cabin door.

"A short time, my lady. I did not want to wake you," he answered quietly.

She sat up, feeling annoyed and aware that her clothing and hair were unattractively mussed. Scowling, she tried to discern his mood, his voice having given no clue to it and his expression being cloaked in the growing dimness. "Why are you here?" His sudden presence flustered her, making her question unintentionally sharp. She had hoped she would have time to gather her composure before their next meeting, but here he was uninvited, making her feel inadequately prepared and disconcerted.

He extended a bulging pouch and continued in the same flat, colorless tone. "Your purchase price into the Whitelaw house. Your thirty pieces of silver."

Cautiously, she rose and reached out to take it from him,

but his hand withdrew. His green eyes were so hard and aloof it was difficult to imagine they had ever shared any intimacy.

"Is this some game, Captain, or have you decided not to honor your word?" she asked coolly. His strangely detached mood was unnerving. Was this yet another facet to his many-sided personality, this remote, emotionless stranger?

"I have no intention of breaking my word. I would recall an offer you once made to see if you are still of a mind to honor it."

"What offer, Captain?"

"One I hastily dismissed as not enough. Now I know better." His voice now low and silken but still oddly toneless, he purred, "Yield to me, Merri. For the return of your dowry, become my mistress until your return."

Merrit went white in shocked outrage. "That was not part of our bargain," she said with difficulty.

He only shrugged. "You see, my lady, it matters not to me. I need not feel obligated to return the pearls at all. Remember what I am."

She held back her retort and glared at him with a jaundiced eye. Was he serious? His calm, handsome features were no help to her, and this was a risk she couldn't take. She had to have the pearls and he knew it. He played the game all too well leaving her no choice. With a flash of cornered anger, her spirit rebelled against his casual demand. If it was a whore he wanted, a whore he would get.

"I yield, Captain, as you knew I would, but for this night only. You will then give me my dowry and never lay a hand on me again."

"Done, my lady."

He watched, unmoving, while she shed her clothing, letting the pieces drop about her feet indifferently until she stood, a glowing pearl in the waning light. Green eyes swept over her petite figure, so lush, so soft, so inviting, and he trembled at the perfect sight, keen desire thawing his eyes and softening the firm line of his full mouth. One night, he thought unhappily. One night instead of a lifetime. Yet he could not deny the powerful need that had led him to maneuver her back into his bed. He had won her once, perhaps he could again.

He came to her, cupping her chin and lowering his head to seek the sweetness of her kiss. She twisted her face away and in a voice that nearly froze his ardor said, "Take me if you must, but do not try to make love to me."

Her words crushed any tenderness he felt, her cold denial flooding him with the frustrated feeling of being cheated. Even though she had rendered his emotion impotent, his need for her still raged. If she didn't want to be loved, so be it, but he still meant to have her.

Roughly, he pushed her down on the bed and claimed her without preamble, using her like a nameless, faceless woman of the streets to ease the painful pressure in his loins, angrily spurred on by her lack of response and her refusal to accept his kiss. He should never have allowed himself to think of her as anything but a tool, yet he could not shut out the feeling of her beneath him, the scent of her, the taste of her. It was all too much, sucking him into a vortex of longing, of need, of love, of hurt. There was no pretending she was an unimportant tool for his pleasure, she was pleasure incarnate and only the spiraling fires she brought him would satisfy him.

Merrit lay alone in the darkness, hugging her arms about her trembling form. It wasn't his angry possession of her that had provoked her tears but her own inability to remain unmoved by him. He had brought her explosive delight when she would deny it. In her fury and confusion, she had overlooked much, how very much she loved him, in spite of his lies, in spite of what he was. His hesitant words, spoken with such husky emotion, came back to her. They had been so difficult for him, he could not even meet her eye. He did love her, of that she was certain for his treatment of her had been so different from his callous reaction to her rejection. Had he really lied to her? Hadn't he warned her of his own shortcomings? Hadn't she promised to accept him for what he was? Who then was at fault, him for being himself or her for wanting to believe she could change him?

Rufe looked cautiously at the dark-haired man who joined him at the rail and took the mug of ale he offered without comment.

"Would you prefer something stronger?"

Nicholas glanced at his friend then at the mug. Without having tasted its mellow contents, he shook his head. "This be fine," he said quietly. "I apologize for the bite of my words earlier. I was not myself."

"No need," Rufe assured him, thinking Colley still looked far from himself. His eyes were too bright and sharp as if he walked on a narrow ledge and the struggle for balance was taking a wearying toll.

"I was thinking that once we leave off the lady, we shall sail south. Captain Hornigold tells me there should be some rich Spanish galleons off the Florida coast."

"Whatever you want, Colley."

"I want to get away from here — as far and as fast as I can," he said with sudden passion. "I want only the sea around me, a heartless whore beneath me, and my crew behind me. I'll never look for more again." He dashed an impatient hand across his eyes, then his voice deepened, its natural Spanish intonation growing marked. "Then I will see to the White-laws. Once she has married them, I will have another means to crush them beneath my heel especially if she spawns a green-eyed Spanish bastard."

"Colley, do not include Lady Merrit in your dark plans. She does not deserve such treatment."

He looked up fiercely, the scars across his cheek growing pale as his features tightened into a cold vengeful mask.

"Why show her any special mercy. She goes to them willingly."

"Perhaps. Perhaps not. You forget she saved your life, that she loved you."

Emerald eyes blazed, changing him into something dark and unpleasant, and his friend swallowed in the face of such rage. "No. I forget nothing. If she cared for me, she would not be leaving. I owe her nothing but my contempt."

"Colley?"

Rufe turned in surprise to the lady who had approached them silently. Her soft voice momentarily shattering Nicholas's poise as if it were fragile crystal, but then he grew rigid, refusing to look around.

"I would speak to your captain alone, Rufe," Merrit repeated in the same quiet tone.

Rufe bowed slightly, acceding to her wish, and whispered low as he passed her, "Go carefully, Merrit."

She pressed his hand with a nod of thanks and understanding, then turned her full attention to the back of the foreboding figure at the rail. "Will you look at me when I speak," she requested simply, and as he slowly turned she repressed a shiver. The dark side, Rufe had called it.

"I can see nothing else that needs pass between us, my lady," he told her frigidly.

"Only this."

Her mouth was on his before he could object, moving insistently over his cool, impenetrable lips as her fingertips brushed his taut cheeks and then slid into ebony hair. She pressed against him fully, deliberately seeking to provoke some response, some spark of feeling, but he remained tense, scarcely breathing, his eyes open and staring through her. Finally they drifted slowly closed and a low painful moan rumbled deep in his throat as he snatched her up in his arms to kiss her with dizzying, consuming passion until they were both breathless and trembling.

"Don't leave me, Merri," he pleaded, the words tumbling

251

out. "Please. I need you. I need you, Merri. Don't leave me now or ever."

"Quiet. Hush now," she whispered against his panicked kisses. "Shh. Colley, I love you. Hush now. We must talk."

"I don't want to talk," he mumbled petulantly. "I want you to love me."

"After we talk."

"No, now. Now." His voice was so intense, so urgent that she let herself be lost in his embrace and in his wandering kisses. Slowly, he began to calm, the frantic rush of his mouth stilling for a long deep kiss that locked them together while an eternity sped by. "Tell me again that you love me," he urged quietly, leaning back so he could look into her dark, liquid eyes.

"I love you. I will always love you. That will never change. But I cannot stay with you. Can you understand that?"

He frowned, black brows lowering until they formed a heavy V over the bridge of his nose. "No, Merri, I can't. You say you love me yet you don't want to be with me in the same breath. How can that be? Can't you forgive me for being so stupidly thoughtless? I care so much and you are hurting me so badly."

"Love is not enough."

His frown deepened in confusion. "I give you everything but love and you beg for it alone; then when I give you my heart, you say it is not enough. What do you want? What would be enough for you? I give you my life. I give you my love. I give you everything that I am. Why is that not enough? Why?"

She took his large calloused hands up in hers, kissing each knuckle in turn and then his damp palms. "Colley, it is not what you give but who you are," she explained. "We are too different, you and I. You are the sleek, fast ship that needs a strong wind behind it to sail in search of danger and excitement. I am a quiet harbor with still waters, deep and placid, waters you stir too violently in passing. I cannot roam and you cannot be still. I would not take your gusty winds from you, and I am not strong enough to cut all ties and fly with you. I want too much to have so little of you."

"I won't give you up," he vowed with terse emotion. "You are more important than all else. I need only you."

"You may believe that now, but in time you would look at me differently, blaming me for stealing you from the sea, and regret would make you bitter. We would end up hating and hurting each other."

"I would never hurt you," he said hastily, then paused realizing how empty the words were and how many times he already failed them.

"You wouldn't mean to and neither would I, but we cannot help what we are. What we have together is heaven and hell, and the constant change from one to the other is too hard for me to bear. Maybe I am not strong enough or wise enough or old enough, but I can't stay. Can you understand even a little of what I've said?"

Though his scowl didn't lift, he gave a slight almost imperceptible nod. His generous mouth pursed thoughtfully. "What if I choose not to let you go? I could keep you with me be it your wish or no. I am a pirate bound by no codes of gentlemanly honor, you know."

"I know," she agreed with a smile. "But you would not keep me against my wish. It would hurt your vain image to be forever subduing an unwilling woman."

"But I would enjoy doing so and you would not long be unwilling." To stress his point, his forefinger tracked from her chin down her graceful throat to the shadowed crevice at the edge of her bodice, making her shiver with a chill of anticipation. "Fool whom you will, my lady, but I know your blood runs as hot for me as mine for you."

"Then let us not waste the heat, pirate."

In compliance, he drew her into the circle of his embrace, warm mouth eager on hers. Before she could protest, one arm swept behind her knees to scoop her up into his arms.

"Come below with me wench," he said with a rakish grin, carrying her easily across the deck while his crew chuckled in the shadows, coin exchanging hands.

In the gently rocking bunk where they lay together, his words were spoken in a low rough whisper heavy with the musical Spanish lilt.

"I love you, Merri. 'Tis either love or madness, for you feed on my heart and mind like a fire that burns out of control devouring all in its path and leaving cold ashes in its wake. Once you are gone, I will never be warm again."

"Colley, no," she began softly. "You will find someone —"

"No." His reply was flat and final. "There was only one small spot of weakness in me and you wedged yourself there. I've no room for any other. I cannot, I will not open myself to this exquisite torture again. I will be as I was before. No, that is not true, for I will have the precious gift of our time together to hoard and cherish. Thank you, Merri, for bringing light and love. You have proved my greatest treasure and I am loath to give you up. 'Tis the first time I ever wished to be other than I am, but for you, I would become beggar or king if it would hold you. Don't forget me too quickly."

She rose up to meet his lips with her own to halt the words that twisted her emotions so painfully. In a sudden fierce voice, she said, "If I could reach out and still the heavens to stop time, I would be here in your arms forever, but time is our enemy so love me now. I will always be yours, my vain pirate captain, yours to take whenever you hold out your hand. Take me now."

"No one will ever love you as I do, Merri. No one. And no one will ever make you feel as I do," he vowed almost angrily, then his voice deepened throatily. "We were made for one another. See how well we fit." His hand cupped one rounded breast possessively. "How well we fit," he murmured again, filling her fully and completely until she caught her breath in a small sob. "I love you, Merri, and that love is for

254

you alone."

In the muted haze of predawn shadow, Merrit lay head propped on raised elbow, watching the sleeping man beside her, painstakingly studying his every sleek line to etch his image on her heart and mind. He was so handsome of face and so awesomely perfect of form that he could have been fashioned from the romantic dreams of countless virgins. He was her angel, her beautiful love whose looks were flawed by the errant stroke of her hand and the cruel kiss of the Navy's lash. Flawed as well was his character, which had been twisted by hardships and hatreds, still he stirred her love. But had she made a mark on his heart as well as his scarred cheek? Would he remember their moments together or would she be quickly forgotten and replaced? She smiled at her own insecurity, knowing full well that he loved her as much as he could and would feel the pang of their separation as keenly as she herself.

Although Merrit had never known love aside from that she felt for her family, she had fallen deeply and painfully in love with Colley, experiencing in a short span infinite sweetness and bitterness. From this unlikely man, she had learned of great passion and jealousy, of stirring desire, aching need, and tender consideration. Again, she raised the fearful question that plagued her: could any man, any touch, bring her such delight or only this man, only his touch?

Rufe approached his moody captain late in the day with an offer of brandy which was gratefully accepted.

"We'll be nearing the Capes by nightfall, Colley."

"I know."

He observed the clean profile of his captain in a moment of silent reflection, then asked, "Do you mean to give her up to the Whitelaws?"

Colley's expression darkened. "I've no choice. It is her wish. It is better for both of us. Her presence there can better serve my purpose."

Rufe frowned at the cold meaning of his words, unable to understand how he could close off his heart so completely. "Have you told her who you are?"

Green eyes flashed up in brief alarm. "Have you said something to her?"

"No. I thought it should come from you." Rufe saw the tense features relax. "Are you going to tell her?"

Colley frowned and looked back over the water. "She will know soon enough. I seen no need to tell her now." Selfishly, he had no wish to disturb the warmth of what lay between them, for the truth held untold dangers. He would deal with it when necessary.

"She is going to marry him, Colley, is going to become his wife."

"I don't need you to remind me of that," he said frigidly.

"Will you be able to watch her on his arm, knowing she is in his bed and will bear his children?"

His eyes darkened until they were almost black with torment and rage. "She won't have me, Rufe. There is nothing more I can do. If she were going to anyone else, I could bear it with better grace."

"Could you?" his friend challenged softly. "She is in the middle of it all, and you are going to hurt her. He will be her husband and whatever grief you bring to them will befall her as well. Have you thought of that?"

"Of little else," he said in heavy misery.

"Cut loose then. Let her go and forget them all. It serves no purpose now. Nothing will change. Forget the past and leave her what happiness she can find. You delight too much in your own scourging. Spit out the bitter taste and drink from it no more. Let go for both your sakes."

"I cannot," he whispered fiercely. "Justice must be met and

I will dispense it without mercy."

"Justice or vengeance?"

"They are one and the same."

"Then be done with it quickly and get on with life."

Colley took a long breath and slowly let it out. "So be it."

She found him at the bow, a strong motionless figure bathed in the glow of the day's end. He felt her beside him and squeezed the fingers she slid into his.

"Twilight," he said softly. "If ever I were to look for proof that there was a God I would find it here in the lingering death and rebirth of each day. For a short while, I can breathe free with no threat of the past or fear of the future. See how pure the light is, so intense and warm, yet it surrenders without a struggle to the darkness, going calmly, silently to be swallowed up and extinguished, knowing that it will return with the new day. What a comfort that must be. Can nothing in this life be so perfect and certain?"

"That is the way of my love for you," she told him in a hushed voice. "Though we may be parted, its strength will never waver."

His abrupt release of her hand told of his disbelief. "And will your love for me guide you in your marriage bed?"

His chilling speech made her blanch then flush hotly, the mounting silence finally bringing his eyes to meet hers.

"How dare you play the aggrieved party here, bemoaning my ill treatment of you. 'Twas none of my doing. 'Twas you, my lord pirate who snatched me from my ship and coaxed me into your bed, well knowing I was meant for another. 'Twas you who agreed to return me to my betrothed for your freedom. 'Twas you who lied and took advantage of my love. Don't you dare lay the brunt of the blame on me. I go to my intended stained and used, and perhaps already breeding a pirate's bastard babe. My lot is to lie to him about my chastity and pray he will take me in so my family and I can have our honor restored. You leave me with the fear that your shadow will always be crossing my happiness. I go to live a lie with a man I have never met, leaving the only love I have ever known for the uncertainty of honor. So don't you dare find fault with me."

Before he could speak, she fled the deck, blinded by insistent tears that burned for release until she cast herself upon the bed. Then they flowed freely, wetting the pillows and his shoulder when he gently lifted her up and held her close.

"Forgive me, Merri. It seems I am as selfish in my grief as I am in my love. Merri, don't go. Don't leave me. If you must, let me return you to your family. I will make it right with them. Only do not go to the Whitelaws. I cannot bear to hurt you further. Merri, please, if you love me as much as you say, do not go to them."

"Why? Can you tell me why? You have oft asked me to yield to you, but you yield me nothing. Why can't you trust me with the truth?"

He paused, his beautiful green eyes searching her face, softening then becoming hard as emerald chips once more. "I cannot."

"And I cannot stay."

He stood stiffly, cool and remote. "As you wish, my lady, but know you this, once you go there is no return. I will put my other plans in motion and there will be no turning from them."

Merrit looked up at him, her dark eyes wet and glittering like dark jewels, "So be it," she said faintly.

He paused for a long moment, his eyes clouded with a flood of the emotion he'd had no experience in dealing with. She was going to leave him, the only light that had ever come into his life, and he could not—would not—stop her. He suddenly wished that she wasn't so achingly lovely, that she wasn't such a delightful mix of sweet innocence and sharp wisdom, that her petite perfection didn't yield such wonderful pleasures and that her depthless eyes didn't shine with love for him. He wished he could walk away from her, but he couldn't. Not on this last night. He didn't have that kind of strength. And so he bent to kiss her.

The early morning was crisp and clean, wet with the fog rising off the glassy river and alive with the sounds of the Virginia wilderness. Merrit saw the Whitelaws' dock ahead, the end of her journey. She felt his hand tighten on her elbow as they crossed the deck to where Rufe waited by the landing boat. At his sudden wide smile, Merrit stepped into his engulfing embrace.

"Good luck to you, Lady Merrit," he said softly. "Thank you for the return of our captain." That meaning could have been simple, but it wasn't.

"Take care of him, Rufe," she whispered fiercely and stepped back.

"I will take you ashore, my lady," Nicholas said in a low voice.

"Don't tarry long, Colley. These are not friendly waters," Rufe warned as he lifted Merrit into the small craft.

They didn't speak as he rowed them to the dock. Silently, she watched him ply the oars, thinking of how such a short time ago he had been taking them to freedom and now he was returning her to captivity. The boat bumped against the sturdy pylon, and he stood in the tipping craft to help her mount the ladder. She hesitated on the bottom rung, desperately wanting to climb back into the boat and sail off with him but knowing sadly that she couldn't.

Holding her hand in both of his, he looked up at her, his beautiful green eyes expressive. "You are tearing the heart from me, Merri."

"And it will break mine to hear they have hanged you, so spare me that agony for as long as possible." She put her other hand to his smiling face, touching the torn cheek with gentle fingers. "I love you, Colley."

"And I you, my lady."

With a soft cry, she stepped into the boat and hugged him, to become lost in the firm, masculine feel of him and the scent of salt that clung to his skin. His kiss was sweet with sorrow and painful longing as his lips moved over hers in a lingering farewell, tasting her willing surrender for perhaps the last time. Reluctantly he held her back, studying her fragile beauty with a faint smile.

"A good life, my lady," he murmured.

"And a long one, Captain," she replied.

"As I promised," he said, extending the pouch. He reached up to take the pearl from his ear but she stilled his hand.

"My gift for all you have taught me of love and life," she told him, her voice suddenly heavy and quavering. "Oh, Colley." Her arms went about his neck, holding him, loving him, wanting him. As she pressed herself to him she felt the beat of his pulse, as rapid and uncontrolled as the pirate drums. "I will love you all my days and miss you every night. God speed, Colley."

She released him and climbed the ladder before the temptation he offered proved too great. He looked up at her, then flashed a cocky grin, once more the confident Spanish Angel. As she watched through the haze of mist coming off the river and through her tears, he returned to the *Merri Fortune*. That was the picture she would hold in her heart whenever she began to doubt her choice, Colley standing bold and free on the deck of his sloop with Rufe at his side, the pretty Angel, the pirate captain, her first and eternal love. Gradually, the mists of the James River swallowed the sleek lines of the ship, returning them to the sea and Merrit to her duty.

# Chapter Twenty-one

"Was that him? The Angel?"

Merrit gave a startled gasp and turned to face the youngest Whitelaw, her hand quickly brushing the moisture from her cheeks, but the girl's dreamy eyes were on the distant fog that had consumed the sloop.

"How beautiful he is," Letitia sighed, then her strangely adult expression centered on Merrit. "If you love him so, how could you bear to let him go?"

"I cannot," Merrit admitted raspily, gratefully accepting the child's comforting hug. "Perhaps you will understand when you are older. Perhaps then I will too."

With a last look down the cloudy river, they walked arm in arm to the great silent house which hadn't awakened. Letitia's bare feet made wet imprints on the fine wood floor. Having seen the masts of the pirate vessel skim down the river in a hide-and-seek between the overhanging trees, Letitia had hastily donned a robe and had scurried down to the dock. The chill that had her teeth chattering was a small price to pay for what she had seen. When they parted at the head of the stairs, Letitia gave Merrit a quick squeeze.

"I will see you at breakfast. Welcome home."

Merrit gave a bittersweet smile. Home. For her, home would be wherever her captain sailed.

For a moment, Mildred regarded her wordlessly, taking in

the tiny figure in the gold and gaudy gown, then she embraced her, feeling the girl sag in a brief instant of weakness, a tremor shaking her fragile shoulders before she recovered her new control and simply leaned wearily in her arms.

"I truly did not know if I would see ye again, pet," Mildred murmured, her voice gruff with emotion.

"I have come to do my duty to my family." How martyrish that sounded, Merrit thought, as if she were an unwilling sacrifice, returning against her will.

"And how be ye, child?"

"I am well, but in need of clothes and a strong bar of soap." She stepped back with a wan smile.

"And our pirate, how does he fare? the older woman asked, seeing the girl's dark eyes shimmer in her oddly remote face.

"He kept his word to you, Mildred, and brought me back."

"Bless ye, pirate. Ye be a man after all," Mildred muttered to herself. Then she steered the tired girl to the dressing table, sitting her down with an authoritative hand. "Get ye out of that tawdry garb while I ready yer bath. Word will soon reach herself and she'll be wanting a word with ye. And the dowry? Did the pirate return it to ye?"

Merrit smiled wrily. "My thirty pieces of silver, all safe and ready to buy my future."

Puzzling over the bitterness in her youthful voice, Mildred saw to the bath, frowning. When she returned, she found Merrit still dressed and looking sheepishly reluctant, as if shy of exposing herself. With a snort, Mildred began to take the bright gown off her, wondering at her uncomfortable blush.

"Child, I have seen ye in yer all together since ye were out of swaddling. Why be ye so timid now?" she chided, but one look at her charge's creamy skin yielded her answer, for it was still blotched and bruised from the pirate's angry possession of her and there was no mistaking the origin of the marks.

"I am not ashamed, Mildred," Merrit said faintly, her face flushed an agonized crimson.

Mildred's response was not the expected shocked rebuff but quiet understanding. "Then hold up yer head, girl. Did ye think me naïve enough to believe ye'd hold yerself from him?" But the harshness of the marks made her frown at the suggestion of rough treatment. "Was he good to ye, Merrit?"

The younger woman's features softened, her dark eyes glowing cloudy once more. "He loved me, Mildred."

"How could he not. And yet he let ye go?"

"Not by choice," she answered quietly. "I wanted to do what was right, but now I am not so sure."

Mildred shepherded her into the hot tub and began to soap her luxurious hair, feeling the tension slowly ease from her. With a voice that was filled with fond admiration, she said, "How proud yer father and mother would be of the woman ye've become, as I am proud. Ye've a great heart, me lamb."

"What good be a heart if it be broken and lies cold and untouched?"

The older woman smiled gently at the girl's misery. "He'll not prove to be the only man to stir yer heart, Merrit. That's not how life was intended to be. Give yer betrothed a fair trial. Ye've too much love to give to be so stingy with it. Do ye think your fair-faced pirate will pine away in the cloisters for ye?"

Merrit was silent for a second, eyes closing as she heard his words echo warmly in her heart. "Perhaps he will, Mildred."

Mildred gave a sensible snort of disbelief. "Ye be dreaming, miss, but hold to it if it makes ye happy. Just don't be making that pretty green-eyed devil into a saintly angel worthy of yer lifelong desire. Think of him as he was, a fine passing fancy, no more."

263

But he was more, Merrit argued to herself. So much, much more. To please Mildred, she keep that assurance to herself and pretended to accept her counsel. With a resigned sigh, she stepped from the tub to dress once more in stylish fashion, to be powdered and pampered with fine silks while she thought yearningly of sand between bare toes and the tangle of loose-flowing hair.

With an impish grin, Merrit asked suddenly, "How did Captain Neville take our departure?"

Mildred laughed heartily and related how the red-faced captain had stormed the deck, threatening to flog every crewman for allowing his prize to escape. However, Mildred had been able to convince him that Merrit had been taken as an unwilling hostage. The forbidding weather had delayed pursuit of the smaller craft, and by morning, Neville had had to accept a very bitter loss. There was no possibility of negotiating Nassau harbor without the Angel's protective shield, so he fervently expressed his hopes that the conniving pirate had drowned.

Merrit shivered at how close his prediction had come to being true, then gave Mildred a sketchy version of their difficult voyage and the following days, leaving gaps large enough to fall through, but wisely the older woman did not press for details. The girl's wistful eyes told her more than she wanted to know about that interval. She only prayed that Winston Whitelaw would prove man enough to erase the memory of the bold pirate.

The meeting with Sophia Whitelaw came at an unprecedented hour, before breakfast was served in the austere drawing room. Surprisingly, the sharp-faced woman didn't seem an imposing threat as she had on earlier occasions, and Merrit was able to meet her without hesitation.

"Lady Whitelaw, I present you with my dowry, complete and as agreed." She failed to mention the single pearl that was set in a pirate's ear. Let her count them if she was of a mind. "I have met my end of the contract and I hold you to yours."

Sophia's pale eyes narrowed at the young woman's commanding tone, such boldness from such a slight girl was disconcerting. She took the bulging pouch and examined its contents, an involuntary smile of greed coming to her lips, then looked up once more.

"Word has spread that you were abducted from Captain Neville's ship. Is that true?"

Merrit didn't hesitate, but held the other woman's eyes steadily. "No. I arranged for the pirate's escape. Neville tricked me and was not going to see to his end of our bargain. I promised Captain Angel his freedom for the return of my dowry, and I kept my word as did he. The proof of that is in your hands. Now, do you plan to keep yours or do I return to England on the first ship? I would have your answer without further delay."

Sophia stared at her gaugingly. True, the dark stigma of being a pirate's captive still shadowed her, but on the positive side, the girl had great courage and initiative. She had also proven herself a confidante of Governor Spotswood. If the story was handled properly, Merrit Ellison could be made to look the heroine and that could not help but promote her son's ambitions.

"Winston returns at the week's end. When he does, the banns will be posted and a date set for your marriage."

Merrit nodded, yet felt oddly empty of any sense of satisfaction. It was done, her future was sealed and set.

News of Merrit's return and impending betrothal spread through the household, and by noontime was fueling the talk in Williamsburg kitchens and taprooms. Her circumstances made for colorful speculation, and no one was without an opinion. Sophia Whitelaw's carefully planted

265

facts did much to put the petite, fragile lady on a pedestal, to make her the object of admiration and envy. As a result Merrit was immediately deluged with cards of invitation to teas and to the nightly balls which heralded the Publik Times, the annual spring gathering of lawmakers and judges that swelled the town of Williamsburg from a prosperous eighteen hundred inhabitants to a cramped four to five thousand people. Sophia and Gabrielle basked in the young woman's popularity, for they were automatically included in the social courtship of the new figure about town, while Letitia giggled and accused them, unkindly to Merrit's ear, of riding on her coat tails.

Merrit cordially declined invitations for the first week, citing fatigue and the absence of her fiancé. Though Gabrielle was miffed, Sophia could only applaud her judgment. The girl had uncommon sense for one so young and the makings of a fine politician's wife. She was busy plotting out Merrit's engagements with wealthy local planters and strategic dinners with prominent figures in government. There were new gowns to be ordered, and an extravagant ball to be planned to announce the engagement. With all the arrangements to be made, it was easy to forget Merrit was even in the house.

Though she'd been thrust into the social limelight, and her position in the Whitelaw house was now well established, Merrit had never felt more alone in her life. Fittings for new gowns, meetings with friends of the Whitelaws, and interactions within the Whitelaw family filled her hours with painless distraction, but her nights were long and sleepless in the empty bed. The calm river drew her at twilight. She would walk down to the end of the dock to look toward the sea until Mildred or Letitia came down after her, to find her dry-eyed but torn by loneliness and heartache. She had given up seeking sleep until the predawn hours, and spent her evenings in restless pacing or curled on the window seat as she stared out into the emptiness of the night, lost in

dreams of a green-eyed lover. If she had known the separation would be such anguish to bear, would she have chosen a
different course? Even now she could have been awaiting
him in the small room over the tavern, still alone but
knowing that he would be returning to her. Here there was
no such hope, no sweet reunion to look forward to, only
endless, meaningless hours. Her sole possibility of rescue
was the impending arrival of Winston Whitelaw. Perhaps
her future husband could shock her from this brooding
melancholy that served no purpose but to strengthen the
ache of her loss and the bittersweet memories of love.

Mildred was at a loss as to how to deal with her charge's
despondency. The closeness that had bound them together
since Merrit's childhood had thinned and frayed into an
alienated mood of courtesy. Merrit shared none of her
feelings or thoughts with the older woman as had once been
her habit, but kept to herself. So Mildred quietly saw to her
needs as she watched Merrit closet herself in misery, longing
for her impossible dream. She cursed the flamboyant pirate
daily for taking her child's vibrant soul with him when he
had sailed, and leaving her this hollow, emotionless shell.
Even in his absence, Merrit chose him above her, leaving
Mildred slighted and grieving.

A ruckus in the household woke Merrit early one morning, stirring her from her lethargy. Peeking curiously out her
window at the grand coach below, she saw a footman open
its door and a tall, slender man emerge. He was resplendent
in a fine peruke wig under a three-cornered hat of dark
beaver. His coat, stylishly cut with stiffened fan-shaped
pleats, opened to revel a heavily embroidered waistcoat and
close-cut breeches. He took a casual pinch of snuff, then
fluttered a frilly handkerchief with an expert flourish. As if
he felt her stare, his head tilted back and his eyes went
straight to her window. She gave an embarrassed gasp and

drew back but not before recognizing his fine, haughty features, the cool blue eyes and jutting cheekbones, the wide thin lips and cleft chin. A masculine image of his mother, Winston Whitelaw had come home.

Merrit rose from her deep curtsy, giving her fiancé time to eye her boldly. Her tiny portrait had not done her justice. She was beautiful, her delicate features an intriguing combination of smooth youthfulness and sharp maturity. Heavily fringed dark eyes rose to his with a doelike timidity, but the allure of her soft mouth and full creamy bosom held his glance. Either the pirates had been blind, impotent old men or she was lying, for no sane man could stand near her and not want her. He would extract the truth from her before leading her to the altar. If he found her unpure, perhaps he would keep her as his mistress. After so long with the buccaneers, she would most likely be eager to yield to a worldly gentleman's touch.

"Good day, Master Whitelaw. 'Tis a pleasure to finally meet you."

"Indeed a pleasure, Lady Ellison. I, too, have been impatient at the wait, but had I known what I was missing, I would have fallen prey to madness." His was a deep, husky voice, oddly out of place in his lean frame.

Merrit gave him a cautious smile, assessing him carefully. So this was the man whom she would marry, be bound to for the rest of her days, lie with and love and bear children for. Yet he was a stranger to her and such intimate thoughts made her uneasy. Not that he was unpleasant to look upon or speak with, but she had somehow thought that when she met her betrothed, there would be some immediate, comforting rapport, a kindred warmth. There was nothing. He was a stranger with a familiar title. He was not going to provide her with relief from her tormenting desire for her pirate lover, but in time perhaps he could make the longing lessen. After all, he was going to be her husband.

He took her elbow in a large, warm hand and led her to her breakfast chair. They were alone at the table. After seating her, he took the chair opposite her, his eyes still scrutinizing her with interested candor.

"I trust you have recovered from your ordeal with the pirates," he began in a low, easy voice.

"Oh yes, though I fear the people in town never shall. They can talk of nothing else when I would as soon put it behind me."

"And the Spanish Angel made no attempt to harm you in any way?"

Merrit repressed her frown at his tone, so blunt and harsh. "In no way. That seems to surprise you. Why?"

Winston gave her a disarming smile to ease her defensive posture. "The blackguard seems to have some absurd vendetta against our family. He pillages our ships until we are lucky to get one in ten through to England. He has an uncanny ability to know when they will sail. I have yet to understand it. I am only surprised that he did not seek to use you in some twisted plot of vengeance."

Merrit was silent for a moment. Perhaps he had, by bedding her and snatching the love of his enemy's intended. That could prove a sweet revenge if the truth were known, but she and Mildred and the pirate crew alone knew that truth. "What does the Angel hold against you? What have you ever done to him?" she asked abruptly.

Winston gave her a shrewd look, noting her high color and bright eyes as if the subject had brought on a sudden flush of excitement. The subject or the man, he wondered wryly. "In truth, I have no idea. No one seems to know who he is or where he comes from, that is unless he said something to you."

Her delicate brow rose in a high arch. "Why would he tell me anything? I was his prisoner not his confidante." There was enough truth in her statement to convince him.

"Of course you were." The faint edge to his words gave Merrit pause. Did he rightfully suspect her of telling less than the truth? Sensing that he was quick minded and intelligent, she warned herself to keep careful check on her words lest she give him reason to doubt her. Winston Whitelaw was her future, the Spanish Angel her past. She would have to accept that fact and transfer her thoughts and affections from one to the other if she was to know any happiness.

They talked for some time of their families and of trivial matters before Merrit excused herself, pleading a trip to the dressmaker, and hurried upstairs to where Mildred anxiously waited with a lifted brow.

"Well, what do ye think?"

Merrit gave a long thoughtful sigh. "He seems pleasant enough, with a sharp wit. He's ambitious and no puppet to his mother, and he seems to favor me. I think all may work out for the best."

Mildred gave a quick prayer of thanks, then accepted Merrit's impulsive hug.

"Thank you, Mildred, for being such a friend to me. I know how difficult I've been this past week with my self-pity and moodiness. Forgive me. What is past is past. I need you to help me look to the future. Winston may not be the flashy pirate who appealed to my imagination, but he is real and will be mine. I must concentrate on that and nothing else. I want to be happy, Mildred. I am so tired of being lonely. I want Winston to want me for a wife, and I want to be a good wife to him. No more dreams. I must live in the present. Will you help me, dear Mildred?"

The older woman's solid arms tightened about Merrit, her eyes clouded with grateful tears. "Aye, me lamb." She had her sweet child back.

Winston met with his mother in the drawing room. After

exchanging a dutifully cool kiss, he sat opposite her and poured himself a generous brandy.

"What do you think of Lady Ellison?" Sophia asked, pleased when her son gave a slow smile.

"She is better than I had hoped, perhaps better than I could have chosen myself. She appears a quiet beauty, but I suspect there is much more beneath that docile surface and I will enjoy discovering what." His eyes grew crafty, his smile thin and speculative.

"I think she will be an asset to your career with her loveliness and poise. She has a gift of handling people, charming them with her innocent appearance and then gaining the advantage with her uncommon quickness. Her cleverness will be a boon to you if you control it quickly. Spotswood is a family friend and that can do no harm, and there is the attitude of the townspeople as well. They have made her into a heroine. Take advantage of their high opinion, my son, and begin looking to the governor's seat."

Winston's smile widened, his rich voice silky and low. "I've every intention of taking full advantage." He wet his lips, thinking of Merrit's luscious figure. A man could do much worse. "How soon can we announce the betrothal?"

Sophia gave her rare thin-lipped smile. She had done well in raising her son. He was the perfect prodigy, with none of his father's weaknesses. Behind his beguiling face and smooth charm, he was as cold and calculating as she, greed and ambition his driving force. He would take her to the governor's mansion, and through him, she would rule Virginia. Nothing would stand in the way of that carefully plotted course. But then, she made the mistake of underestimating the will of Merrit Ellison whom she never thought to consider.

On the ride to Williamsburg, Merrit was guiltily aware that she had ignored Gabrielle while cloaked in her self-indulgent misery. The girl was quiet and withdrawn, seemingly as alone and unhappy as she. With a sudden smile, she clasped the girl's slender hand, feeling her jump at the contact.

"Tell me, Gabi, when is your Captain Seward due to return?" she asked brightly, and was immediately rewarded by the flush of color that appeared on Gabrielle's wan cheeks.

"Oh soon, I hope. He is so busy it is hard to hold him to a date."

"Even a marriage date?" she prompted mischievously.

Gabrielle blushed and fairly trembled. "Marriage. How I long for it. I envy you the year that separates us. Mama will not hear of a betrothal until I am seventeen."

"Has the captain asked for your hand?"

"He's made his intentions quite clear," she said breathlessly. "He wants me for his wife. Me. How lucky I am. Merrit, have you ever been in love?"

Her dark eyes grew pained, but she forced her smile to remain steady. "No, I never have, but I hear it is glorious."

"I think I am quite in love with Captain Seward. I cannot wait for you to meet him. Perhaps the four of us can go off on some gay adventure. Mama is so strict about allowing me any time alone with a gentleman. Perhaps that will change now that you are here."

As the girl's blue eyes rose hopefully and trustingly, Merrit forgot her own troubles. "I will do my best to play Cupid for you and your captain."

"Oh, Merrit, hurry and fall in love with Win. You should be as happy as I am."

Gabrielle made it sound so easy. And maybe it was if only she could allow herself the freedom to feel again, to lower the barricade of remorse about her heart. It had been so sudden and sure with her captain, and so it might be with her fiancé if she gave him a chance.

Her opportunity came that night after an austere dinner.

272

Winston asked her to accompany him on a walk in the gardens. For a moment, she rebelled at sharing her twilight dreams with another, but then she smiled and accepted his arm. He guided her easily through the small but neatly planned beds of blossoming flowers, not speaking until he sat her down on one of the stone benches and faced her, boldly taking her hands in his.

"Lady Ellison, I know this is too soon to be proper and beg that you will not take offense, but I would very much like you to be my wife."

Merrit was silent, her eyes huge and dark in a suddenly pale face that betrayed no reaction. Taking her lack of protest as a sign of encouragement, he proceeded with more confidence.

"I know we are strangers to one another, but believe me when I tell you that you have quite captured my heart. I must have you, Merrit. Say you will marry me and make me the happiest of men."

Her reply was faint but without hesitation. "I will."

Winston's smile was quick and smug. "I will make you happy, Merrit, I promise you. Together we will sit in the governor's palace. With you by my side, all things are within reach."

Her face still white, she asked in a small voice, "Would you kiss me, Winston?"

Still smiling, he touched her cheek with his fingertips, feeling a heated rush as her eyes slid closed and her soft lips willingly parted. It was with difficulty that he held his mounting desire in check. Not wanting to frighten her, he touched her lips lightly with his own, not dreaming of her quick, eager response, the tender mouth that moved against his in hurried passion. She leaned forward until he felt the exhilarating brush of her breasts against his shirtfront. Hopefully, he seized her shoulders, bringing her closer, only to have her stiffen in modest alarm and struggle to pull away. He released her gradually so his surrender of her would not look like an apology. Looking down on her flushed features, eyes half-closed and lips moist, he felt a chill of anticipation. He wouldn't have to wait for the marriage bed. He recognized sensuality in this woman. Merrit Ellison was a ripe, tempting little miss, and her instinctive reaction to his kiss told him he would have no fear of a frigid bed. Just as she had begun to succumb to the rise of passion she had pulled away, not out of coy shyness but from confusion, as if fearful of her own response, a response Winston was eager to rekindle. Soon.

On her solitary bed, Merrit tossed restlessly, her mind a turmoil of anguish. She had her answer. The kiss had told her all. At the first touch of his lips, she had felt a burst of want and need flood her senses. For an instant, she had been in the familiar heaven of warm, titillating sensation, then he had touched her and those bold unfamiliar hands had shattered the spell in which Winston Whitelaw had become her Spanish lover. Once she had separated the two men in her mind, her desirous need had been replaced by cold rejection. It was not her fiancé's touch she longed for, not the feel of his too-narrow lips she wished to yield to. She was not just mildly disconcerted, but was violently denying what she saw as a violation of her body and emotions.

Words came back to haunt her, spoken in a husky timbre. *No one will ever make you feel as I do.* How right he had been and how well he had known her. Able to read her slightest shift of emotion, he had controlled her will with a mere glance, her desires with the brush of his hand. What foolishness it was to think another could replace him in her heart when he was everything she wanted in a lover, a companion, a man. Yet she had pushed him away from her. If she could turn back time, she would step back onto the ship to sail with him into the mist. But she couldn't. He was gone and Winston Whitelaw was to be her husband. Those were the facts she had to live with.

"Oh, Colley, you warned me. Why couldn't I have listened?" she whispered into the darkness, rolling onto her stomach to hug her fat down pillow as if it could miraculously assume his firm familiar shape. "Where are you, my love? Do you think of me at all? Come back to me. I made a mistake. I need you."

If she had known how close he was at that moment, she never would have succumbed to an exhausted sleep.

For a moment, she was sure she yet dreamed. Her hand searched beside her to find only empty darkness. It had been so achingly real her pulse still throbbed with a steady racing beat, leaving her trembling with frustration in the heat of the almost tropical night. Flinging herself from her lonely bed of torture, Merrit began to pace the confines of her room, rubbing her temples in an effort to free herself of that continuous echoing rhythm, the heartbeat of the night, of her passion—the sound of New Providence. She stopped suddenly, remaining deathly still. She listened, for the sound was not from within her but carried on the humid Virginia night. A name low on her tremulous lips, she rushed to the window, throwing the sashes wide and leaning out as far as she could. In the still of the evening the rumble of pirate drums rolled like quiet thunder.

"What be that infernal noise?" Mildred asked irritably from her side. When Merrit looked to her, the older woman caught her breath, fearing the girl had been possessed by some demon for she was quivering visibly and her eyes, hot and bright, dominated her pale face as her parted lips curved into a rapturous smile.

"It's Colley," Merrit breathed in excited anticipation. "He's come for me."

Damn ye, pirate, Mildred thought fiercely, can't ye leave her in peace? Aloud, she said, "Come away from the window, pet, before you catch a chill." She draped a shawl about the younger woman's trembling shoulders, but Merrit would not be moved, her blazing eyes intent on the darkness. Mildred's voice sharpened, in it a note of dismay, "Stay away from him, me lamb. Find yer happiness here where ye should be."

Merrit's glance was brief and scornful. "I've no happiness here. It lies wherever he is."

"Ye mean ye do," was the tart reply.

"Think what you like."

"Merrit do not throw aside yer future for a tussle with yon pretty pirate. Think of what ye be doing. Ye've been pledged by yer own word and by that of yer father. Would ye shame him with yer frivolous lusts?"

Merrit frowned at the desperate ploy, but she was drawn back to the night and to the echo of the drums that held a promise of passion. "Nothing matters but him," she said with quiet determination, her features becoming serene. "I was wrong to leave him. He is my life, Mildred. Can't you try to understand that?"

"Aye, I understand but what kind of life? As his harlot until he tires of ye? Is that what yer poor parents raised ye for, to tend the fickle passions of a thief and a criminal, to be used as his whore? Ye be trusted into my care, and I'll not let ye disgrace such good folks. Hate me if that be yer pleasure but ye'll not go to him."

"You cannot stop me," Merrit declared softly. "I do not seek to dishonor those that love me, but I know not what else to do. I have tried to be their sacrifice. Would you see me tied to an existence of lonely misery? That is what I have in this house."

Mildred put a comforting hand on her shoulder. "Ye've not given it a fair chance. Yon fair-faced pirate clouds yer senses with his dark lure. Pay it no heed. He'll bring ye misery for sure."

"I'd as soon be miserable with him than empty here. At

least I'd know I was alive. With Colley, I am alive."

Mildred sighed as she gazed at the girl's dreamy expression. She would do what she could to play on her conscience, but it was Merrit's choice. She could only hope the wisdom of her upbringing would steer her to the right course. She could talk in circles, but Merrit was right, she couldn't stop her. Only Merrit's own standards could do that, and they were bending like supple grasses before the pirate's enticement. Cursing him, Mildred hugged the shivering girl and prayed for the best.

# Chapter Twenty-two

"My lady, there is a messenger below asking to see you."

Merrit looked up at the maid in her dressing-table mirror, her dark eyes belying her outward calm. "I will be right down."

"Do not go, child," Mildred warned softly when they were alone. She was exhausted, having spent the long hours of the night trying to convince Merrit that duty outweighed desire without dissuading the girl from the dangerous path she'd selected.

"I go where I long to be," Merrit said evenly.

"Will ye be returning, me lamb?" Mildred asked in sudden fear.

"I do not know, Mildred. All depends on him. If he says go, I will go." She accepted the older woman's fierce hug with a fond smile. "Try to be happy for me."

"How can I be when yer throwing yer life away for the likes of him."

" 'Tis my life and I love him."

A fidgety Freddy Moffit stood in the foyer. Merrit almost didn't recognize him in his colorful livery, for he was clean shaven and freshly bathed. Propriety kept her from embracing him and squealing delightedly. Despite the early hours someone might be about.

"The captain sent me to bring ye to him," he said simply.

Merrit simply nodded and then followed him from the sleeping household to the shiny carriage that waited in the side yard. With a puzzled smile, she settled onto the cushioned seat, trying to hold her mounting anxiousness in check as Freddy guided the matched pair away from White-lawn toward all her dreams. Lost in her excitement, she paid no heed to their destination until the carriage pulled up at a neighboring plantation house. She looked up at the newly erected mansion. Its majestic size patterned after a country villa, the dwelling was set in a contrived imitation of a natural Italian campagna. She had often admired it in passing and its name had always given her pause, Twilight. Surprisingly, Freddy escorted her into its elegant interior. Her jittery emotions were momentarily stilled by her awed admiration of the house.

Constructed in the new rococo style that replaced stuffy pomp with elegant grace, its interior was scaled down to charm and invite rather than impress. Cavernous marble was replaced by wood, rich and warm and carved in flowing serpentine lines from which realistic leaves and tendrils stemmed to asymmetrically adorn a panel or curl over a frame. Even the furniture was made to look as though one piece grew from another, the decorative designs on each piece flowing unbroken over the joints, the bombé surfaces overlaid with oriental lacquer, carved leaves curving to form unobtrusive handles.

In the informal drawing room, the heroic Baroque mo-tifs — shields and gilded bronzes depicting heroics — were superseded by pipes and tabers carved or painted in pastels and warmed with light touches of gold. They gave the room an intimate and domestic air, yet also were reminiscent of a pastoral idyll. The scrolling S-shaped lines of the carved moldings were accented by the paintings that hung on the walls: a Hogarth, Gainsborough and a Watteau. The creamy opalescent tints of the Gainsborough struck Merrit , and when she turned from it, he stood in the open doorway. He had been admiring her beauty, thinking it surpassed any on the canvases surrounding her. Merrit's rich chestnut hair entwined with beads and partially covered by a close cap of lace, was drawn back from her lovely face. Her flowing gown of pale silk, as sensuous and feminine as the woman beneath it, rippled at her slightest movement, its light free lines revealing more than they concealed from his sweeping gaze. Seeing her rocked him, but he was able to keep his emotions under control until she turned and those dark, depthless eyes rose to his.

"Good morning, my lady," he murmured in a voice remarkably aloof considering the clamor of his desire.

"You sent for me, Captain?" Her tone was equally cool, making him cautious. Though they were separated by the width of the room, the heat between them was instantaneously sparked, flaring across that distance in an all-consuming rush. Slowly, he closed the doors behind him.

"It was not my plan to seek you out," he began quietly. "I had meant to stay away long enough to purge you from my soul, but I could not close my eyes without seeing your face, I could not listen to the wind without hearing your voice low and soft upon it, I could not lay upon my bed without wishing you were between it and myself. You plague me like some consumptive sickness until I can neither eat nor sleep. I am useless to my crew and to myself. Have pity on me, Merri, and let my weary heart find some relief in your arms."

Soundlessly, she came to him, hugging the hard familiar strength of him, so solid and good after her many empty dreams. For a time she was content just to hold him, breathing in the clean scent of sea and sun that clung to his crisp white linen shirt. Then in sudden urgency, she insisted, "Colley, kiss me."

Long tanned fingers curled about the delicate line of her jaw, tipping up her chin so their lips could meet, and Merrit was beset by a trembling so abrupt and fierce she clung to his shirtfront to steady the weakness in her knees. Oh Lord, she thought giddily, how could she ever have believed any other man could wreak such total havoc on her senses? His full sensual mouth possesed her with bold, unquestioning domination, demanding her passions be rendered up to him as if he were her master and lord. And indeed she was his to command.

She heard her name called once, low and crooning, then again questioningly. She forced down the strange shivery emotions she felt and opened her eyes. His face was close enough to feel the warm brush of his quick breath, and his incredible green eyes held hers until she felt she was sinking in them as in the sea.

"Do you love me still?" he asked quietly, waiting anxiously for an answer as she hurried to gather up her scattered wits to respond.

"Aye, my bonny pirate," she replied to calm the look of shadowed apprehension that had begun to cloud his expression. "You hold my heart as tightly and jealously as always. And you? I would know the same of you."

His generous mouth pulled into a pout as if he were insulted that she would need reassurance. "I gave you the pledge of my life and my love. Isn't it enough that you alone have heard that from me?"

" 'Tis enough," she assented with a soft smile, touched and amused by his awkward anger. She couldn't resist lightly chiding him. "For the vain, selfish Angel, you show a curious lack of confidence."

"Because you make me crazy, you temptress. Your girlish guile hides more woman than I have ever known. See what you do to me." He held her hand flat against his breast so she might feel the frantic racing of his heart.

But she was momentarily distracted, glancing about the rich room as if fearing discovery. "Colley, this house—"

"No questions. They can wait until later. I cannot. See what you do to me," he repeated, drawing her close so he pressed boldly against her silken skirts. His kiss was hot and breathless, searing her with a wild shock of pleasure.

Molded to him, she experienced the welcome fires of longing, her skin tingling in anticipation beneath the silken finery, impatient to be free of the barriers that kept her from the press of his warm flesh. His arms slipped about her waist, and holding her tightly, he lifted her feet from the floor and walked with her across the room, tipping her back until she felt the low, broad settee beneath her. As his weight carried her down onto its well-upholstered softness, his mouth left hers to trail along the ivory column of her throat. She arched up in response to the caress, her eyes flickering, then coming into sharp focus.

On the low lacquered table sat an exquisite music box, a fantasy work of spun gold filigree. She knew its cheery tune just a surely as she knew the inscription on the base which read "May this be the music in your heart. Happy birthday."

Her mind flooded with questions, Merrit sat up abruptly, sending the amorous pirate on a slippery slide to the floor. Ignoring his look of injured surprise, she lifted the small box. The inscription was there. The tinkling tune was the same.

"This is mine," she uttered, turning a curious eye to her lover as he picked himself up with prideful dignity to join her on the low couch.

"I know, love. I brought it for you. Now set it aside and thank me properly."

She evaded his determined kiss with an uncharitable laugh. "You expect a reward for returning that which you stole from me?"

"Aye," he said in a husky tone. "A sweet generous reward. I have all your things. I got them all back for you. Does that please you?"

She looked away from his heated eyes, the temptation of the flesh momentarily forgotten as she again studied the room, so elegant and inviting. She thought it curious that a pirate would be trying to make love to her in this surrounding without fearing discovery.

"What is this place? Whose house is it?" she demanded a second time.

A frown creased his handsome face, then a flicker of another emotion crossed it. Uneasiness, perhaps even fear. His arm curved about her trim waist drawing her to his chest, and his mouth possessed hers. She could not break away immediately; his lips were too sure, too persuasive.

"Colley, wait," she managed to protest, pushing her palms between them for leverage.

"Wait?" he gasped. "By God, Merri, I cannot wait. Yield to me now and I will tell you all after."

She dodged his eager mouth and, wriggling out of his embrace, placed more distance between them. "Tell me now."

His eyes were a smoldering jade, murky with hunger for her. He was breathing heavily, and his full lips, moist after leaving hers, began to thin in frustrated annoyance. "What game are you playing with me, Merri?" His tone was curt and she knew he would not long be kept at bay, but while she had the advantage, she would take it. He had taught her that. Once they had lain together, she would have no bargaining power and he might choose to tell her nothing.

"I would have you answer my questions now, then I will yield you all you seek. And more." She wet her lips in sultry promise bringing a low moan from him.

"Merri, please. Let me love you. You have my promise I will answer all you want to know." There was a strain to his words that puzzled her, but she would not relent.

"You want my trust when you give none? Trust me a little."

His eyes searched hers for a long, unhappy minute, then he rose with a quiet, "It is mine."

"What is?"

"This house, everything you see." He paused, seeing the look of doubt and amazement on her face.

"But how? You are—"

"A thief? A pirate? Aye, but a good one. A wealthy one. For years I have squandered a double share of fabulously rich prizes. The benefit of being the popular Spanish Angel is that I rarely pay my own way, others are always eager to do that. So I bought the land, had it planted, had this house built."

"Why? For what purpose?" She couldn't imagine him harboring dreams of retiring from the sea to become a Virginia planter. There was too much of the restless Angel in him. But the hard look that stole over his eyes bespoke another reason.

"Why to be a good neighbor of course," he said smoothly.

"To the Whitelaws," she murmured in sudden understanding. She looked up at him, at the profile cold as a marble bust. "Who are you? What do you call yourself? Surely you didn't have all this built in the guise of the notorious Angel? Who then, Colley?"

There could be no further evasion of her query. Trust her, he told himself glumly, turning to meet her dark eyes. He could face her anger but not her hurt, especially when he was the cause. Knowing he could well lose her, he spoke slowly, softly, and with great care.

"By my rightful name."

"What name? Who are you?"

"Colley to you and Rufe. To my crew and on the seas I am the Spanish Angel. On land and to the Whitelaws, I am Nicholas Seward."

"Captain Seward?" Her voice trembled incredulously. "Gabrielle's Captain Seward?" He made no move to confirm or deny the hoarsely asked question, looking away from the tormenting picture she made, her face ashen with shock and tears welling in her pain-filled eyes. He was unsure of what to say to ease her anguish. The only way he knew to comfort her was with the strength of his embrace, the tenderness of his kiss, and the sharing of his body; but she would be more likely to interpret such moves as seduction rather than compassion. So he stood silent, waiting for Merrit's numbed surprise to cede to her volatile temper.

There was a whisper of silk as Merrit came to her feet, drawing herself up rigidly before him, her damp eyes black with hurt. With a clenched fist, she smote him hard on the center of his chest, the gesture causing more hurt than the blow. Glaring up into his calm, guiltless visage, she felt a frightening rush of violence surge up, hot and bitter, demanding a harsh revenge. But this time she was able to control it. Stinging tears scalded down her cheeks as she forced out her accusations.

"How could you? Why didn't you tell me? My God, I've been bedding my future sister-in-law's fiancé. She's my best friend, she trusts me. I've listened to her pour out her heart over her handsome, gallant Captain Seward and all the while she was speaking of you, the bold villain I pined for all those long empty nights. How could you let me come to you and so betray that friendship?"

"Leave off, Merrit. You didn't even know the girl when we first lay together," he argued in his own defense.

"What be your excuse the second time and even now when you try to buy my favor with my own belongings?" Her words like a viciously wielded lance ran him through, though his features remained impassive.

"I didn't want to lose you," he replied in simple honesty. After a pause, he asked softly, "Have I, Merri?"

She wouldn't answer. "Do you want to laugh?" I even wished her a good and happy life with you. Oh, Colley — or should I say Captain Seward — you play these games of the heart so well when you can stand aloof and fear no danger to that cold dark lump that hangs so heavily in your chest."

He flushed, his eyes narrowing chillingly. "You are a harsh accuser, but you gave no thought to the promises you made to another."

"That is a different matter," she corrected frigidly, furious at his quick counter accusation. His defenses were instinctive and hard to penetrate. "I had never met Winston. It was a pact agreed upon by our parents. But you, you smoothly woo another with sweet promises and then take me without conscience to satisfy your lusts. Colley, she loves you, and you used me to betray her. I can never forgive you for that."

In quiet desperation he said, "She means nothing to me. You are everything."

"Rufe warned me you would crush all in your path without a thought. I didn't want to believe that included me. I wanted to think I was something special to you, that I mattered." Her fragile chin quivered as her anger gave way to anguish.

Seeing her barriers crumble, he breached them quickly, enfolding her in his arms, where she sagged limp and unprotesting. "You are special. You do matter. I love you, Merri. These plans were set in motion long before I looked into your lovely eyes. I never meant any hurt to come to you. I tried to keep you from it. I asked you not to come here."

She looked up at him, eyes bright and feverish. "Then take me away from here now. Someplace far away where there is no shadow of the Whitelaws. Give up whatever it is you plan if you want me, if you love me."

She felt his answer in the stiffening of his body, the swift spasm of denial that made him tense and withdraw without actually moving away. It took longer for that decision to register in his eyes. His love for her was not strong enough to overthrow the longstanding bitterness in his soul. His feeling for her was too new, too fragile.

Before he could speak, Merrit pushed away from him, choked with hurt and resentment. "I would like to return to Whilelawn," she said in a strained voice as she drew herself up proudly.

He hesitated, reluctant to let her go, wanting her with an insistent ache and wanting to bridge the gap that was widening between them. "What of the things I brought you?" he asked softly.

Her soft mouth pulled into a narrow line. "Your price for stolen goods is too high, Captain." With that, she whisked to the double doors, jerking them open to confront a surprised Rufe. Her laugh was as sharp as shattered glass.

"This is all too amusing. A nest of pirates under Williamsburg's nose. That is rich." Her dark eyes flashed to the motionless figure in the room. "Think what a sight you'd all make with your toes dancing on the breeze. Ridding the colonies of you could be quite the heroic deed for my future husband. It would guarantee him the governor's seat. Don't get too comfortable." With that warning, she swept out to the waiting coach.

Rufe looked after her with uneasy dismay. "Colley, she could see us all hanged."

"Rest easy, Rufe. For all her harsh words, she loves me still. She would not see me hurt. I can trust her more than she can me." He gave a restless sigh, still heady with the fresh scent and the soft feel of her. "She'll not keep me from that which I have coveted for so long. I'll have the bitch's daughter and her son's wife as well. My time has come to have that stranglehold on them and I will enjoy the tightening."

His bitter hatred was purifying. It eased the ache of losing Merrit and cleared his mind so everything was in sharp focus, all black and white with Merrit Ellison the only gray. Try as he would, he couldn't force her to one side or the other. He could not let his desire for her cloud his purpose. First, he must deal with the past, then perhaps there could be some hope of a future for him and the lady who held his heart captive.

Mildred gave an audible sigh of relief at the return of the pale-cheeked waif whose eyes were red and swollen, holding Merrit easily in a solid embrace while the unhappy young

287

woman's slender shoulders shook.

"All did not go well with the pirate?" she asked in quiet sympathy.

"I hate him. I hate him," Merrit vowed fervently, her pride and her faith cruelly abused. I'll make him sorry for his thoughtless games. He'll not hurt me so again. He gave me his life and I can have it taken wherever I please."

"You don't mean that child," Mildred soothed.

"I do. I do. He'll not treat me like a harlot to be bought with some trinkets and a pretty smile, asking for my love when all he does is lie and deceive."

"He cannot help what he is, pet," Mildred said, in a surprising defense of Colley. "He knows no better."

"But he does," Merrit protested, pulling back to look up in anguish. "He can be so different, so loving and kind, so eager to please and care for me. Why must he complicate things so?"

"There is no such thing as a simple man. What ye know of men and life can barely scratch the many-sided surfaces of both and our pirate has more facets then ye can count. Ye've much to learn before trying to chip away his sharp edges. A smooth polished piece takes time and care, but in the end is flawless and without a price."

Merrit's expression lightened with fragile hope. "And you think his edges could be rounded."

"If any one could turn the task, ye'd be the one, lass."

"Why, Mildred, you sound almost as if you approve," she teased with a sudden smile that brought a gruff look.

"Bah. Of that scurvy rogue? He may be peerless in face and form, but I'm betting ye'll soon grow weary of the task of taming him and look for a man less convoluted."

Her words sparked a challenge. Intended or no, Merrit took them as an invitation to change the pirate from a rough-edged rock to a smooth bright gem, a flawless emerald, irresistible. "We shall see who yields first."

But as the day progressed, the difficulty of her task began

to grow more weighty when Gabrielle bounded into her room aglow with the news of her handsome captain's return. Merrit schooled her features to receive the expected tidings with a look of pleased surprise. It crossed her mind that she might tell Gabrielle everything, including her part in the bold pirate's deception, but she could not deal out such hurt. Besides, there was the matter of protecting his anonymity. Should Nicholas Seward be found to be the Spanish Angel, she would not be able to save him from the gibbet, and losing him to Gabrielle was preferable to that.

"Nicholas—I mean Captain Seward—is joining us for a late supper," Gabrielle gushed excitedly. The flush of emotion brought an attractive color to her normally pale cheeks, and her light blue eyes were animated. What a pretty face hers is, Merrit thought with a twinge, wondering if Colley thought so as well. "I cannot wait for you to see him so you can tell that little snip Tisha that he far surpasses your pirate in looks."

Merrit blanched. As far as she knew, Letitia had never told anyone of the embrace she had witnessed at the dock.

"She imagines the Spanish Angel to be perfection in a male form but you can settle her on that," Gabrielle continued proudly. "Only you would know the truth of it."

"Your captain must cut quite the swath, for Captain Angel is very fair of face." Merrit mused on how this new guise of gentleman would suit him.

Gabrielle continued to chatter on until the hour grew late and she scurried off. Relieved to be alone, Merrit soaked in a leisurely tub hoping unsuccessfully to ease some of her nervousness. She pondered long over what to wear, finally settling on a silken sacque with treble Watteau pleats falling from the neckline to merge into the folds of the gown. The shimmering fabric draped fluidly over a panier that extended nearly eight feet in a wide flattened bell. Its soft dove color with a spicing of scarlet trim accented the healthy glow of her skin which had faded from that painful red of New

Providence to a blushed gold. Now her giddy anticipation served to increase the warm hue. Taking a long breath to strengthen her composure, which was shaken by alternate waves of guilty pleasure and anger, she started downstairs.

Winston stood at the foot of the steps, smiling up at her like a smug cat awaiting its prey. How strange that she should interpret his look as sinister when before it had seemed pleasantly charming. Was it the pirate's moody darkness that had made her wary of the Whitelaws? She was unable to refrain from shivering when he tucked her hand into his elbow. He smiled wider, thinking it a sign of her eagerness.

"Come, my dear. I'll introduce you to our guest."

Had it not been for the startling green eyes, she would have thought him a stranger. He was every inch the colonial gentleman. His elegant wear was splendidly adapted to his slight athletic build, disguising all vestiges of the swarthy Angel. The simply dressed powdered wig had a short front and side wings, its back tresses being tied by a velvet ribbon at the nape of his neck. It hid his close cropped hair and softened the foreign cast of his complexion, changing him from blooded Spaniard to well-weathered Englishman. Careful attention and expense was evident in his choice of clothing. The dark three-vented coat was cut close to the firm line of his body, extra fullness added to each side so that it came almost to his knees. Its sleeves were widened from shoulder to wrist and turned back in opulent split cuffs; the buttons were fashioned from flawless malachite only a shade lighter than his eyes. Indeed, his embroidered waistcoat was almost as long as the generous coat, its design of running vines reminding her of the graceful lines in the rich wood of his home. His shirt was of the finest Holland linen, its frill of lace evident under a pleated stock. Fine roll-up stockings were drawn over loose knee breeches and fastened by a garter of ribbon, and he wore glossed buckled shoes.

Merrit's eyes swept him from head to toe in amazement.

As they rose, they met his bright emerald gaze which was aglitter with amusement.

"Lady Ellison, a pleasure to meet you after having heard of your daring exploits."

"Captain Seward, I, too, have listened long to praises of you."

Their polite exchange contrasted with the snap of current that warmed them both as he cordially took up her hand to kiss it. She repressed a gasp as the outwardly correct gesture concealed the way his heated lips drew on her knuckles as his tongue traced quickly about them. His eyes lifted, bold and teasing. If he had not removed the pearl he'd worn at his ear, he would have looked very much the pirate despite his fine clothes. To Merrit's dismay his attention was quickly diverted as the Whitelaw women joined them.

Sophia was frigid winter in her icy silver satin gown, Letitia earthy fall, her plump figure swaddled in brown silk, and Gabrielle was freshest spring, airy and virginal in a blush of pink. Her enraptured gave froze as her perfect dream of a man turned toward her.

"My Lord," she exclaimed gracelessly, "what has happened to your face?"

Nicholas's hand rose to the nearly forgotten marks, her horror reminding him of the disfiguring scars that ruined his flawless image. Merrit may have been the only one to notice the brief tensing of his features before he smiled disarmingly.

"I had an unfortunate tangle with a bottle of brandy that must have traveled poorly and was disagreeable enough to burst as I was opening it," he said smoothly never once looking at Merrit.

Gabrielle continued to stare at him in mute revulsion until Merrit was tempted to pinch her sharply for her rudeness. Finally, the girl's manners returned and she accepted Nicholas's arm as he escorted her to dinner.

When guests were present, the dinnertime ritual of silence

was preempted. Like the others Merrit was captivated by Captain Seward's tales of his latest trade endeavors, though she knew all he said was a lie. He spoke with the same easy charm he exuded when fabricating tales for the pirates, his manner almost flirtatious. It was disturbing to watch him project sincerity while knowing it was as false as the clothes he wore and the heavy clipped English accent he used. She could almost be cajoled into believing he was piloting his ship along the Continent while she had been with him in the Caribbean. Thaddeus's jolly laugh boomed often, and even Sophia was teased into relaxing her rigid manners to smile and occasionally chuckle at Nicholas's amusing antecdotes. Only Winston remained withdrawn and impervious to Seward's appealing charm. He regarded the other man narrowly, watching and waiting until he saw the green eyes meet those of the woman at his side. The look they gave Merrit was charged with a flash of instantaneous desire that came and went as quickly a sizzling bolt of lightning. Winston saw the teacup tremble briefly in Merrit's hand, then Seward's gaze shifted and she brought it smoothly to her lips.

Merrit was in a quandary. Feeling a part of some elaborate charade, she sat next to her fiancé and across from Nicholas Seward's betrothed, hungering for Nicholas with a need so strong she nearly writhed in her seat. She watched his lips as he spoke and laughed, thinking of their delicious warmth against her own, and she followed the movement of his well-manicured hands as he gestured to punctuate his storytelling, remembering the feel of them upon her skin. He seemed oblivious to her in his courting of the Whilelaws until his eyes caught hers with in a glance so intense it nearly shattered her poise. Thankfully the meal soon ended and the men retired to the drawing room for brandy and a smoke while the women were shepherded into the parlor, where Gabrielle sank into one of the champagne-colored chairs.

"Oh, his face is horribly ruined," she nearly sobbed. "I can hardly bear to look at him."

Her voice sharp with annoyance, Merrit chided, "You'd think you laid more claim to the looks than the man."

Gabrielle sniffed. "Of course I don't. 'Twas just a shock. He was so handsome before."

"He still is, a true rival for the fair Angel."

The younger girl flushed with a possessive pride but was still doubtful. "You don't think the horrid marks make him ugly?"

Merrit's hands clenched in the folds of her gown. Ugly? The little fool. Didn't she know what she had? In a gentle voice that opposed her inner irritation, she replied, "On the contrary. They lend a mysterious rakish quality, don't you agree?"

Gabrielle thought for a moment then was quick to be swayed. "Now he is much more manly than the pretty Angel."

Merrit smiled tolerantly, but Letitia gave a snort of disbelief. "You would not say that if you had ever seen him."

"And when pray tell did you ever see the Spanish Angel?" Gabrielle countered snidely.

"I — I haven't."

Merrit let out her breath. "Enough arguing? 'Tis impossible to compare things so unlike, a gentleman to a rogue."

"And which do you prefer, my lady?"

Merrit, wary of the question, turned to Sophia who had been listening wordlessly. " 'Twould depend on the man, madam," was her evasive answer.

# Chapter Twenty-three

The study was filled with the pleasant odor of tobacco and brandy, but the atmosphere was far from relaxed. Thaddeus had found a comfortable retreat in his favorite chair while the two younger men regarded each other cautiously, each knowing instinctively the other was a sham.

"What do you think of my fiancé, Nicholas? Wouldn't you say I am a lucky man to possess such a perfect piece?"

"Indeed lucky." Was there a sudden glitter in the bold green eyes or was it a trick of the lamplight? "And fortunate that she remained untouched and yet a virgin after such a lengthy stay with the pirates. I understand it is a rarity for them to pass up the sampling of so fair a lady, especially the Spanish Angel who has a way with women."

Winston flushed hotly, the words too closely echoing his own doubts. "Are you saying that the lady is lying?"

Dark brows rose in an innocent sweep. "Oh, I would not presume to slur her name. I do not know the lady, only what I hear."

That was no consolation. Winston frowned in irritation. How he despised the shallow, fair-faced Nicholas Seward. The man was an effeminate dandy who traded on his looks and simpering charm. He had no political leanings, no opinions of interest and he seemed to prefer the company of women to that of men. A weak loathsome individual. And yet there were brief instances when his vapid face took on a sudden sharpness, his placid eyes grew hard. It was in those moments that Winston felt a chill of suspicion and wondered if Captain Seward wasn't a man to be closely watched. He found himself curious about what lay beneath Seward's unruffled charm, and about what it would take to penetrate his smooth exterior.

"Perhaps you should not listen to such untrustworthy sources. If I did not believe her, I would not have asked her to marry me."

"Are you to be congratulated then?" The question was asked with a smile, but Winston felt the cutting edge to the words.

"She has said yes."

"You are indeed a lucky man. And when is the happy event?"

"As soon as it can be arranged. Can you blame me for an eagerness to assume my husbandly duties?"

Aware of Winston's purposeful stare, Nicholas kept his features relaxed in an easy smile though a snarl of fury was clogging his throat. The brandy tipped dangerously in his glass as the muscles of his arm contracted. Had it not been a game of such high stakes, he would have tossed the contents into Whitelaw's smug face. Instead, his answer was silken and two-fold.

"No, I cannot blame you. A toast to you and the Lady Ellison. May your marriage be a fruitful one and your first child born full term."

Winston went white with rage as the handsome Captain Seward raised his glass to empty its contents, mocking eyes meeting his over its rim.

"Time to rejoin the ladies," Thaddeus announced with remarkable timing. Rising from his chair in a haze of drink, he walked between the two men never feeling the hostility between them.

His smile once again guileless and inoffensive, Nicholas

bowed, his eyes never leaving Winston's. "After you," he said smoothly.

His face mottled with fury, the tall blond man had no recourse but to comply, stiffly following his father from the room, his back growing rigid as he heard what sounded suspiciously like a chuckle disguised as a soft cough.

Merrit gave a start when cool fingers closed over her elbow; then she smiled hesitantly up at Winston. His color was unusually high and his pale eyes seemed to pierce hers, alarming her with their fierceness and the unspoken accusation in them. Her lowered gaze slid to the captain, but he was engaged with Gabrielle who clung to his arm and looked up at him with dewy eyes. As Merrit sulked in secret, he presented the calf-eyed girl with a gift. Excitedly, Gabrielle tore away the paper and gave a squeal of delight. Merrit's teeth snapped together with an audible click to grind in silent rage as Gabrielle held up a short string of pearls, then gave her fiancé an impulsive hug Sophia quickly put an end to.

As the matriarch assessed the gift with shrewd eyes, a gready smile touching her lips, Nicholas's glance met Merrit's, but his expression was unenlightening. Lips tight with anger, Merrit spun away to retreat to the cool shade of the open terrace. Damn him, the cur, the liar, the heartless thief. He had kept out part of her dowry to flaunt before her as a gift to another. She choked back her humiliation, but the hurt was a heavy ache in her chest. He was buying Gabrielle with her dowry meant for Winston.

"Are you all right, Merrit?"

She turned to Winston with a quickly composed smile, seeing the suspicion behind his concern. "I am sorry if I worried you. I was a bit warm, 'twas all. I am not used to your humid clime."

He seemed to accept that, for his eyes warmed with a

different purpose, lingering over her delicate features then plunging to the ripe bounty revealed by the low cut of her gown. She flushed with irritation at his bold appraisal, the flutter of her fan increasing.

"The pearls were exquisite, were they not?" he said, his eyes finally ceasing their lustful appraisal and returning to her face.

"Captain Seward appears to be very generous to your sister," she observed carefully.

"I can be as well."

She had time only to utter a small gasp as he drew her to him for an impassioned kiss. For a moment, she was slack-jawed with surprise and Winston took advantage of her pliancy to slip his tongue deeply into her mouth to taste its softness. That sudden intrusion freed her from her shock, and provoked a surge of cold rebellion. Yet he paid no heed to her sounds of protest, her struggles. The probing kiss went on until she feared she would swoon.

"Oh, I beg your pardon."

Winston released her with an abruptness that left her wobbly, and turned hotly to face Nicholas Seward whose handsome face was as bland as ever.

"I meant no interruption," he began smoothly with no hint of apology. "I did not realize you were not alone."

"What is it, Seward?" Whitelaw snapped, vexed nearly to violence at being pulled from the tempting exploration of his bride-to-be.

"I was going to ask if you were planning to run that gelding you are so proud of in Saturday's race. I have a horse I think will equal it."

Winston's thoughts turned from soft pleasures to the glitter of a challenge. "Are you proposing a wager, Nicholas?" His smile was cunning and greedy. His roan stallion was well known for its fleetness, and Winston lined his pockets from the bets of the foolish. His grin widened. It would give him great satisfaction to take the captain's coin.

"We can discuss the terms Saturday. Don't risk anything you cannot afford to lose." Green eyes slid to the still-shaken Merrit, then back. "I believe your mother was seeking you inside."

Winston paused, looking from Seward to Merrit, but neither seemed inclined to move. Reluctantly, he bowed to the pink-cheeked woman. "Later, my dear."

Repressing a shiver, Merrit silently watched him go, then looked to her rescuer who could well prove the more dangerous man.

His face still carefully devoid of expression, Nicholas lifted his hand to wipe the moisture of the kiss he had witnessed from her lips, and speaking in the oddly accented voice, he said noncommittally, "I did not mean to halt your pleasure."

"Did you not?" she argued sharply, angered that he would dare criticize her actions when his own were flagrantly cruel.

The crisp English tone dropped to a husky cadence. "Merri, they were not your pearls. I only kept the one you gave me. I never thought you would believe that until I saw your eyes. I am sorry for your distress. You must think little of me to believe I would so hurt you."

When he turned to leave her, she reached out to catch his wrist, saying softly, " 'Tis I who am sorry. 'Twas easier to think the worst."

He gave her a rueful smile, his hand twisting so that his finger twined about hers. "I fear I have done little to dissuade you from thinking that." His fingers began a distracting massage, and when she tried to pull away, his grip tightened almost painfully.

"Let me go. Someone might come," she protested, her eyes going to the door.

"I must see you, Merri."

"Later, but for now let go." Her hand squirmed in his grasp, but she could not free it. "Please."

"Tonight then. I will come to you."

"In this house?" she gasped apprehensively. "No."

"Do not worry. I have friends among the staff who will see you are not compromised. Say it is all right." He leaned forward, eyes searching hers persuasively, until his close proximity made her uncomfortably aware of him and of their position. "Say yes." His lips parted invitingly, about to dip down and claim hers.

But upon hearing footsteps, Merrit pushed him away. "All right. Yes."

He instantly released her hand and took several steps back to greet Gabrielle with an easy smile.

"Oh, Nicholas, here you are," she began wonderingly as her eyes as yet without suspicion, darted between the two of them.

"I came to speak to your brother, and promised to keep Lady Ellison company until he returned."

"That was kind of you, but you must call her Merrit for she'll soon be my sister," Gabrielle instructed, smiling fondly at Merrit.

"I did not want to appear too familiar, but Merrit it is."

Merrit returned his smile sourly. Then, eager to escape before her fiancé had time to make any further advances, she put a hand to her temple, exclaiming, "I seem to have developed a dreadful headache. I think I will retire. Would you make my excuses to Winston?"

"Of course," Gabrielle agreed in quick sympathy. "Get a good night's rest and you'll feel much better."

"I'm sure you will," the captain remarked mildly.

"Good night then." As Merrit turned away, the image of Gabrielle possessively holding his richly clad arm, cut her savagely as did the green eyes that followed her as if the clinging girl at his side did not exist.

Her troubled thoughts left her silent as she bathed and slipped into the wispy lawn nightdress Mildred had laid out for her. Pleading the same excuse, a headache, she had dismissed Mildred and now sat curled at the window, her bare feet drawn up childlike as she stared out into the silent evening. The hour was late, but she felt no weariness, her stomach tight with anxiety and excitement. When the door to her room opened softly and whispered closed, she remained unmoving for a moment, then slowly turned to see him standing in the mellow glow of the single lamp, seeing not the flashy Angel or the dapper Nicholas Seward but Colley, her lover. The faint light gleamed off the bronze of his face, playing on his high cheekbones, glittering in his eyes, and casting a sheen on his short dark hair. He was easily the most breathtaking sight she had ever seen.

"Good evening, Captain," she called in a low voice, straightening her shapely limbs to stand. The fragile gown floated about her slender form creating an alluring silhouette against the backdrop of the night.

"My lady," he replied in an oddly stilted voice, remaining by the door as if suddenly uncertain of this lovely wraith. Her haunting beauty paralyzed his senses, the stunning awe it evoked abruptly making him afraid to boldly take what he had known well and often before.

Puzzled by his awkwardness, Merrit crossed to her night table. "Some brandy, Captain? I smuggled it up for you."

"Thank you." He waited silently for her to pour two glasses, then took one from her and touched it to hers. "A toast to your upcoming nuptials. Whitelaw confided his eagerness to bed his new bride." He drank the contents of his glass in a quick swallow.

Merrit frowned. "What would you have me do? I had no way of knowing if I would ever see you again. You confided nothing to me. He was the only acceptable choice."

"What I offered you was not acceptable, of course." Colley's statement held the bite of bitterness, and a slow chill began to take over his eyes. "And now that you have seen me?"

"I don't know," she cried in hostile anger, his criticism rankling her for she didn't feel it her due. Sparked by the need to retaliate, she hissed, "At least I can trust Winston."

300

She heard his sharp intake of breath, then he replied searingly, "If your Winston be such a paragon, why are you sneaking behind his back to invite me to your room?"

"I did not invite you. You invited yourself," she clarified hotly, glaring up at him defensively.

For a long, silent moment they regarded each other narrowly, like wary combatants, then he asked curtly, "Is it your wish that I leave?"

She opened her mouth to say yes but heard herself saying no. She wanted him to stay. Desperately.

He gave a heavy sigh, the tension ebbing from him as he ran a hand through his close-cut hair. "It was not my intention to exchange such hurtful words with you," he said quietly.

"And what was your intention, Captain?"

"Lord, I've missed you, Merri," he proclaimed throatily, the gruff timbre of his voice giving her a tingle of expectation. "My memories and dreams were but a poor substitute, so let me look upon you now."

"You only mean to look?" she teased huskily.

His eyes grew heavy, darkening with sultry passion as he lifted one slender hand in both of his, to touch his lips to her knuckles, then turn her hand over to brush her palm with them and finally her wrist, feeling the hurried tempo of the blood he had stirred. Still holding her hand, he bent to lightly touch her lips with his in an infinitely gentle gesture, leaning back when he felt her response. Bewildered by the chaste kiss and by his withdrawal, Merrit's eyes opened questioningly to find him regarding her, strange quiet in his expression instead of the expected desire. Still not embracing her, he sough her lips once more to savor their softness in a brief caress. When he stopped, Merrit gave a murmur of protest, reaching for him only to have him grasp her hands, keeping the distance between their bodies. His light kiss came again, his mouth lifting only slightly from hers. She gave a fitful shiver as the tip of his tongue traced a lazy circle about the contours of her lips without seeking to penetrate their inner softness. This time, Merrit moaned aloud, parting her lips in welcome to have him coolly retreat. She tried to close the gap between them, but he used his grip on her forearms to hold her at bay. What kind of punishment was this, some crafty torture he had devised to torment her with tempting samples of the hearty fare she desired.

He raised one hand, grazing her cheek with a fingertip and then letting it glide with feather lightness down the column of her throat and over the gauzy front of her gown, provoking an excited quiver as the trail ran between her breasts to end maddeningly at her navel. Her flesh was all atingle, painfully sensitive and longing for the bolder touch he withheld.

"Colley, love me," she insisted hoarsely. When he didn't answer or respond, she cried softly, "What are you doing to me?"

"Nothing, my lady," he replied in a silken caress. "I would not want to spoil you for your fiancé with my unworthy touch."

So he hadn't gotten over his jealous pique. He meant her to suffer for it. And she was, grievously. She ached for his closeness and familiar warmth.

"Don't play with me like this, Colley," she pleaded, twisting in his relentless grasp.

"Be satisfied with the bed you chose to lie in, my lady. 'Twas not the one I offered you. You seemed pleased enough with his kisses. You are not a timid virgin. Go seek him out if you hunger for loving. He is most anxious to oblige you. He is your chosen, not I."

Her eyes narrowed as she growled in frustration, "Damn you, Nicholas Seward, or whoever you are. I didn't choose him. You know well you are my choice. He leaves me cold. You know I love you, want only you. Why are you doing this?"

302

"You are the one with the harsh condemning words, my lady. Would you refute them now and take me knowing what I am?" His green eyes held a challenge, daring her to prove herself, and his hands loosened slightly, allowing her to pull free.

"Yes," she sighed and was instantly molded to him full length, her mouth taking his with the aggressive force of pirates boarding a prize, refusing to be put off by his meager response. Her lips roved across his face, burning his closed eyes, searing his temples, nibbling down the short bridge of his nose, and kneading the fleshy part of his pierced ear. His reserve was shaken, and though she felt a sudden tremor run through him, it didn't crumble. Her fingers raced down the front of his linen shirt, then rose to push it from him, her hands eager to reacquaint themselves with the sinews of his arms, the taut cording of his neck and shoulders, the lean muscles of his chest. Her fervent lips burnt along the swell of his shoulder, then pressed hotly to his throat, feeling him swallow hard. His slow breaths had become quick and shaky, but still he stood motionless in stubborn denial of her tempting seduction, fighting the painful pressure in his loins that demanded precedence over his pride.

Merrit hugged him tightly about the neck, suddenly still. Her voice, warm and soft against his skin, was barely a whisper. "Please don't hate me, Colley. Don't torment me for being caught in a trap that was not of my making. Love me this night so I might have the strength to face tomorrow without you."

His large hand rose to rest atop her glossy head, his fingers twining in its rich, soft glory. He murmured something low and deep in fluid Spanish, the unfamiliar words heavy with feeling.

"What does that mean?" she asked quietly.

"It means 'Heart of my heart you will never be without me for I love you beyond all reason.' I will love you this night and every night, for I haven't the courage to face the

303

emptiness of a life without you. Never again turn from me as you did this morning. Do not trample so carelessly on my love when it is for you alone. What I do is not what I feel, Merri. Perhaps someday you will understand that, but until then, trust me if you are still able to, and know that I value you above all things."

"Even above your hatred for the Whitelaws?"

He frowned slightly at her shrewdly phrased question, then murmured simply, "I love you, Merri."

Before she could press him further, his mouth was on hers, moving slowly and fully, parting her lips to seek a deeper union, his tongue slipping in to stroke hers in a tantalizing caress that purged all doubts and questions from her mind. As she shivered, she felt him smile against her lips.

"If you be chilled, my love, let us light some fires." He held her tightly to him, drinking in the ecstasy of the feel of her. "Are you certain you wish to pass the night with a pirate when you could have a lord?"

"I have all that I want right here," she purred heavily.

Her night dress pooled about her feet in a wispy flutter and he lifted her out of its circle, carrying her to the waiting bed. There was a pause as he tugged off his boots and breeches, then the mattress dipped as he joined her upon it.

"The light," he muttered as she rose to kiss him.

"Do not fret, pirate, the only powder kegs are within me, and you have already lit the fuse. Join me and feel the heat."

He complied quickly, and often throughout the hours of the night, smothering her helpless sounds of passion with his kisses lest they be heard. No more words were spoken except those whispered low, their lips and hands and bodies communicating all that need be said, time and place losing all meaning until his reluctantly spoken words made her hug him to her in protest.

"I must go, Merri. 'Twould not do for me to be discovered here."

"Stay," she pleaded quietly, pillowing her head on his shoulder and stroking his chest convincingly. "Sleep the night beside me. I've not known peaceful rest since we've been apart. Please, Colley. I'll see you safely up and out before anyone rises. Please."

"You ask us both to risk much," he said hesitantly, then closed his eyes as her hand caressed the planes of his face. "But it is well worth it."

The decision made, he drew her close to his side, brushing a kiss against her temple.

"Sleep well, my love."

# Chapter Twenty-four

Balancing a tray on her hip, Mildred crossed the darkened room, an indulgent smile on her face.

"Up with ye, ye lazy child," she called, dropping her hand down to shake the single figure beneath the sheet. The tray rattled perilously as she leapt back. That hard-muscled flank did not belong to Merrit. Uttering a dark curse, she went to throw open the curtains and then stared fiercely into groggy green eyes that squinted in protest against the early morning light.

"What in heaven's name are ye doing here?" she demanded, chiding herself for being fooled by Merrit's cleverness.

"I was sleeping blissfully until you so rudely fondled my backside." He yawned hugely in the face of her towering rage, then wrinkled his nose in sudden interest. "If that be coffee you have there, would you be kind enough to pour me some."

Obligingly, Mildred lifted the silver pot and extended it over the center of the bed, repressing her smug satisfaction as he scrambled into a sitting position, his knees drawn up to protect the more vulnerable portions of his anatomy. They were eying each other warily when Merrit slipped into the room, addressing him as she quietly closed the door.

"Mildred must have slipped by me. I couldn't find her."

She turned and stood riveted, her eyes round in surprise, her mouth forming a small O.

"I found her or she found me," Nicholas said in good humor, arranging the sheet over his knees with a nonchalant air. "She was about to pour me some coffee. In a cup. Right, Mildred?"

"As you say, pirate," she retorted drily, passing him the filled mug, unable to contain the grudging smile provoked by the mischievous crinkle of his eyes.

Cautiously, Merrit skirted the older woman to sit atop the covers, modestly holding her robe together as if that prim gesture could rectify the fact that she had a man in her bed.

"Hurry with that, Colley," she urged, keeping a careful eye on Mildred's scowling features. "We must get you out of here."

Contrarily, he took a leisurely sip, then reclined against the headboard, casually placing an arm about Merrit's shoulders to draw her down to his chest for a long, thorough kiss.

"Thank you for last night, Merri," he murmured, his lips grazing her cheek as his eyes teased the outraged Mildred. "And you, Mildred, I've not yet thanked you for helping save me from the noose."

"I'll wring yer treacherous neck meself if ye compromise me pet. Get yerself out of that bed," she snapped.

The green eyes blinked once. "But I have nothing on," he protested mildly.

Mildred remained undaunted. "I'll not be leaving the two of ye alone so move, pirate. I've seen ye buck naked before so ye'll be doing me no great favor."

Brows raising, he said, "As you wish," and tossed back the sheet.

Merrit giggled naughtily as Mildred's eyes quickly rose heavenward and she spun on her heel. Catching her lover's face in her hands, she kissed him warmly with a whisper of, "Thank you as well. I love you."

307

As he pulled on his clothes, a curious expression crossed his face at the feel of a heavy weight in his pocket. "Oh, I'd nearly forgotten. I've a gift for you, Merri."

She gazed at the long slender box with a jaundiced eye. "Not pearls, I trust."

He laughed softly. "Never pearls."

She opened the box, her gasp of awe bringing Mildred around to see an exquisite necklace and eardrops fashioned of dazzling emeralds, the three pieces set in a fine web of gold. She held them against her palm, where they glittered, flashing highlights the same color of his eyes.

"Never wear them in London," he warned, then chuckled at her frown. "In all honesty, I bought them for you, though do not tell anyone. Pirates are not supposed to pay for what they can steal. I didn't think you would be pleased with something stolen."

Mildred said curtly, "Stolen jewels, stolen money, wherein lies the difference?"

"In his heart, Mildred," Merrit said quietly. "Thank you, Colley."

He flushed with pleasure as she kissed his cheek and hugged him about the neck, the embarrassment of purchasing them legitimately lost in that warm embrace.

"I must go," he said, holding her back, his eyes searching hers intently. "Remember how much I love you." Turning, he seized Mildred's hand and, before she could manage a protest, pressed a hot kiss on it. "Good morning, ladies."

They waited anxiously for some time, but no cry of discovery sounded. Mildred turned to the dreamy-eyed girl with a rueful smile. "A bold, charming rogue, that one," she muttered, her hand still tingling from the touch of his lips.

Sighing contentedly, Merrit lay back on the bed, holding up the necklace so that the light winked on the stones. "Smooth flawless edges," she mused to herself. "Priceless."

Knowing she was not referring to the stones, Mildred frowned and prodded her sharply. "Up with ye, ye brazen chit. Ye cannot afford to whore away the night and sleep through the day."

"I wasn't whoring with him," she objected, hopping from the bed and crossing defiantly to her full-length mirror.

"What be ye calling it then?"

Hands resting lightly on her belly, Merrit said quietly, "I carry his child, Mildred. Does that make me his whore?"

For a moment, Mildred's mouth opened and closed soundlessly, then she said tartly, "No, that makes ye a fool. Are ye sure?"

"I've missed two flows so I am fairly certain." She turned to Mildred with large teary eyes. "You don't hate me, do you?"

"Land no, child," the woman clucked, all traces of harshness disappearing as she enfolded the shivering girl in her arms. "Have ye told yer pirate yet?"

Merrit's glossy head shook. "I don't know if I should. Oh, Mildred, what am I to do? I love him so and I love this new and growing child, but I cannot trap him if he doesn't want me. I know I'm being punished for my wickedess."

Mildred rocked her charge soothingly, but her mind raced ahead. "We must think of ye and the babe first, and of what's best for ye. Ye've been bedding the man like a woman full grown so now ye must act the part and take responsibility for the result. Yer in a mighty fix, miss, but I'll help ye and we'll make the best of it. Now dry yer eyes and drink some of this noxious brew while we decide what to do."

Merrit's slender arms tightened briefly, then she stood away, fondness overcoming her anguish. "My real wealth lies in your friendship, Mildred. I don't know what I'd do without you."

"Posh," Mildred said gruffly, her eyes clouding and then becoming serious. "Sit yerself down."

As Merrit sipped the strong coffee, she listened to the alternatives Mildred listed, her eyes on the rumpled bed and her thoughts half on the pleasures she had found there.

"If the seed was sown that first time ye spent with him, the babe will be here by Christmas. With yer small shape, 'twill not be long before ye can't hide the fact. If it weren't for the babe, what would ye be wanting?"

"Colley," was her quick unhesitating response. "I would leave here today to live with him wherever he was if he would have me."

Mildred frowned at her unwavering stare, but continued impartially. "Would he marry ye if ye told him of the babe?"

Merrit chewed her lip, forcing herself to detach her answer from emotion, gauging what she knew of the man. "I fear he would not. His plans do not include me as a wife bearing his child."

So much for the selfish pirate. "Then the most ye could hope for is to become his mistress if he would have ye heavy with child, to bear a nameless babe and hope he does not soon tire of ye both." She ignored the girl's angry glare at the blunt words. "Lamb, a wailing babe can ofttimes cool a man's ardor. If he casts ye out, ye'll be alone and penniless with a bastard child. Yer parents be good-hearted and would most likely take ye in, but what chance would ye have to become anything but a burden to them. If ye care not for yer own situation, ye must now think of the wee one."

"Colley loves me," she stated firmly, but her dark eyes would not meet the older woman's.

"If he be loving ye so much, why is it ye fear to tell him what he's done to ye?"

Merrit didn't answer, her grievous expression saying more than her words could. She didn't trust Colley. With his swings of mood, she couldn't be sure he wouldn't run from the responsibility she represented.

"If ye went to him and he took ye in, think of how ye'd raise the babe, the child of a pirate with no name. Ye couldn't bring it up in society, not with a papa fleeing the gallows. And when that noose catches him, what then? How will ye provide for the needs of the babe? Think of what ye want for yer child, Merrit. Is it the life its papa leads?"

"No," she moaned softly. "I want my baby to grow up a fine man or woman, to live in a proper home, to be safe and happy. I will not ruin this precious babe's future because of my own passions. Oh, Colley, forgive me." Her face dropped into her hands, but the time for tears was past.

The last thing Merrit was prepared for was looking into the face of Nicholas Seward over the breakfast table. Heart fluttering wildly, she took her seat, not objecting when Winston's hand lingered on her shoulder and then ran down her arm in a light caress. Her objection was to hard green eyes. They sought hers questioningly, but it was too soon, too painful, for her to meet them, so she concentrated on the man who would become the father of her child, finding a cheery exchange with him easier than bearing up to the smoldering looks sent her from across the table.

"Merrit, I ride into Williamsburg this morning to see to the posting of our banns. Would you care to ride in with me?" Winston was saying warmly, the promise and invitation in his eyes hard to miss.

Ignoring the narrow glare from Captain Seward, Merrit forced a smile. "I'd enjoy an outing. I've not much of an appetite this morning, so if you'll excuse me, I'll go ready myself."

Nicholas tried unsuccessfully to catch her eye, to read some meaning in her gaze; then he brooded silently in her absence. What game was she playing now, leading on the priggish Winston Whitelaw who was eager to get her alone and treating him as if he were the man he pretended to be, a stranger, the fiancé of her intended sister. A hang tugged at his sleeve a second time before, with a touch of annoyance, he acknowledged the girl at his side.

"Nicholas, you promised we would ride over to visit with the Copeland's this morning. You have not forgotten have

311

you?"

For a moment, looking into the insipid face of Gabrielle Whitelaw, he almost snapped out a curt refusal. Then he regained control of himself and took up her hand, pressing a light kiss to the back of it. Her fingers trembled in his, increasing his irritation.

"I had not forgotten, little love, but if you will forgive me, this time I must beg off. I've other pressing matters to see to this morning. I promise to make it up to you," he murmured silkily.

Winston was a charming escort on the ride to Williamsburg, chatting with an easy humor she would not have expected of him as he handled the carriage reins. Merrit found herself scrutinizing him, wondering how she would have viewed him had she not been abducted by the pirates. He was conventionally handsome, with fine features, a pleasing deep voice, and a rather dry wit. To compare him to the darkly fascinating Spanish Angel was unfair, but against all others he would do well. Had she come to him untouched in body and heart, he might easily have moved the innocent she had been. But she could not turn back to that unspoiled state, nor would she have forgone her interlude of passion for peace of mind now.

Winston Whitelaw, her fiancé. She could do worse. He was ambitious and intelligent, with an eye on his future and no questions as to how to obtain what he sought. Apparently, he felt she would be an asset to him. She was to become the wife of a prominent politician, to aid him in his career. And what was she bringing into the marriage? A heart filled with love for another and a womb filled with the child of that love. She was filled with guilt over that unfair bargain, but no matter what direction she took, someone would be hurt and she was determined it would not be her unborn child. She would do whatever was necessary to protect that blameless reminder of her one true love. If it meant denying that love, she would have to find the strength to do that.

"How would you like to live in the palace, Merrit?" Winston asked suddenly, gesturing to the estate Alexander Spotswood was having built, so dubbed by the taxpayers who resented the added levies that were paying for it. It was a stunning, gracious house constructed of brick, its steep roofline broken by a multitude of dormer windows, a cupola perched above the balustraded roof. Castellated walls enclosed the forecourt and the elegant gardens, the first of Georgian Style in the Americas. Crushed oyster-shell walks bordered with dwarfed boxwood ran throughout the formally designed flower beds, square and rectangular, and through the beginnings of a holly maze.

"It is overwhelming, but your home is quite suitable for me," she said simply, uneasy at the brightness lighting his pale eyes as they ran hungrily over the nearly completed estate.

Those avaricious eyes slid past the Raleigh Tavern to the capitol building, a half-smile touching his lips. "I mean to serve there, Merrit, and with your help, I can be there sooner than I had dreamed. You will help me, of course."

Like his mother, Winston made what should be a question an order, and that annoyed Merrit. Her response was a trifle cool. "In what way?"

"The Governor's Council is appointed by the King on the recommendation of the governor. Usually it is composed of elder members of our tidewater aristocracy, but perhaps Spotswood could be persuaded to let in some new, younger blood. It is widespread that you curled him about your fingers to obtain the release of the pirate." His smile was a scheming one as he coveted the turret-shaped wings of the capitol. Behind the medallioned windows of one wing sat the Burgesses, in the other wing the General Court met; the members of which were also on the Governor's Council.

Merrit repressed a frown. Was he only interested in her political connections? Perhaps she wasn't coming into this marriage without bargaining power after all. However, if he thought he could manipulate her so easily, he was due for a sharp setback but not now when so much hung in the balance. What would be the harm in promoting her husband to a lofty position that would bring respect to him and safe, comfortable surroundings for herself and her child? Not an unfair exchange. Why let her vague uneasiness about his overzealous ambition stand in the way? They would both be getting what they wanted.

The first of the banns was posted at the Bruton Parish Church, and after spending some time greeting Winston's acquaintances on the now crowded streets, they began the journey back to Whitelawn. Winston fell strangely silent as the carriage rolled smoothly down the well-traveled road, and the quiet gave Merrit time to let her mind wander ahead to the birth of her child. Yet unseen, it would one day become Lord or Lady Wexington. Her thoughts were broken when Winston guided the carriage into a copse of shade trees. When she turned to him questioningly, her slight form was roughly crushed against that of the eager Earl of Wexington whose lips snared her as a clever trap snares a hare. It was a moment before she could gather her wits to pull back from the hot, seeking mouth and protest.

"Winston, please," she gasped. "You mustn't."

His voice raw with passion, he answered, "But I must. I want you, Merrit, and it cannot wait until the marriage bed. Why spend a few weeks in impatient agony when we can enjoy each other now. I will have you."

Reading the truth in his bold statement, Merrit twisted from his embrace and foolhardily leaped from the high carriage, managing a solid landing. Gathering her voluminous skirts up to her trim knees, she fled in panic into the trees, realizing too late how much more danger she was in there when she heard him in pursuit. Her dainty slippers were not made to withstand such rigors and she soon fell, sprawling on the grassy carpet of green. Before she could regain her feet, he was upon her, straddling her midriff and rolling her onto her back to see her stare in alarm at his flushed, purposeful features.

"You lead me a merry chase, my sweet, but now I insist you yield to your captor," he panted, then smothered her reply with a wet consuming kiss.

Merrit gagged at the intrusion of his tongue, and struggled beneath his pinning weight. But there seemed no escape. Tears of fear and loathing streaked her cheeks as she felt his hand upon her rounded breast, pushing inside the confines of her bodice. His knee shoved up her skirts and petticoats until her thighs were bare and vulnerable to the determined quest of his hand, which prodded and pinched, seeking to separate her tightly clenched legs. The sudden invasion of her woman's flesh made her shriek in outraged helplessness, the sound barely escaping her lips before Winston clamped his other hand over her jaws.

His eyes as enflamed with urgency as his loins, Winston murmured fiercely, "Don't fight me so. After this first time, you will beg me to take you again."

Merrit's eyes rolled wildly. If she had her dagger, she would have sent him to as quick an end as the pirate Bob met. She continued her thrashing, then abruptly went rigid, her eyes growing huge and round in horror and dismay. Reluctantly, Winston followed her riveting gaze to where two men sat on horseback. With a growl, he rolled from her and stood to face the cold green eyes of Nicholas Seward and his hulking manservant, while on the ground behind him, Merrit, crimson with shame, struggled to shield her modesty.

"What the bloody hell do you mean intruding where you have no right to do so!" Whitelaw shouted. Twice now his intentions had been sabotaged by the foppish captain, and his rage was insurmountable.

"No right?" Nicholas repeated softly. By God, he'd kill the fool for daring to touch that which by his word and hers belonged to him. His hand went to the pistol he carried tucked in the band of his breeches against the curve of his spine, only to have it gripped in Rufe's paw and compressed until pain shocked sense back into him.

Teeth gritted behind a faint smile, he said, "My apologies for intruding yet again. We came across the empty carriage, and when we heard the lady's cry, we mistakenly thought it was one of distress."

Her gown now in a semblance of order, Merrit looked up at him, her eyes wide and pleading. "As you can see, Captain, your concern was unwarranted. I but twisted my ankle. I trust we can rely on your discretion in this matter."

He regarded her unblinkingly for a moment, in his eyes a distant chill. There was no mistaking the scene he and Rufe had come upon, the sight of Merrit's white legs bare and trembling as she writhed beneath Whitelaw's weight. But had she been willing? She was obviously shaken, but was that from fear of Whitelaw or dismay at being discovered in such an untimely fashion? As much as he wanted to believe her innocent, he couldn't banish the sight of those creamy thighs open to another's touch.

"Of course, Lady Ellison," he said smoothly. "Again, we beg your pardon and wish you a good day."

Seeing the accusation in his eyes, Merrit longed to rush to him, to assure him that she was a victim not a participant, but she could not betray either of them. Let him draw his own conclusions based on whatever trust he had in her. As she watched in stricken silence, he reined his horse about and returned to the road.

Alone with Winston once more, Merrit began walking purposefully to the carriage, her anger and embarrassment outweighing her intimidation. When he caught her arm, she spun to face him, glaring up at his towering height fearlessly.

"How dare you treat me like some dairy wench to be

316

chased and bedded in the woods. I am the lady who is to become your wife, not some casual whore. Pray do not forget that again. Take me back this instant and I will forget your knavish behavior. Perhaps in time I will even forgive it."

He stared at her narrowly for a moment, then his features took on the appropriate humility as he muttered, "I beg your pardon, my lady. I was overcome by sudden madness. You have my word it will not happen again." At least not while there was a chance they would be interrupted, he thought, still certain if he had been able to complete his plan, this degrading apology would not be necessary. Damn Nicholas Seward. He was the one who would not be forgiven or forgotten.

Over his mug of ale Rufe watched his captain battle to piece together the fragmented threads of his concentration. Colley's hands were unsteady, but his eyes were cold and calm. When he spoke, his voice was low and even, detached from inner upset.

"A shipment goes out tonight, fat and heavy in the water. If we leave by first light, we can catch her by midday and be back by midnight, much wealthier."

"The Whitelaws'?"

Nicholas Seward's expression tightened, his eyes taking on a bright, dangerous glitter. "The loss will hit them hard. It will be a crippling, perhaps fatal, blow. I will watch their lofty pedestal crumble. Its pillars were built at my expense, and I'll show them as much mercy as they showed me. They spit on me, and now I will grind them to the dust."

"And your lady?" Rufe asked softly.

Colley's eyes held an edge of uncertainty as they dropped to the murky ale. "I will do what I can to keep her from harm, but it is her choice to be where she is. Again he felt the anguish of nagging uncertainty. He tried to shut out the sight of Merritt in Whitelaw's arms, of her lying beneath him in their woodland tryst, but the memory was a constant provocation. It would be easier if he were totally convinced of her duplicity. He should have been, for it was his nature to be suspicious and mistrusting. But he was torn. Part of him instinctively, unwittingly, believed in her, in her pledge of devotion, in the willing surrender that had sealed her vow. For once in his life, he wanted to believe in something — someone — and he wanted that someone to be Merrit Ellison. But wanting did not always make things so, his cynicism insisted. Trust was for fools. Captain Fool? A frown creasing his brow, he drained his mug and called for another.

# Chapter Twenty-five

"What happened to ye, me lamb?" Mildred cried in alarm, seeing Merrit's rumpled, grass-stained gown and the cloud of rage that darkened the young woman's features.

"The proper Lord Whitelaw decided to take the liberty of sampling the charms of his bride-to-be in a woody thicket," she announced indignantly, stripping out of the irreparably damaged gown. "Pour me a bath. I feel quite soiled."

"That puppy. Was he successful in his black intentions?"

"No. There was a timely interruption by a certain pirate captain." Her dark eyes softened, then became edged with worry as she remembered Colley's accusing look. Would he, as usual, believe the worst?

Mildred pursed her lips. "I'm sure that sent yer bonny lover into a fine rage."

Merrit's face lit vengefully, and she felt very much like a distressed damsel rescued by her chosen knight. "I thought he was going to murder Winston on the spot." She almost wished he had. She envisioned Colley sweeping her up onto his noble steed and carrying her off. Then she sighed. This was no child's tale. Her knight wore tarnished armor and would leave her to the dragon's mercy. "I set the amorous Master Whitelaw back a step, but I will do well to keep out of his reach until after our vows are said. I do not care to suffer his rutting passions any sooner than I must."

Merrit sank wearily into the tub, her delicate brows furrowing anxiously. "Oh, Mildred, what am I to do? His touch leaves me so revolted I want to retch, yet I fear he will be most insistent and enthusiastic in his marriage rights. I do not know if I can endure it after knowing such tenderness."

"It will get better, child. Many a man and woman are made to marry while yet awkward strangers. It takes time to learn to love one another, for the awkwardness to abate."

"I can never love him," Merrit vowed huskily. "There is only room in my heart for one, and that will not change with time."

Mildred was about to make some doubtful retort, but something in the intensity of the girl's tone halted her condescending words. With a frown, she said instead, "Then ye will learn to tolerate him and, perhaps, grow fond of him. Ye must surrender yer romantic notions, child, and accept what ye must."

Merrit's lips trembled briefly, a tear slipping from her tightly closed eyes. "But he hurt me, Mildred, and shamed me until I wanted to die. Not being a virgin does not ease the horror of rape, and that is what it would have been — will always be — with him."

Torn between her young mistress's plight and her own sensibilities, Mildred said somewhat shortly, "There be no rape between husband and wife. Ye will submit dutifully and without complaint, and I'll listen to no more of this whimpering from ye, my lady."

Merrit's shoulders stiffened and her soft voice became brittle. "I will do what I must, but I need not like it."

"Yer selfish wants are not to be considered here, and the sooner ye come to terms with that, the better. Yer part of the bargain, signed and sealed, and ye'll honor it the best ye can in spite of yer sullied condition."

Merrit continued her bath in brooding silence, not seeing

the damp eyes of the woman who stood at her back grieving over an unhappiness she could not change.

The chill of the late spring night prompted Merrit to seek out warmth, by burrowing into the covers and up against the solid heat beside her. For a moment, she basked in that familiar comfort, content and smiling softly, on the edge of slumber. Then her eyes snapped open with sudden shock, as she realized she was not alone in her bed. She rolled toward him, her mind set on a harsh objection, but his warning shush silenced her before he rid her mind of protest with a long, deep kiss. With a soft sound of acquiescence, she pressed close, her hand sliding over his smooth, muscular arm and shoulder so she could cup the back of his head and hold him to her as she feasted upon his lips.

When the kiss ended, Nicholas said quietly, "I sail at first light, and I could not go without seeing you."

Though his words made her tremble, her voice was low as she asked, "How long will you be gone?"

"Only a day, love, not long enough for you to miss me." His long fingers played over her fine features in an easy caress, feeling the lines of worry at the corners of her eyes and mouth. "You've no cause to fear for me, Merri," he whispered.

"I cannot help it," she replied faintly, laying her cheek against the firm expanse of his chest. Her fingers kneaded his neck and shoulders in unspoken agitation. "I've no guarantee you'll come back to me."

"Of course I will," he assured her warmly. "There's nowhere else I'd rather be. I am the Spanish Angel, remember, and the Angel always sails with Lady Luck." He felt her smile against him.

Her voice light and sarcastic, Merrit inquired, "Are you never without some woman clinging to you?"

His hand cupped her chin, lifting her head so he could

look upon her delicately boned features in the dim light. "But you are the one I choose to be with."

Merrit hesitated, pacified by his declaration but still bothered. "I would explain about that scene in the morning," she began timidly.

"Shh. No. You need say nothing," he insisted. "I trust you without explanation." And amazingly, he did.

"Thank you for that trust," she sighed, gratefully seeking his lips but troubled by his distracted tension.

"I heard you cry out, Merri," he said tightly. "Did the bastard hurt you? If he did, I swear I'll carve out his heart and make him choke on it."

Hearing the hatred in his tone, Merrit was given pause, then said softly, "I was surprised and overpowered 'tis all, not hurt. I have no fear of him trying any further liberties. As you said, my lord pirate, I am no timid virgin."

He squirmed at that response. "Do not feed me my words, Merri. They are far too bitter to swallow."

"And to hear as well," she admonished gently, as her hand lingeringly stroked the ridge of his spine to pause in surprise. "Why are you still half-dressed?"

He chuckled. "I was not sure how you would receive me, my fiery wench, and had no wish to be tossed naked from your window by you and your nanny."

"Consider yourself welcome," she told him with a soft laugh, then her tone deepened. "I am glad you are here with me."

"I would stay with you 'til daybreak if that be all right, my lady."

"Please stay," she whispered against the press of his mouth.


Merrit shivered in the folds of her thin wrapper, then snuggled gratefully into the curve of the Spanish Angel's arm as they stood together at the end of the dock, searching the cold shrouding mists for the *Merri Fortune*. She didn't

322

speak for fear her words would become pleas that he not sail and she had no right to hold him, no right save her love and his child growing within her. She wondered if knowing of it would hold him, not begrudgingly or bitterly but willingly. Looking up into the bright, anticipating eyes of the Angel, she thought not. He would not relinquish the rush of excitement for domestic tranquillity, a yoke that would become as tight about his restless neck as the noose. She would let him go without ties because he needed the freedom of the seas surely as he needed air and nourishment.

The rapierlike bowsprit of the pirate sloop pierced the heavy rising mists, gliding toward them through the silent haze, a haunting specter gliding up the river Styx, come to claim her lover. In sudden reluctance to render him up, she clung to him, her arms slipping beneath his open coat to encircle his bare midriff as she pressed hot kisses to his throat.

"Oh, Colley, my Angel, my love, promise you'll return to me. Promise," she demanded fiercely.

"On my love for you, my lady, and that is not a vow I make lightly." His hands trapped her face between them. "Do not fear, my lady. My eagerness to return to you will guarantee my safe return."

"Nonsense, pirate," she scoffed, a brave smile on her face. "You will forget me the moment you set foot on your other mistress, your *Merri Fortune.*"

"Jealous of some sails and wood and of my crew?" he teased, his green eyes intent on hers.

"Aye, of anything that takes you from me," she admitted gruffly, covering his warm hands with her own cold ones.

"I think I like that," he mused, then kissed her hard, bruising her lips and her heart.

"Colley, let's go," Rufe called from the landing craft.

She could feel a sudden hesitation on her lover's part as if he were pulled between her and the lure of treasure. "Wish me luck, my lady?" he asked softly, almost hopefully.

"No, but I will wish you a safe return," she countered.

"Good enough. I love you, Merri," he said simply. But he was already distracted, his mind on the ship that waited in the mists.

"Go, pirate," she urged huskily, "while I'll still let you." She stood away, freeing him of his ties to her, allowing him to become the Spanish Angel. "Go Colley, but a favor for me?"

"Your pleasure, my lady."

"Fire two rounds upon your return so I know you to be safe."

His smile was quick and dazzling. "I love you," he vowed. Then he crossed to the ladder and was consumed by the fog.

Chilled through by cold and worry, Merrit slipped into her room and drew up with a small cry of surprise to find Mildred standing arms akimbo and holding the pirate's forgotten shirt. Her chin lifted defiantly at the severity of the older woman's look, and crossing to take the shirt, she hugged it to her as if its owner were still inside. The two women walked back to Merrit's chamber in silence.

"Be there no end to yer shameful ways, miss?" Mildred began once they were safely behind closed doors, but Merrit cut her off quickly.

"Please dear friend, no scolding today. Colley sailed this morning, and if you are mean to me, my heart shall be quite broken."

Mildred paused in her tirade, and Merrit almost believed she saw concern in those sturdy features. "Off to do his thieving is he. How long will he be absent from yer bed?"

Merrit frowned at the searing tone and replied coolly, "He will be back tonight."

The older woman gave a heavy sigh. "Me lamb, cease this madness. Ye risk all by bringing him into this house to lust with him under the nose of yer intended. If ye have no conscience, then at least have a care. If the man finds ye cuckolding him, he'll likely slay ye both."

"I am bound to Winston only by word not law. Once we

324

are wed, I will be a true wife and give him no reason for shame.

Mildred snorted. "So say ye now. And what of yer pretty thief? Does he know his days of pleasant tussling beneath yer sheets be about over, or have ye let him believe ye'll still take him after ye've put on another man's name?"

"We haven't talked of it," Merrit said stiffly, clutching the shirt tightly to her as if it were a symbol of her unwillingness to give up even a part of Colley.

"Then ye'd best be talking. The man has a right to know what yer playing him for, using him as yer whore 'til ye be wed."

"Enough," Merrit snapped, her face darkened with a heated flush. "Leave me, Mildred. I want to hear no more of this."

The great head shook slowly from side to side. "I thought I had raised ye better, my lady."

Alone in the empty bed, Merrit buried her face in the folds of the shirt and trembled. Were Mildred's words true? Was she leading Colley on for her own selfish pleasure, too greedy to relinquish the physical rapture he brought her like some treasured gift? Was she wise enough to separate love from lust, or had they reversed themselves in her thinking? She had never thought of herself as the one doing the using, but had laid the blame on him. Was she, in fact, trading on his fragile emotions to fed her own insistent desires?

"No," she whispered. "It's not true. I love you, Colley. I do. I do." But she realized that the pretense could not continue. They had much to discuss upon his return . . . if he returned.

Merrit spent a restless day, her nerves so frayed by worry she snapped unkindly at Gabrielle for the girl's ceaseless praise of Nicholas Seward, unable to bear hearing more of the girl's fond dreams. Then, looking into the stricken girl's eyes, she was assailed by remorse. Gabrielle was not to blame for her own illicit love affair with her perfect captain.

"Oh, Gabi, forgive me and my sharp tongue," she pleaded in anguish. " 'Tis just that I am overwrought. What with plans for the engagement ball, the wedding, and all else, I fear my head is quite spinning."

Gabrielle gave her a quick smile. "Of course. I forgive you. I am only thankful that when I am in the same situation, I will have your wisdom and friendship to rely on."

Eyes abruptly teary, Merrit hugged her, almost choked by the ever-tightening web of guilty deceit. How could she abuse the poor girl's trust so cruelly? There had to be a way to end these lies, to spare Gabi needless hurt, but she didn't want to face it, knowing it would mean turning away from her love.

The Whitelaw's small evening party was an agony for Merrit. The time crept as she watched Gabrielle fidget anxiously over the lateness of her escort. With a wooden smile, she endured the idle chattering of the ladies and Winston's solicitous chivalry, yet inside her nerves were screaming, Where is he?

There was a distant rumble, its rolling echo followed by a second volley, and Merrit sank weakly into a chair, her fan fluttering like the wings of a frail bird.

"Oh, thank the Lord," she whispered reverently.

"Did you say something, Lady Merrit?" Sophia asked, observing the girl's high color and trembling hands.

"That it is overly warm," Merrit murmured quickly. "I think I need some refreshment."

Winston hovered over her at the buffet table, availing himself of every opportunity to touch her or brush against her until she wanted to slap him in annoyance. Covertly, her eyes stayed on the door, and she was silently counting the minutes. Finally, unable to bear any more of Winston's polite mauling, she excused herself, saying she needed to touch up her hair, and hurried from the room.

326

As she swept into the foyer, she came face to face with the faultlessly garbed Nicholas Seward. They regarded each other for a brief, timeless second, then he cordially took up her hand and raised it to his lips.

"Oh, Colley," she breathed hoarsely, fighting the impulse to cast herself in shaky relief upon his shirtfront.

"Lady Merrit, how nice to see you again," he said, his voice cool, warning in it.

"Captain Seward," she replied, taking his cue. "I fear your tardiness had Gabi in a fine tizzy. You should never keep a lady waiting."

"Sound advice, my lady. My love," he added in a faint whisper then moved past her without another look.

Merrit sank down in a broad circle of hoops on the bottom steps of the sweeping staircase. He was safe, but her distress was far from over.

"I see he's returned."

Merrit gave a start and swiveled to look up at Letitia who was crouched on the curve of the stairs in her nightdress. Her huddled figure obscured in shadow, she had good view of what happened below.

"Tisha, shouldn't you be in bed?" Merrit scolded, oddly uncomfortable under the girl's bright eyes.

"I was waiting for him as well."

"Who? Captain Seward?" she demanded, in no mood for childish games.

"Captain Angel," she said simply.

"Letitia you are speaking nonsense," Merrit snapped, face alarmingly pale.

"I wasn't sure at first until I heard you call him Colley like that morning on the dock."

Merrit scrambled up the steps in a jumble of whalebone and fabric. "Tisha, what are you suggesting?"

"That Captains Seward and Angel are one and the same."

Merrit gripped her shoulders in desperate hands. "Tisha, this is no game. Such knowledge could cost him his life."

The girl smiled easily and said, "You've no reason to fear I'll say anything. I find it all very romantic, you playing at being strangers while so much in love. Foolish Gabi contents herself with the shallow surface when the true man goes much deeper. You have that man, don't you, Merrit?"

She nodded vaguely seeing no need to lie when Letitia knew all. But if she had discovered the link, perhaps others could as well. It was becoming too dangerous. "Tisha, you must forget all this. 'Tis no romantic game but life, harsh and real."

"I am no simple child, Merrit. I know that," Letitia chided. "You've my promise that no one will hear of it from me. I only wish you would not surrender such a man to my silly sister who has no appreciation of what he is. You give up too easily, dear Merrit." With that, she scurried up the stairs to her room.

Distressed and uncertain, Merrit joined the gathering, feeling disassociated from their gaiety. Nicholas Seward was obviously its focal point. He was animatedly relating an amusing tale, and had the guests chuckling at his cleverness. Gabrielle hung on his arm, her eyes large and mooning, her irritation apparently gone. Merrit stood apart for some time observing them, the way his fingers absently caressed Gabi's arm as she leaned against the hard line of his hip. Then his eyes rose to meet hers fleetingly. Reading her discontent in the thinned line of her mouth, he casually disengaged himself from Gabrielle's possessive grasp on the pretext of getting a drink. He stopped at Merrit's side to pour himself a liberal brandy from the heavy sideboard.

"You look particularly aggrieved, my lady," he said softly. "Is something amiss?"

"I would speak to you alone," she murmured without looking at him.

"I will come to you—"

"No." Her sharp reply brought his eyes up to study her tense expression. "In the gardens after everyone has gone.

Await me there." Without giving him time to reply, she moved away, slipping her arm through her fiancé's and evoking a surprised smile from him.

Nicholas rolled his glass in his hands restlessly, his smooth features betraying none of his uneasiness. Her tone had awakened an alarm within him, but he could think of no reason for it. Their night together had been spectacular and intense, and their parting that morning touching. Her joy at seeing him was unquestionable, so why the sudden chilling retreat to Whitelaw's side? What had he done to pique her stormy temper this time? He had only to wait, bracing himself for the onslaught to come and wishing fervently he weren't so slow-witted when it came to the charged emotions of the Lady Ellison.

After the last of the guests had driven off and the Whitelaw family retired to their rooms, Merrit slipped out into the fresh night air to hurry through the fragrant spring garden which laced the breeze with the scents of jasmine, wisteria, and plum blossoms. Her eyes searched the shadows, and she gave an involuntary gasp as her wrist was snatched up and she was spun about and pressed flush against a lean form. His heated kiss caught her off guard. Her body's response being much quicker than her stunned mind's, she parted her lips for him and became supple clay in the hand that rested low on her back, urging her closer still, while the other roved warmly over silk-clad breasts. For a moment she resisted any idea of protest, savoring the deliciousness of his mouth, which tasted of brandy and more bitterly of ale. The faint odor of gunpowder clung to his skin, not quite overpowered by the dusky scent he had applied to disguise it. Finally, when her sensibilities prevailed, Merrit pushed away from him, flushed and breathless but determined.

"We need to talk," she insisted as his embrace tightened and drew her back to his chest with vise-like strength.

"I thought we were communicating quite well," he argued,

his lips once again lingering over hers with agonizing results.

"Colley, please don't. I have to talk to you and we'll get nowhere this way," she protested weakly.

"On the contrary, we'll get everywhere."

"Please." This time her appeal gave him pause, and loosening his grip he let her step back from the consuming heat of his taut body. "This cannot go on. I cannot allow it to happen."

"What, my love?" he asked innocently, his eyes warm and inviting.

Swallowing hard, she forced out, "I cannot—will not—meet with you again."

He smiled somewhat nervously, but his eyes were searching hers. "Merri, don't tease me like this. You are being very unkind."

" 'Tis no jest, Captain. I am very serious."

"I don't understand. What has happened? What have I done? What can I do? Merri, tell me."

"What we've been doing is wrong and it must stop. We are both pledged to another. Hasn't that given your conscience any trouble?"

Nicholas frowned and instinctively drew away from her to protect himself from hurt, hurriedly covering his emotions and barricading them behind a cool, green-glass stare. "I have no conscience, Merri. I love you. You claim to love me. I see no wrong in the expression of our love."

She sighed in exasperation, seeing the narrow scope of his feelings. "There is if it has to be hidden like something vile and disgusting."

"Is that it how you view our relationship, my lady?" His tone was deceivingly smooth.

"It's wrong and it will hurt us all, especially Gabrielle and Winston who are not at fault."

His frown deepened, and he became sullen and arrogant. "What do I care if they be hurt?"

"You are speaking of the woman who will be your wife."

"What has that to do with anything?" he insisted crisply.

"She loves you. Have you no feeling for her at all?"

"For that insipid little mouse? She bores me to distraction with her clinging devotion. I didn't ask her to love me, nor have I ever suggested to her that I love her. I am not responsible for her stupidity."

Merrit winced at his insensitivity, and she wondered how she could love such a cold, shallow man. "Yet you will marry her and trap her in a loveless snare."

"It will be a tender trap. I don't plan to abuse her. She will have everything she desires."

"You?"

His features congealed in an unpleasant expression of loathing. "No, never me."

"What of love and children?" she persisted to his growing annoyance.

"Let her get them where she can. I won't stand in her way. I don't expect her to be a brood mare. The thought of her milk-faced whining brats does not please me. Let someone else father them. Indeed, I care not if she goes to the grave a virgin. I've no desire to breach that arid ground."

"Do you plan to tell her how you pay for your fine home?" Merrit asked tartly. The woman in her was pleased by his profession, but she couldn't help but feel sympathy for Gabrielle and her hopeless dreams. "How will you explain a drawing room full of pirates or the ring you wear in your ear?"

He smiled mockingly at those questions. "Gabrielle is hardly a woman of great astuteness. She will see only what I tell her to and will be pleased with the pretty trinkets I bring her. She'll not question where I got them. She can be the mistress of my house but not me. Only you can be that, Merri."

The green eyes flared brightly as he pulled her to him, bringing a gasp of surprise from her as she met his hard chest. His kiss was equally hard and demanding, momentarily overwhelming her resistance. Feeling her slight response, his mouth softened to generous warmth, sapping her will with frightening ease.

Seeing the couple entwined in the garden, Gabrielle began to withdraw tactfully then paused, recognizing Merrit and realizing the man with her was too slight to be Winston. Scandalized but curious, she ducked into the shadows to spy upon the tryst, exhilarated by the passion of the pair. What secret love had Merrit been concealing all this time?

"Colley, no," Merrit protested faintly, twisting away to rest her head on his shoulder, weak from battling the insistent desire his touch stirred in her. "I will not yield to you on this."

"Merri, you are a stubborn wench and sometimes very foolish. You know you'll not resist me. You cannot any more than I can you. Save a little of your sympathy for me. I need your love as well. Would you deny me that?"

Gabrielle frowned. His voice was low and rich, enticingly foreign yet familiar. When he stepped back, she nearly shrieked, but clasped her hands over her mouth to seal in her cry of wounded trust, for it was her beloved captain in her brother's fiancé's arms. Too stunned to move, she stayed in the darkness and listened to softly spoken words not meant for the ears of others.

"Find it in your wife," Merrit snapped harshly, more stirred than she cared to admit by his plea. She had to get him back on the defensive for his husky passion was far too dangerous to her. "Why else would you marry her?"

His features grew cold, a magnificent portrait of ice. "I have my reasons, Merri. You had your chance and you threw my offer back at me like a slap."

"What did you offer me?" she sneered. "Surely not the name you would not tell me. I cannot live as your whore, Colley, on your half-truths."

"You seemed to enjoy it well enough last night and on

many nights before that," he countered frigidly, unaware of the tears those words brought to their unseen hearer. "Why the sudden protest? It is not as though I were trying to steal your maidenhead. You gave that willingly enough. Why condemn me when you made no attempt to bar me from your bed? You have a betrothed as well, yet you had me as your lover. You are not blameless, my lady."

"Please," Merrit cried, unable to withstand his bitter anger. "Just go and leave me in peace."

"If I go now, I'll not be back," he stated coldly, then hesitated knowing the corner he had backed himself into. "Merri, think on it. Please."

She looked at his extended hand, wanting to clasp it tightly, but she slapped it away along with the love and trust he held out to her. "No," she whispered. "Not this time."

"Merri?"

"Colley please be kind to her. She is an innocent."

"As you once were?" he said softly. "Good-bye, my lady. The decision was yours to make. It is too late for regrets." He bowed stiffly and strode from her, the swaggering Angel now alone with his fierce pride.

Merrit stood trembling, biting her lip to keep from calling him back. She had to let him go for the sake of the child they shared, for the unsuspecting victims of their lust, and for his own sake, for if she didn't release him now she wouldn't be satisfied until she had more and more of him. Woodenly, she returned to the house, passing within feet of the silently sobbing Gabrielle and then climbing the darkened stairs to her room.

"No companion on this fine night?" Mildred asked tartly.

"He won't be coming again."

Mildred stiffened at the faint, hoarse words. "Oh, Lord, he hasn't gone and gotten hisself killed has he?" she cried in genuine horror.

"No. What was between us has died," Merrit concluded stoically, and oddly there was no emotion left in her.

Mildred sighed in audible relief, then with a shake of her head, said, "Child, all the waters in the sea couldn't put out the fires in that man's eyes when he looks at ye."

"Perhaps, but his arrogant pride won't let him act on his feelings."

"Rest, pet. Sleep and let the fires cool. 'Tis best for now that ye be apart to think on what ye must do."

"I know what I must do and the knowledge gives me no rest."

She lay awake long into the night, restless on her lonely bed, wishing he were there if only to hold her and give her the peace she drew from his enveloping strength. But she would not have to bear a solitary bed long. Soon she would be sharing one with her new husband. Rolling into a tight ball of denial, Merrit shivered fitfully, for that thought was frightening. The idea of being intimate with Winston terrified her; the memory of his penetrating kiss and hurtful hands made her quake. Without love, the act of love held no appeal, but she knew as his wife she would have to submit to him. More importantly, if the child she carried were to bear his name the marriage would have to be soon. That was what she had to concentrate on, the best interest of the child that would become the center of her world.

In the great house, another lay awake, troubled. Merrit, she thought with disbelief, the only friend she had had, the only person who had ever taken the time to listen to her and share her thoughts was also sharing her man. Gabrielle's pale face darkened with hurt betrayal. Nicholas had been right. Hers was not a quick mind, but what she lacked in intelligence, she made up for in cunning. She couldn't understand how Merrit had managed to steal away her beau in the few days since his return but she was determined her brothers fiancé would not keep him. She would not relinquish the prestige of being on the arm of the most handsome man in the Colonies nor would she forfeit the extravagant gifts he brought her. Oddly enough, the concept of love never occurred to her, only that Merrit would not take him from her. She would be the wife of Nicholas Seward, but now she knew she could not afford to wait a year as her mother had demanded. The marriage must take place immediately. As her pale eyes slitted craftily, she became a younger image of her mother. There was a way. She would have his name and his fortune, not Merrit, her deceivingly sweet friend. Smiling coldly, Gabrielle closed her eyes.

# Chapter Twenty-six

Gabrielle demurely arranged the folds of her skirt on the blanket he had spread beneath the shady umbrella of tree. Nicholas had greeted her idea of this isolated picnic with his usual indulgent smile, little knowing the plan she had conceived, the carefully camouflaged trap her limpid blue eyes, innocently inviting, were luring him into.

"Sit by me, Nicholas," she purred, extending her slender white hand to draw him down next to her. His nearness made her heart race; and her mind was full of excited, naïve thoughts of what she was about to do. He had never really kissed her, not the way he had the deceitful Merrit. And she realized that he had never said that he loved her, but then he must if he'd asked her to marry him. He had always been a figure of awe to her, his beautiful face and aloof manner keeping her at a respectful distance, but that was about to change. Boldly, she put her hand on his arm and he made no move to withdraw. How muscular and firm he was, she thought with a nervous thrill.

Nicholas never felt her touch, for his thoughts were heavy and brooding. He'd been drinking with Rufe until dawn, and his head pulsed with a dull ache that echoed the pain in his chest. He had tried to ease his hurt with liquor, with anger, with cold denial; but still it seemed to grow. Merrit had encouraged him to awaken these strange, powerful feelings, but now, without her, they prowled restlessly over a spirit he couldn't calm or control. Silently, he cursed her for unleashing the fearsome demons of love and trust, feelings he had never wanted and now could not rid himself of. She had revealed their binding strength, then left him alone with them, to be lost in and consumed by their vastness.

He turned involuntarily as Gabrielle spoke his name, his thoughts scattering in surprise when her lips fastened eagerly over his. He remained motionless, stunned by the sudden passion in this vapid girl; then with a cold click, he froze at her touch. He almost had to wrestle her away, her strength and determination yet another surprise.

"Gabrielle, please," he protested with a smile. "You cannot expect a man to remain a gentleman under such temptations."

She pressed against his restraining hands, her slight bosom heaving and her face highly flushed. "I don't want you to be a gentleman. I want you to kiss me, to love me as a man does a woman."

Inwardly, he shuddered, but his words were gentle. "I cannot betray the trust your family has placed in me. As difficult as it may be, we must wait until we are wed."

Panting with newly realized desire and frustrated because her plan was not working, Gabrielle sat back, her calculating shrewdness taking control. If he would not love her, neither would he return to Merrit. She dropped her gaze to murmur primly, "You are gallant to wait, Nicholas, but you needn't. I wouldn't think any less of you or of myself. You know how much I admire Merrit, yet she went to lie with my brother last night and that was not the first time."

Gabrielle glanced up at his perfect face, seeing no change in his expression but hearing the harsh intake of his breath as if he were in sudden pain. Smiling slyly, she embellished her clever lie. "After hearing her tell of the pleasures she found in Win's arms, I am impatient for you to show me the same joys. Love me now and Mama will have no choice but

337

to let us marry to save my honor. Love me, Colley."

She saw him become rigid at her use of that name, his eyes growing so hard and brilliant that she felt a shiver of fear.

"Never call me that," he said in a low shaky voice.

"I am sorry, Nicholas," she stammered weakly. "I did not mean to displease you." Suddenly, he was a stranger and she was afraid of his response to her spiteful baiting. The threat of violence in him, his abrupt shift of mood, made her want to flee him in panic. But he seized her arms in a hurting grasp, crushing her to his unyielding chest, and her cry of fear was smothered by a savage kiss which turned it to a throaty moan of excitement.

Why not? he reasoned coldly. Take her now and be done with it. She would be his wife and his vengeance against those who had hurt him most deeply. He used his weight to press Gabrielle down upon the blanket. As he deepened his kiss and put a hand over one small breast, he felt her tremble in virginal eagerness. Independently of his mind, his body responded to the inviting wriggle of her slim hips as her impatient hands seized one of his and led it to the damp heat beneath her petticoats. She urged him on with breathless whispers, peppering his face with hot kisses.

Had she been still and silent, he would have taken her then, but the more insistent she became, the more he recoiled. Nothing was right, not her sweet cloying scent or her wet darting tongue, not the surprisingly bold hands that sought entrance into his clothing or the hard, bony hips that pressed against him. She wasn't Merrit. That realization was an icy shock to his system, an abrupt denial of desire. Sickened by what he had almost done, he pushed away from Gabrielle's grasping hands and lurched to his feet, unable to look upon the figure that lay waiting for him.

"My apologies, my lady," he said roughly. "I lost my senses. I'd best take you home now."

He would hear none of her protests, but bundled her into

the carriage, where she pouted and remained silent on the ride back to Whitelawn. As he lifted her down, she declared emotionally, "Nicholas, I love you."

He met her admission with an unflickering stare, his eyes flat and opaque. Finally, he raised her hand, never touching his mouth to it. "Good day, my lady" was all he would say.

The raised voices coming from the study made Merrit pause outside its closed doors, curious as to what would spur Winston to such a rage.

"Are you sure it was him?" he was shouting.

Another man answered, his voice unfamiliar. "It was the Angel, all right. I could tell by his accent and manner of dress."

"Did you get a close look at him?"

"He didn't board us himself."

"Damn the villain to hell. How does he know what ships to take? He sailed off merrily with a year's profits. We can never make that up. If not for the dowry, we'd be nearly penniless."

"Not quite." That was Sophia, her tone strident and upset. "A stop must be put to him. Offer a sizable reward for his capture. Those pirates are a greedy, disloyal lot. One among them should be willing to turn him in for a profit."

Merrit's knees trembled weakly for she thought of Durant and of those like him, but Winston's words were even more frightening.

"Not yet, Mother. I've been conceiving a plan. It will cost us nothing and will bring us his neck for the breaking. I'll have him dancing by the end of the month, caught in an irresistible trap."

Hearing someone enter the house, Merrit hurried away from the closed doors, schooling her unsettled features to reveal none of her anxiety. Gabrielle's appearance gave her pause, for the girl's face had a feverish cast, her eyes were wild and bright when they lit on Merrit.

"Good heavens, Gabi, what has happened?" she gasped in alarm, fearing the trembling girl was about to have a fit.

Gabrielle's pale eyes slitted and she gave a crazy laugh. "You want to know what's happened, my dear concerned friend? I'll tell you. Nicholas and I spent the morning making love to one another. That's right and he was magnificent. Shall I tell you about it, my dear friend, how he kissed me and undressed us both right out on the open ground, then loved me until I begged him to stop?"

Merrit's face went deathly pale, the image Gabrielle's gloating words conjured up in her tortured mind crushing the breath from her. She wanted to shriek liar at her, but the panting girl's swollen mouth and suspiciously rumpled clothing seemed to support her claim.

"He and I are lovers now," Gabrielle went on hysterically. "He'll never come back to you. He told me how easy you had been and how bored he became with you once there was no challenge. We laughed at you, Merrit — you fool, you whore, trying to steal my man. Well, you won't have him now. Not ever. I will see that he is never bored enough to seek you out again."

Merrit's head began to swim with a sudden dizziness and she reached out blindly to grasp the stair rail to steady herself. Yet through her growing haze, she knew something was not right about Gabrielle's story. Not certain if it was the girl's frenzy or her own innate trust in the man she loved that made her doubt it. "Tell me, Gabi, if you two were such intimate lovers, what did you think of his back?"

"His back?" the girl echoed blankly. Then she sneered. "A fine, nicely tanned back to match the rest of him."

Merrit stared at her long and hard. If she had been telling the truth, she would know about the scars Colley bore from that long-ago beating. Why would Gabrielle lie so vindictively except to taunt a rival? Stung by the girl's cruelty, Merrit hissed, "I don't believe you. He is not interested in

340

you, Gabrielle. You will have his name, but you will never, ever, have his love. That is mine. Do you hear me? You can be Mrs. Nicholas Seward, but I will be the one he loves."

Gabrielle's face lost its animation, becoming pasty and stricken. "Why couldn't you have stayed with the pirates? Why did you have to come here?" she cried pitifully. "Oh, how I hate you."

Realizing the full force of her angry words, Merrit was aghast at her own spite. Seeking to make amends, she started up the stairs after the fleeing girl, calling her name, only to be assailed by another spell of giddy faintness. Her vision growing dark, she sank down on the steps and closed her eyes as beads of sweat dotted her forehead. She sat quietly until the dizziness passed, then slowly climbed to her room, where she sobbed in shame, regretting her hateful words that could never be withdrawn.

The next two evenings Williamsburg was filled with balls, delightful crowded affairs that were totally unappreciated by at least three of those attending. A nervous, hostile Gabrielle clung to the arm of her fiancé, steering him away from Merrit and becoming petulant and demanding whenever he glanced her way. Lost to his own turmoil, Nicholas, oblivious of Gabrielle's mounting upset, was annoyed by the way she constantly dragged him from the woman to whom he was tragically drawn. Merrit's presence left him coiled into a knot of emotions—love, anger, betrayal, hurt, and jealousy foremost among them. Most of his anger was directed at himself for having succumbed to her sweet entreaties to trust her when doing so was against his very nature. But he had trusted, and the pain and folly of it was a relentless cancer. He was a fool for wanting her, a double fool for believing in her. Yet knowing she had played him false didn't keep him from desiring her, from wanting to hear her soft-spoken words even if they were lies.

For Merrit, being the focus of angry stares from both Nicholas and Gabrielle was a double torture. Gloomily, she kept to Winston's side, playing the pretty, charming figure-head he wanted in a wife. Determined not to hurt him as she had his sister, she was careful to give him no cause for suspicion, smiling up at him dutifully and promoting him to all they greeted. She would become his wife and anything in the way of that goal, including the alternately hot and cold green eyes that pursued her, had to be pushed aside and ignored, though doing so wore her down bit by bit until at the evening's end she was too exhausted to think.

Winston was not untouched by the tensions of those about him. He felt it in Merrit's arm beneath his hand, in Gabrielle's withering glare, and in Nicholas Seward's unusually rigid stance. Something was sorely amiss with the three of them. His sister's plight was of no interest to him — she was a silly whining creature who'd surprised them all by snagging the wealthy Captain Seward; Winston had never been able to understand that. His concern lay in what had transpired between his bride-to-be and his sister's much touted catch. There was nothing he could point to, only little glances now and then that snapped with energy. It was enough to contend with the Spanish Angel's seizure of the Whitelaw cargoes without having Seward trying to steal his bride.

Purposefully, he sought Nicholas out, feeling Merrit's reluctant pull on his arm as she lagged behind, her eyes downcast to avoid Gabrielle's accusing gaze and the cool emerald eyes that feigned indifference.

"Nicholas, are you still of a mind to lose your wager tomorrow?" Winston said amiably despite the sharp challenge in his look.

The other man gave a low chuckle and a slow smile. "I have no plan to lose, sir, but I am more than willing to let you try and best me." His tone clearly said that he didn't worry about the possibility Winston had suggested. Despite his casual posture, Merrit's nearness had him in a quandary, however. He dared not look at her, knowing he could not

342

keep his heart, still so newly broken, from his eyes.

"Have you decided on the stakes yet?"

"I will let you know tomorrow."

"Fair enough. Tomorrow then. And may the best man win all."

Green eyes glittered. "He usually does."

The midday horse race was but one of the events of that busy Saturday. The day began with a fair and bazaar, which were followed by a picnic lunch and a traditional springtime gala at Whitelawn. It was a day of casual outdoor celebration, the Virginia clime contributing a warm hazy sunlight. Merrit and Mildred rode in one of the four Whitelaw coaches, finding the streets of the usually staid town full of gaiety. With Winston busy talking politics with the visiting lawmakers, Merrit was free to roam through the booths under Mildred's watchful eye, and Letitia became her incessantly chattering companion, which made the morning more enjoyable. With her childish enthusiasm, the girl wanted to miss nothing, especially the tasty samplings of sweets which she indulged in wholeheartedly when not under Sophia's critical eye. She vowed she didn't care if she never had a trim figure like her sister. In her mind being plump and happy was far better than being thin and miserable.

The race took place at mid afternoon and was the focus of much speculation and gambling. Four local men and three outsiders were vying for the prestige of winning the grueling cross-country race. Winston was by far the favorite, but his popularity waned with the arrival of Nicholas Seward's horse. Pieces of Eight was a beautiful creature with a gleaming silver coat and long high-arched tail. The animal was slight and sleek much like its owner, with a deep powerful chest and well-muscled haunches, its small triangular head with wide-set eyes and dainty pricked ears bespeaking its Arabian lineage. Nicholas rode the spirited beast with an easy mastery, something of a spectacle himself in his silver-trimmed riding wear. His handsome rakish air drew many a maiden's eye and brought a gasp from a surprised Mildred.

"Good Lord," she exclaimed, shocked to see the pirate mixing so boldy with the gentry on whom he preyed.

"Captain Seward is Gabrielle's intended, Mildred," Merrit explained, realizing she had forgotten to prepare her companion for the sight of her lover in his new guise. She herself was not prepared for the sudden quickening of her pulse or for the ache of longing that his absence had only strengthened.

"Steady now, miss," Mildred cautioned crisply struggling to hide her dismay. "Ye'd best save that look for yer intended."

"A kiss for luck," Winston called to her as he walked over, leading his leggy roan stallion. Merrit could not very well refuse. She stretched up to press a quick peck on his cheek, but to her embarrassed dismay he caught her fully on the lips. To pull away would cause undo speculation, so she endured his caress with a dignity she was far from feeling. She could have cried had she realized Nicholas Seward was coolly assessing the embrace from horseback, his knee looped casually about the pummel of his lightweight saddle.

"I am ready to wager, Whitelaw," he called out smoothly, causing Winston to reluctantly withdraw his attention from Merrit. "If I lose you shall have my horse, but if I win, as I expect to, I will have the first dance with your lady this evening."

Ignoring Gabrielle's gasp of protest and Merrit's frown, Winston hesitated, regarding his opponent with narrowed eyes. On the surface, it seemed a highly profitable bet so why did he feel as though he was being cheated?

"Done, Captain. Your little pony will be a nice addition to my stable." His good humor fled when Nicholas's handsome face was split by a flash of white teeth. Glittering eyes swept over Merrit in a bold caress before Seward swung his leg back over the saddle and abruptly encouraged his mount to prance away.

"Pirate rogue," Mildred muttered as he stood in the gathering crowd while the horses drew abreast of the starting line. She pursed her lips at the look of desire on Merrit's face. There was no question of where her allegiance lay.

A single shot was fired and the crowd roared as seven horses leapt forward. In the sudden crush, Winston's crop rose, slashing across the nose of the silver stallion in what could have been, but was not, an accident. Pieces of Eight neighed in pain and, lunging to one side, crashed into another horse, sending it and its rider down in a tangle. Nicholas was jarred from the saddle losing his stirrups as he slid precariously. Only his tenuous grip on the lengthy mane kept him from falling beneath panicked hooves. For an uncertain moment he struggled, almost losing his mount then he was able to regain his seat. His heels nudged the skittering horse forward, his sure grip on the reins bringing the animal under control. By that time, Pieces of Eight lagged far behind, but when Nicholas bent low into his wind-whipped mane, urging the horse to give its all, the silver stallion dashed after the others in long, ground-eating strides.

Alarmed by the near tragedy, Merrit clung to Mildred's hand, silently cheering Nicholas on as fervently as Gabrielle was rooting against him, in fear of the bet. Rufe was still smiling in the background, and covering wagers with bold confidence. His smugness proved to be well founded for the small horse closed on the others, urged not by whip and spur but by hand and voice. Slowly the silver stallion edged by the trailing horses, it sights set on the leader, the tall roan.

"Come on, Captain," Mildred roared with enthusiasm as the horses rounded the last bend and headed into the drive to the finish, forgetting her biases in the excitement of the moment and cheering for her favorite. Merrit gave her a startled look, then grinned. What a fraud she is, she thought fondly.

Winston cursed as he saw the bleeding muzzle of his rival's horse draw up beside him until the riders were neck and neck. He flailed mercilessly at the lathered flanks of his roan, but could not force it to pull away from the smaller steed. Snarling in fury, he swung the crop across the back of Seward's hands, but his opponent's grasp never loosened. The bitter exchange was missed by the crowd that thronged the finish line and burst into loud hurrahs as the fleet-footed Pieces of Eight swept across a full stride ahead of the roan.

Fearlessly, Rufe stepped in front of the plunging stallion to seize the reins and jerk it to a halt, patting its dripping muzzle as his friend vaulted from the saddle.

"Is he all right?" Nicholas asked in concern, reaching for the stallion's velvety nose which was flecked with a crimson froth.

Rufe intercepted his hand, frowning as he examined the gash that laid Nicholas's knuckles bare. "Are you?" he countered, pulling his neckerchief off so he could wrap the wound.

Nicholas grinned. "Bloody painful, but worth the price," he declared.

"Ah, yes, the price," his friend mocked.

Before Nicholas could respond, he was hoisted to the shoulders of a couple of enthusiastic men and was carried into the cheering crowd. Rufe gave a start when a small hand pulled at his cuff, bringing his thoughtful gaze down to the petite woman at his side.

"Lady Merrit," he murmured in no little surprise. Nicholas had not told him what had happened between the two of them; but he had guessed its magnitude by the devastating effect it had had on his friend.

"Rufe, give a warning to your captain," she said softly. "Winston is planning some trap that would see him hanged

346

by month's end. I would not want that to happen."

"Nor would I, my lady," he agreed quickly. "I will pass the word to him, but I know not if he will heed your caution."

Merrit nodded, her dark eyes large and anxious. "Do whatever you can to keep him safe."

"I will, Merrit. Thank you." He stared after her as she rejoined the family of the man she'd spoken against, wondering what had caused her to betray him for a pirate.

Winston was in an ill-concealed rage. Losing the big race of the day was hard enough, but watching the swaggering Nicholas Seward bask in his victory was too much to bear gracefully. He hated being second and he hated Seward. The combination was too bitter a bile to swallow. He threw the reins of his winded stallion to a groomsman and stalked to where Merrit stood with his family. Lips thinning unpleasantly, he gripped her arm roughly, seeing too late the rebellious glint in her dark eyes.

"Come. We leave for home," he snapped. He was about to lash out at her for balking at his command when she slid her hand over his and spoke with an undebatable reason.

"Winston, a man of your prominence cannot afford to show poor sportsmanship. Your rudeness would be remembered longer than who won this race. If you wish to make a favorable impression, you must smile and heartily congratulate the winner."

He looked at her long, gaugingly. Though the idea of admitting defeat to Seward was distasteful, he couldn't overlook the opportunity to stand out as a man of honor and generosity. "Of course you are right, my dear, and I thank you for your astuteness. You have the instincts of a politician's wife."

Merrit smiled in response to his praise, relieved to have successfully manipulated his anger.

"Come my dear. Let us be gracious." Winston took her arm, his expression becoming smooth and amiable. She arranged her face in mild, smiling lines as if the prospect of coming face to face with Nicholas was not one that made her tremble with forbidden anticipation and an all too painful anguish. Those emotions caused a hard knot to form in her throat as Colley turned to them, his eyes briefly touching hers before settling on the tall man at her side.

"A good race, Nicholas. Congratulations on your win," Winston stated diplomatically, extending his hand.

Green eyes slowly rose from Whitelaw's outstretched hand, and looking into them, Winston decided he would never again make the mistake of seeing Nicholas Seward as a harmless, good-natured dandy. The man's burning stare smoldered with a violent hatred that sliced through the thin veneer of his meaningless smile. Winston blinked once and that look had vanished but he was certain he had been allowed to see the danger the man presented. The captain was not what he seemed, and he wanted Winston to know it.

Finally, Nicholas grasped Whitelaw's hand with his own injured one, never wincing as it was ruthlessly crushed in the other's brutal grip.

"I shall come to collect our wager," he said. Then he spun away in an arrogant dismissal.

# Chapter Twenty-seven

Whitelawn was alive with music and tantalizing scents. Musicians played on the broad portico, and tables ran the length of the great house, groaning under heaping platters of pickled oysters, batter breads and biscuits, crisp fried chicken, deviled crab, and sweet-potato pie. Madeira was served in sterling cups to the ladies, and frosty pewter goblets of ale were provided for the men. Every year, for this one day, the barriers of class and social position were dropped, and gentry mixed with servants, sharing the same tables and even dancing together, their usual segregation lessened by the free-flowing spirits. Carriages and sturdy wagons from neighboring plantations lined the drive. The annual event always filled the lawn with merrymakers who would celebrate late into the evening, many of whom would remain overnight, being unable to negotiate the journey home.

Seeing Rufe and Freddy Moffit as well as other familiar faces from Twilight, Merrit searched the crowd for the one face foremost in her thoughts. Her heart gave a twist of envy when she found him, Gabrielle ensconced on his arm. The pair were sampling the offering set out on the banquet tables. They seemed to be thoroughly enjoying each other's company and she was pricked by a sudden doubt that Gabrielle had been lying. As she looked away, her heart heavy, Merrit missed the look Nicholas gave her, his eyes softer and more caressing than Gabrielle would ever see them.

Seeing Merrit was like feeling the warming touch of spring after a severe winter. She looked so fetching and vibrant in her calico of painted chinz. The short jacketlike bodice molded her high firm breasts and tiny waist, then extended into a hip-length basque, and the skirt moved freely as she walked, swaying gracefully over her short petticoat. Beneath a straw milk-maid hat, her chestnut hair was simply arranged, and a full apron with large pockets added to the carefree appeal of her appearance. With a wistful sigh, he thought how different the evening would be if her small hand were tucked into his elbow and her dark eyes were smiling up into his. Increasingly intolerant of Gabrielle's childish prattle, he longed for Merrit's low, sweet voice and mellow laugh. Just looking upon her as she wove her way across the crowded lawn was a balm to his restless anger. Had she not been at Whitelaw's side after the race, he would have given way to that insistent call for retribution, would have struck his enemy's insincere face. But his vengeance had been carefully plotted, and though waiting was hard, it would yield a result worth the price. Except, argued a small involuntary whisper, the loss of Merrit Ellison. Had he been a man given to optimism, he would have considered the possibility of sharing a future with her, but her unswerving stance gave him little hope of that. To him, their separate ways could not meet.

Once the guests had eaten their fill, the food was taken up, to be replaced by casks of brandy and smoothly cut rum. Torches were lit in defiance of the seeping darkness, and the music began to lure adventurous couples to spin beneath the starry canopy in each other's arms. Merrit felt a touch of melancholy occasioned by the happiness she saw all about her. It set her apart from the others, isolated her in loneliness. Then she saw a palm stretch out before her in invitation, and her eyes flashed up.

"I've come to collect my wager, my lady."

Her hand slipped across the roughened familiar plane of

his palm. Then they moved, as if in a dream, into the torch-lit circle of well-trod grass. Lacing his fingers in hers, Colley lightly drew her to him by pressing the fingertips of his other hand to the curve of her waist. As he led Merrit in the slow, stately dance that kept a formal distance between them, his touch seemed to burn her, the gleaming heat of his eyes absorbing her thoughts and will until nothing was real but the dark emerald depths she stared into. She glided in his arms, unaware of the music that guided them until she imagined it had subtly changed, its rhythm deepening to the beat of a heart, its pulsing tempo growing ever faster and spinning her thoughts back to warm sand between her toes and a bold bare-chested pirate trying to cajole her out of her ill temper. His swarthy teasing face blurred in her memory, blended into the one that grew ever closer. She began to notice the tightening of Colley's grip on her hand as his other hand moved to the small of her back to bring her near enough to feel his movements against her skirts. As his steps quickened, she realized that she hadn't imagined the sultry hint of pirate enticement flavoring the traditional music. Several of the bandsmen had been on that fire-flushed beach, and they were kindling that same blaze here on the grassy terrace of Whitelawn.

Caught up in that primal rhythm, Merrit rested her head on his shoulder, her eyes lost in his as he whirled her about, their dance skirting the edge of propriety but charged with an excitement that soon had the other dancers pausing to watch. Finally they danced alone, pressed so close that she became the shadow of his steps, Merrit was increasingly aware of him, for he used the dance and the suggestive movements of his body against hers to heighten her sensitivities. Flushed and breathless, her desire almost out of her control, she had to struggle to keep her sense of time and place, to keep from reaching up to taste his tempting mouth now parted in a slightly mocking smile. The beat of her heart raced wildly with the tempo of the music, the night becoming suddenly close and unbearably hot. He dipped her back over his arm until her head nearly brushed the ground and it took her a moment to realize the music had stopped. When he brought her up, it was like surfacing in a deep pool; everything was wavering and out of focus except his glorious features, the eyes burning down into hers. Just as she was about to speak his name and declare her love, he released her abruptly letting her stand on trembling legs.

"Thank you for the dance, my lady," he said simply in a level voice. Then he strode through the applauding throng, past a white-faced Gabrielle, to seize the bridle of his silver stallion and gallop into the night.

Had Mildred not come to tug on her arm, Merrit might well have stood rooted until morning, numbed and shaken beyond thought, her eyes staring in a rapturous trance in the direction of Twilight. She took the mug Mildred pressed into her hand and drank obediently, choking on the rum as it seared down her throat, tears and awareness coming to her. She let Mildred lead her into more subdued light, ready to endure her merciless upbraiding.

"Where did ye learn such a lewd and immoral dance? Surely not in the drawing rooms ye should have been in. Ye might as well have let him strip ye naked and bed ye down right in front of all them ogling eyes. Ye think they all be blind, child, not to see what was between ye and yer pirate, especially yer intended."

"I don't care," the girl whispered. The tingling warmth excited by his touch was replaced by an insistent ache. Had she been cold and scheming like Gabrielle, she would have sought out Winston to fulfill her needs, but she was thinking with her heart not her head and she knew her fulfillment lay wherever Nicholas Seward was. Silently, she passed the emptied mug to Mildred and began to walk, unconsciously at first, then fully aware of her destination.

Frowning, Mildred started after her, but she stopped and sighed heavily an unwilling smile curving her lips. Let her go, her heart insisted, and soon Mildred's attention was drawn to the welcoming smile on the face of one of the pirate crew who was masquerading as a groomsman at Twilight. He was pleasing to look upon in a rough-hewn manner, and the night was long. Returning his smile, she accepted a mug of rum and raised it in a toast to the darkness that had taken in her young charge.

Rufe had seen Nicholas's abrupt departure, but he was reluctant to follow him for that meant leaving the soulful-eyed beauty on his arm. With mixed feelings, he saw Merrit glide into the darkness, knowing full well where she meant to go and how she would be received. But he grinned and pulled the mahogany temptress close. Let the lady see to the calming of his captain's mood this night. Perhaps Colley could find some peace if only for a short time. That would leave him to his lovely Dulcie. "Thank you, my lady," he vowed silently.

Winston had endured the dance between Nicholas and Merrit with ill grace. The pair's movements had been charged with a raw sensuality that went far beyond the fulfillment of the wager, and Winston was not willing to surrender higher stakes. Relieved by Seward's departure, he was about to collect his fiancée when a beefy hand caught his arm.

"Who was that man?"

Annoyed he looked at the ship's captain he had been dealing with, but something in the man's bright stare changed his irritation into sharp interest. "Nicholas Seward. He's a planter and merchant captain."

Captain Whitney mopped the sudden perspiration from his brow with an unsteady hand. "Aside from his finery and the scarred face, he be the image of the Spanish Angel."

Winston looked long at him. "What are you saying?"

"That there cannot be two men so fair of face. I might be wrong, but by Gad, I swore I'd never forget him. If he is not the same man, the resemblance is the work of the devil."

"If that were true, wouldn't Lady Ellison be aware of it?" Whitelaw demanded, his pale eyes growing cold and hard in speculation.

"She'd have to be. She was a lot closer to the Angel than I. I mean as his captive and all," Captain Whitney added quickly with awkward diplomacy.

"Who would know for sure?"

"Captain Neville. 'Twas from his noose that your lady freed the Angel. Neville vowed to see him dead."

Winston Whitelaw gave a slow, fearsome smile. "Perhaps we can arrange that," he mused thoughtfully.

Nicholas Seward sat on the edge of his dock, watching the slow moving James as his bare feet trailed in the water. In the sudden oppressive heat, he had stripped off the confining fopperies to don a pair of white canvas breeches. The sounds of music and laughter were carried faintly on the sluggish current, a mocking reminder of what was denied him. The dance had been a mistake. The chafe of longing had been hard enough to bear, but having her in his arms again had awakened all manner of demons that tormented him in body and spirit. He wondered dejectedly if he went to her on this night, would she be willing or would she fillet him with her sharp tongue and cast him out. Or worse yet, would she not be alone? What had he seen in her dark eyes as she moved so easily in his embrace? Lust for the pleasures he could bring her or desire for him as a man?

He froze as he heard a soft step on the planks behind him and, without looking about, lifted a welcoming hand. Her cool fingers slipped inside it as she settled beside him on the dock pulling, off her shoes and stockings to dangle bare toes in the river. For a time, they were silent, only their hands touching, as if they were afraid of shattering the fragile contentment that lay between them. The laughter carried from Whitelawn suddenly seemed far removed. He shifted slightly and obligingly, and Merrit leaned into his side, pillowing her head on his shoulder as his arm formed a solid support behind her back.

"I have missed this," he said softly, as his cheek brushed her fragrant hair.

"I, too," was the brief reply.

Feeling awkward and hesitant with her, he looked up into the heavens to murmur, "We're in for a storm tonight. Perhaps you'd best go back now."

Merrit's hands came up to press the heated skin of his chest and back. "Surely, not," she argued faintly. " 'Tis a fine clear night."

"A calm surface can hide many dangers, my lady."

"Don't send me away, Colley," she asked quietly, unwilling to relinquish their closeness and the feelings it stirred.

"I couldn't if I wanted to, Merri," he answered, his voice husky. "Come up to the house for a time and share a glass with me. There is much I want to tell you. I promise I won't compromise you."

"Your word as a pirate or a man?" she teased, flashing him a smile.

"With you, 'tis always the man."

She took his arm and let him lift her up. Then they stood toe to toe, looking into each other's eyes. She waited for him to kiss her, but he didn't. Instead he took her elbow and led her up the winding path to Twilight. She felt oddly conspicuous in her damp bare feet and with her half-dressed pirate escort amid such elegant surroundings but Nicholas was unaffected by them. He guided her into the warm wood-paneled room in which they had been reunited, and she took the fragile stemmed glass he offered, her fingers brushing his and thereby eliciting the shock of excited pleasure. The air about them was heavy and crackling with expectation and desire as intense and searing as the heat lightning that streaked across the Northern skies.

"What was it you wanted to say to me?" Merrit asked finally, seeking to slow the downhill race that would inevitably end in his arms. She saw the quick flicker of caution in his eyes, and frowned. He would not tell her. Nothing had changed between them. He didn't have the capacity to trust her, to love her without restraint, and she felt mildly cheated.

"I would show you instead," he said. His fingertips brushed the planes of her face, their light touch reaching to the very quick of her and setting her atremble as his eyes darkened with the smokey heat of passion.

"Colley, please," she whispered brokenly, her eyes closing. He looked long upon her face, then started to draw back, uncertain. But she grasped his hands tightly and concluded, "Please love me."

The distance between them evaporated as their lips met in an urgent press to create that magical elixir that would heal the hurts and scars made by sharp words and unkind thoughts. Drifting on the ebb of their melding kiss, Merrit lay her head on his shoulder as he lifted her easily and bore her up the curving flight of stairs. He shouldered open the door to one of the rooms and carried her inside. The bed he placed her upon was covered with a velvet spread, that, much like her stormy-eyed lover, could be either silken or rough depending on which way it was rubbed. But his persistent attention gave her little time for further thought about their surroundings. His hands parted her from her clothing while his maddening tongue teased her lips and her closed eyelids. Colley's lovemaking matched the imaginings of her lonely dreams. It was tender yet passionate, sweet yet savage, the persistent play of his touch arousing her to her body's demands. In the smothering heat of the darkened room, they could well have been on an island paradise isolated from the world for they were in the haven of their ecstasy.

At last, they were sated, and drenched from the heat without and within. It was a long time before either of them could move; then he managed to roll to one side, flopping onto his back with a weary sigh.

"What are you doing to me, witch," he mumbled hoarsely. "I want you more now than ever, yet I haven't the strength even to kiss you."

"Just hold me then," she whispered, burrowing into his side and closing her eyes as his hand played through her hair.

After a moment, he asked softly, "Do you love me?"

"Always."

"Then do not take offense when I ask you to move away. I am near to dying from the heat and you are an overstoked fire."

Chuckling, she crawled from the bed and tottered somewhat shakily to the window. Even after drawing the heavy velvet drapes and throwing open the sashes, there was no relief from the still, humidity. She returned to sit beside him, sympathetically mopping the moisture from his forehead with the hem of her discarded petticoat.

"I need some air," he moaned miserably. "I feel like a fish too long out of water. Damn this sweltering place anyway. I hate this heat. Rufe tells me its because my Spanish blood runs too hot already."

Merrit laughed and kissed him lightly, feeling scorched by his body. "I can vouch for that, my pirate love. Come. I've an idea. Have you something I can put on?"

"Put on? Why?" he protested, his eyes sweeping over the opalescent glow of her bare skin.

"No questions. Just come with me." She rummaged about until she discovered a lounging banyan and slipped the loose garment over her head. Its billowing folds of Chinese silk enticingly caressed her nakedness. After turning the cuffs back several times, she took his hand and tugged relentlessly. "Come."

With a reluctant smile, he rose, pulled on his trousers, then followed her down the wide staircase and out into the night. It was only slightly cooler there, the air still heavy and thick with the rain he knew was coming. Merrit raced ahead on the soft carpet of pine needles, her barefeet flashing beneath the raised hem of the robe. His spirits heightened by her childlike gaiety, Colley pursued her down the winding path, pausing when he came to the dock. There was no sign of Merrit, only a bright puddle of silk at the dock's end. Curious yet wary, he went to stand beside it, finally catching the gleam of her body as it glided along the surface of the lazy river. She bobbed on the slow current, tossing back her damp locks to grin at him.

"It's wonderfully refreshing. Come in," she called naughtily.

He viewed the placid surface with a skeptical eye. Are you not satisfied with nearly drowning me twice?"

She laughed and dipped below the surface, coming up to splash him. "I won't let you drown. I promise. Come in."

He paced the end of the pier like a nervous cat, sullen yet agitated. "Is this some sort of fiendish revenge for abducting you?" he growled, eying the inviting prospect of her nudity as she floated upon the cooling waters.

"What's this?" she teased. "The bold Spanish Angel frightened of getting his feet wet?"

"I am not afraid," he replied with stiff dignity, but he paused at the edge of the planking.

"Then jump," she challenged. "Coward."

He took a determined step forward, and the dark water drew him down like a plummeting stone, instantly rekindling the remembered terror of that night in the sea. But she was there to bring him to the surface. Gasping for breath, he flailed about, not bothering to pretend he was not terrified.

"Don't let me go, Merri," he cried in a low, unsteady voice.

"I won't." She kissed him reassuringly until she could feel some of his tension lessen. "Come, Captain. 'Tis time you learned to swim." Seeing the uncertainty in his wide, darkened eyes, she added, "Do you trust me or not?"

"Enough to foolishly jump in," he countered.

"Then relax and learn to be as at home in the water as upon it."

The lesson, a gradual one, was liberally interspersed with caresses and kisses of encouragement until his fear became a shaky confidence, the water rinsing away the sticky heat of their passion and becoming a welcoming balm on the sultry night. As they held to each other buoyed by the gentle current, the distant rumbling drew near and rain came down in an abrupt deluge, pocking the surface of the river. By the time they reached shore, the air had become chill, the downpour cold and slashing. Hand in hand, they ran laughing to the house, and once they were in the dry foyer, Nicholas drew her dripping and shivering into his arms, his features serious.

"I cannot send you back in this weather," he declared. "Stay with me. Be mine a bit longer. Merri, I don't want to be alone tonight."

Mildred frowned as she watched the rain pelt the windowpanes. It had been difficult enough to convince the suspicious Winston that Merrit had retired early, but what would she tell him in the morning, that his fiancée had spent the night in the bed of her pirate lover?

"Ah, child 'tis a dangerous game ye play, and with dangerous men," the loyal woman said softly.

# Chapter Twenty-eight

The warmth of the fire dried them and eased the chill as Nicholas and Merrit sat on the floor staring silently into the cheery blaze. Soothed by the presence of the woman tucked against his side and the heavy bulk of Beelzebub over his bare feet, Nicholas let his thoughts wander and before he realized it, he was speaking them aloud.

"Had things been as they should, I could have given you a great house like this honestly. You, my lady, would bear a fine, proud name, and I would not dread the morning light which will take you from me again."

"How should things have been?" she prompted gently, brushing her lips over his injured hand. Dared she hope that he was going to trust her with whatever haunted him so mercilessly?

He shifted slightly so that her head rested upon his shoulder, and began to speak in a low conversational tone that belied the tension in the hand that stroked her hair. "My mother was of the royal house of Spain, my father an English earl who had come to negotiate during one of the many conflicts between the two countries. He stayed with her family and they fell in love with one another. I'm sure you are wondering how such pedigreed lines could produce a lowly pirate like me."

"They didn't marry?" she asked softly.

"Oh, no. They did, and that was the problem. My mother had been pledged from birth to a nobleman, and when her family discovered she had married an Englishman, they cast her from their house for the shame she had brought them. For a time, she and my father were happy and didn't care. They traveled the Continent for several months until they found she was with child, whereupon my father decided they should return to England so she could be safely delivered at his family's estate. But before they left Spain, he contracted a sickness and died within the week. Heavy with child, my mother went to her family but they would not receive her. They said they had no daughter. Since she had no money, she wrote to her husband's family in England, explaining about the child and her circumstances. When she heard nothing, she wrote again and again. The letter she finally received denied a marriage between the earl and his Spanish whore, and stated that her husband's family would not accept a bastard as heir to their fortune. They vowed any further letters from her would go unopened, that her ploy to get money from them had failed."

He paused to take a long swallow of brandy before continuing in the same even tone as if he were describing someone else's past. He told her of his birth in a famous Spanish bordello. Desperate and destitute, the unfortunate Maria had ended up there, having been taken in because of her uncommon beauty. She promised to work out the year in return for food and a place to stay, and the women there saw to her birthing and aided her to recover her full health. By the year's end, she had become a favorite of the court and lived for the next eight years in luxurious apartments furnished by the men who kept her. During that time her son had the finest tutors and was even shown off publicly by some of her lovers who enjoyed his quick wittedness. They were years of fine living, but they didn't last. Marie fell victim to a consumptive disease, and her beauty began to fade away, as did her generous supporters. She and her son were forced to move from their grand suite of rooms to a dingy hovel over a tavern where Maria worked in the early hours of the evening serving drinks. Later she entertained men in the small, one-room apartment. While she was involved with business, her enterprising son became a shadow in the back streets, returning in the morning with enough food to last them the day and sometimes longer. Maria never complained about her situation, but she regretted the life her son was forced to live. When the boy brought her the stolen gifts, she wept silently, because the son of an earl lived like vermin on the streets of Spain . . . ."

Colley's hand was far from steady as he lifted the brandy, and his voice became so low and so heavily accented that Merrit had to struggle to understand him.

"She was so proud, wearing her ragged clothes like they were the finest silks, entertaining the scum from the tavern as if they were proper gentlemen, and insisting I behave in a way that befit my name. My name, what a joke. Finally she became so ill she could no longer ply her trade. There was no money for doctors, and she was in much pain. I cut the purse of a nobleman so we could afford some medicine. She — she slapped me and threw away the coins telling me that I should always do whatever I had to but that I should never surrender my dignity, to remember who I was, that my name was Nicholas Edward de Fonte Seward, that I was the son of a noblewoman and an earl."

His words were choked off by a hard swallow, and for a moment the crackle of the fire and his deep, shaky breath were the only sounds. Merrit took up his cold hands, pressing them to her own wet cheeks, but she didn't embarrass him by meeting his eyes.

"She was dead by morning. They buried her in a plain box in an unmarked pauper's grave and I stood over it. I spat on her coffin and damned her for leaving me, for being too weak to demand what should have been ours. I cursed her for lying to me about dignity when she let herself be bought like an animal. I hated her weakness and I vowed I would never be weak, that no one would ever take anything from me.

"Nothing ever hurt me like that slap. It was the only time she'd ever struck me, and I never felt pain like that again until I met you, Merri."

With a soft sound, she turned to embrace him, holding his dark head and feeling the hot, dampness of his cheek upon her shoulder. "She must have loved you deeply to have gone on in such a life. It was the only choice she had," Merrit told him quietly.

He sighed heavily. "As a man, I know that. I have made my peace with her, but a ten-year-old boy does not have that kind of understanding. Her dying was a betrayal, yet I was determined to settle things for her. I stole aboard a ship bound for England and searched until I found them. My grandfather had died and my father's sister was in control of the estate until her son came of age. How naïve I was. I marched up to the door and demanded I be given my due. I could barely speak English and all I had to prove who I was, was my father's signet ring."

Merrit smiled into Colley's short hair, thinking how little he had changed. She could well imagine him as a proud, swaggering little boy facing down a cold matriarch, using cocky bravado to cover his fear of being alone in a strange country.

"She laughed at me, Merri, and told me to go away, but I wouldn't leave without the ring she took from me. She wouldn't return it, saying I had probably stolen it and that it belonged to her son now. She called to some men and told them to take me out and discourage me from ever making any claim on her family again. She said her son would be the Earl of Wexington. The title would not go to some dirty-faced Spanish bastard."

"But that's Winston's title," Merrit blurted in confusion. Then it all made sense. "Was it Sophia then?"

He nodded, leaning back from her. "So now you understand." In the firelight his face was all planes and shadows, but his eyes shimmered with reflected flames as if their heat was within him.

"Colley, I—"

He put his fingertips to her lips. "Let me finish," he insisted. Once more he gathered her in the circle of his arm, then he poured them more brandy. His voice was calm again, but the accent remained, a testament to his background. "Her discouragement cracked my skull and most of my ribs. I doubt if I would have survived the night in the open sewer where they had dumped me had I not been found and taken in by another misfit. He'd been prowling the backstreets for several months, having escaped his indenture."

"Rufe?"

Nicholas's tone grew warm. "He stole food for the both of us until I mended enough to forage with him. He taught me English and I taught him refinement. It was his idea to go to sea with the Royal Navy. By then I could almost speak without an accent and, with my father's eyes, make a passable Englishman. Had it not been wartime, they wouldn't have taken us. I was twelve and looked all of eight, whereas Rufe's color made for a touchy situation. But he was strong and able-bodied enough to impress them into overlooking it. What a miserable eight years that was. The discipline was brutal, the food and water always bad, the wages low, and the voyages long. We made terrible crewmen, Rufe because of his coloring and me because I could never take a foolish order gracefully. But I loved the sea too much to give it up. Finally, after a particularly harsh voyage, the one that earned me my stripes, eight of us took a ship. We sailed as privateers during wartime and took to piracy when we could no longer obtain commissions."

"And so you became the Spanish Angel," she concluded.

" 'Twas far better than begging or starving on land. There was no livelihood for a seaman in peacetime. The merchant fleet couldn't absorb us all and privateering was illegal. I didn't know how to do anything else."

"You didn't want to, you mean," she scoffed, her harsh words softened by the gentle brush of her fingers across his smooth tanned chest.

Nicholas grinned. "True enough, my lady. I wanted no one to be my master save the winds and the tide." His tone lowered as he went on to describe the voyage that changed the course of his carefree existence, the one on which he'd found cargo bearing a certain crest; he remembered it being on the ring. Seeing it again had awakened his submerged fury and had revived the nightmare of watching his mother sink from the most beautiful woman in Spain to the wasted corpse he'd seen laid in a nameless grave. He became obsessed with finding his father's family, and traced them from their estates in England to their new home in Williamsburg.

"But what of your mother's family? Didn't you ever seek them out?"

"They were gone, their lives taken in an epidemic much like the one that claimed my father. Their land and monies had been divided amongst lesser relations with whom I had no quarrel. But the Whitelaws, I wanted them to pay for my mother's suffering. I hated them for making her look the way she had. I knew I could not rest until she looked beautiful to me again. I pillaged their ships, but stealing their goods wasn't enough. I wanted them to know who it was who was impoverishing them. I went to their door, but Sophia didn't know me. When I told her my real name, she

365

assumed I was some distant relation. That was when I decided how to seek my vengeance. I had this house built, paying for it with their money, and I courted Sophia's daughter. After I marry Gabrielle, I will go to that cold bitch and demand my ring and my title. If she refuses I will make it public that her daughter is the wife of an infamous pirate. Either way, they will be ruined."

Merrit was silent, feeling his rage in the tenseness of his body. His consuming hatred of the Whitelaws was justified, but how far would he go because of it? Her voice soft and hesitant, she asked, "And what part do I play in this vengeance?"

"You are no fool, Merri. You would know I lied if I said I hadn't been tempted to use you. Meeting you was a stroke of providence until I lost my heart to your melting eyes and soft lips." He stroked her cheek with the back of his hand. "Exposing you as my lover would have been a master touch and I would have, had I not fallen in love with you. I do love you, Merri. You've no part in this and I am torn with fear that you will suffer because of my plan. As Whitelaw's wife, I cannot spare you. I mean to ruin him and his family, and I will do no less. I would understand if you went to them and told them all I have said."

He fell silent; almost able to feel her thoughts. Now that he had spread his secrets and shadows before her, he was vulnerable. She had asked for his trust and he had given it, full measure. It was too late for cautious doubts to protect him should she decide to see to her own interests. He would understand, but he would never forgive.

She straightened so she could meet his searching gaze, tracing the pale crescent scars with the tip of her finger. "I will not betray your trust, my lord pirate. What then are we to do?"

"At this moment I plan to take you upstairs and love you fiercely. All else can wait 'til morning. Come to me, witch, and convince me that I am not crazy to risk so much for you."

The storm-cooled breeze wafted in, stirring the velvet drapes and bearing the fresh scent of the rain to where Merrit lay awake on the great bed, Nicholas's body pressed against her back. The brush of his breath on her neck was slow and heavy as he slept, but there was wary possessiveness in the arm looped tightly about the curve of her waist. There was something so right, so sure about them being together in the darkness. She tried not to think of the fast approaching time when the familiar form molded to hers in such perfect symmetry would be replaced by another.

Nicholas Seward. What a fascinating, compelling man ruled her heart and thoughts. He was an earl, a pirate, an avenger, a lover, all these parts of him merging into one man. Knowing of his ill-fated past only made her love him more, especially since he had trusted her with it, with all the buried emotions and the coveted hatreds that churned within him. As he had promised, now she did understand the reasons for his confusing, often harsh, actions. While his chosen method of vengeance was not one she could approve, she could not blame him for it. He was not as heartless as Sophia, who had had a child beaten and left to die so she might grasp all of the family's fortune. Merrit couldn't help but remember the message from the Whitelaws denying her ransom. How fitting it was that wealth so coveted should be taken so cleverly. She felt hatred for Sophia Whitelaw and a surge of protectiveness for her noble pirate lover. Even though it might mean her own ruin, she wanted to see him gain back what should have been his.

Things had taken a confusing turn. Now Colley was being truthful with her and she had become a liar. Moved by the plight of the proud Spanish woman, she could identify with

367

Maria's choices. The child within her would not go unnoticed for long. She had to secure a future for that babe. She no longer doubted that Nicholas loved her but was his love for her stronger than his need for vengeance? Did she have a right to ask him to choose between them?

"What is it, Merri?"

She started in surprise as he whispered against her ear, having been unaware that he was awake or that she had been crying softly. She rolled toward him, pressing her face to the valley of his throat to avoid the search of his too keen gaze, and tremulously said, "Hold me, Colley. I don't know what to do and I am so afraid."

His embrace was quick and crushing as if its strength could protect her from anything. "Tell me what I can do," he demanded. "Anything, Merri. Name it and it be yours if it will stop your tears. The wound of your weeping cuts too deeply. What can I do?"

Marry me, she longed to plead. Make me your wife and put an end to my turmoil. Instead, she replied, "Just hold me and love me."

He knew there was more to her anguished sobs, but was at a loss for she would not name their cause. With a frustrated sigh, he hugged her shivering form. "I do love you, Merri. I am yours whenever you need me."

"I need you now" was her hushed reply.

He rose up on his elbows trying to see her expression, but the light was still too poor. His lips, soft and sweet upon hers, moved with a tenderness he could express no other way to this fragile, precious woman. He loved her with a slow, quiet passion, hearing her moan his name as she found her pleasure. Then he cradled her in silence as she soundlessly sobbed herself to sleep.

"Merri, wake up. 'Tis morning."

368

Merrit gave a mumble of protest, refusing to open her eyes and admit the traitorous daylight. If the sun was up, she would have to leave and she was much too comfortable to return to Whitelawn to face Mildred's questions concerning her whereabouts.

"No, it cannot be," she argued. "Close your eyes and it will go away."

"I am afraid that as much as I would like it to, it will not oblige us. Come, before Mildred arrives to fetch you."

Smiling, she looked up to see him standing at the bedside fully dressed. "I do believe poor Mildred has you quite bullied."

"She has a very strong arm," he reminded her, touching his cheek as if he could still feel the weight of the good woman's slap. "Rouse yourself, you lazy wench."

"I am aroused," she purred, her eyes growing sultry and tempting, "and wondering why it is that you've already dressed."

"To avoid temptation, my lady," he said primly, while his gaze wandered over contours the sheet concealed.

Her mouth pursed saucily as she sat up, letting the sheet slide to her waist. "And have your chaste garments relieved you of temptation?"

With a grumbling growl, he pounced upon the bed, making her shriek with protesting laughter as he snatched her wanton nakedness to him and rolled them both across the tangled sheets until she ended astride him, pinning his wrists to the mattress on either side of his dark head.

"Anxious for me to leave are you?" she taunted, provocatively wriggling her rounded buttocks upon his narrow hips and grinning wickedly when she felt his well-defined answer through the fabric of his trousers.

"But 'tis daylight, my lady. Have you no shame?" he mocked, willing to remain her captive for at least a bit longer.

369

Merrit looked down at him, her desire surprisingly fading into something deep and achingly permanent. She stared long and lovingly at his face, at the generous mouth curved up in a smile and the green eyes heavy and warmed beneath the black brows. Even so close, his features were perfect, except for the haunting scars, but the sharp, arrogant beauty he purposefully sported was softened now, its edges smoothed by happiness. She wondered if anyone other than Rufe knew this man existed, and felt awed that Colley had let her behind the barriers, had trusted her to keep his secret in her heart.

"What are you thinking?" he asked with a bemused smile, no longer pressed by the urgent need of her but content to bask in her loving gaze.

"Angel, Nicholas, Colley," she listed fondly. "My bold chameleon, do you never fear you will forget who you are and change to the wrong color?"

"I have played a dangerous game too long for that. The threat of the noose keeps me alert."

Merrit frowned, and the hand that brushed his throat shook slightly. "I hate to think of this fine neck cruelly broken. Colley, have you never thought of retiring your Jolly Roger? Surely you have an ample fortune. Your revenues from this plantation must make you legitimately prosperous."

His brows lowered thoughtfully. "I do not know. I've hired others to see to the land so I could be on the sea. That won't change in me, Merrit. For your sake, I almost wish it could."

"Almost," she echoed wistfully; then her eyes grew speculative. Now that she knew the man he truly was, now that she'd been welcomed into his inner circle of trust, she loved him without restraint. She wanted him, all of him, even the most unpleasant facets, because they made such an intriguing whole. She wanted more than his love, more than his trust. She wanted the permanence of his name. Before she must go to the altar with Winston, she would do everything in her power to make him want her with the same intensity. If he couldn't be swayed, she would give him up, but not without one determined fight.

"I love you, Nicholas," she said with fervor. Then, seeing his eyes darken with pleasure as her lips lowered to his, she kissed him in a firm, candid claim. He would be hers in spite of himself. She was not fooled by his willingness in her arms. It would be a struggle to wrest him from his single-minded purpose, and he would fight her if she confronted him directly. The only way to win him was his way, by throwing out the rules and relying on trickery and subtlety. That she had learned from him, the master.

"Colley, I must go," she insisted, drawing away with a sad smile as his response grew more impassioned. "You know I cannot stay to see this out though it would be my wish."

Sullenly, he released her, reluctance plain in his smoky eyes.

Merrit rose, determined to weave her silken web around him. As she began to dress, she gave a delighted cry of discovery, for on the dressing table all her stolen belongings were neatly arranged, her scents, her jewels, and even her most minor trinkets.

"I told you I had everything," he said with a pleased smile, his eagerness for her approval evident in the meticulous collection. "A well-kept ledger has other advantages beyond keeping guests from discovering their paintings hanging on my walls."

"Why have you put them all here instead of bringing them to me at Whitelawn?"

There was a touchingly innocent hesitation in his bright emerald eyes. "I had hoped you would spend your nights here. This room is for you. Last night was the first I have spent in it. I usually sleep on the sofa downstairs."

"Mine," she said quietly, then snapped in abrupt annoyance, "Isn't it going to be a bit difficult explaining that to your new bride?"

The softness left his eyes in a blink, his dark brows lowering to a scowling V. "That won't be for another year."

"And then I would be expected to pack my belongings and go," Merrit stated coolly. "I think not. I will not be one of your stolen prizes to be shifted about to avoid suspicion."

Merrit was halfway down the sweeping staircase before she heard him hurrying after her. He caught her arms, turning her to face him, his mouth full and demanding against hers until she relented, her slender arms rising and her fingers slipping into his close-cut hair.

"I love you, Merri. Please remember that," he requested earnestly.

"I know you do," she replied, but her response gave him no satisfaction.

They were silent on the ride to Whitelawn, Merrit perched on Pieces of Eight's saddle and Nicholas sitting behind, his arms loosely encircling her waist as he controlled the reins. He drew the horse up finally when they were as close to the house as he dared go, and gave her a crushing hug.

"When can I see you again?" he asked, his lips caressing her hair.

"At church this morning," she replied deliberately misinterpreting his meaning.

"Alone," he clarified rather crisply.

"I don't know. Perhaps we shouldn't." She smiled to herself as his arms tightened in rebellion. "Perhaps tonight. We shall see. Let me down, my pirate lord, but kiss me first."

He turned her head with gentle fingertips, and took her lips thoroughly, his command of her leaving her breathless. "Your kiss, my lady. Now off with you." Clasping her hands firmly, he lowered her to the ground with a careful ease, and pressing a light kiss to his bandaged knuckles, she sprinted toward the house, turning once to wave a hand before slipping inside.

From the doorway to the breakfast room, a red-eyed sleepless Gabrielle watched as Merrit lightly darted up the stairs, her narrow gaze not missing the fact that her rival still wore the same clothing she'd had on the night before. She shed no tears, but a cold hatred of the woman who had claimed to be her friend seeped through her. Merrit had been with him again, had gone to him brazenly, knowing he belonged to another. Her pale face mottled unattractively. Well, she would put a stop to it. No dainty-faced tart was going to take what she had dreamed of for so long.

## *Chapter Twenty-nine*

The Bruton Parish Church in Williamsburg had a pew reserved for the governor and his twelve councilors and transept pews for the burgesses. It was the governor's seat Sophia Whitelaw coveted for her son and he, just as zealously, for himself. Their passport to that select position was the lovely Merrit Ellison whose fortune and political ties would see their ambitions met.

Merrit stood demurely at the end of the family pew with Mildred serving as a staunch buffer between her and her fiancée. The stocky woman had been oddly silent, making no judgments or scathing comments upon the girl's early morning return.

"Good morning, my lady. Again," said a low voice as Nicholas slipped into the pew beside her. "Good day to you, Mildred."

"Heaven help us," Mildred mumbled sourly. "He'll bring the roof down upon all our heads."

Nicholas gave her a wry look of appreciation, then nodded his greetings to the row of family members, thankful for the ladies full skirts that wouldn't permit him passage to join his fiancée. He was quite content where he was.

Try as she would, Merrit could not concentrate on the rector's droning voice because of Colley's disturbing presence at her side. She glanced up at him as the congregation sang the opening hymn. He looked like a pious angel as he sang the words of commitment in a rich, pleasant voice, but as they moved into prayer, he stood unbending, his eyes moving in restless derision over the elegant parishoners who claimed such devotion on Sunday then disavowed the commandments on the other six days. At least, he was no hypocrite. His eyes dropped to the woman at his side, her head reverently bowed and her face filled with a calm serenity. He studied her expression curiously. Stirred by her sincerity and humble quiet, he looked away uncomfortably, feeling an intruder, and as he listened unmoved to the spoken words, he wondered what she heard in them that brought her such a look of peace, a bit envious of convictions that were so foreign to him. Perhaps he would get her to tell him of them someday.

Merrit was in misery, the heat in the crowded building tormenting her body and the words, her soul. She cringed in her pew as the rector spoke vehemently on the wages of sin, her hands going consciously to her still-trim waist line and her eyes to the lover who stood boldly beside her. She felt as though their presence mocked the sanctity of the holy gathering. The minister's condemning words became an unpleasant buzz as her head began to throb and reel, and a dizzying sickness made her overheated skin grow suddenly cold. She felt a strong hand on her elbow as the room began to spin and darken, but she was barely aware of moving her feet as Nicholas lead her from the pew.

"I'll see her home," he told Mildred softly, as the woman made a move to follow. She looked at him long and hard, then nodded silently, agreeing to hold the family at bay so he could escort Merrit from the church.

"The heat, poor child," Mildred murmured to Winston as he turned in alarm to see his fiancée being led from the church. Annoyed, he was of a mind to follow, but found Mildred solidly blocking his way. "The captain will see her safely home."

Unable to get by her without using force, Winston angrily remained in his place, scowling darkly and planning all modes of retribution on the too helpful Nicholas Seward.

Merrit retched miserably in the grass, mortified as Colley held her easily, then gave her his handkerchief and chuckled low.

"Do not fret, my lady. I am not of a queazy nature. I've seen the contents of many a stomach after a long night's celebration."

She moaned in abject embarrassment, unable to look at him as he loosened the stomacher of her gown and waved her lacy fan until the heated flush began to subside in her otherwise pasty face.

"Do you think you can stand, my lady?" he asked finally. " 'Twould not do for them to find you on my lap outside their church doors."

Horrified, Merrit struggled to rise but the nausea had not yet abated and the sudden movement brought her to a near swoon. Her protests went unheeded as he lifted her in his arms to deposit her gently upon the seat of his closed coach. After speaking briefly to the driver, he climbed in opposite her, the width of her skirts keeping him from joining her on the same seat.

"Are you all right?" he asked solicitously, chafing her chilled hands and anxiously awaiting the return of color to her cheeks. "I didn't know you were ill."

" 'Tis not illness," she assured him faintly, unable to halt her words in time, "but a natural state in my condition."

Nicholas jerked back as if she had struck him, his eyes growing large and round as the meaning of her words hit him with the force of a roundhouse punch. For a brief moment his face lit with unrestrained joy, then darkened as the poison of doubt tainted his elation. His question was unforgivably blunt.

"Have you told the father yet?"

Her face grew even whiter, then fused to deep crimson,

her eyes nearly black with outrage that he would dare ask such a thing. "I am telling him now," she frostily replied.

The tight line of her lips and her flashing glare told him he had made a grave error and his mind scrambled quickly to make amends. In his haste he made matters worse. " 'Twas a fair question from what I have been told," he muttered in defense of his faux pas.

Her voice was deadly calm. "Just what have you been told and by whom? Who would the sire be if not you?" She mistook his silence, and had her head not been so giddy, she would have struck his expressionless face. Did he truly believe she was carrying the child of another or did he wish to avoid his responsibility. Her words were low and shaken. "I have been with no man but you. The babe is yours. I cannot force you to believe that."

The image of her lying beneath Winston on the ground rose to taunt him. For a moment, he struggled with that picture, then he met Merrit's eyes and the doubts were purged. "Of course, I believe you," he answered flatly. He leaned back in the seat in a daze. "You took me by surprise 'tis all."

Only slightly mollified, Merrit said sarcastically, "Surely you were not unaware of such a consequence when the Caribbean is most likely populated by your green-eyed bastards. What is one more?"

Her barbed words brought a frown to his handsome face, lessening his charitable feelings. "Yours will be the first to my knowledge. Pirate women are careful to avoid that trap."

"Leave it to a foolish virgin to be caught up in it. You'll have to be more cautious with the next maid you initiate." Her eyes grew shimmery, but the cold look in them kept him from comforting her. "Who were you willing to lay credit to? Winston, I assume. How could you be so stupid?"

"It seems a natural state for me where you are concerned," he confessed in surly humor. Then his brows lowered in sudden suspicion. "Of course. I wondered why she would call me Colley. Gabrielle must have overheard us talking together."

"She knows we were once lovers. She accused me of it when she was confiding to me that you had deflowered her."

"What?" he gasped in surprise, but the near truth of the girl's claim brought a guilty flush to his face that gave Merrit pause. "She lied and to me as well. She tried to provoke me into succumbing to her seduction by telling me you were bedding her brother." He let out his breath in a harsh rattle, eyes closing at the thought of his gullibility.

"And did you?"

His eyes opened. "Did I what?"

"Succumb."

His answer was succinct. "No."

"Does the thought of this child displease you terribly?" Merrit's question was soft but weighty with importance.

Sighing, he admitted, "I do not know. I'm not certain yet what I feel. And you, my lady? What of you?"

She met his searching eyes with a calm smile. "I am not displeased by your child. It will be born of our love if not in your name. And I will have a name to give the child. It will not be called bastard."

"What be your plans, my lady?" His eyes dropped, as he waited reluctantly for the noose to close about his neck, but she surprised him.

"If I marry right away, Winston may be convinced that the babe was conceived in wedlock. I can only pray that the child will be small and in no great hurry. You need have no fear that I will involve you."

"You would give him my child?" Nicholas asked dully. His thoughts were slow, and muddled by her sudden revelation. It was too much for him to absorb quickly, the magnitude and consequence of the situation out of his scope of quick reasoning.

"I would give my child the Whitelaw name. After all, you will be able to see it often as you like. You will be its uncle when you marry Gabrielle, and then you can have your own children, legitimate ones. No one need ever know that this child is yours save us. And Mildred."

Nicholas was silent, feeling himself being slowly strangled on an unseen noose. He weighed the arguments from the heart that demanded he claim the child and those from the mind that told him to take the escape she offered. His emerald eyes took on a hard sheen as cold logic took over. "And if I were to wait until he boasted of the fine child of his loins, then claimed it as my own, how sharp a vengeance that would be."

"Would you treat me and your child so harshly, Colley?" she asked softly, fearing the fiery brilliance of his stare.

She touched his knee and that glassy stare wavered, beginning to melt as he looked into her dark liquid eyes. "No, I would not, Merrit," he said quietly, and reluctantly enough for her to believe him. "What do you want of me?"

It was the question she had longed to hear but the time was wrong. She wanted him to come to her freely. "Nothing, Colley, save your promise that you'll not interfere in my plans."

Her hopes soared as he balked at her request, but then he answered in a low voice. "You have it, my lady." He took up her hands, pressing hot kisses to them, then holding their palms to his face as his eyes searched hers. "But what about now? I want you, Merri."

"I will come to you as often as I can until I marry. Once I wed, I can see you no more. What we do now is a sin of passion, but I will not commit adultery for you. Will you abide by that?"

Looking into her eyes, he knew she meant what she said, that she would be lost to him once her vows were spoken, but there was still time and he would make the most of it. "Aye, my love. I will."

Merrit pulled her hands from his as the coach turned into the drive at Whitelawn, and dismissed his offer to see her to the door, saying, "I feel quite well now, and I need some time apart from you to think on what I must do."

"Come to Twilight tonight, Merri," he urged in an eager tone. "Or let me come here to you."

"You mustn't come here. 'Tis too great a risk. I will come to you if I can. You must satisfy yourself with that, my pirate lord."

"Tonight, Merri."

After being told that Merrit was resting after a bout with a stomach disorder and did not wish to be disturbed, Winston stormed into the study to pour himself a liberal drink. The last thing he was interested in was the banal chatter of his sister, but for once his fierce glower did not discourage her.

"Why are you so patient with her, Win? You treat her as if she were something fragile that would break when handled, but I can assure you that is not the case."

"What are you prattling about, Gabi?" he demanded in irritation, but something in the girl's insinuating tone caught his attention.

Gabrielle gave a crafty smile. Merrit's plan to feign illness and lure Nicholas from the church had nearly blinded her with humiliation and fury. Nicholas was clearly just an unwilling victim. Once Merrit was out of the way, he would turn back to her. It was time to take care of her brother's fianceé.

"You treat her as if she were some tender virgin, but that is not true."

Winston's pale eyes narrowed dangerously, taking on a cold glitter. "None of your gossipy tales, Gabrielle. You make a serious charge."

"It was from her own lips that I heard it."

"And whom did she name as her lover?"

Gabrielle thought rapidly. Knowing she could not name

Nicholas, she seized upon what she thought was the substitute. "Why the Spanish Angel, of course. He forced her and she was in fear of her life, but she was his lover. I know if I had been in such a position, my Colley would marry me at once to save me from any hint of scandal. After all, you would not want to lose your fortune."

Vapid little twit that she was, for once Gabrielle had shown remarkable insight. Haste was vital to Winston's cause if he was to secure his bride and her dowry, but he was not fool enough to believe his sister was concerned for him. He knew she feared losing her pretty captain. It was time to deal with Seward as well.

"Thank you, sister. I will take care of everything. Now excuse me. I am expecting an important visitor."

His guest arrived shortly, obviously annoyed by the abrupt summons.

"Captain," Winston began. "I understand you share an interest in ridding the waters of a certain Spanish pirate."

"Angel," the man spat out. "He escaped my noose with the help of your fair lady, but I will have him again."

"What if I said I could deliver him to you?" Whitelaw poured two glasses of wine and held out one to Captain Neville, smiling at his sharpened look of interest.

"Go on."

"Describe the Spanish Angel to me."

"He is deceivingly small and fair of face, with the exception of a scarred cheek I hear your lady gave him. His looks are dark and Spanish, but his eyes are green from crossed blood."

"And what of his relationship with Lady Merrit?" Seeing the captain's hesitancy, Winston was curt. "Come man, the truth. I am no fool."

"She was very protective of him. I would say they are great friends—if not more. She spoke with him very familiarly, calling him by name."

"What name?"

"Colley? Something like that."

Winston gave a slow smile. "Ready your ship, Captain, and prepare to hang a pirate."

Rufe raised an eyebrow in curiosity at hearing his captain loudly and resonantly, singing what sounded like a hymn, humming the tune when he lost the words. Nicholas strolled into the study, twirling his formal wig by one false curl until it was so ravaged it would need a barber to comb it back into shape. He grinned when he saw his friend's puzzled stare and perched the wig upon Rufe's head.

"Good morning, my lord quartermaster. Come join me for a toast."

Rufe removed the wig, brushing the powder from his hair with a bemused smile. " 'Tis a bit early to be so drunk, Colley."

"I am not, not yet, but I plan to be if you will help me on my way." He splashed black rum into two large goblets, and passed one to his friend. "Drink a toast with me. To my impending fatherhood."

Rufe's smile dropped in dismay. "I thought you had no plan to bed the wench."

Nicholas gave him a bewildered look, then gasped in matching horror. "Good God, no. Not that simpering chit. My toast is to the Lady Merrit."

The beginnings of a frown on his face, Rufe touched his glass to Nicholas's. So she had won the captain after all. "She trapped you into marriage, did she?" he asked quietly.

Emerald eyes dropped to the contents of his glass, and Nicholas spoke, betraying no emotion. "No, as a matter of fact she plans to marry Whitelaw and pass the babe off as his."

Proceeding cautiously, Rufe said, "So your plans continue undisturbed."

"Damn my plans," he muttered harshly, draining his glass

382

and pouring another. As he sipped it more leisurely, his thoughts grew dark and brooding. An uncle, not a father. There was little satisfaction in that. He thought of Whitelaw bragging as Merrit's figure ripened, of him holding the wailing newborn child, holding that child as it slept upon his shoulder—thought of the child, his child, calling another man Father.

"Damn," he growled, and began to pace, his mind spinning in agitation. Now there was more than Merrit to consider. Any ruin he brought on the Whitelaws would be felt by his child as well. A picture of Merrit rose to torment him. Her features tragically aged by hardship, she was dressed in tattered finery, a child at her side, one that looked like him, a child who had to roam the streets, steal in order to survive, if one could call that survival. "No!"

His glass shattered against the fire grate, splintering like his emotions into tiny, broken fragments. The pieces were coming apart even as he struggled to hold them together— the free Spanish Angel, the dirty-faced street urchin that spat on a nameless grave, the affluent Nicholas Seward, and the man who laid his head in the lap of the woman he loved. He couldn't find the common thread that stitched them all together.

"What is it you want, Colley? What's most important to you?" Rufe asked quietly, seeing the battle raging within the tense figure.

"I do not know. All has been confused since I met her. I love her, Rufe, and I cannot bear to let her go." The admission was softly spoken, yet heavy with emotion.

"If she be that important, then marry her."

He scowled. "And become what, landlocked gentry? All I know is the sea, and that is no life for a missus and child."

"Then go back to the sea and forget all that's here. It will be your child who is the next earl. Is that not satisfaction enough?"

"No," he snarled, beginning his restless pacing once more.

"They'll not escape with a slap of the wrist. I want their throats in my hands." His knuckles cracked as he demonstrated what he would do.

"Then let Merrit marry him and you wed the pale-faced daughter. Take their fortune and their honor, then you and your lady can go and live your own lives. You would have it all, Colley, your vengeance and your lady."

Nicholas pursed his lips thoughtfully. The suggestion was a promising one, but he soon sighed heavily. "She would not go with me. She has said as much. She won't live the life of a pirate wench, and I want no child of mine to become as I am."

"She would go with you into hell if you asked her to."

"Yet isn't that what I offer her in a life with me? I want what's best for her, yet I am too selfish to let her have it. What am I to do?"

"Have you asked her what it is she wants? Not what she thinks you want to hear, but what she really wants in her heart? She may yet surprise you."

Nicholas chuckled. "You surprise me, Rufe. I did not think to see you come to her defense. I thought you preferred things as they were."

"I did my friend," he replied with a smile. "But if having her will take the bitterness from you, then I will raise a toast to her." He lifted his glass, wresting a smile from the glum captain. "Time will provide you with your answer. You have only to wait to see which wind will fill your sails."

"But have I the time?"

Both turned as the double doors opened and Freddy Moffit appeared in his full livery. "A lady to see you, Captain."

Nicholas felt his anxiety fade. She had come after all. Smiling, he strode to the door, then drew up short, his exclamation of welcome freezing on his lips.

"Good day, Nicholas. Are you surprised to see me?"

Disappointed would have been closer to the mark, he

384

thought as he forced a smile. "What brings you here, Gabrielle?" Uninvited, his eyes added.

Gabrielle's enboldened determination waned somewhat in the face of his less than enthusiastic greeting. She had only been to his home twice, both times on social occasions and at his request. Now she began to doubt her wisdom in appearing unannounced. It was the first time she had seen him so casually, his head bare and his shirt open to show a good deal of browned chest. He looked so naked standing there, his black close-cut hair making him appear strange and foreign like his voice when she had heard him speak to Merrit. Aside from that, his manservant was also present. The hulking colored man always made her uncomfortable with his unconscionable familiarity with his master and his too brazen eyes.

"I—I came to thank you for your kindness to Merrit this morning."

He gave her an easy smile. "It was my pleasure. You did ask me to treat her like family. Is she quite recovered yet?"

"I am sure she has from whatever strange and sudden malady overcame her. I would not have thought her to be the sickly type," Gabrielle added critically, casting a sharp glance at Nicholas's handsome impassive face.

"Appearances can be deceiving," he responded blandly. A lengthy silence followed, during which she waited for him to extend some hospitality, but he only asked, "Was there anything else, my dear? I am quite busy at the moment."

"You could have your man offer me some refreshment. It is a hot day and the trip was rather dusty." Her fan fluttered to attest to her frailty as Nicholas raised a finger and the silent servant moved to the sideboard. In a lowered but hardly discreet voice, she confided, "Nicholas don't you think he is a bit unsuitable for the house?"

Seward's green eyes widened and flashed to Rufe's turned back. "In what way?"

"He is so unpolished and so—so huge he quite alarms

people. He should be working in the fields where you could make use of his size. I could find you a genteel valet if you've no objection."

"How thoughtful of you." He took the glass of sherry Rufe extended without sparing him a glance, noting how gingerly the lady accepted the fragile crystal from his friend's enormous hand. "Since you have broached the subject, are there any other changes you would make?"

Not catching the cynicism in his voice, Gabrielle warmed quickly to what she felt was interest in her opinion. Her eyes swept the tasteful room, secretly impatient to call it her own. "You are a man of great influence and are the focus of many eyes. Your home and your appearance are under constant scrutiny from your peers. Your staff, well frankly it is an odd assortment hardly befitting a man of your stature. Folk have thought it curious that they be all men and such an unsavory lot. Why your cook is half-blind, your driver is lame, your groomsman has but one eye. I would cast the lot of them out and find acceptable help. After all, a man and his wife are judged by the household they keep."

He sipped his drink casually as he listened to her, the angles of his face becoming more prominent as his jaw tightened and his lids drooped until cool emeralds peered, glittery, from slits. "So you find my household lacking. And me as well, my dear?"

"Oh, no. I could never find fault with you," she said quickly.

"Only with my judgment. It is not my wont to consider how I am viewed by those I have no regard for." He set down his glass, then looked up at the girl in the frilly, expensive gown that did little to soften her shrewish nature. He saw a spoiled, thoughtless child whose interest would never extend beyond her own wants. In fact, she was a lot like himself. This was the woman he was to share his life with, and his bed. Her strident voice would greet him each morning, and her narrow body would bear the children that would carry his name.

His voice low but with an unmistakable edge to it, he said, "I will tell you this only once, Gabrielle, and I trust you will hear my words and understand them well if you plan to live in this house. Firstly, Rufe is my friend, not my lackey. He plays the part because it suits my purpose and it amuses him. You will treat him as a guest, not as a servant who hasn't the wits to understand that you are speaking rudely about him. As for the staff I have chosen to employ, I will tolerate no interference from you. They are here because it is my wish—not to please the neighboring gentry or you, my dear. This is my house and you will not question how I choose to run it. Though you may live here, you will not take advantage of being its mistress. Make no mistake about that."

Gabrielle heard his speech with an ashen face, unable to believe he would talk to her in such a manner especially in front of servants. Injured pride far outweighing her sensibilities, she snapped pettishly, "Is that because you already have a mistress in your house?"

Restraint fled beneath her derision, and Nicholas's swarthy face grew black with rage. It was with difficulty that he kept from shaking her. He bit out between clenched teeth, "My mistresses are also none of your concern. I will not answer to you for anything I do. You will have my name, but that gives you no right to make demands on me. I will see that you are well provided for and have all you desire, but never criticize me and never question me. My personal life is my own. I will not interfere in yours and you will not in mine. In the future you will not come here unless by my request, otherwise you will not be welcome and will not be allowed in. Do you understand all that I have said to you?"

Gabrielle nodded jerkily, suddenly very frightened of this strange cold-eyed man whose words were flavored with a rich accent. She felt the slut had clouded his affection for her

387

and made him treat her like a common kitchen maid. That will change, she vowed to herself. Merrit Ellison would never set foot near her husband or in their home. With a last confused look at his handsome angry face, she fled the room, tears prickling her eyes and a fierce spite in her heart.

Nicholas watched her go with a sneer of distaste. "The price is becoming very hard to bear," he said heavily. "I wonder if saddling myself with that stupid snake-tongued chit is a harsher revenge upon me. Am I being a fool, Rufe?"

"You'd not like my answer, Colley, and time will give you yours."

Clad in a silken wrapper, her face still lacking its usual color, Merrit received Winston in her sitting room, waving him into the wing chair opposite her own. The sudden intensity of his gaze gave her cause for alarm, but then he smiled easily.

"I trust you are feeling much better, my dear."

"Yes, thank you. It must have been the rich food I had last night. I am sorry if I caused you any distress."

Looking at her lovely wide-eyed face, it was difficult to believe she was such a liar, that there was a deceiving heart behind those sweet lips and innocent looks. But what she was wasn't as important as what she could do for him, and he didn't want to lose her.

"Merrit, I don't want to seem overly bold, but I can wait no longer to have you at my side as my wedded wife. Permit me to announce our engagement on Friday. We could then be married in less than two weeks' time."

Two weeks. Her mind was awhirl. In a moment of panic, she wanted to cry a crisp denial, to beg for more time, but she knew her expanding figure would not allow her the respite.

"That would please me very much if it would not put too

388

much of a strain on your mother to make the arrangements in such a short time," she said quietly, her dark eyes betraying none of her upset.

"I have already discussed it with her and she will see to everything. You have made me the happiest of men, Merrit. I will be away until Friday. We have a ship sailing to England on that day, carrying the goods that will guarantee us a comfortable life. At their sale, we should want for nothing." He provided the information casually while watching her expression. She showed no undo interest, but then she was skilled at concealing her thoughts. The information would get to her lover, he was sure of it, and Neville would be anxiously awaiting him.

With a small smile, he bent to kiss her, annoyed by the subtle turning of her head that granted him only a smooth cheek. For now, he would play the game, but later she would be his.

## Chapter Thirty

The figure in the doorway stood out in sharp bias against the darkness of the night, an unidentifiable shadow until the silken hood of a capuchin was pushed back to reveal the face of his haunting dreams.

"I was not sure you would come," Nicholas said quietly, unable to do anything but look upon her with appreciative eyes. Then he smiled and extended his hand to her. "I've had a late supper prepared if you'd care to join me."

Her fingers closed warmly about his. "I would enjoy that," she answered, her eyes filled with him and her heart suddenly accelerating with a leap of excitement. In this candlelit backdrop of warm, welcoming panels and soft opalescent paintings, a small corner of the endless dining table became an intimate island furnished with sterling, crystal, and Irish linen. Except for the absence of a wig, Nicholas could well have been the earl he was entitled to be, clad as he was, elegantly, in deepest blue with heavy gold trim and stitchery, and buttons of jeweled lapis. His features were dark and exotic in the dim light, and above the snowy stock and lace-frilled shirt, his gleaming cat's eyes gave him the look of a sleek, glossy panther. Those bright eyes mocked the genteel image he presented, hinting at the treacherous eddies beneath his deceivingly smooth surface. But Merrit could now look easily into the deep, sometimes murky waters of his soul. To her, his eyes were as calm and clear as the Nassau cove as they roved caressingly over her while one of two liveried men seated her. He took his place at the table's head and gestured for their meal to be served. As a surprising number of dishes were set out on the sideboard, Merrit rose.

"You may go. I will serve your captain."

Used to taking orders and hearing firm authority in the lovely woman's voice, the men didn't question her words but faded like shadows, into the recesses of the banquet-length room.

Nicholas leaned back in his chair, watching Merrit, a trace of a smile playing over his full mouth as she filled his plate and then her own before pouring a rosy wine into fine-stemmed goblets which had been carefully chilled. After eating in silence, their eyes devouring each other even as they feasted on the delicacies upon their plates, she cleared the table and bent over his shoulder to refill his glass. Her silk clad breast brushed his arm and her tantalizing scent teased his nostrils with a waft of jasmine. The sudden heat in his loins urged him to seize her trim waist and pull her onto his lap for a hearty kiss, but, with difficulty, he ignored those lustful stirrings. He wanted to sample more of her infectious charm before savoring her delightful person.

"Come, my pirate lord. Let us go into the drawing room and enjoy this fine bouquet of wine and the warmth of a fire while the evenings are yet cool enough to encourage one."

He followed her wordlessly, intrigued and bemused by this woman who seemed so comfortable and gracious in his home. And the feeling was a most pleasant one. She seated him on the settle then went to kneel at the fire grate to cajole a blaze from the neatly arranged kindling. Watching her, he was assailed with a rush of warmth and contentment. He had ordered the house built with every luxury but never had it seemed a home to him until he saw her gentle figure bent over his hearth. She could enhance a meager ship's cabin or a bawdy Nassau tavern by her mere presence. Sipping the wine, he mulled over the prospect of seeing her daily moving thusly about the great house, her slender form rounding with the weight of their child—thought of her remaining beside him as the sun rose high, no longer a slave to time and the hours of darkness that passed so quickly.

His musings were interrupted by Rufe's arrival. The huge man halted inside the doorway, his eyes flashing between the two of them.

"I beg your pardon," he said quickly. "I was not aware you were here, my lady. I had some things to discuss with you, Colley, but they can wait."

"Nonsense, Rufe," Merrit insisted, rising gracefully in a ripple of pale pink silk. In the months ahead, that would become no easy task. "You are here now. See to your business whilst I pour you a glass."

"Thank you, my lady."

Nicholas smiled. So Rufe felt it too. Merrit assumed the role of his hostess with a natural ease, and it pleased him that she would want to. As he listened to his quartermaster's efficient categorizing of the stores and repairs required by the *Merri Fortune*, his eyes continued to rest warmly on the petite chestnut-haired beauty as if he were mesmerized by her every move. He was unaware that Rufe was observing him just as closely, but with a reluctant amusement. Rufe saw clearly that the lady was indeed about to trap his friend so skillfully that Colley had not even seen the snare. Had she made demands on him, he would have backed away warily, but her silent acquiescence drew him to her, a willing, unsuspecting victim. She was clever in the weaving of her silken net, and had he not seen her purpose, Rufe would have shaken his friend and captain roughly awake. But Merrit loved him. She was bearing his child. She treated Rufe with unquestioning equality, showing him an unaffected acceptance he had found only once before in a beaten, yet unbroken, Spanish boy who called him friend. If Gabrielle Whitelaw became mistress of the house, Rufe would no longer be welcome in it despite Nicholas's words and their years of unrestricted friendship. That did not sit well with him. Nicholas would soon have to choose, make a decision that would irreversibly change his life, and Rufe knew where his captain's real allegiance lay.

"Well, I'll take up no more of your time. I can see the lady would much rather have you to herself while you can still be together." He looked past Nicholas's brooding frown to grin broadly at Merrit, seeing understanding and silent thanks in her faint smile and warm eyes. "Good evening to you."

While there was yet time . . . Nicholas chafed beneath that thought, feeling he was being uncomfortably rushed into something he was unprepared for. He wanted to cling to the present, to dig in his heels stubbornly against his enemy time, but it was a useless struggle. Defeat was something he could never accept gracefully. He managed a moody smile as Merrit settled herself beside him. She kissed him softly at first, then more deeply as she sensed his need. When he moved to embrace her, she intercepted his hands and guided his head down onto her silken lap.

"Rest yourself, Captain," she crooned, beginning a firm, exquisite massage of his knotted muscles. "Close your eyes to all about you and place yourself in my hands."

Obediently, his eyes closed and he rolled onto his stomach, releasing a pampered sigh as he let her fingers knead the tension from his neck and shoulders as well as from his thoughts.

"Merri—"

"Shh, no more talk," she instructed. "Just relax."

Surprisingly, he found that easy to do, he who was so consistently on edge, so unused to dropping his guard. With Merrit, there was no need for pretense. She didn't expect him to be the bold Spanish Angel or the smoothly confident Nicholas Seward. She accepted him, not as a glossy image but as a man touched by insecurities and doubts, a man who was more vulnerable than he would ever concede. The release from pressure to be more than he was brought him an unusual peace. Smiling in contentment, he didn't realize that he had just sprung her trap.

Feeling the unmoving heaviness of his dark head on her lap, Merrit allowed herself a smile. "I have you now," she whispered to the sleeping man. "You will yield to me, Colley. You must. There is no more time for reluctance. You must take me now or let me go. I pray that you take me, my love. I will make you happy. I swear I will. Surrender your hatred and have my love instead. I know it is much to ask, but trust me and believe in my love." As her fingers lightly stroked his smooth bronze cheek with its curving scars, he muttered softly in his sleep and then turned onto his side, his head sliding from her lap as he curled up defensively as if in denial of her words. "Very well, my pirate lord. Have this evening to yourself, but I won't let go so easily." Pressing a faint kiss to his forehead, she collected her cloak and slipped into the night.

The evening was cool, the full moon a silvery beacon on the shadowy path between the two estates. Merrit was unhurried, knowing morning to be hours away, and the darkness felt good to her, the night breeze as soothing as the cool hands of a gentle lover. The leisurely walk calmed her unsettled emotions and eased her uncertainty about the future. She had done all she could to prove herself. She would not beg him. It was his choice, and she would make the best of it without bitterness or regrets.

A sound on the path behind her made her turn, then give a cry of alarm as a large silver shape loomed out of the night to bear swiftly down upon her. Her breath was expelled in a gush as she recognized Pieces of Eight being ridden bareback by his rather harried-looking owner.

"Merri, why did you go? I awoke to find you'd left me. Why didn't you awaken me?"

She smiled up at Colley, gratified by the hint of panic in his voice. "I wanted some time to think, and you no longer had need of me so I decided to return to Whitelawn."

"You were mistaken there, my lady," he told her quietly, extending his hand to her. "If you are returning, I will see you there."

She grasped his hand, letting him lift her up in front of him so he might hold her in place by placing an arm about her waist. Her head sought the comforting hollow of his throat as her own arms slipped about him.

"What prompted you to flee from me?" he asked, nudging his stallion into a slow gait.

"Winston and I are announcing our engagement at a ball Friday. We will be married a week thereafter."

He sucked in his breath noisily, stunned in silence for a long moment. When he spoke, his voice was low and noncommittal. "That should please you. I know you are in haste because of the child." His large hands moved across her midriff. "When is the babe expected?"

"By Christmastide," was her soft reply. His strangely quiet acceptance was not what she'd expected—or hoped for.

His caress lingered over her flat belly as his thoughts strayed to the tiny seed that flourished beneath his palm. "What better gift could a man ask for than his first-born," he reflected. His hand stilled. Merrit's silence made him continue. "When will I be able to feel it move within you?"

His genuine interest made her smile. "I should be able to feel it within the next months, but 'twill be a bit longer before its kicks are hearty enough for you to notice."

"Not so long. 'Tis a strong healthy babe and 'twill be as restless as its father." His arms tightened constrictively as he said, "I am the father of this child. 'Tis not right that another should claim what we made between us."

Merrit pulled away so abruptly she nearly lost her seat. Her voice was aghast and frightened. "No. You promised, Colley. You cannot call this child your own."

In the hazy moonlight, his eyes glittered like fresh-cut gems as his expression grew severe. "You ask me to ignore the fact that I sired the child that will be the Whitelaw heir?

395

You expect me to forget the nights we spent together to conceive that miracle you carry? You asked before how I felt. I can tell you now that I am pleased. You please me. The thought of our child pleases me even more. You cannot take that from me, Merri."

Her tears were glistening trails down her upturned face., the sight of them unnerving him despite his bold words. "I must if I am to have a future to give this babe. You will give me nothing, so do not prevent me from seeking it elsewhere. You have no right."

"No right?" he thundered, then relented when he felt her trembling with sobs. "I love you, Merri. I give you everything I am and all that I have. Come live with me, let me take care of you and our child. Let me raise it to know who its father is. If you want Twilight, it be yours. Anything only don't leave me again. Don't take from me that which we share together."

"What are you asking me?" she demanded, suspicious of this proposal that wasn't quite a proposal.

"Come with me. Be with me. Nothing need stand in our way. I want you, Merri. Nothing else need matter to us. I will see you have all you need."

She understood him now, and her words shook with fury. "You are asking me to be your mistress, to bear your bastard child. No. Never. I will not be your whore."

"Dammit, Merri, what do you want of me? What?"

In her anguish, she threw subtlety to the wind and cried, "Your name, Nicholas. Give me your name. Make me your wife. Marry me and forget the past. Make me and your child your future."

Even as she spoke, she could feel him tense with rebellious denial of what she asked.

He withdrew to a defensive position behind cold green eyes. "No," he replied curtly.

Choking back tears of regret at her rash outburst, Merrit looked away, and her voice fragile with grief, she said, "Very well. I am sorry I spoke of it. I will not do so again."

Nicholas reined in his mount, surprised to find them on Whitelawn's terraced grounds. He was stunned and deeply shaken by Merrit's request, especially by how close he had come to giving her a different answer, and before he could catch her, Merrit slid from the saddle and ran to the house without a word or a glance for him. Wanting to call to her but not daring to, he cursed unhappily and wheeled his horse about, urging it into a reckless gallop. He rode throughout the rest of the night, restless and agitated, afraid to stop lest his thoughts catch up with him. He traversed his extensive property, galloping from the forests to the turgid shoals where cattails grew in profusion. This coast was the home for thousands of redwing blackbirds and many shore animals with rich pelts—muskrats, raccoons, and otters. Colley had heard the waters were rich with sturgeon, herring, and shad, as well as lobster and crab, but he had never been stationary long enough to try his hand at fishing or trapping. Those were things one did with one's son, he thought. As he roamed through the golden fields of tobacco that spread out for miles, he became slowly aware of just how little he knew of these vast lands or of the revenue they brought him.

Exhausted and smelling strongly of exertion and horse, he strode into his house—his home—and shouted for Rufe as he poured himself a liberal glass of rum. He grinned wryly at the look of curious dismay his appearance provoked, and surprised his friend by saying, "Find me my overseer. Wake him if you have to, and bring him here with lots of strong coffee. Tell him to bring his books."

Nicholas then spent the early morning hours poring over ledgers with a sleepy-eyed overseer who was at a loss to understand his master's sudden interest, though he was surprised by Sewards' acumen. When the overseer left, impressed by the man he had never seen before, Nicholas leaned back in his chair, his mind overtaxed by the enormity of what he'd taken for granted. He looked up over his umpteenth cup of strong coffee, and mumbled to Rufe, "By God, have you any idea of how wealthy I am?"

"Enough to set aside your pirating, I assume," Rufe replied with quiet astuteness.

Nicholas frowned at him in irritation as if his friend spoke treason. "If I chose to. I had no notion about all of this."

"What set you to looking into it? You had no interest before now." Rufe had his suspicions, but he wondered if his friend knew what drove him.

"I was but curious 'tis all," Nicholas bit out in a tone too hostile to permit further questions. But Rufe's knowing grin made him uneasy, and plucking at his sweat-stained shirt-front, he grumbled, "I'm in sore need of a hot bath and a year's sleep, but the sleep will have to wait. I've apologies to tender this morning."

"To Lady Merrit?"

"No," he replied brittlely. "Why would you think that?"

"Because you are here alone, tired and dirty, and she is probably pacing her rooms restlessly. Colley, when are you going to make your peace with her?"

"Leave off, Rufe," he growled in foul temper. "I'll not be pushed by you or her."

Gabrielle received her errant fiancé with a cool reserve that held no little trace of fear. Seeing him in the Whitelaws' stately parlor in all his elegant finery, she could almost believe that the man who had revealed himself to her had at Twilight was another, for surely this handsome, attentive gallant was not the fierce-eyed stranger who had nearly thrown her bodily from his home.

"Thank you for seeing me, my little one. I know I do not deserve such consideration after the shameless way I treated you yesterday. I have come to beg your forgiveness for the unforgivable, and to plead with you to accept this small token in recompense for my knavery."

Forgetting her compunctions, Gabrielle eagerly took the small box he extended, exclaiming breathlessly over the pearl bracelet, and the matching string for her neck.

"Oh, Nicholas, thank you. How can I not forgive anyone so generous?" she gushed hugging him exuberantly.

He withstood her embrace gracefully, then peeled her from his shirt-front with a strained smile. "I would be pleased to see you wear them on the night of your brother's engagement ball. I thank you for the invitation I received this morning."

"I know it is a bit hurried, but can you blame them considering the risks they've taken."

Her tone was so modestly proper that for a moment he stiffened, almost believing her until he conjured up Merrit's earnest expression as she vowed she'd been with no other. He repressed a sudden urge to slap Gabrielle's scheming face and merely smiled indifferently. "The wages of sin, I suppose. Where is your brother, by the way?"

"He's off seeing to some important venture. As you know, we've lost quite a bit to those marauding thieves, so he went to make certain this ship would get through. If we lose this cargo, we'll be ruined. Win is so clever about these things," she babbled carelessly, letting slip in careless ignorance the very information that could cause her family's financial collapse. Secure in her own fantasies, she had never thought throughout their courtship to question Nicholas's subtle probings about the coming and goings of their ships.

Not clever enough to keep his plans from his foolish sister, Colley thought to himself. Containing his excitement with difficulty, he asked, "What kind of cargo does he send?"

"Merrit's pearls, for one thing. The rest I am not certain of. He will use what is realized to buy up political favors and to repay what he borrowed to make up for cargoes stolen in the past. I think he is quite in debt, but do not fear, my own dowry is secure."

"Rest assured, Gabrielle. It is not your dowry I am

interested in." He pulled her to him, giving her a hard kiss in reward for the information that could finally secure him his vengeance. When he released her, Gabrielle staggered back in a near swoon, powerless to call him back as he bowed to her and took his leave.

Merrit knelt in the neat strawberry patch, having a difficult time seeing well enough to pick the ripe plump berries because of the haze that kept returning to her eyes. She dashed away tears with a shaky sigh and began her task again, trying to find some serenity in the simple chore though it had begun to strain her back sorely. She needed time alone, and was not likely to be disturbed here. Not with Winston gone and Sophia, Thaddeus, and Letitia in Williamsburg for the day and Gabrielle entertaining her caller in the parlor. She sniffed loudly, indulging in a bit of uncharacteristic self-pity. She was wont to meet a challenge head-on, but Nicholas's terse refusal had badly bothered her confidence, and had left her poor-spirited and weepy-eyed. It must be the babe, she concluded, drying her eyes once more, then gasping as a sudden shadow crossed her.

"Good morning, my lady. You make a most fetching sight there among the other tasty fruits."

She glared up at him, squinting due to the bright light at his back. She was in no mood for his flippant charm this particular morn, not with her swollen eyes and her teary disposition. "What do you want with me, Captain?" she asked softly. "I thought your business was inside."

"Business, yes, but not my pleasure," he responded with a rakish grin that touched her despite her sensibilities. He looked so calm and self-controlled while she felt so acutely miserable. "I thought I could coax you into giving me a bite of one of those succulent beauties." His grin widened as his eyes dipped to her bosom which had grown fuller and was straining against the simple calico of her gown.

Tempted instead to slap his leering face, Merrit rose,

pressing her palms to her back with a grimace, then scowling at his look of concern. She selected a large berry and held it out to him.

"Your taste, Captain."

He leaned forward and bit the strawberry in two, then took the remainder along with the tips of her fingers in his mouth, swirling his tongue around them and sucking off the juice. Merrit jerked back her hand, but now before he saw her shiver of desire. All the light-hearted teasing gone from his hot emerald eyes, he said huskily, "Do not be mean to me, Merri. If we've only two weeks, then let them be glorious ones. Come spend the day with me and all the nights to come. Don't deprive me of that."

"I will not deprive either of us," she confessed, her eyes downcast and her face drawn into a frown as if her weakness for him made her unhappy.

"Are you able to ride in your condition?" he asked soliciously, finally eleciting a smile from her with his naïveté.

"I am with child, not infirm, Captain."

He smiled at her sarcasm, encouraged once more. "Come with me, then. There are some things I would show you. I will wait for you at the end of the path."

Some minutes later, Merrit ran lightly down the stairs, a striking figure in her riding habit, its coat and waistcoat of blue camlet trimmed and embroidered with silver and her petticoat of the same fabric. Her Steinkirk cravat was twisted up to loop carelessly through a buttonhole in the coat, and her smartly cocked hat, edged with silver and sporting a sprightly feather, allowed only an errant curl or two to brush against her animated face. She couldn't suppress her excitement, though she knew she should be angry and hold herself from him. She had two weeks and would make full use of them. Perhaps she could convince him yet, but never again would she make the mistake of pressuring him.

"Going for a ride?"

Merrit looked up in surprise to see Gabrielle. The girl had barely spoken to her since their confrontation on the same stairs. "I thought I would. The house seems so empty with everyone about. I quite enjoyed riding at my own home."

"I think I would like to join you . . . if you've no objections."

Merrit wanted to shriek in annoyance but she forced a placid smile. "If you wish. I'll have a horse readied for you." She couldn't mistake the hard gleam of suspicion in the girl's pale eyes, and wondered with a touch of alarm and guilt how much Gabrielle knew and how much she was supposing out of hurt and anger. Whichever it was, the girl was determined to prevent a rendezvous between Merrit and the man she thought of as her stolen love. Cursing beneath her breath, Merrit went to the stable. Then she began to smile. If Gabrielle wanted a ride, she would have one.

The two women rode side by side in silence that was not an easy companionable quiet. Finally Gabrielle turned to Merrit, her one-time friend and said coldly, "I hope my decision to join you didn't interfere with your plans."

"What plans, Gabi?" she asked, with an innocent lift of her brows. "In truth, I am glad not to have to ride alone."

"And is a solitary ride what you had in mind?" The girl's lips thinned nastily changing her into a caricature of her mother.

"I beg your pardon?"

"You were going to meet him, weren't you? Too bad I foiled your scheme. You won't have him, Merrit, even if I have to expose you for the whore you are and have you driven back to your family in shame." Her eyes were bright with malicious promise, there could be no dismissing her spiteful words. She was cornered, and as dangerous as any defensive creature. Merrit stood in the way of what she

402

wanted, was an obstacle she would not tolerate.

"Gabi, please. You saw me as your friend once. That was no pretense. I had no idea he was your intended when we met or I would never have allowed anything to happen between us. You must believe that," Merrit said softly, her heart breaking for the girl.

"Believe you?" Gabrielle scoffed. She sneered unpleasantly. "You whore about with my fiancé under my nose, pretending to be my friend and making a fool of my brother then plead that I believe in your innocence? Oh, please. You may have fooled me once, but now I know you for what you are. Slut! Hussy! Making us feel sorry for you, the poor pirate captive, when you were probably happily whoring with the entire crew all the while."

Merrit's face went from white to flaming crimson, only pity for the unhappy girl keeping her from striking out. "You don't know what you are saying, Gabi. I don't blame you for hating me. I deserve your anger, but I am no loose-moraled whore. I love Nicholas. He is the only man I've ever been with. It should never have happened, but it did and I beg your forgiveness. I say this to you as a friend. You would do well to find yourself another man. You don't know him. He is not what he seems and will hurt you."

"I know him very well," Gabrielle snapped fiercely. "It is you who have corrupted him with your cheap offer of your body. I don't blame him for that weakness, but the words for you are many and too vile for me to say. Do not try to belittle Nicholas to me just so I will leave him because I won't set him free. He will be my husband. *I* will share his house and his bed and his many children, not you. Not you!"

Her words brought back the icy sweat and dizziness as they echoed with bitter truth. Grievously, Merrit cried out, "You are right. You do have him. It is you he will marry, so leave me alone. I need none of your taunts to remind me." Eyes burning with tears, she wheeled her horse about and

403

kicked it into a reckless gallop.

When Gabrielle reined her mount around to follow and hurl more hate-filled accusations, her saddle slipped perilously, sending her sprawling to the ground on her backside. By the time she neared the edge of the path, the sting of the encounter had faded some.

Merrit felt crushed by it, however. All that Gabrielle had said was true. While she might claim his love, it was Gabrielle who would have the man. The fact that she hadn't known about his ties to the girl lost its meaning, for she had allowed the affair to continue after she knew and was even now hurrying to meet him—his willing whore.

She dashed a trembling hand across her eyes, then straightened when she saw him ahead, lounging on the back of his silver stallion. The quick infusion of warmth into his handsome face should have pleased her, but it made her more unsettled yet.

"Where have you been?" he asked, taking her hand and pressing it to his lips. Her fingers were freezing. "Are you all right?" His eyes searched her face, seeing her pallor and the puffiness around her eyes. She had been crying again. "Merri?"

What could she say to him that wouldn't sound like a complaint meant to provoke sympathy? Instead, she managed a colorless smile and said, "Gabrielle insisted on accompanying me."

"Where is she?" he asked in irritation, looking down the trail.

"Most likely making the walk back to Whitelawn. Somehow her cinch worked loose."

Nicholas gave a hearty laugh of appreciation, then leaned over, his hand clasping her behind the neck and bringing her to him for a firm kiss. He was surprised by her momentary stiffening. Then her lips moved against his with a matching fervor and he forgot that instant of reluctance.

Seated back in her saddle, flushed and breathless, Merrit

asked faintly, "What did you wish to show me?"

"Ride with me."

They followed much the same route Nicholas had traveled during the early dawn, crisscrossing his properties, Merrit awed and Nicholas beginning to feel a strange stirring of pride and ownership.

"What do you think?" he asked finally as they looked over the tobacco fields. "It's all mine."

"I am very impressed. You have a sizable holding."

He swung one leg over the pummel of his saddle, and leaned on an elbow as he looked at her intently. "What would you suggest I do with it all?"

Her eyes swept the miles of fertile ground, and she smiled. "I would look into the best prices on the tobacco market, and use my own ship for transport to cut the costs. My father would know buyers to whom you could speak. If you have a good overseer, learn as much as you can from him. You have a talent for handling men and getting the most from them. Use it and stay in touch with those who work your fields. I would fence off that upper crop land and breed that fancy pony of yours. Judging by the race Pieces of Eight ran, that would be a profitable venture." She blushed slightly when she saw his smile, not certain of its meaning, wondering if he was making sport of her enthusiasm.

"So you would see me a wealthy planter." He chuckled when she didn't answer but looked away uncertainly. "And what do you think of my household staff?" There was an odd edge to his question as if it were a test of some kind.

"They are all pirates, aren't they?"

"Does that bother you?"

"Why should it? If they're aground, they're no longer thieving, though I cannot understand why they are not at sea."

"According to the articles of my ship, if a man be maimed or otherwise unfit for sea duty he is recompensed with eight

405

hundred pieces of eight and given lifetime employment here, that lifetime being his or mine."

She failed to share his rather grim jest, and he continued soberly.

"They are all good men and served me well on shipboard. There's not one among them I wouldn't trust with my life. They are loyal and discreet. Could you think of better virtues in a servant?"

"Only they're not just servants, are they?"

"They are my friends, and that wouldn't change whether they worked for me or I for them. Any one of them is welcome in my drawing room for a drink."

Merrit smiled then and remarked wryly, "The only difference now is the size of your quarters."

His white teeth flashed briefly, then all traces of humor were gone as he asked, "Were you mistress of my house would you accept that?"

She frowned and looked away so he wouldn't see the wetness in her eyes. "Don't tease me, Colley. That will never be the case."

"But if it were," he persisted.

She sighed heavily. "Lack of limb or sightedness does not lessen the man. I was well treated by your crew aboard ship. I don't see why that would change in your home. I fear I've grown used to having pirates about me."

A smile played across his mouth and his eyes grew thoughtful.

# Chapter Thirty-one

While a reluctant Mildred covered her absence at White-lawn, Merrit spent that night and the three that followed at Twilight. Though she came to him and loved him with a passion that left him drained and shaken, Nicholas became increasingly frustrated for each night she lay curled in his arms weeping softly until sleep came to her. No amount of questioning could make her name a reason other than the child for her moodiness, but except for those moments when she was lost to the exhilaration of their love, she remained strangely silent and withdrawn though maintaining the outward pose that nothing was amiss. He would catch her watching him with anguished eyes, but still she would name no cause.

By the eve of her engagement party, Colley was a bundle of raw edges. She had clung to him, tears dampening his chest, her silent sobs tearing through him mercilessly until at last she had fallen asleep. He slipped away from her and began to pace the floor in bewildered agitation, finally seeking solace from a bottle of brandy. Sipping the warming liquor, he gazed down on her calm profile, on the smooth cheeks that still showed traces of moisture. What had he done to hurt her so? He loved her. She knew that. She knew the reasons behind his plan for vengeance and accepted them. She wanted him, yet wouldn't come to him on any terms but those which she knew could never be. Or could they?

He sat on the edge of the bed and lifted a chestnut strand to rub it between thumb and forefinger, remembering with a smile when he had first felt that silken weight. How afraid she had been of him then. How strange that he should now fear her. He couldn't deny it. Since she had asked him to marry her, he had been in a quandary. He knew he should stay away, yet each time she touched him, he wanted her all the more. Tomorrow night she would pledge her future to Winston Whitelaw. She had spent the day being fitted for her ball gown, then had come to give herself without reservation. Although her marriage wouldn't deter him, he knew with a certainty that she would never lie warm and familiar beside him after her wedding day.

Frowning, he thought angrily, she's just a woman, a woman who would pull me from the sea with her demands, bind me to a suffocating life of drudgery. He scowled at that picture, but a part of him knew it was a false one. Any ties would be of his own making, for she had asked for none. He thought then of what he truly had and was willing to forfeit, a woman who loved him unconditionally, who knew him and still wanted him, who saw him off to sea with a kiss and no complaints and then welcomed him back with tears of gladness. She had taught him of love and trust and truth, had lightened his spirit with her warm humor, gentle graciousness, quick understanding, and unwavering loyalty. Now she carried his child proudly, and she asked only for his name, not his riches, not for him to change what he was. His name was good enough for her, the name of a half-caste pirate who lived too many lives and was accepted for himself in none of them. But she accepted him. She loved him.

"Ah damn," he growled, and shook her roughly awake. When she appeared up at him, groggily questioning, he said gruffly, "I need to hear that you love me."

408

She sat up, arms encircling his neck and face pressing into it. "I love you, Colley. I love you," she said softly.

He hadn't planned to tell her but heard himself saying low and gently, "I sail at first light." Her arms tightened convulsively but she was silent. "I will be back in time to see you before you make your pledge to Whitelaw. Perhaps then I can change your mind."

"I will not be your mistress," she stated faintly.

"Do not be so sure that is what I mean to ask you."

Merrit jerked back, her eyes wide with disbelief and sudden hope as they searched his for a confirmation. "What are you saying?" she asked in a voice so low he could barely hear her.

"Nothing yet. I cannot lose you, Merri. I couldn't choose before, but perhaps now I won't have to. This venture could satisfy my quest and free me."

Merrit's face was pale. "You're going after the Whitelaws' ship."

"You knew of it and did not tell me?" There was a faint bite of accusation in his tone, then he smiled to relieve it. "No, of course you wouldn't, my honest little love. Fortunately Gabrielle has no such compunctions." His eyes grew teasing. "Was it truly your wish that I give my love to Gabrielle, that I hold her like this?" His arms tightened, crushing her breasts to his hard chest. "And kiss her like this?" Lips possessed hers, his tongue slipping between them to tantalize her wickedly. "And love her like this?" He pressed her down to the mattress, half his weight upon her as he kissed her again in that wild, wanton manner until she tore away to catch her breath. "Is it, Merri? Would you send me to another with your blessings?"

Her dark eyes held his as she panted slightly, "You know it is not. I'd rather strangle her than see her in your bed. A part of me dies to think of you touching another. Oh, Colley, I want you and I want to be yours alone. Why must we be apart?"

"You are all I want, Merri. You are the only woman for me, and this is the only soft flesh I ever wish to touch." His hand caressed her lingeringly and then rested on her abdomen. "My child," he whispered thickly as he lowered his head to the smooth expanse that would soon begin to plump with life. "Oh, Merri, you are my life. Please don't leave me. Don't ever turn me away. Don't ever say no to my love. Promise me."

"I do. God forgive me, but I do," she moaned wretchedly. There was no point in pretending otherwise. She was his. She would always be his.

The sudden shriek brought him upright, a clammy sweat on his face and the nape of his neck bristling. Instinctively, even before his eyes opened, his hand darted to the night stand to grasp the primed pistol he kept there. His eyes flashed about seeking some threat, but they were alone in the still darkened room, and a close look revealed that Merrit was sleeping. Shakily he replaced the pistol and turned to the tossing woman. He gathered her in his arms and woke her gently.

"Merri. Merri, wake. 'Tis only a dream," he called, but her reaction sent a chill through him. Her dark eyes flew open, round and bright with terror, then they flooded with tears when she saw him. She hugged him about the neck, half choking him. "Merri, it's all right. I'm here. 'Twas a dream."

"It was no dream," she cried fearfully. "I saw you in a cage on the waterfront, your neck cruelly broken. Winston brought me to see you, so he might gloat over having had you killed."

"It was a dream," Nicholas insisted, though his spine had gone rigid at her carelessly blurted words. "I am whole and

410

here with you now."

"Colley, please don't go. I know you won't be returning to me. Not alive. Promise me you won't go."

"No one is going to hang me, love. I'll come back as I always have," he soothed, stroking her tossled head and trying to warm her chilled, trembling body.

" 'Twas an omen. A bad omen. Something terrible will happen if you sail. Let them go without you this time. Please, Colley. If you love me, don't go."

Rocking her gently like a frightened child, he crooned softly, " 'Tis because I love you that I must. I want to be with you, yet I cannot until I make peace with my past. Say no more of this foolishness, Merri. You will feel better in the morning."

She said nothing, but clung to him with all her strength, more afraid than she could ever remember being. He lay back slowly, holding her comfortingly, but she would not be comforted and the image would not leave her. Shivering fitfully, she nestled against his side, feeling the heavy throb of his heart beneath her cheek. When dawn came, she still lay like that, unmoving and frozen with fear, though he had readily fallen back to sleep.

There was a thump on the door and Rufe called, "Colley, wake up. 'Tis time to go."

Nicholas stirred slowly then came fully awake, mumbling a satisfactory reply and turning his face into Merrit's hair. "Good morning, my love," he said in a low warm voice, filled with the remembered joy of her promise not to forsake him. He frowned when he felt her begin to tremble. "Merri?"

"Colley, please don't go."

He chuckled and gave her a squeeze. "Don't begin that again. It was a dream, love, nothing more. Don't be such a goose. Now give me a kiss and wish me well and Godspeed."

But she refused to look at him or speak until she saw he was readying to leave. Then she leapt from the bed to cling to him like a half-crazed Cassandra. "Please stay. I will be your mistress. I will live with you. Anything, only don't sail today."

With a jaunty grin, he caught her chin in his hand. "My love, you always make these offers at the damnedest times. I love you, Merri and I will be back." His mouth moved slowly and convincingly upon hers, the quiver of her lips and her quick response touching his heart. His large hands moved from shoulder to hip tracing the supple softness of her, and he wished he had more time. He leaned back and kissed the salty dampness from her cheeks. "Look especially beautiful for me tonight," he said huskily, his eyes a dark, dusky jade. "I must go now."

When she saw Rufe and her love to the dock, she kept a carefully stoic front, though her hand clung to Nicholas's in a desperate possessiveness. She felt Rufe's huge hand on her shoulder and gazed up at him in ill-disguised panic.

"I will see to the captain, my lady, and will bring him, safe, back to you. You've my word on it."

"Your word as a pirate?" she asked with a tremulous smile.

"Aye and as his friend and yours."

She looked at her handsome love and the fear surged back again. "Be careful, Colley," she whispered.

"I will," he promised with a tender smile. He didn't dare kiss her again, afraid he might succumb to her tears if they began, so he lifted her hand to his lips and then turned to follow his quartermaster to the small boat tied at the dock. They rowed out to the *Merri Fortune* which lay hidden in the concealing mists of early morning. Once on deck, he let the confident Spanish Angel dismiss his doubts as he called for the ship to make sail.

The day was warm, yet a swift wind filled the parade of canvas mounted on the lengthy bowsprit and square topsail, speeding them along at better than eleven knots. The captain stayed on deck cleansing himself with the crisp smell of the sea and the flap of the breeze in the sails. The excitement of the chase was quickened by his lust for retribution. By night fall he could well have all or nothing. He thought of how pleased Merrit would be to receive as a gift her dowry pearls magnificently strung, for she would not need them to buy herself a husband. She would share no marriage bed with Winston Whitelaw. He would see to that. The Whitelaws would be crushed by the ravishment of their ship, for Colley intended to sink the vessel after setting her crew adrift. Then he would burst into the Whitelaws' home and claim all that was his — Merrit and his title — before all their well-to-do friends. The Whitelaws would be ruined and humiliated, and that would satisfy him.

"Ho, Angel. The ship."

Nicholas's head jerked up, eyes glittering. For a moment he was torn between the desire to rush in full tilt and crush his prey and the need to fulfill his responsibility to his crew and vessel. After a brief hesitation, he called out his orders.

"Bring her alongside. Wait to strike the colors. We take her by surprise."

But the pirates were the ones taken unawares. The sluggish merchant normally carried a crew of nineteen, barely enough to handle three guns but on a close look, she had a cannons in each of her sixteen mountings. By the time they were seen, it was too late.

"Steer clear," Nicholas shouted as the first volley ripped into the hull of the *Merri Fortune* sending him reeling against the rail. How did they know? The colors had yet to be unfurled. Merrit's prophesy flashed through his mind. A trap. "Fire on them and run to open water."

The two ships exchanged fire, the pirates frantically trying to repel any boarders and make good their escape. They were outgunned, their only chance lying in the sea on which their sleek craft would outdistance the lumbering commercial vessel. Partially lashed together, the ships shuddered as their cannon belched smoke and acrid powder, clouding the air with an unbreathable haze. Through the mist of bitter destruction, Nicholas looked to the opposite deck and surprise made his face blank for an instant, then a fierce snarl rose in his throat. On the other ship, his harsh features drawn into a grin of savage pleasure, was Captain Neville, the man who'd sworn he'd see the Angel hang. The foes stared at one another for a long moment, each seething hatred and knowing that this would be their final meeting.

Nicholas tore himself away to call, "Cut the ropes. Fire all guns at once and steer hard aport. Time to go." When he looked back across the narrow expanse of water, he saw the pistol in Neville's hand, and the man's thin lips moved in an epitaph.

"Not this time, Angel."

The pistol spat and the pirate captain staggered back, a bright spot of crimson blossoming like an exotic deadly flower across his shirtfront. Green eyes registered amazement, then chilled with purpose as he pulled his own piece free and sighted down the barrel at his startled nemesis. Then he fell to the deck.

"Colley. No!" The thundering roar of grief and fury came from Rufe who reached down to seize the pistol from his friend's still fingers. Neville was smiling triumphantly even as Rufe's shot tore through his throat, ending his life in an instant.

All the starboard guns roared at once, their blasts propelling the lithe sloop to one side as the wheel spun and the wind caught the fore and aft sails. The light ship slipped out to sea. Even badly damaged the *Merri Fortune* nimbly glided away to freedom.

Rufe knelt down heavily beside the sprawled figure and whispered hoarsely. "Oh, Colley, what do I tell your lady?"

Merrit sat at her dressing table, freshly bathed, powdered, and fragrant with the scent of spring. She had done as he had asked. She was exquisite to behold. Her glossy chestnut hair was dressed in small neat spheres of bubbling curls atop her head, and was covered by the merest wisp of lace entwined with delicate jasmine blossoms that echoed the haunting smell of her perfume. A bunch of the fragile blooms rested between her full breasts. The pale yellow damask gown she wore was tucked into a treble row of Watteau pleats flowing loosely about her while the outfit was stiff-bodied beneath. Cut scandalously low to expose the ripening swell of her bosom, the gown had wide skirts that billowed due to the support of extravagant painiers, so that Merrit looked like a graceful ship under sail when she moved. Lavish flounces of yellow lace fell from her elbow to merge with the matching gloves which left her slender fingers bare. About her neck and in her ears, emeralds glittered like living green fire, and as Merrit looked at them, her heart gave an uneasy twist. The terror of her dream had subsided to a dull nagging anxiety she could not dispell. It gave her features a sharp edge, tightening her usually mobile mouth and warm dark eyes. Though Merrit had not spoken of her fears, Mildred knew something was amiss and stayed close, fussing cheerily while keeping a cautious eye on her charge. Smiling in appreciation, Merrit closed her fingers over the large-boned hand of her friend. That fond exchange was shattered by Letitia's abrupt arrival.

One look at the child's grief-twisted features froze Merrit's heart. "What is it, Tisha?" she asked faintly, her pulses already racing with the certainty of what she would hear.

Tears spilled from the button-brown eyes as Letitia blurted clumsily, "I heard Win talking downstairs and thought it best I tell you this first. He's been killed, Merrit. Your Angel is dead."

415

Surprisingly, there was no hysterical reaction. Merrit sat quietly, her fluttering hand rising to clasp the bright stones that were the color of his eyes. She felt no pain, no loss; a numbing blanket covered her in a protective shroud. It was Mildred who gave an emotional wail, her arms flying about the motionless girl.

"Oh, me pet, me lamb. 'Tis sorry I am for ye. What will we do?"

Merrit patted her friend's solid arms in a detached, comforting manner, and said colorlessly, "I must get through this night. I pray to God I can. Thank you, Tisha, for your kindness. I will be able to bear the news now. I must go down or they will wonder what's keeping me."

She rose calmly and smoothed out the folds of her gown, quelling her sudden inner trembling. They must wait — the grief, the tears — until they could come out safely. She knew once the mourning began, it would consume her. She clenched her fan and moved with a stately grace from the two weeping females, steeling herself for the ordeal ahead.

Winston met her at the foot of the stairs, his light eyes boldly administering her beauty. He took her cold gloved hand in his and kissed the dainty fingers.

"You are astonishing, my dear. I have missed looking upon you. But soon we will never be apart again," he crooned. "Come, greet our guests with me."

It was an extravagant affair, at which the powerful and the landed gentry of Virginia quaffed imported wines and nibbled delicate tidbits. Even Colonel Alexander Spotswood was there to pay tribute to the daughter of his old friend. He came to plant a fatherly kiss on her rather pale cheek, and reluctantly shook Winston's hand. Personally, he had no use for that ambitious ruthless pup, but he was determined to be pleasant for Merrit's sake.

"Have you heard the news, Governor?" Winston gloated, a smug smile on his face. "Today I have rid your Capes of a

416

vile pestilence."

"Oh? Speak plainly, good fellow," Spotswood insisted, irritated by the younger man's cocky manner.

"I devised an elaborate trap and it's been neatly sprung. I've netted you the Spanish Angel." His eyes rested on Merrit to gauge her response, but she only raised a brow in feigned interest.

"Have you captured him then?" the governor asked sharply.

"He's dead, shot by my captain, Neville." Winston was impressed by Merrit's demeanor upon hearing of her lover's death. She had barely blinked, then had spoken in an even tone.

"I'll admit I am a bit regretful. He was most considerate of me when I was his captive, but still I am sure it will be of relief to those whom he plundered," Merrit declared.

"A toast then," said a low voice behind them. "To the demise of the dreaded Spanish Angel."

The blood rushed to Merrit's temples and she would have swooned if it were not for the sudden fierce grip of Winston's hand on her arm. The pain of his grasp returned her to her senses, and she slowly turned to face the mocking emerald eyes of Nicholas Seward.

Winston's surprise ebbed first, his face mottling with a frustrated rage. "What the devil are you doing here?" he choked out.

"No need to be rude. I assure you I was invited," Nicholas replied coolly, his eyes challenging. "I would not miss the opportunity to congratulate my future brother-in-law on his charming fiancée." With a taunting smirk, he lifted Merrit's hand to kiss it. As he bent, her other hand brushed quickly past him. He winced at the sharp tug on his earlobe then repressed a smile at seeing his gold earring safely encircling her finger. He had forgotten to change all his colors.

Merrit's shock had been too deep for her to respond

417

immediately to the relief that swept over her in a cleansing tide. It was with difficulty that she stood at Winston's side while her resurrected lover introduced himself to the governor and then exchanged pleasantries with an affable charm. She wanted to reach out and clasp him to her breast, to kiss him, to feel his strength, to assure herself that he was indeed here. Though he was impeccably dressed as usual, his face was flushed and his eyes had a strange bright glimmer. When he had taken her hand, Merrit had noticed a clammy chill to his normally warm fingers. Was he drunk then? His speech seemed clear, but there was a stilted awkwardness to his movements when he left them to rejoin Gabrielle.

The rest of the evening swirled by like a hazy dream, the gaiety leading to the purpose of the affair, the announcement of her betrothal. The music began, and she was led about in countless dances until she found herself face to face with the one she sought. He turned her around the crowded dancefloor with strangely uncoordinated steps, leaning upon her until she feared she would stagger under his weight. When his head lolled forward to rest heavily on her shoulder, earning them several scandalized looks, Merrit was prompted to scold. "Captain, even your obvious drunkenness will not excuse such a breach of decorum."

"You are most beautiful, my lady," he muttered thickly, his words slurring together.

"Oh, Colley, I thought they had killed you," she almost sobbed.

"I may not disappoint them," he mumbled, lifting his head with an effort to regard her with a quizzical smile. His face was dappled with sudden sweat and his eyes seemed to lose their focus. "Merri, get me from here. I'm going to faint."

Swallowing her questions, she steered him through the throng of dancers, struggling to keep him on his feet until they reached the secluded foyer by the stairs. There, he sagged down on a low bench, the sound that escaped him unmistakably one of pain.

"You've been hurt," Merrit gasped in alarm as she propped him back against the wall, fluttering her fan before him as he abruptly paled and his eyes rolled up, revealing only white. Heart pounding frantically, she opened his waistcoat, then bit her lips to seal off a wail of horror. The breast of his snowy shirtfront was stained with fresh blood, the ominous circle ever widening. When she reached to undo his shirt, he caught her hand weakly.

"Don't," he rasped. "Leave it for now. Get me home, Merri." His wandering gaze lit on a chubby girl in a nightdress kneling before him.

" 'Tis all right, Captain," Letitia assured him quickly. "I am a friend. Is it bad, Merrit?"

"I—I don't know. Colley, how did you get here?"

"Rode," he said simply, his eyes closing halfway.

"Where is Rufe? He let you come here like this? I'll have his head," Merrit promised fiercely, bringing a wan smile from him.

"He left me at Twilight and went to see the ship secured. He didn't think me fool enough to move. Captain Fool, eh, Merri?" He gave a low chuckle that ended in a gasp, his breath now coming in quick, shallow pants. "Barton in the stables is my man. Have him bring round a coach."

"Tisha, see to it, and fetch Mildred. I'll need her help to move him."

Letitia leapt up and raced barefooted up the stairs. Then, with a soft cry, Merrit embraced Colley, holding his head to her shoulder while she pressed her lips to his dark hair.

"Next time I will listen to you, my lady," he vowed in a gravelly voice.

"Hush now, my love. Be still and save your strength."

They sat together in the shadowed quiet, the music from the ball within hushed and distant. Yet as precious minutes ticked by, the risk of discovery grew.

"Here now, pirate. Have the decency to die somewhere else," Mildred said curtly as she knelt before him.

Nicholas leaned back with a lopsided grin. "I will do my best to oblige you, madam."

"Are ye hurt badly, laddy?" she then asked in genuine concern, worried by his pallor and uneven breathing.

"Bad enough to know we'd better go soon or you'll have to carry me." His right arm slipped about Merrit's shoulder but when Mildred took his left, he gave a short cry, his eyes squeezing shut and his breathing quickening. After a brief pause, he nodded and the two women brought him to wobbly feet. With Mildred's sturdy arm about his middle, they were able to hurry him unnoticed from the well-lit house into the shadows of the night. Letitia, wrapped in a robe, waited beside an enclosed coach. By the time they reached it, Nicholas was drenched with a cold sweat and his lips were pale, but he was able to muster his charm to take up the girl's pudgy hand. He stared into her round, awed eyes and murmured, "I am deeply in your debt, my lady. Thank you." He kissed her hand in all sincerity, causing Letitia's mouth to slacken in frank adoration before, with a flustered giggle, she ran back to the house.

"Another conquest I will have to fight for you?" Merrit teased gently to lessen her own anxiety.

"You need fight no one for me," he said huskily, touching her cheek with unsteady fingers. "Go back to your party, my lady. You will be missed."

She clasped his hand tightly. "I don't care. I want to be with you. I cannot leave you like this. Mildred, help me get him into the coach."

Between them, they boosted him none too gently into the seat. Merrit tried to climb in after him, but was hampered by the width of her hoops. With a grumble, she fumbled beneath her gown until the pannier collapsed in its graduated whalebone rings. Then, pointedly ignoring Mildred's disapproving glower, she settled on the seat beside Colley. He looked ghastly in the uneven light, slumped back against the seat, his breath hissing from between clenched teeth and his lids sagging over cloudy eyes. Gently, she undid his cravat and unbuttoned his ruined shit. The wadding he had pressed to the wound was saturated so she removed it, carefully laying bare the oozing hole beneath his collarbone. It was low enough on his chest to make her fear for his life. Though she said nothing, that fear was plain on her face.

Seeing it, Colley gave her a shadow of a smile.

"It seems I am forever breaking my promises to you," he muttered.

"You won't break this one, Captain. I won't let you," she vowed, folding the cravat into a small square and using it to staunch the frightfully steady flow of blood. "Don't you dare die. I would never forgive you that. Never."

The coach jerked forward, pushing him down beneath the dark eddied waters of unconsciousness.


As Winston Whitelaw began to look for his bride-to-be in the crowded room, he was intercepted by his mother.

"Where is Lady Ellison? 'Tis time to make your announcement," Sophia said, catching his arm and frowning at his tense expression.

"I have not seen her. She was dancing with the guests then — Where are Gabi and Captain Seward?" he asked in sudden comprehension. He roughly pushed his way across the dance floor to find his sister pouting in a corner. She was alone. "Where is Seward?"

Her pale, puffy eyes rose in wretched pettishness. "Off somewhere with your little tart," she snapped petulantly. "I saw them go into the foyer, but they were gone by the time I went looking. It would seem she has flown, your precious little dove, and made you look the fool in front of all your friends."

"Shut up, you simpering idiot," he hissed, his eyes growing hard and narrow. "I will kill him myself for this," he promised, scanning the room filled with prominent people waiting to hear the announcement that he was powerless to make. Even the governor had come, and would chuckle at his expense. Yet he would bring the bitch to heel for this humiliation. No one made him look the fool and not pay for it. And her lover would pay with his life.

## Chapter Thirty-two

The door of the coach was jerked open, and Rufe's golden eyes peered in from the night, going quickly to the pale face of the man Merrit coddled in her arms. He exhaled in heavy relief when he saw the shallow movement of Colley's chest. Without a word, he scooped him up gently from the seat and carried him to the house. When Merrit stared after them, Mildred caught her arm.

"Merrit, he is in good hands. Let his own take care of him. Think of yerself and of yer future. This is the night of yer engagement. Ye must return or all will be for naught."

Merrit put her hand over Mildred's. Sensible Mildred, her words were soft but strong as tempered metal. "I've no future without him, dear friend. I must stay. He could yet die and I cannot leave him until he is free from danger. I can make things right with Winston tomorrow, but tonight nothing exists for me but my love and I will be here with him. Please try to understand."

"I'd best remain with ye then, in case ye've need of me," Mildred relented, winning a grateful smile.

Nicholas was conscious and lay shifting uncomfortably on the bed he had shared with Merrit that morning, such a long time ago. His dulled eyes fastened on her when she appeared in the doorway and she quickly went to take the bloodstained hand he lifted to her. He tried to speak, but his throat seemed tightly closed and dry, blocking the effort. Forcing a swallow, he tried again, bringing her ear down to his lips to hear his raspy whisper.

"Merri, don't let me die until I see our child. I now fear going into hell alone. Keep me with you a bit longer. I love you, Merri."

"And I you," she soothed, brushing her hand across his sweat-beaded brow. She fought back tears as his fingers tightened in a sudden spasm of pain and he held his breath, releasing it in light, fast pants.

"Don't leave me," he mumbled thickly, having difficulty finding her in the confused, twisted shadows all about him. "Merri?" He heard her soft voice, low and sweet saying, "I am here. I won't leave you," and his panic quieted. Closing his eyes to the meaningless shapes, he clung to the secure warmth of her hand as fire lanced through his chest at every breath. He drifted hot and disoriented for a moment, then heard Rufe call to him from a great distance, his words oddly hollow and slow.

"Colley, can you hear me? You still sport that piece of lead, and it'll have to come out before the poison sets in. Do you understand me?"

He managed a jerky nod.

Rufe passed Merrit a bottle of dark rum. "Get him to drink this, all he'll take," he said grimly, then turned to the silent Mildred. "Be you here to help or watch?"

"What be ye needing?"

"Boiling water and a sharp blade. Lots of towels. And some strong men to hold him. He won't be that drunk."

Mildred left to see to Rufe's requests while Merrit forced the harsh liquor down the injured man. "Rufe, what happened?" she asked finally. "I heard Neville was involved."

"It was a trap, my lady. They knew who were were and were lying in wait. Someone knew we were coming, some-

424

one who knew Colley would sail after the bait without caution."

He raised his golden eyes to hers and she gasped, "Surely you don't think I would send him to his death."

"No, Merrit. I never thought that."

" 'Twas Winston. There was never anything of value aboard that ship. He sent Neville out to kill the Angel. What of Neville?"

"It was his bullet that laid Colley out. I killed him."

"Good."

Rufe looked at her in mild surprise, seeing the hard, ruthlessness in her that demanded blood in payment for her captain. There was a fierce protectiveness in the tender gesture as her hand rumpled Colley's wet dark hair and Rufe smiled. She would make a fine lieutenant for the Spanish Angel for there was a hellcat beneath the fluffy kitten.

When Nicholas was muttering insensibly from the drink, Rufe motioned to the two burly men at the bedside. "Hold him down. A movement could kill him." He took the long thin-bladed knife from the solemn-faced Mildred and glanced at Merrit. Her set features were very pale, silent tears making unnoticed streaks down her face and then forming dark blotches on her gown. "My lady perhaps you should wait below. 'Twill be very hard on him."

"No," she said with a quiet strength. "I won't leave him."

"Then release his hand lest he break your fingers."

As she withdrew her comforting grasp, the green eyes snapped open in brilliant alarm. "Merri?" he cried out, his hand groping through the haze of rum and pain. Her cool fingers guided his hand to her forearm so he could hold to her.

"I'm here Colley."

He nodded, then looked groggily to Rufe and said, "See to it."

Merrit opened her eyes to a cool darkness, uncertain as to where she was until she heard Mildred's soothing voice.

"Easy, me lamb. Just lie still."

She lifted an unsteady hand to the cold wet cloth on her brow and moved it aside. She was stretched out on a comfortable bed in an unfamliar room, but where? Then it came back to her, the thick smell of blood, the hoarse terrible cries, the fingers biting into her arm, and lastly the swirling darkness she had succumbed to.

"Colley?" she blurted out, trying unsuccessfully to sit up as Mildred caught her shoulders.

"Yer pirate's resting easy. He bade me to see ye did as well." Warm admiration filled her tone as she thought of the barely conscious man insisting his lady be taken care of. "Ye fainted, pet. 'Twas too much for ye in yer family condition."

"I must go to him," she insisted, pushing aside Mildred's restraining hand and placing her feet on the floor. Her head swam with a dizziness that she overcame with sheer resolution. Still light-headed, she made her way to the master suite, to find it awash with muted candlelight and stale with the smell of rum. Rufe sat at the bedside, a bottle in one hand and his friend's limp fingers in the other. He looked relieved to see her and quickly rose to give her his chair.

"Speak to him, my lady. He refused to sleep until he knew you to be well."

She nodded, touching his arm briefly. "You get some rest, Rufe. I'll sit with him 'til morning."

Rufe hesitated, seeing the deep weariness etched in her face, but the set of her gentle mouth would brook no interference. It seemed he had to take orders from two now, heaven help him when their wills crossed. "Call if you need me or if—if there is any change."

She nodded and dismissed him from her thoughts as she

426

sat down and turned her attention to the man who moved restlessly beneath the fresh sheets. There was no trace of the pretty Angel in his ravaged face, its features in too sharp relief against the sunken hollows of his cheeks. His ebony hair lay flat, plastered to his head by sweat, and his vague eyes, bruised and red around muddied irises, moved in slow, sightless circles. When Merrit lifted his hand she felt she was grasping hot coals wrapped in dried parchment. His fingers tightened weakly when she said his name, and his head turned toward her, his eyes searching with sudden purpose until they found her. He wet his lips and spoke in a raw voice.

"Are you all right?"

"I am fine. I'm sorry if my weakness upset you. I'm here now and I won't leave you again."

"Am I going to die, Merri?"

Tears sparkled in her tired eyes, and her hand rested light and cool on his flaming cheek. "No, my love. We won't let you. You gave me your life, remember, and it is not my wish to surrender it now."

He turned to brush her palm with his burning lips. Then the cloudiness returned to his gaze, and he seemed to drift off only to jerk awake, his hand frantically clutching at hers. "Merri, don't go," he panted, his features tensing with pain from the sudden movement.

"Shh, lie still, Colley. I am here."

"Wanted to ask you—to ask you—" he muttered brokenly, struggling with his weakness and slipping awareness.

"Ask me later, love."

"No, now," he protested, agitation causing him great pain.

"Ask me what?"

"Ask you—" His words trailed off in confusion.

"Sleep now, Colley. Tell me in the morning. I will be here when you wake. Sleep now," she urged in gentle persuasion, stroking his flushed face until his eyes closed and didn't

427

reopen. Slowly his finger grew loose in hers. "Don't die," she whispered. "Please don't leave me."

Holding his hot hand between hers, she settled back to maintain her vigil until the pink of dawn lightened the shadows and exhaustion finally took its toll on her. Soft voices awoke her sometime later and she opened her eyes, perplexed to see Mildred and Rufe chatting over breakfast like old friends. Nicholas lay resting quietly, his color better and his breathing easier.

"Good morning, me pet. You look as though you could use a bite of something to eat and some strong coffee." Mildred said softly, a smile on her face.

"Thank you, Mildred," Merrit murmured, stretching to ease the strain of her uncomfortable position. Her hands reached out to rest lightly on Colley's cool forehead and she gave a faint smile. "He's better."

"He'll be fine, my lady," Rufe assured her, his relaxed posture convincing her more than his words.

After Merrit had eaten a few biscuits and enjoyed a cup of harsh coffee, Mildred hovered over her solicitously. "Go home, pet. Ye'll be no use to him soon if ye don't get some rest. I'll stay and watch over yer pirate for ye if that'll comfort ye."

Tilting her head onto the strong hand resting on her shoulder, Merrit asked, "You would do that? And send for me if he should need me?"

Mildred smiled gruffly. "I said I would, now go. Ye'd best slip in unseen."

Merrit followed the older woman's glance to her elegant gown, the one in which she had looked so beautiful for the sake of her lover not her betrothed. The damask was creased and splotched with Nicholas's blood and sweat, the hem tattered from being dragged about in the absence of hoops. Like the flowers in Merrit's hair it had long since wilted, now appearing as limp and crushed as she felt.

With a sigh, Merrit nodded. She had to rest and think before she confronted the Whitelaws. Reluctantly, she bent and touched her lips to Colley's damp brow, whispering soft words he didn't hear before turning to Mildred in anguished indecision.

"Go, Merrit," the stocky woman instructed firmly. "I'll see to him for ye. Now go."

Shortly after she had gone, Nicholas woke with raspy request for water. Mildred brought it to him, slipping a hand behind his dark head so he could drink from the cup. When she eased him down, she noticed that his eyes quickly searched the room, even that slight movement bringing a pinched look to tighten his features.

"Merri?"

"She's gone back to Whitelawn, pirate," Mildred told him simply.

"Gone?" He lay back, contemplating that with a frown.

"For the moment. Do not fret. She'll be running back to yer side in no time.

The woman's disapproving tone deepened his frown, but he was satisfied with her answer. Nose wrinkling slightly, he strained to peer over the edge of the bed to where the breakfast tray sat. "Is there coffee on that tray, Mildred?"

"Aye, and I be supposing ye'll want breakfast as well," she grumbled. Her complaint was softened by the careful way she lifted him and slipped several pillows behind his back. Watching him attack the food with awkward enthusiasm, she grinned wryly. " 'Tis plain to see ye've recovered yerself."

"I did not want to aggrieve you with my absence, madam," he murmured silkily.

"Do not trouble yerself, pirate. Yer loss would not devastate me," she parried crisply, removing the empty tray and slipping him a brief wink.

Smiling faintly, he looked to Rufe and then grew somber. "The ship?"

"Crippled badly, but I think she'll mend," his friend responded quickly.

"Did you see to her safety?" He relaxed at Rufe's nod, but asked quietly, "How many did we loose?"

"The surgeon, Charlie Stewart, and two others were left lame."

His eyes shut briefly then opened, hard and glittering. "And Neville?"

"Dead by my hand and your pistol."

That alone did not satisfy him. "I heard someone say this was Whitelaw's doing."

"Yes."

"See to the ship's repairs—we may need her—and to the injured as well. I don't want to be long aground."

Rufe nodded and went to see to the orders.

Sipping his coffee in an unsteady hand, he noticed Mildred's glower and raised a brow questioningly. "Madam, you have something to say?"

"Aye, pirate, and it's not to my liking. Since ye'll soon be back at yer thieving, what about Merrit?"

"What about her?" Colley shifted uncomfortably under her stare, the movement awakening the dull agony in his chest.

"What about her indeed? Do ye ever think about her and what she suffers each time ye go out on the seas? 'Twill be worse now that she's almost lost ye. It may be fine for ye, but I be the one that has to stay behind with her and watch her fretting over ye like ye was worthy of her misery."

"She has not asked me to change what I am," he answered in wary defense.

"Nor would she. She's too afraid ye'd cast her off if she asked anything at all. She loves ye, the foolish child, and be willing to pay the price of being with ye."

"The price," he murmured to himself, lowering his eyes in deep reflection.

"And would ye change for her if she asked ye?"

The green eyes came up sullenly. "And be what?"

"Man enough to keep her. I'm fond of ye lad, but I've no use for pirates. They prowl the waters in reckless anger, being in love with the smell of danger and greed, hiding from the hardships of life behind the guise of adventure. I would say they put on a brave show to hide their cowardice. Be that a fair description of yerself?"

He scowled and grumbled, "You could show me a little mercy since I am injured."

"If ye want to be spared, do nothing. Merrit will go back to the Whitelaws and marry into their family, and ye'll have no one to answer to save yerself. But I think ye've long since stopped listening. Ye'd be doing her a favor to stay clear if ye be a pirate. She said there was more to ye, but I'm guessing she was wrong."

"You would prefer to see her with a man like Whitelaw?" His annoyance and upset provoked a throbbing ache in his chest, but he ignored it as best he could.

Mildred's sturdy features twisted into a distasteful grimace. "That whole lot leaves a sour smell, though I cannot name a reason. Better an honorable pirate than a scheming gentleman, I'd say, but 'tis not me ye'd have to ask."

"Why won't she have me? I love her, Mildred. I would do anything for her."

Mildred was silent for a moment, her loyalties torn. Merrit's well-being had been entrusted to her by the Ellison's, good, honest, and respectable folk. How would they feel about her encouraging the union of their precious child with a pirate rogue? On the other turn of that coin, she'd never seen two more in love or better suited, the captain a flashy gemstone held securely in the delicate but unbreakable setting of Merrit's devotion. Her rough cut emerald.

"Have ye asked the right question of her? She deserves better than a pretty lover who'll care for her handsomely and keep her plump with his bastard children. I shun ye if ye be pirate, but as a man, she'd do no better than ye. The only fault I lay on ye is being fool enough to let ye go ahead with this farce of a marriage. She loves ye too much to let ye go, yet ye'll be breaking her gentle spirit every time she comes to ye in sin. Do ye want to see her hurt like that? Do ye care what she'll be feeling every time she goes against what she believes in order to steal some time with ye? She'd make ye an unhappy mistress but a fine wife, and I wouldn't mind living in this great house and acozying up to yer lusty crew. Ye'd best decide what ye be wanting before it be too late."

Nicholas lay back, eyes closed. She wouldn't be gone. Even if she married Winston, he would still have the pleasure of seeing her, speaking to her, and lying with her. And he would be able to see their child grow within her and without. Yet he would have no responsibilities. His life would continue unchanged, but what of hers? She would be forced to live with a man he knew she loathed, forced to lie with him and endure his attentions. And he would have to deal with that as well. And the child . . . uncle not father. Without her, would anything else matter? His thoughts shifted from himself to her, everything fell into proportion. If nothing mattered without her, then what was he struggling to hold onto? What would he lose? He was standing on the brink, toes dangling, and she was saying, "Jump, coward."

"Ah, damn," he muttered in resignation, then his eyes snapped open, bright and calculating. "I've not much time." Setting his teeth, he pulled himself up, the effort bringing beads of sweat to his face and a panting shortness to his breath.

"Here now, Captain. Lay yerself down. Yer in no shape to be moving about. Killing yerself won't be solving anything," Mildred chastised, worried by his loss of color.

"If I don't go now, it won't matter anyway," he vowed

432

staunchily, his voice wheezy with strain. "Will you help me, Mildred? I cannot let her go, and I may not be able to make it to Williamsburg alone."

She met his hopeful glance with a snort of disbelief. "Ye'll be lucky to make it there alive. But she'll be miserable without ye, and I've grown to like yer pretty face so I'll be helping ye."

His smile was dazzling. "I could kiss you, Mildred."

"Save yer strength, pirate. I'd best be finding ye some clothes."

# Chapter Thirty-three

The large house was strangely silent after the previous night's gaiety, all signs of the festivities already removed by the servants. It was as if nothing had happened at all. But Merrit knew better. She climbed the stairs to her room with a heavy heart, stopping one of the timid maids to ask that hot water be brought for a bath. She had deserted Winston without a word, had left him to face his influential guests with no fiancée and no explanation. How embarrassed and angry he must have been. She didn't enjoy the thought of bringing him such shame.

Her shoulders sagged wearily as she shed the ruined gown and lay down on the bed, closing her eyes in a futile attempt to dismiss the tormenting thoughts. She had done nothing but bring grief to all since her arrival. Though she had no special feeling for Winston, that did not excuse her flagrant abuse of his forthright proposal of marriage. Now she had endangered his political career. Would it be any better once she'd married him? Or would the situation simply worsen? Could she be a wife to him, dutifully see to his interests and desires while her heart was bound to another man? What kind of wife would she be? One that pretended devotion while lusting for a lover? Which was the greater sin, an unfaithful wife or an unmarried mistress? The moment she had seen Colley injured and had faced the prospect of losing him, she'd known she could never give him up. She would go to him regardless of vows or laws or even of her own conviction that it was wrong to do so. Each minute she spent with him was complete, a lifetime unto itself, and she would not surrender that no matter how selfish it was.

The bath water arrived, and Merrit indulged in the luxury of not thinking while its penetrating heat soothed her body and spirit. By the time she stepped from it and dried herself, she had made her decision. She donned a fresh cheery gown of painted chinz, its warm shade of rose giving her weary features a false color. She was not cowardly by nature, but she dreaded the coming confrontation. It had to be done quickly and as kindly as possible, but it must be done. She admitted to herself that she could not be near Nicholas and not want him; the pull was too strong, the magnetism too right. She would ignore any barrier, moral or legal, to have him, but she could not live with that kind of dilemma long. She would take a chance and trust to his love, placing herself and her child in his hands and hoping that she was not ruining both their lives. She had ruined too many already.

Merrit discovered Winston in the austere confines of his study. He was going over several ledgers. His expression was so grave that she almost relented, but before she could silently withdraw, he glanced up.

"My lady, I did not hear you. I'm glad you are here. Come in and close the doors. We've much to discuss, you and I."

Merrit hesitated. Something in his silken tone and his cold blue eyes gave her a chill of warning. Reminding herself that the sooner she put this meeting behind her the sooner she would be free, she shut the heavy doors and advanced boldly.

Winston observed her coldly as he rose from his chair, but even the knowledge that she had deceived him didn't dampen the fires her beauty stirred.

"You placed me in a most awkward position with your untimely departure last night," he began frostily. "It is rather difficult to announce a betrothal when your intended is not at your side. There are several things we have to set straight between us, Merrit. If marriage to you did not hold such attractions, both physical and political, I would not hesitate to name you for what you are."

Merrit blushed deeply from guilt and rebelliousness. "I promise I will not disgrace you so again," she began, but he interrupted curtly.

"No, you will not. My sister may be a fool but don't mistake me for one. I'll allow you no indiscretions when you are my wife. If I even suspect Nicholas Seward has resumed his role as your lover, I will kill him." He ignored her gasp, giving her a disgusted sneer. "I know all about your sordid little affair, but it is over, done with. If that idiot Gabrielle still wants him, she's welcome to him, but I'll not have his eyes resting on you, let alone his hands. The wife of a politician can not afford to be made the subject of gossip. Is that understood?"

Merrit's voice was surprisingly firm when she replied, "I will not embarrass you again. I am freeing you from your obligations. I have brought dishonor to your house with my behavior and I own up to it now. I cannot remain when I know I will continue to be a source of grief. I love him and I am going to him. I should never have left. I tried to abide by an agreement that was not meant to be, though I guess I knew in my heart I could not hold to it. I lay no blame to you. My own weakness is the cause of it. I did not want to love him, but I cannot stop and I cannot live without him. I am sorry, Winston."

His reaction was not at all what she had expected. In two great strides, he was before her, gripping her forearms and shaking her furiously. "You little tart. You'll not ruin me. Do you think I'll let you jilt me and leave me a laughing-stock? My plans include you as my wife and my wife you'll be. Your contract is legal, and the dowry has been spent."

Swallowing her fear of the raging figure that towered over her, she said in protest, "Keep the pearls. 'Twas I who broke the bargain and so I will pay the price. You cannot mean to keep me knowing I love another, that I could never love you."

Winston took her chin in his hand, his grasp rough, and his thin lips curled in a nasty smile. "Can't I? Think again, my lady. What has love to do with it? I am not such a fool as to stake my future on something so useless. I never loved you, but I do want you. I don't care what you think of me. We will be wed at week's end, my dear. You will visit each of the guests who attended last night to tender your personal apology for the sudden illness that prompted your disappearance — and you will be convincing. You will do exactly as I say or I will see your lover hang, Gabrielle be damned."

"W-What are you talking about. You'd hang him? For what crime? For trying to steal away your fiancée? I do not think that is a hanging offense," Merrit bluffed boldly, as she tried unsuccessfully to free herself from his hold.

"But piracy is, my love. Captain Seward, Captain Angel — two sides of one coin. I always knew there was more to the man than a preening fop. He played the game well. Neville was a fool to let him escape, but I hear his aim was only slightly off. Letitia told us with a little persuasion that Seward was badly wounded. She was quite reluctant but Gabi can be ruthless when provoked, and you and Seward provoked her mightily."

"Please, you mustn't do anything to hurt him," Merrit pleaded in a subdued voice. Now she was truly afraid. Badly wounded and without a ship, Nicholas was terribly vulnerable. Winston could take him with ease and he would hang. The horrifying vision from her dream returned. She could not let it come true, not at any price. "I will do anything."

"I know you will," he said smugly. "You will be my

437

beautiful bride, my loyal supporter who will see me governor. In public you will be sweet and devoted, and in private, you will be my wife in every way. You will never speak to your pirate again. No more midnight rides. You will both be watched from this moment on, day and night. I will keep his neck safe only as long as you please me. And you will please me, won't you?"

Merrit remained stonily silent as her mind sought a means of escape for both her and Nicholas. She had to stall for time. "And what of the remaining terms of the contract? What of your obligation to my father?" she asked brassily as if she still had some leverage in their bargain.

"I will meet them as long as it is to my advantage." Winston released her and went to pour himself a liberal brandy. As he regarded her over the rim of his glass, he could almost see desperate ideas fluttering behind her dark impassive eyes. Her quick intelligence aroused him almost as much as her lush figure and fair face. He felt a dark coil of anger upon remembering how she held him at arm's length while she'd rushed in secret to bed her Spanish lover. The thought of Sewards smug taunting cat's eyes made his blood beat hot and savage in his temples. That he should be denied the sweet pleasures that man enjoyed seemed a gross injustice—one he would rectify immediately.

Deep in frantic thought, Merrit failed to see his intent until his arm clasped her tightly about the waist, imprisoning her so his free hand could wander over her taut breasts. Her shock was promptly replaced by fiery indignation, and she slapped his cheek with all her strength. In return Winston dealt her a stunning blow, sending her reeling to the floor. The violence only increased his desire to have her, and he jerked her up by the hair, smothering her painful cry with a kiss that went on and on until she sagged in his embrace, weak and shivering yet filled with fear and hatred. He held her back, his pale eyes bright and demanding.

"Now you'll be mine and mine alone and you'll know what

it's like to have a real man take you," he growled.

There was a rending of cloth as he split the front of her gown from shoulder to waist. The sight of her rose-tipped breasts barely shielded by the thin fabric of her chemise made his nostrils flare wildly and his eyes blaze with purpose. Using one hand to piece together her bodice and the other to try to hold Winston at bay, Merrit's eyes flashed about seeking some avenue of escape. She had to get away, had to warn Nicholas that his identity was secret no more. She ducked under Winston's arm and rushed for the door, but as her fingers closed on the knob, she was seized by one shoulder and spun away so roughly she stumbled and fell upon the wide sofa. Before she could catch herself, he was upon her, his weight smashing her into the yielding cushions. She fought him fiercely, wishing she wore the protective circle of her hoops instead of layers of petticoats that offered no resistance to his insistent hand. She pummeled his back and head until he relented, panting down upon her with hot, fast breath.

"Is this how you play with your pirate, with protests and fire? And how does he take you? Is it a good rape you need to show you who is master?"

"Whoreson," she spat, twisting beneath him frantically, her eyes dark fire. "He doesn't need to rape, but that's the only way you'll ever have me. You are no man in comparison to him."

Merrit's angry words were halted by another stinging slap. She had never in her life been struck so cruelly, and tears of pain and shock sprang to her eyes. In a panic, she realized she couldn't resist his strength or stop him with her struggles. Faint with revulsion, she endured his probing kiss, but when his greedy mouth fastened on her barely covered breast, her efforts redoubled. Desperate to halt the degrading treatment, she cried, "You mustn't. I'm with child."

Wintson's weight was instantly lifted, and Merrit scrambled up to huddle in trembling defiance against the arm of the couch, watching in dread as fierce emotions crossed his face.

"You whore, you bitch," he hissed, following his harsh words with another slap. His hands gripped her torn bodice shaking her until her tears sprayed in a salty shower of fear and hurt. "When? When is your bastard due?"

"December," she wept hoarsely.

"You came here already breeding the pirate's whelp?" He flung her back against the cushions and rose in agitation to pour himself another drink, calculating as he did how much time would pass before her condition would be obvious. "You'll not ruin all for me. No. I've worked too hard and spent too much to let a carelessly planted seed rob me of all. I'll send for someone to purge you."

"No," she cried, hugging herself protectively. "You'll not harm this child. I'll die first. Do you understand me?"

He stared at her long and hard, wondering why she would go to such lengths to save a bastard child. Then he drained his glass thoughtfully, his pale gaze resting on her mercilessly. He was his mother's son. No child would keep him from his ambitions.

"Have your brat then," he began slowly. "We will go abroad when your time is near and you can be delivered in secrecy. If the babe be born with your fair face, I will claim it as my own, but not as my heir. But be warned, if it be birthed with his pretty looks and green eyes, I will give it to another to raise, and we will return childless."

"You cannot do that," she wailed in horror. "You cannot punish a blameless child."

"I can do anything I like. You will be my wife, and I will tolerate no slur upon my name or reputation, especially not from the fruit of your indiscretion. I have every right. Rid yourself of the babe now or agree to my terms. You've no other choice."

No choice. Her head spun. There had to be a way out, but she could not find it. Her instinct was to protect her

440

child and her love, and the only way to do so was to accept the abomination that was proposed, knowing in her heart that he would never take Nicholas's child from her. Never.

"I agree," she said faintly, "providing you will not harm the child or Nicholas."

"My word on it," Winston swore, his eyes hard and glittering. He had already decided that Nicholas Seward would meet with an unfortunate accident as soon as it could be arranged. Now that he had the child to use as leverage, he need never look on that pretty face again.

# Chapter Thirty-four

Mildred frowned as she observed the figure slumped in the seat opposite her. He had remained unmoving and silent since they had left Williamsburg, his eyes closed, his face sweat drenched. She could tell he was conscious from the restless movement of his hands and the tensing of his features whenever the coach jolted, but the high color of his face and the shallow breaths he was taking made her fear he was bleeding again. If he had a weakness in his character, lack of courage was not it. He had borne up under the tortuous journey and lengthy interview without complaint, and only on this return trip had he shown any sign of discomfort, saving his reserve of strength for when it would be needed. Mildred already knew he was hurting, so he didn't bother to pretend with her. In return, she voiced none of her apprehensions. If Merrit didn't appreciate what he was suffering for her, she vowed she would thrash the girl soundly.

Nicholas's eyes opened when the coach turned into the drive of Whitelawn, all outward signs of weakness disappearing as his features sharpened and he straightened in his seat. More than thoughts of Merrit brought the fierce brilliance to his emerald eyes, he was anticipating the settlement of a debt long overdue. His chest was afire, breathing a dull agony, but he could endure physical pain more easily than the memories that tormented him. The hatred that had smoldered in him for so many years flared. Hotter than the fever that throbbed in his temples, it raced through him like flames through dried grass, all-consuming and destructive. He climbed down from the coach, waving off Mildred's hand, and strode up to the impressive residence, the type of home he should have lived in with his mother instead of rat-infested slums and plague-ridden back streets. His walk became a swagger, his bearing proud and arrogant. The Spanish Angel come to call — the angel of retribution.

The Whitelaw ladies looked with a mixture of surprise and fear at their unannounced visitor. The man who had once been a sought-after guest was now a threatening intruder, a loathsome pirate. He looked much like he had when Letitia had first seen him on the dock, clad in a scarlet coat, a heavy cutlass riding on his hip, his head bare and a pearl in his ear. The girl went to him fearlessly, however, her upturned face sporting a swollen lip and a rainbow of bruises. Her usually mirthful eyes swam with tears.

"I'm sorry. I didn't mean to tell them anything. I tried to keep your secret, but I couldn't," she sobbed as he folded her easily in the curve of his arm.

"Who struck you little one?" he asked softly, his eyes regarding the other two women with dark menace.

"Gabi," she declared, her small voice muffled in his colorful coat. "She was so angry. Then Win made me tell him the rest. I tried to be braver."

Wiping away her tears, he said gently, " 'Tis all right. We are never as brave as we'd like to be." He chucked the girl under the chin, and then turned her over to Mildred before he crossed to where Gabrielle cowered on the divan.

"Nicholas," she began flatteringly.

He slapped her sharply with the palm of his hand, then with the back of it in a return stroke. "Not very pleasant is it?" he said in a low angry voice. "Don't ever raise a hand to

443

your sister again. She is the only decent thing your family can boast of."

Sophia Whitelaw rose imperiously, her height topping his by several inches. The chill in her pale eyes showed no trace of alarm. "Just who do you think you are coming here to make threats against my children, after dining in our house while robbing our ships? I will see you hanged."

"You should have seen to it eighteen years ago and spared us both much," he told her in the heavily accented voice he reverted to unthinkingly. "Who am I indeed? You didn't recognize me when I returned here. I am no distant cousin. A relation, yes, but of a much closer nature. Look at me. Look at me closely. Peer into my eyes and tell me you cannot see your brother there, my dear aunt."

For a moment, Sophia was stunned speechless, seeing in Nicholas's swarthy face a grimy little boy in torn clothes, a lad who clutched a heavy ring in one grubby hand as he had made an audacious claim in a thick Spanish accent. Something in his bold green eyes had sparked a shiver of panic in her then. She had known that his outrageous story was true, but she had refused to turn over the vast wealth of her family, the future of her son, to a foreign beggar boy. Who would believe a half-starved Spanish boy once she had taken away his only proof? He had fought wildly to keep that ring, and the burning hatred she had seen in the boy's eyes that day now shone from the eyes of a man.

With an unfaltering voice as cold as her stare, she said, "So you are one of Edward's baseborn bastards."

"You know who I am, madam," Nicholas snarled. "I am his lawful son. His only son. His first-born. His heir. You knew that when my mother wrote you, yet you turned away her cry for help. You knew that when I came in her stead, and you ordered me beaten."

Sophia sneered contemptuously. "Your mother was a Spanish whore. How do I know she did not take my brother's life so she could steal his fortune with her lies?"

444

Nicholas's face went white and he began to tremble. The dam that had held back his emotions since he'd stood over his mother's grave gave way, releasing an uncontrolled flood of hurt and grief and hate.

"You lie," he roared, seizing Sophia Whitelaw by the throat. "You lie, you bitch. She was no whore. She was your brother's wife. The proof was in the ring. You killed her with your indifference. You stole our fortune. You stole my title. And you stole her life. She lived in hell and died there because of your greed. You killed my mother."

His hands tightened from the strength born of madness. Through his blinding rage, nothing reached him, not Sophia's choking pleas, not her daughters' fearful weeping. Then he heard Merrit's voice, low and clear, touching his reason.

"Colley, no."

As he turned toward her his fingers relaxed, and he took the full brunt of Winston's punch. He reeled backward, falling hard only to rise to his feet with surprising agility. In a slight crouch, he held the room at bay like some savage, wild-eyed beast, a sleek panther, wounded, cornered and dangerous. His eyes flashed between Sophia and Winston, his hatred for them seething in his every hurting breath. Suddenly, he staggered, weakness making his head swirl. Blood, warm and fresh, splotched the toes of his boots and made a bright pattern on the floor. He struggle to catch his breath knowing that there would be no escape if he lost consciousness. Yet he was drowning. Instinctively, his hand reached out and was firmly taken in a cool, caring grasp. That a familiar hand had seen him through many a storm. Merrit's arms went quickly about his middle, supporting him as he leaned heavily on her shoulders.

"I came for you, my lady," he said thickly, letting the tension and violence be absorbed by her gentle yet strong spirit.

"I will go with you. I will stay with you. I love you,

445

Colley." She felt him sag in relief as her arms tightened in a careful hug, but his temperature had soared from overtaxing his system, leaving him wobbly and wet with a sheen of perspiration. "Let me take you home, my love," she suggested worriedly, not sure how long his strength would keep him on his feet and feeling courageous in his presence.

"You are not going anywhere," Winston said coldly. He straightened, having assured himself that his mother had finally recovered her breath and her coloring. "You'll not leave here with him, not ever. Remember our discussion, my lady."

Merrit hesitated, torn between love for the man she held and fear for him. She had to see him safe no matter what the price. "Your word guaranteeing his safety?" she insisted. She felt Nicholas recoil in puzzlement and rebellion, and she struggled to contain him in her embrace.

"Don't let him go, Winston," Sophia rasped, holding her bruised throat. "He is dangerous."

"I will stay if you promise to give him safe passage," Merrit repeated firmly, feeling the undercurrent in the room and anxious to get Colley clear of it. "Mildred, take him to the coach."

Before Mildred could catch his arms, Nicholas reeled back, stumbling slightly and then finding the strength to draw himself up. "You think I would run and leave you behind to save myself? If a price is to be paid, I will pay it, not you, Merri. You're coming with me." His eyes widened, then narrowed into glittering slits as he noticed for the first time the state of her gown and the welts on her face. Awkwardly, he shrugged out of his coat, and ignoring her fearful gasp, draped it about her shoulders to conceal the tear in her bodice. He refused to follow her alarmed stare to his shirtfront where a vivid crimson had spread from shoulder to waist.

Seeing that stain emboldened Winston further. Seward was obviously gravely injured so what kind of resistance

446

could he possibly offer? "Merrit, you would forfeit being the wife of an earl to become the mistress of a pirate? You are a fool. I will see your family in the poorhouse and your lover hanged; then what will you do with your bastard child?"

The Whitelaw women gave a startled gasp at that as Merrit looked between the two men in anguish. What choice did she have? Winston's threats were real. She cared nothing for his title or wealth. It was the hurt he could do to others that concerned her.

Nicholas's emerald eyes never flickered. "No. I'll not have her for a mistress." He ignored Merrit's soft cry of bewildered upset and the clutch of her hand on his arm. "She *will be* the wife of an earl." He took up her hands and smiled faintly into her hurt confusion. "You will be my wife, Merri."

With a cry of gladness, Merrit hugged him fiercely, and he cheerfully endured the pain it brought him. Over her shoulder, his eyes taunted Winston.

"Enjoy your celebration," Winston snarled. " 'Twill be a short one. You cannot marry a man who's been hanged for piracy."

Merrit's eyes filled with panicked tears. She couldn't lose Colley now. His unconcerned smile only made her puzzlement greater. Didn't he realize they knew who he was?

It was Mildred who answered her unspoken questions with a low chuckle. "I see no pirates here. The Spanish Angel is dead, killed in a trap ye laid for him, my lord, and by yer own admission. Colonel Spotswood agreed to accept that death. He reasoned it was to his advantage to have a wealthy planter contributing to the prosperity of the colony rather than a pirate stealing it away."

"Colley?" Merrit asked softly, stunned by the import of the words.

"I have retired, my lady. The governor gave me his full pardon, and by the way, he sends you his regards and best wishes for our wedding." Nicholas turned to Winston, his expression smug and arrogant. "You lose. Again. I have taken my lady and now I shall have my ring."

Winston frowned, following Nicholas's gaze to the large signet ring he wore. It bore the crest of the Earl of Wexington. He recalled Seward's fascination with it when they had first met. "What the bloody hell are you talking about?"

"Tell him, madam. The truth."

Sophia didn't meet her son's eyes, but stared up instead at her brother's son, her face pale and her shoulders sagging. "I should have known you'd come back. You were too much like Edward. He was so rash and rebellious. He had no sense of family pride, running off to marry that Spanish woman and then expecting us to welcome the creature and her pup into our bosom. I couldn't allow our proud tradition, our heritage, to be defiled by his foolish act. Our name had to be protected. I should have let them kill you, but I couldn't. I was weak. You were Edward's son. You see why I did it, don't you?"

"All I see is that you pushed your son into my place over the corpses of my parents. My mother's life was worth more than all your proud, dead ancestors. We would have brought no disgrace to you and your fine heritage."

Sophia hung her head, too weary to suppress her haunting shame for betraying the brother she had loved. Her greed and her father's earlier repudiation of Edward had prompted her to commit an unforgivable act. "Give him the ring, Winston," she said. " 'Tis his by birth and right." Her voice was low and broken.

"Never," Winston swore fiercely, seeing all his hopes and plans crumbling beneath the grinding heel of Nicholas Seward. "I'll give him nothing but what he deserves." He yanked a rapier from a wall display and charged the hated enemy whose mocking face had thwarted him at every turn.

Nicholas pulled his cutlass free, shoving Merrit to Mildred as he met the fierce attack. His unwieldy sword was

448

a poor match of the lightning-quick foil, and the weight of the blade and the strength needed to meet each waspish jab was more than he could manage for long in his weakened state. It would have to be a quick duel, or he wouldn't survive it. Already he was nearly blinded by sweat, his heavy pants of exertion stabbed through his chest, and blood flowed warm and sticky beneath his shirt. He gripped the hilt of his cutlass with both hands and gave a savage cry, swinging it with all his might. The heavy blade snapped the thin rapier in two. Taking advantage of Winston's brief hesitation, Nicholas caught his wrist and twisted it until the blade was released. Then he laced his fists about the metal butt of his sword and swung, dealing a felling blow to his opponent's temple. Winston went down with a groan. Nicholas dropped onto his chest, the cutlass quickly inverted in his hands until he held it high like a huge dagger.

"Yield to me what's mine or I'll kill you."

"Kill me then, for I'll never give you the satisfaction."

"Then I'll see you in hell." Nicholas's eyes held the chilling brilliance that was the last thing Durant had ever seen, the fierce promise of death, quick and certain. His hands swung up, but their downward plunge was halted by the smaller hands that covered his, stilling him not with strength but with quiet emotion.

"Colley, don't do this. Our future lies ahead of us, clear and free. If you take his life, they've won. Don't you see? You'll be what they've made you, not what you can be, what you will be. I love you. Don't go back. Leave this and come with me. The time for old hurts is past. 'Tis our time now. Let it go, Colley. Please."

Merrit's voice, low and steady, was the ballast in his dizzily rocking world. He no longer needed the blind hatred to sustain him. His reason for being was here, not in the past. It was the loving soul of Merrit Ellison and in the shared gift she would bear. With an undulating wail of long-fed anguish and helpless rage, he drove the cutlass deep into

449

the planked flooring next to Winston's head, deep into the heart of the vengeful demon of hatred that had plagued him. He took the hands Mildred and his lady put down and let them hoist him to his feet, tottering between them like a newly foaled colt. The weakness he was feeling didn't touch his crisp stare as he looked to Sophia Whitelaw.

"I give you your son. 'Tis more than you ever gave me. Keep your title and your precious family pride. 'Tis clear it has never brought you any good. All I want is here beside me. The Spanish Angel is dead. If you try to revive him, I will show you no mercy. I would happily dredge your spotless name through filth that has a stench you could never rid yourselves of. Mark that as a promise."

Sophia nodded jerkily, exhaling. Scandal could be averted. All would be well again.

"Colley, what of my pearls?" Merrit asked softly. "The dowry's been spent."

"Blast the pearls. I need no bribe to take you for my wife. What you bring me is wealth untold. Our fortune." He began to smile, but the gesture was never completed, his eyes doing a slow loop and his knees buckling. As the two women struggled to hold him, Winston gave a sudden cry and surged to his feet, wrenching the cutlass from the floorboards. That frightful sound of warning brought up Nicholas's head, and his eyes sparked in an instinctive reflex of self-perservation. But he was not in time. Merrit shrieked as she saw the gleaming blade draw back, the murderous intent Winston's pale eyes.

"No," she screamed in fierce denial.

It was over in an instant, but it had seemed to flow in a strangely slow-motioned pace, like a lethargic nightmare. As the sword swung back in a deadly arc, Merrit stepped in front of Nicholas, her arms encircling his neck and pulling him to her. She made her slender body a shield to ward off the approaching blow. Winston's mind registered that change, but he could not stop the momentum of his arm.

Nicholas had time only to hug her to him and squeeze his eyes shut, waiting for them both to be struck dead. But there was a roar and the smell of powder, and Winston was thrown back, the ball from Rufe's smoking pistol having gone clean through his shoulder.

A tender touch on his fevered cheek woke him. His hazy green eyes blinked rapidly in surprise as everything swung about him in great dizzying swoops. Merrit's gaze was the only steadying point in that tipping world.

"I love you."

He heard the words echoing far away as he murmured in a thick voice, "Merrit, take me home." Then he felt Rufe's huge hands on his shoulders and darkness washed over him, cool and silent.

# Chapter Thirty-five

There was a sharp bite of winter in the air as Merrit lumbered down the well-trod path to the river. She paused at the foot of the dock, drawing her woolen cloak more closely about her as a buffer against the crips winds. Her features softened as she looked out to the man who stood at the end of the pier, for she felt a warm surge of love at the sight of her husband. He was bareheaded and in shirtsleeves, disdaining the elements as he waited for twilight to sink into darkness. His eyes were turned, as always, up the wide river to the unseen sea and he made a striking picture in the fading light, standing straight and proud with that arrogant tilt to his chin — the bold, free Spanish Angel, feet on a tipping deck and sea green eyes searching the horizon for easy prey. She saw his shoulders rise and fall in a heavy sigh, that gesture tugging at her heart for she knew he still longed for the freedom of those restless seas while she bound him to the land. But when he turned to her her doubts were swept away by the simple devotion in his expression. That changed him from a pirate to her husband.

"Regrets, my lord?" she asked softly as he came to her.

"Only that I must be kept waiting to see if it be a son or daughter that holds me at such a distance," he replied easily, leaning over her massive belly to place a quick kiss on her forehead. "You shouldn't have come down, love. 'Tis too far and 'tis freezing."

She smiled at his concern, then chafed his hands in hers. "And so are you," she scolded, seeing him shiver as if suddenly aware of the temperature. "Warm yourself. There's room for two inside this cloak."

"There are already two in there," he teased, his hand resting possessively on the protruding bulge that would soon render his first-born. "Besides that kind of warmth would cause more discomfort that it be worth."

She laughed unkindly at his distress, and flippantly replied, "Calm yourself, my lusty pirate. 'Twill not be long before you can resume your husbandly duties. Do you think I rest any easier with you so warm and tempting at my side?"

The ache of loving her spread slow and deep, and he leaned forward, his fingertips gliding along her delicate jawline as their lips met to kindle fires that grew more painfully insistent. Finally he broke away, panting unevenly, and groaned, "You witch. You torment me most cruelly. If not for this plump babe, I would take you down right here on the docks as a teasing wench deserves."

Merrit's dark eyes glowed with excited promise, for she was far from immune from frustrated desire. "Patience, Captain. This babe will not be between us forever."

"It only seems that way," he grumbled petulantly, but the circle of his arm was strong and reassuring. The past month had been a torture, Merrit sleeping peacefully at his side while he writhed in miserable need. Actually his suffering was one of his making, for he had refused to move to a separate bedroom despite Mildred's tirades about propriety and decency. To be barred from one of the great pleasures of their marriage left him sorely strained, but it did not occur to him to turn to another woman to ease his need for no

453

other woman existed for him. He would wait. Impatiently.

Feeling him relax, Merrit snuggled into his side, smiling blissfully as his cheek rested atop her head. The summer and fall had sped by in a glorious whirl, filled with the wonders of beginning a new life with the man she loved. Increasingly she felt the vigorous stirrings of that new life within her. That the babe would be early in coming caused no unkind speculation. The Sewards had been fondly embraced by Virginia society, and the small community was thrilled by whispers of a romantic scandal in their past. They were constantly sought after, Lady Merrit for her beauty and her witty charm, and Captain Seward for his outrageous tales and fair face. The rumors that he might have been the Spanish Angel only added to his aura of mystery. The sudden change in the wedding plans of the two couples had provoked much curiosity, but no answers had been offered by the principals. As Merrit grew round with child, there was no question of parentage. Nicholas strutted about proudly as if he were the first man to father a child, and his tender solicitation of his wife made many a matron envious. His unwavering love for his petite bride was obvious in his every glance and in his lingering touch. His obvious devotion was enough to make a youthful maiden sigh.

"Are you happy, Colley?" Merrit asked suddenly, his faraway look disturbing her. "Do you miss being the unfettered Angel?"

As he leaned over to her, she felt him smile against her cheek. "Those were glorious times," he told her quietly. "I was free to live above the law and beyond man. Things were easy, rules were simple. It was like being a child — greedy, selfish — and I loved it. Aye, I miss it, the excitement, the quickness, the mindlessness of it. It's like an ache in my soul when I smell the salt in the air or when Rufe's visits bring the taste of the sea back to me, that restlessness." He glanced at her to find her eyes downcast, chin trembling. His hand cupped that elfin chin to lift her shimmering eyes to his. "I miss it, but I would not go back to it. I am a child no longer. I've a fondness for the past, but you've taught me that you live it and then go on. The sea is my past, you are my future. You make me happy, Merri, and I am content to be wherever you are."

She looked long into his eyes, then smiled, secure in her belief that he was telling her the truth. She was proud of him for his adjustment to being a husband and a respectable planter. During their first months together they had indulged in utter passion and selfish enjoyment until the sudden clash of wills Rufe had predicted brought all to a halt. It was Merrit's insistence that what they had on their walls be legally purchased that sent Colley into furious rebellion. When they spoke, their words were unkind and both were in a pique. Pouting and surly, and unused to being questioned or criticized, he withdrew from their bedroom to sleep in the drawing room. To his mind, his sweet wife was unreasonable to demand that the spoils of a lucrative career by dismissed as tainted. He felt she was including him in that summation. They argued and shouted, neither willing to compromise. Finally one evening, he stalked from their home, sporting his scarlet coat and gold earring. Mildred put an end to any thoughts Merrit had of pursuing him, so she huddled miserably in the big empty bed, sobbing with fright and loss. Shortly after midnight, Rufe carried him in. He reeked of alcohol and bore a huge bruise on his jaw.

"Your husband, my lady," Rufe announced casually. "He somehow fell in with pirates and I thought it best I help him find his way home."

She had wakened in the morning to find him gone from her, and when she had gone downstairs, the walls and shelves had been stripped nearly bare. It was an early

455

Christmas for those around Williamsburg who woke to find their plundered belongings heaped on their doorsteps. The only exception, she would discover later, were those valuables belonging to the Whitelaws. Those he had burned. When he met her for breakfast, it was with a kiss of tender fierceness. They never spoke of the incident again.

From that morning on, Nicholas had settled in without complaint to the daily routine of a planter. It wasn't the drudgery he had once thought, for there was little difference between dealing with merchants and competitors and dealing with pirates. He charged into the world of business headlong, but tempering intuition with caution, he grew richer. And Merrit's father prospered as his distributor. Victor Ellison proved an excellent channel for Nicholas's ventures, and the two men were looking forward to a meeting when Nicholas took Merrit and the babe to England in the spring for a visit. He was nonplused to find his in-laws more accepting of his being a reformed pirate and of his presenting them with an unseemingly quick grandchild than they were of him being godless. To please them and Merrit, he let her inundate him with theology, teasing her in the face of her solemnity by saying that she would have to look long and hard to find a soul worth saving in him. But she was determined and undiscouraged, and he didn't mind the hours spent stretched out with his head in her rapidly disappearing lap listening only to the melody of her voice at first and then to the words she spoke. He was at peace with himself and he was happy.

After long hours in the hot sun, he grew to respect the rich fertile earth as much as the rolling seas, and much to his neighbor's dismay would often shed his shirt and join his men in the fields, often inviting them up to the house, filthy and strong with sweat, for a round of cooling ale. His was an unconventional household, and Merrit ran it masterfully for him, handling everything from elaborate society balls to a drawing room full of pirates rowdy with drink with equal aplomb. She took no exception to serving the hands from the fields as graciously as the governor. The house had been beautifully refurnished, grudgingly out of the pocket, and he had to admit she had created a harmonious display that soothed the eye. If he was a success as a changed man, it was due to her steadying influence, he felt. She spoiled, pampered, and flattered him outrageously, anticipated his thoughts and made their bed into a secluded paradise he was loath to leave in the mornings. And she carried his child. As her slender shape ripened, he was enthralled by her new glowing beauty and contendedness, liking to curl up beside her with his hand resting on her round belly, awed by the vigorous stirrings of life beneath his palm. In those quiet times, Merrit felt her life couldn't be any more perfect.

She knew what a difficult time he had starting this new life, curbing that wandering undisciplined spirit that drew him to the dock at twilight to give that heavy sigh. It was for her that he had changed and she was ever amazed by the strength of his love. His many aspects had finally merged, blending into a man who, along with their child, was her life. He was the Spanish Angel when with his men, easy tempered and a natural leader. He was Nicholas Seward when they mixed socially, smoothly charming, and flagrantly flirtatious but only when his wife was near enough to keep any miss from being overly encouraged. He was the man she had always wanted, her Colley, whose smoky jade eyes would follow her about the room, a man who delighted in the movement of their unborn child and who came to her at night with kisses so sweet she wanted to sob her happiness. And the dark side of him was there as well, buried and controlled but still flaring hot and fierce when they were thrown together with the Whitelaws, which happened with uncomfortable frequency. Merrit thought bitterly that it was purposefully arranged by them in the hope of provoking a confrontation. The entire community knew that both men had been treated for pistol wounds within hours of each other and found it maddening that the facts were never revealed. But Nicholas would not oblige the gossips, though often his hatred for the Whitelaws boiled when Winston flaunted the heavy ring beneath his nose. The light touch of Merrit's hand on his shoulder always quelled his violent urges, however his eyes would rise to hers, and looking at her, he knew he had all he desired and his hatred would fade to a vague disquieting ache.

The darkness had grown complete as they stood together, drawing warmth and contentment from their closeness. Nicholas gave a low chuckle, bringing up her gaze.

"What will we tell our children when they ask us how we met? That their father was a pirate captain who abducted their mother for ransom?"

Merrit laughed at the dilemma, then rested her head on his shoulder and hugged him tightly. "They would never believe us. By then all you scruffy buccaneers will have become respectable."

He gave a shudder at that thought. "Respectable. What a frightful name to bear."

Her fingertips caressed the scarred cheek that brought back memories of wilder times. "But like it or not, you are my lord, and I fear soon Rufe will be as domesticated as you. I've seen him eying Dulcie and noted how frequent his visits have become." She didn't voice it, but having Rufe off the seas would be a great relief to her, not only because she worried over his safety but because of the temptation his way of life presented.

"Don't tease him about it, Merri. 'Tis embarrassing for a bold pirate to be captured by a mere wench."

"But you survived it, my proud Angel," she teased, then sighed as his mouth moved gently over hers, the light flickering of his tongue making her tremble with impatient longing. Would this child never come?

As if in answer, she felt a sudden pressure and gave a gasp of surprise.

"Merri?" Nicholas prompted, his eyes growing round and uncertain at the sight of the wet stain that darkened the planks at her feet. "What is it?"

She smiled in gentle amusement at his look of abject terror. " 'Tis but the birthing waters, my lord husband. You are about to become a father."

"Now?"

She stilled his panic with a brief kiss. "Soon. You'd best help me to the house lest you want to welcome this child yourself here on the dock."

His teeth flashed white in a sudden grin as he scooped her up in his arms and kissed her hard. "I can wait, my lady, if you can."

Merrit rested fairly comfortably throughout the night, with Rufe pacing the halls and Nicholas at her bedside, while a disapproving Mildred fussed about the room making endless preparations. Near daybreak, a rain began to fall. It turned to heavy sleet by morning, leaving a slick of ice on the roads and making the branches groan with the weight of it. Mildred looked out on the glistening ground with a fretful frown. She hoped there were no complications with the birth, for the inclement weather would slow the arrival of the doctor, if indeed it was possible to fetch him at all. But Merrit was a strong girl and all seemed to be going well for a first delivery.

A sudden squeeze of his hand woke Nicholas from his dozing. He straightened in his chair and looked quickly to his laboring wife. Her lips were tightly compressed, her eyes half-closed in concentration. A sheen of perspiration dampened her hair at the temples and neck, and made her nightdress stick to her. When she relaxed, he pressed her hand to his lips, to be rewarded with a smile and the caress of her eyes.

"How goes it with you, my lady? I did not mean to fall asleep."

"It should be soon now. The babe means to be born whether you be awake or not, but your company does make it easier for me." She shifted on the damp bedding, trying to ease the ache in her back for it was now unmerciful.

"I love you, Merri. I only wish I could do more. I did not know it would cause you such hurt. You are very brave."

Merrit smiled at his honest praise, and chided, "Women have been birthing babies for centuries. I am not special among them."

"You are because you are my wife. I did not love the others," he stated simply, ending the matter.

He stayed with her through the long arduous hours of the afternoon, growing increasingly distressed by her discomfort but forcing himself to remain calm so he might be of some help to her. Mildred adamantly insisted that childbirth was to occur only in the presence of women, and it rattled her staunch sense of propriety that he would not go. But though she was affronted by his presence at this intimate time, she knew he saw to Merrit with a quiet consideration that kept her comfortable and his presence enabled her to rest in small snatches. As the only woman in the Seward household, Mildred had nowhere else to turn for assistance so as the time drew close she didn't relish the idea of trying to persuade Captain Seward to leave.

Merrit bit her lips as cramping pressure twisted through her abdomen, holding in her cry lest it upset Nicholas. Mildred would shoo him away if he caused any trouble. As long as she could hear his crooning whispers of encouragement, a mixture of English and Spanish, she could endure anything, but it was growing so hard. The pains seemed to go on forever now, and she had little time to gather her waning strength between them. When the spasm finally ended, she gave a breath of weak relief and lay limp on the soggy sheets. She could tell nightfall was approaching by the lengthening shadows and the increasing frequency of Nicholas's stifled yawns.

The next pang caught her unaware, wringing a cry from her and immediate consternation from Nicholas. Mildred, too, looked worried though she tried not to show it as she hovered over the bed.

"Merri, are you all right?" he asked in a low shaken voice.

"I don't know," she mumbled faintly, for the pains were all flowing together. "It's taking so long. Mildred, is everything going well?"

The thought that something might be amiss made Nicholas look quickly to Mildred, the somber set of her features giving him little reassurance. The deep creases in her forehead made him think this was no new idea to her. "What is it, Mildred? Why is it taking so long?"

"Give us some privacy, Captain." She raised her hand to prevent his immediate protest. "I need to check the position of the babe. It will take but a minute. Go on. Get yerself a bite to eat and a strong drink." She gave him a slight push to get him started, smiling at his reluctance and giving a nod.

In the study, Nicholas paced, an untouched brandy clenched between his hands, the buffet set up for his benefit untouched. The air was heavy with the fragrant smell of the fir boughs Merrit had had him cut and bring inside to make the atmosphere festive for the holidays. Yet he felt far from festive. Concerned as well but a bit more practical, Rufe helped himself to a huge plate of food, washing it down with an excellent wine; then smiled sympathetically at his friend's agitation.

"Colley, relax. Your lady will be fine. Birthing babes is no ailment. For women, it is a natural state. Calm yourself."

"I cannot. I cannot. Something is wrong. Mildred isn't telling me something. His eyes rose, bright and uneasy.

"Drink your brandy. You're as nervous as a cat. If you are an example of what married life does to a man, maybe I'll reconsider."

Nicholas's mind was briefly distracted, and he smiled. "You're settling in with the fair Dulcie?"

"If she'll have an old shiftless pirate like myself. 'Tis not the same sailing with another captain. Bellamy is a fair man, shrewd in thought and as flowery in his speech as you, but he's not the Spanish Angel. Perhaps I am getting too old, or maybe I am just jealous of a friend who has everything a man dreams of."

Nicholas's smile soured when Mildred appeared in the doorway and gestured to Rufe. They spoke for a moment, then he hurried off. Nicholas's breath caught when she turned to him, an icy fear seeping through him.

The older woman sighed heavily, seeing not a fearless pirate but a man afraid for his beloved wife. How greatly Merrit had changed Nicholas, she thought. She had grown to like and admire the often swaggering and insufferable Nicholas Seward, and she shrank from revealing this news that would tear him assunder.

"Captain, I have sent for the doctor, but because of the weather I have asked Rufe to seek some assistance from the neighbors in case the doctor doesn't arrive in time."

"Mildred, tell me what's wrong?" he demanded quietly.

"The babe is lying the wrong way and preventing the birth. It has to be turned before Merrit gets any weaker. Without a doctor, it can be dangerous," she said plainly.

"How dangerous?" he almost whispered.

"We could lose them both."

He swayed as if the words were a buffeting wind that snatched his breath and robbed him of his senses. After a long second, he shook his head fiercely in denial. "No. I

462

cannot lose her. I won't." His eyes went to the stairway, the angry protest becoming blind panic. He pushed by Mildred to rush up the stairs.

The sight of Merrit checked his mad rush at the doorway of their room. She looked so small and vulnerable in the huge bed, more like a child than a woman about to bear one. When she saw her husband hesitating in the hall, his handsome face almost rigid with anxiety, she raised a weak hand. The whisper of his name brought him to her with a hoarse cry. He sank down at the edge of the bed, his dark head dropping into her palm.

"Merri, don't leave me. You promised me. You promised you'd never leave me," he wept in selfish agony. "What would I do without you? Don't die. Don't leave me alone."

"Here now, Captain," Mildred scolded, gripping his shoulders to pull him away. "Don't be upsetting me lamb with that wild talk."

He struck out mindlessly at her hands, glaring up, his shiny green eyes hostile and fearsome. "Get away from me," he snarled in a voice so threatening that the older woman took a step back, fearing him for the first time.

Merrit interceded, guiding his dark head back down to her and nodding to her agitated friend. "He's all right, Mildred. Leave him be. Hush, Colley. I'm not going to leave you. I bring you your child."

"I don't care about the child. I want you," he cried pettishly.

She cuffed him hard enough to make him wince. "No more of that. I won't have it. Either help me or go."

Swallowing his childlike panic and straightening, he asked softly, "What can I do?"

"Kiss me and tell me you love me. I need that more than anything."

His mouth moved gently on hers, for he now saw her need for tender comfort. She breathed deeply as she went into the

463

next rolling pain, letting the sweetness of his kiss tide her through it.

"Oh, Merri, I'm sorry," he said his voice low and unsteady. "Had I known how it would hurt you, I never would have—"

"Lain with me, Captain?" she supplied with a faint smile. "Do you think I would allow our marriage to be one in name only? When this is done, I will have you again, willing or no. Childbirth is no great price to pay for the joy you bring me."

"You are my life, Merri. Without you, I am lost. I would never forgive myself if my child took your life."

"Promise me, Colley. Promise me you will love this child no matter what happens," she panted, gripping his hands with all her remaining strength. "I want your word."

The green eyes glimmered like precious gems as he managed a stiff nod. "You have it, my lady."

He stayed at her side for some time, holding her hand to his cheek in silence. Mildred had left the room to afford them privacy, and upon hearing her return, he turned to look her way. His harshly drawn breath and abrupt stiffening made Merrit lift her absurdly heavy head to look to where Rufe stood with Sophia and Gabrielle Whitelaw.

"Why have you brought them into my house?" Nicholas demanded in a low, outraged voice. That they should be here to witness his grief and possible loss was too much. He rose to present a figure both protective and threatening.

"I need them to help with the birth," Mildred explained, uneasy about his sudden rigid posture and hard flashing eyes.

"We don't need their help. I'll not have the likes of them touch my wife or my child," Nicholas growled in fierce denial. Hatred surged up in him, bitter and caustic, finding him vulnerable in his weary anxiety. He glared at Sophia and spat, "Do you think I'd let you come here and gloat over my pain? Aren't you satisfied with all the suffering you've

464

caused, or won't you be satisfied until I'm broken and no threat to you?"

Undisturbed by the near madness in his reddened eyes, Sophia spoke coolly. "I came because your man said my help was needed."

"I don't want your help," he ranted. "I don't want you and your bitch daughter here defiling my house and making a mockery of my grief."

With a sudden loud crack Mildred's beefy palm met his cheek, rocking him back and silencing his ugly words. "This is not about what ye want, ye thoughtless fool," Mildred railed. "What kind of man be ye to hold yer stale revenge above the life of me pet?"

He put his hand to his face, eyes glassy and expression blank, and it was from Merrit that the reprisal came.

"Mildred, how dare you strike him," she lashed out, struggling to her elbows and glaring at the startled woman with dark, angry eyes. "He is my husband and your lord, and if you ever again fail to show him respect, I'll have your bags packed and ship you back to England. You will not question him. The decision is his alone, and you will abide by it or get out of my sight. I'll not have such disloyalty in my house."

Mildred's eyes filled with tears of protest, but she said nothing more.

Nicholas turned to his seething wife, kneeling at her side and pressing her palm to his burning cheek. "No, my love. 'Twas me being disloyal, not poor Mildred," he confessed softly. "She was right. Forgive me for forever being the fool. I love you so."

He kissed her palm, holding her eyes for a long meaning-ful moment. Then he stood. There was humble sincerity in his voice as he said, "Lady Whitelaw, I would be most grateful to you for whatever you can do to save my wife and child."

Sophia nodded curtly, then looked to the uncertain Gabrielle and ordered, "We'll need more light and water and clean linens. See to it."

Gabrielle hesitated. She had had to fight her mother for the right to come to the Sewards' home, pleading that she could be of help even if she was ignorant of what to expect. In her heart, it had not been concern for Merrit that had prompted her request but an eagerness to see Nicholas. She hoped he would need comforting. Looking at him now, she saw realized he would never turn from Merrit to seek solace from her. She had thought she loved him. Strange how that love had disappeared the moment he had slapped her, as if he had awakened her from a dream. She knew that even this last futile wish to get him back was wrong. Real love was what she saw reflected in his tortured eyes, the love for a woman she had called all manner of foul things, a love she had sought to destroy with her lies and prayers that Merrit and her child would be safely out of the way so she and Nicholas could be together. How terrible and vengeful those thoughts seemed to her now. Hoping she would have a chance to rectify her mistakes, she hurried to do her mother's bidding.

Mildred came to the weary captain and embraced him as if he were a frightened child in need of reassurance and he clung to her, his breath coming shakily.

"I cannot lose her, Mildred. She is everything to me."

"I know," she said gruffly.

"Mildred, I —"

"No need, pirate. I'll see to yer lady. Go downstairs and wait with yer burly friend." She felt him stiffen in rebellion and added quickly with unquestionable reason, "She's got hard work ahead of her and cannot go about it if she be aworrying about ye. Go on now."

He nodded reluctantly and stepped back to where Merrit lay while Mildred said quietly to Rufe, "Get him plenty drunk."

Nicholas bent over the frail figure of his wife, taking her smiling face between his hands. His kiss was quick, but deep emotion was conveyed in that brief stirring gesture. He looked into the dark pools of her eyes, and said huskily, "I leave you in good hands, my lady. See to your promise to me."

"You to yours as well," she reminded him, giving a breath of relief at his nod. "I love you."

He gave a small reluctant sound, his emerald eyes filling wetly; then he blinked and his control returned. "And I you," was his soft reply.

He rose with a difficultly achieved dignity and left her to the care of the waiting women.

# Chapter Thirty-six

Through the haze of her weariness, Merrit was puzzled by Gabrielle's soft smile as the girl gently dried her face and gave her a wet cloth to suck on. Had she been forgiven then? That hope encouraged her. Immediately, her body tensed at the beginning of another swelling pang, her hands twisting in the damp sheets and shaking with the strain. She heard Sophia's voice, low and competent.

"Merrit, stop fighting the pains. You need to save your strength. Relax and breathe into them slowly and deeply. Listen to me and do as I say. Cry out if it will help. You need impress no one here with your courage. Giving birth is no elegant affair."

Merrit meant to allow herself only a small whimper, but it rose to a moaning wail as the contraction peaked. She did feel better now that she was no longer struggling to keep her anguish silent. Breathing in slow pants, she closed her eyes, concentrating on the angelic vision of a darkly handsome pirate daring her to prove herself a woman by meeting his kiss, on the gleam of the firelight against his golden chest as he swung her barefoot through the wild dance, on the smoldering heat in jade green eyes as he lifted her into his arms and carried her to the cabin below. How she loved the life they had made together. How she loved him. Had these months of happiness been too wonderful to continue? She would not give them up. She'd worked too hard for that happiness with the man who held her heart. So intent was she on these thoughts that when the next wrenching spasm caught her, she cried out his name, then panted until it ebbed.

"You're doing very well," Sophia told her with an encouraging smile that spanned all their differences. "Let's see if we can persuade this child to come to meet us."

At the sound of Merrit's first cry, the untouched glass of brandy slipped from Nicholas's fingers to darkly color the wool carpet. He stood motionless, barely breathing, his eyes on the stairs until he heard her call his name, snapping his fearful trance. His rush forward was halted by Rufe's massive paws on his shoulders.

"Colley, stay put. They don't need you up there. You'd only be in the way. Now sit down and wait. That's all you can do. Be sensible or I will plant some sense in to your hard head with a tap on the jaw. You choose."

The look on his friend's handsome face was one Rufe had never seen before, not in the face of death, not in the heat of battle, not when he'd been a boy floundering about battered and bleeding in a London sewer. It had taken Merrit Ellison to introduce him to fear, to put that haunted glimmering in his eyes, the tremors in his hands.

Nicholas whirled away in agitated panic, and dropped down onto the sofa where he had once tried to woo his love and had later fallen asleep with his head in her lap. Resting his elbows on his knees and his face in his hands, he let the chills of doubt and uncertainty shiver though him.

She was going to die. He had no hope of ever seeing her again, of tasting her sweet kiss, of loving her through a sultry night, of hearing her teasing laughter, or of seeing the flash of fond irritation in her dark eyes. Or of holding their child. He was going to lose them both. Why had he trusted her to keep her promise? She had convinced him to love her, to trust her, and to depend on her, and now she was going to cruelly desert him to a future he had planned for them both. What would he do in it alone? Damn her and his own foolishness. Why couldn't he have let her go? Because he loved her was the immediate answer. Loved her so much that he was cursing her? Would he spit on her grave as well? Had she taught him nothing of love, of trust, of faith — the kind she had, unquestioning and unfailing?

"I yield," he whispered into his hands. "I yield. Just save her. She's the only good I've ever known. Don't take her now." He let his thoughts quiet for a time, waiting for some sign that he had been heard, for some miracle. Then he frowned angrily. Her god was as false as she was.

"Captain?"

His body went rigid at the sound of Mildred's voice, knowing if she had left Merrit the worst had happened. He took a deep breath, trying to still the wailing terror and grief that rocked him, and then said in a flat voice, "Is she dead, then?"

There was a pause before Mildred said formally, "Captain, might I present yer son to ye?"

Green eyes flashed up to fasten in undisguised shock on the small bundle the smiling woman held. "My son," he echoed in dumb amazement as he rose to his feet. The delight of the moment was hampered by another question. "And Merri?"

Mildred's smile faded as she looked into his haggard face. "We've done all we can. The difficulty of the birth has left her very weak and if the bleeding cannot be stopped she won't last the night.

Surprisingly, he accepted the news stoically. Apprehensive of his calm, Mildred extended the child to him.

"Take the babe. I must return to me pet. Pray that the doctor comes in time."

Nicholas took the covered infant gingerly, not certain what to do with it.

"Rufe," Mildred continued. "Merritt wants to speak to ye."

470

"Not me?" Nicholas protested faintly, slighted to think that he would be left to tend the babe while his friend saw to his wife.

"Patience, pirate."

Alone in the room, Nicholas felt excluded and distraught. Why had Merrit forgotten him? Did she think he would prefer this child, a stranger he didn't love, to her? "I will take no substitutes," he muttered bitterly. "I will hate this child if it has taken away my love."

As if the babe could understand the words, his tiny features puckered in uncertainty, readying for a frightened howl. Then the small fingers rose up to curiously knead Nicholas's severe chin, eliciting a reluctant smile.

"Bold little creature," Nicholas mused. "Let's have a look at you. My son." He turned back the swaddling of blankets to cautiously examine the infant. He'd never seen one up close, let alone handled one. "What a beautiful child you are," he said in quiet awe, his emotions taking a sudden proud possessive turn. From the reddish thatch of ample hair to the big cloudy eyes that would turn pure green, the baby was a precious blend of both parents, which endeared him to the father who had been determined to resent him. Those perfect miniature fingers had already closed about his heart to seize his love. "My treasure," he vowed, stroking the mottled cheek with his forefinger. He gave a start as the petulant little mouth caught at his fingertip and began a vigorous sucking. "My apologies, little one, but I cannot help you there. You must wait for your mama." He sighed heavily. "We both must wait."

The sight of Merrit Seward momentarily froze Rufe at the foot of the bed. Even after the horrors he'd seen in battle, the blood soaked sheets and pale, hollowed-eyed woman who lay limply under them, gave his stomach a queasy jolt. Thank God, she hadn't called Nicholas up, he thought with remorse. The sight would have shattered him.

Her tired eyes lifted and a faint smile curved her wan lips.

471

Rufe came to kneel at her side, taking up the cold hand she pushed toward him.

"Rufe, my friend, I don't believe I shall make it," she whispered fragilely.

"Nonsense. You've Colley to think of and the boy."

"I am thinking of them." She paused a minute to gather her strength. "Take care of them, Rufe. Keep Colley off the sea and out of the noose if you can. He will make a good father for the babe. I don't want him to grieve for me. For his sake and the child's I want him to marry again soon."

"Good Lord, Merrit," he gasped in shock. "He only wants you. He'd take no other. He won't grieve; it will kill him. I don't know if I can keep him off the water. He needs you. He may hand the babe over to someone else for care and return to his pirating."

Rufe's words had the desired effect, Merrit's face flushed with angry objection. "He wouldn't dare, the vain, selfish man. He'll not turn his back on our child. He gave me his word and he will abide by it. I will see to it."

"As well you should," he agreed with a smile, seeing more fight in her little body than in those of men twice her size.

"I will," she vowed. "I will."


His thoughts tied up in the cooing child nestled contentedly in the crook of his arm, Nicholas failed to hear Freddy Moffit's arrival and was unaware of him until the homely face bent close and split with a grin.

"A handsome lad, Captain. Your lady has done you proud. The doctor is with her now." He put a hand on the pistol at his hip. "It took a bit of persuading to coax him out on such a night but —" He shrugged and smiled.

"Thank you, Freddy. You may have saved her life."

Freddy drew himself up with a new feeling of importance. "As she once did mine. I would do anything for Lady Merrit. Let me and the men know how she fares. We be

472

waiting to hear the good news."

"I hope I can bring some."

After the gangly boy left, Nicholas turned to his son ruefully. "Your mama has quite a following. You and I will have to be diligent to keep her all to ourselves."

The babe chortled happily in agreement, waving tiny fists and wringing a smile from his weary father.

An hour later he looked up from the sleeping figure of his son in vague alarm to see Gabrielle and the man who had tended his wound some months before. His unasked question hung heavily in the air.

"She'll need plenty of rest and care for the next few weeks," the doctor began as the captain gave a soft cry of relief. "She is a strong woman. I will return to see her tomorrow. Can you have that renegade who abducted me see me home again?"

"I'll see to it," Gabrielle said easily. The sight of Nicholas tenderly holding his child had so moved her she was near tears. He was a total stranger to her, this man Merrit had made. "Merrit is asking for you, Captain. I'll take the babe for a moment if you'll allow me."

He gave the girl a long look, seeing in her genuine feeling which she'd not exhibited before. She smiled with pleasure as he placed the boy in her arms, her pale eyes misty.

"You have a beautiful child, Nicholas, and a wife who loves you. Go to her."

He needed no urging. Bounding up the stairs with an energy that belied his long vigil, he paused in the doorway, his eyes falling on the bed and his heart swelling with a surge of tender emotion and longing. How beautiful she was. She lay still on the fresh linens in her crisp night dress, her chestnut hair tied back from a surprisingly serene face that showed only slight signs of the ordeal she'd been through. Thinking her asleep, he lingered, wondering abstractedly how he could have lived without her.

"Congratulations, pirate," Mildred greeted him, meeting

his smile with a fond grin. "Ye've a bonny fine son to follow in yer footsteps."

His brows lowered into that scowling V. "I'll raise no son of mine to be a thieving scoundrel. And he could not become such under your watchful eyes, I'm sure. He'll be respectable whether he likes it or not. If I can tolerate it, so can he."

"Ye be a good man in spite of yerself, Captain," Mildred admitted.

"Don't be softening me up with praise. My poor heart couldn't stand it," he warned with a grin, his eyes glimmering with mischief. Those green eyes narrowed into a mixture of gratitude and uncertain anger when Sophia Whitelaw approached them. The debt he owed her softened his bitterness, but they regarded each other warily.

"Thank you, madam," he said simply. "I owe you much."

"Not as much as I owe you," she stated. He flinched in cautious apprehension as she lifted his right hand, but he didn't draw away. He stared blankly at the heavy ring she pushed over his knuckle. "For your son, the future earl."

He drew a shaky breath, his emotions too varied and strong for him to speak immediately. The large signet felt weighty and uncomfortable on his hand, a symbol of his crushed dreams that could now be realized for his son. In a hushed voice, he said, "I am not fit to wear it, but I will keep it for the boy. He will be deserving."

His motion to withdraw the ring was halted by her cool hand. "Wear it proudly," she insisted. "You are very much like your father. He would have wanted you to have it."

He dropped his eyes, leaving the ring where it was. "I wish I had known him."

Sophia started to reach out to touch his dark head, but the gap was too great to bridge so soon. Instead, she said simply, "I know there is too much hurt between us for us ever to be close, but I would like us not to be enemies."

Nicholas took a deep breath and expelled it along with a

rush of ill-feeling and past bitterness. "I would like that as well." There seemed no place in the fullness of his life for the harboring of old wounds. It was time to let them heal cleanly.

"Colley, have you forgotten me?"

He turned with a start to the woman who looked up at him with a warm smile, her dark eyes shimmering. Going to her quickly, he sat on the edge of the bed and took her beloved face in his hands.

"Thank you, my lady, for my son and for staying with me. I love you, Merri." He bent and caressed her soft lips with his own.

As the sudden wail of an unfamiliar voice broke them apart, Nicholas smiled. "Your son is hungry, my lady."

Merrit looked to the noisy bundle Gabrielle held so contentedly. "His name is Edward. Edward Nicholas Seward."

Sophia's eyes clouded briefly, then she took the child from her daughter to carry it gently to its mother. "Thank you, Merrit," she said quietly, placing the child in her arms.

"Well, ye've no need for company so we'll be going." Mildred sniffed upon seeing dark eyes locked with green above the downy head. To herself, she added, "I wonder if Rufe has left me any of that excellent rum."

Smiling in welcome, Merrit tossed back the coverlet and patted the empty space beside her. "Join me, my lord husband. You look worse than I feel. Do you like your new son?"

"He and I are already fast friends," he assured her, kicking off his boots before slipping in beside her. Their lips met and held until the whining babe proved a distraction.

"Let me see to this greedy one's breakfast," Merrit laughed in the face of her husband's scowl. But he soon forgot his annoyance when she undid the bows at her bodice and freed a full breast, which little Edward fastened upon with an avarice that made his mother gasp in surprise.

"He reminds me of you, my lusty pirate," she teased, stroking Nicholas's unshaven face.

He kissed her fingertips and settled back on his elbow to watch his son's first meal with curious interest. Sharing Merrit's time would take some adjustment, but he could harbor no resentment toward the rutting infant whose loud smackings of satisfaction made him smile. He looked from the hungry babe to the ring he wore, his brow furrowing slightly as he touched it.

"What is it, Colley?"

He gave a wistful smile. "I was thinking of how different it might have been if my father hadn't died. I wonder if he would have loved me the way I love this little fellow."

"I love you," she said with a simple finality that answered all.

After giving her a smile, he pried open the top of the signet, releasing a catch Sophia didn't know of. Inside the ring was a likeness of his mother and the date of her marriage. His proof.

"Oh, Colley, she's beautiful," Merrit said softly.

His reply was low and reverent. "The most beautiful woman in Spain once more." He snapped the ring closed and touched Merrit's face. "You are everything to me—my future—and I've no regrets."

When Mildred tiptoed into the room, she found the three of them sleeping soundly in the circle of their love, the babe nestled between Nicholas and Merrit. Smiling, she blew out the light to leave them to the sheltering darkness.

476

**Now you can get more of HEARTFIRE
right at home and $ave.**

Preview
Four Brand New
ZEBRA
*Heartfire*
Romance Novels...

# FREE for 10 days.

## No Obligation
## and No Strings Attached!

♥

*Enjoy all of the passion and fiery romance as
you soar back through history, right in the
comfort of your own home.*

Now that you have read a Zebra **HEARTFIRE**
Romance novel, we're sure you'll agree that
**HEARTFIRE** sets new standards of excellence
for historical romantic fiction. Each Zebra
**HEARTFIRE** novel is the ultimate blend of intimate romance and grand adventure and each
takes place in the kinds of historical settings you
want most...the American Revolution, the Old
West, Civil War and more.

# <u>FREE</u> Preview Each Month and $ave

Zebra has made arrangements for you to preview 4 brand new HEARTFIRE novels each month...FREE for 10 days. You'll get them as soon as they are published. If you are not delighted with any of them, just return them with no questions asked. But if you decide these are everything we said they are, you'll pay just $3.25 each—a total of $13.00 (a $15.00 value). **That's a $2.00 saving each month off the regular price.** Plus there is NO shipping or handling charge. These are delivered right to your door absolutely free! There is no obligation and there is no minimum number of books to buy.

---

## TO GET YOUR FIRST MONTH'S PREVIEW... *Mail the Coupon Below!*